PRAISE FOR HAND OF FIRE

"But what is the difference between a *good* historical novel and a *brilliant* one? I suggest you read Judith Starkston's *Hand of Fire* and you'll discover the answer." Helen Hollick Editor *Historical Novels Review*

"In *Hand of Fire*, Starkston's careful research brings ancient Greece and Troy to life with passion and grace. This haunting and insightful novel makes you ache for a mortal woman, Briseis, in love with a half-god, Achilles, as she fights to make her own destiny in a world of capricious gods and warriors. I devoured this page-turning escape from the modern world!" -- Rebecca Cantrell, New York Times bestselling author of *The World Beneath*

"Suspenseful, tragic, surprising and sexy" –Nancy Bilyeau, author of *The Crown* and *The Chalice*

"Briseis steps out from the handful of lines she gets in Homer's epic, and fearlessly tells her own story as healer, war prize, and partner to the famous Achilles--here a godlike hero who manages to be all too human. Recommended!"–Kate Quinn, author of *Empress of the Seven Hills*

"In her portrayal of Briseis, Judith Starkston has cast a bright light on one of the *Iliad*'s most intriguing sub-plots. With her fast-paced story, three-dimensional characters, and fascinating cultural details, Starkston has given historical fiction fans a tale to remember." –Priscilla Royal, author of *Covenant with Hell* and 9 other Prioress Eleanor mysteries

"Starkston breathes new life into an age-old tale in this masterful retelling of the *Iliad*. The reader experiences the terror, bravery and heartbreak of Briseis who now takes center stage in one of the most famous love triangles of all time." Elisabeth Storrs, author of *The Wedding Shroud* and *The Golden Dice*

"Absolutely loved the book. Couldn't put it down. Wonderful writing. And, I see no errors whatsoever as regards the history." –Professor Eric Cline, Chair of the Department of Classical and Near Eastern Languages and Civilizations, George Washington University

"Ms. Starkston's fascinating novel tells the story of Briseis, famed beauty and war prize to demi-god, Achilles. Backed by meticulous research, Starkston weaves an intriguing tale about a brave woman who must bury her heartache, survive amid those who destroyed her family, and rise above the confines of her station to create her own destiny. A must read for fans of ancient Greece, and lively tales of historical fiction." –Heather Webb, author of *Becoming Josephine*

"In *Hand of Fire*, Judith Starkston frees Briseis from the actions of Achilles and Agamemnon and gives her the power to become the heroine of her own story. ... Starkston does a lovely job of bringing the characters to life, and her descriptions of the religious rites, the scenery of Mount Ida, and life as a woman of privilege in the ancient world put me firmly in the story. The love story between Briseis and Achilles is well-rendered, as are Briseis' relationships with her father and brothers, her nurse, and the other women in the city and in the camp. A wonderful new take on a timeless story." –*Historical Novels Review*

"...once one begins this tale one is transported back thousands of years to a time both ancient and modern all at the same time. Reading *Hand of Fire* is akin to entering a time machine. I felt the age come alive through Starkston's subtle manipulation of her research and her narrative skill. These fully fleshed-out characters leap off the page and a time that is far away chronologically becomes all too real. This is a wonderful introduction to both Homer and the late Bronze Age. Any reader from teen-ager on up will find this both a fascinating history lesson and a thrilling novel." –*The Poisoned Pen Fiction Review*

HAND OF FIRE

A NOVEL OF BRISEIS AND THE TROJAN WAR

JUDITH STARKSTON

BRONZE AGE BOOKS

Cover design by Heather Senter

BISAC Subject Headings:

FIC009030FICTION/Fantasy/Historical

FIC010000FICTION/Fairy Tales, Folk Tales, Legends & Mythology

FIC014010FICTION/Historical/Ancient

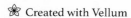 Created with Vellum

Dedicated to my father, Rodman Wilson Paul, 1912-1987, historian of the American West, writer, my greatest inspiration.

CONTENTS

1. Wind and Fire — 1
2. Blossoms and A Groom — 13
3. Warriors — 21
4. Gold and Blood — 33
5. A Goddess's Will — 41
6. A Wolf Curse — 51
7. Handkerchiefs, Herbs, and Sacred Tales — 61
8. Voices — 69
9. Consequences — 79
10. Visions and Sweet, Seductive Flames — 87
11. Veiled Wedding — 99
12. Wool — 107
13. Plowing and Fighting — 115
14. Hurried Preparations and Divine Silence — 125
15. Attack — 133
16. Ash, Fire and Arms — 145
17. Brotherly Loss — 151
18. Wandering in the Shadows of Death — 159
19. Kindness and a Pyre — 167
20. Joined by Fire — 177
21. Warriors at Troy — 187
22. The Choice — 195
23. A Bard's Tale — 203
24. Offering of Love — 213
25. The Rhythms of Life and Death — 223
26. Strong Love — 235
27. A Too-Brief Feast of Fire — 245
28. Freedom and Fetters — 255
29. Plague — 263
30. Holding onto Fire — 273
31. Howling in the Dark — 283
32. Wrathful Fire — 293
33. Implacable — 303

34. Burden of Grief   311
35. Life or Death   321
36. A Father's Kiss   329
37. Wellspring of Life   337

Maps   345
People, Gods and Places   347
Author Notes   351
Acknowledgments   357
About the Author   359

1

WIND AND FIRE

Antiope's breath rasped like a distant wave scouring a rocky shore. *Too faint to sustain life.* Briseis squeezed her mother's hand, then balanced her mother's limp hand on her own, shifting each finger until the two matched up. When had her fingers grown as long as her mother's? It didn't mean she was ready to take on her mother's work alone. She rubbed gently, but Antiope's hand remained slack. Briseis shifted closer to her mother on the bed and adjusted the fleeces cushioning her mother's shoulders from the leather straps pulled across the bed's wooden frame. No response. *What should I do, Mama? Tell me how to save you. You've taught me to be a healer from birth, but I don't know this, the one thing I have to know. Tell me.*

Briseis leaned over to kiss her mother's forehead. Her lips pressed Antiope's skin—cool as bone—and Briseis's red-gold hair brushed against her mother's ashen cheeks. She shuddered at the contrast. The fever was gone. The single worry line had smoothed. These signs, reassuring at other times, tightened the knot in Briseis's chest —intimations of withdrawal, not healing. Her mother had let go.

Months ago she'd discovered her mother's secret illness. She'd begged her to fight it, tried every cure she could discover, even though her mother refused to offer advice, saying there was no point. Nothing Briseis did slowed her mother's decline. Now, Antiope would die if Briseis didn't strengthen that ragged breath.

Why hadn't her father and two oldest brothers stayed home today? The king had summoned them, but still .... All had seemed as usual in the morning, her mother no worse than any other day among the many she'd been ill. This sudden downturn had taken Briseis by surprise. *Wake up, Mama, you can't die now. I won't let you.*

Briseis glanced at the youngest of her brothers, Iatros, seated on a stool at the far side of her mother's bed. He twisted the hem of his tunic first in one direction and then in the other. Normally, she would have pulled him close and told him not to worry—she couldn't today. His fear was well founded. She turned toward her old nurse, Eurome, waiting for something useful to do, her soft, round figure sagging against the doorframe. *What else can I try?* Briseis felt the familiar tightening at her temples. She willed away the threatening headache. *Not now. I need to think.*

The storm that had blown in so suddenly threw wind and rain against the closed shutters of the clerestory windows. So late in the winter no one had expected such bad weather. Would it prevent her father and brothers from returning home? The pounding against the shutters sounded like some beast trying to break in—no ordinary storm. She imagined the squall building up force in some distant, dangerous place like Greece, blowing across the Aegean Sea and flinging itself against Mount Ida's flanks. The frenzy outside mocked her mother's stillness. Inside, the flickering light came from clay oil lamps, causing the geometric patterns frescoed on the mud-brick walls to lunge and recoil.

"She's barely breathing. What do we do?" Iatros said, leaning in to be closer to his mother.

Briseis shook her head. Though already sixteen and a year older than she was, he had a small, tense body and round cheeks, never yet shaved with a scraper. His gentle brown eyes and dark curls, startling against his worry-blanched face, deepened Briseis's dread of carrying on without their mother. Antiope had always sheltered Iatros in a manner unlike her treatment of his brothers. How would he fare without that guidance?

Briseis rubbed her eyes and blinked back the pain pressing behind them. Her hair, escaped as usual from its bronze butterfly clasp, annoyed her and she pushed it out of the way. *Can't you give me a sign, Mama? We always worked together.* Not anymore. Her mother's silence crushed down on her shoulders.

"What should we do?" Iatros said again.

Briseis looked at her mother's slack face. "We give her strength."

"If she doesn't breathe, how can she be strong?" Iatros walked around the bed and stood beside his sister, staring down at the still figure.

What have I missed all these months? Any moment, that small breath will stop. I have to do something. Briseis hunted in her mind for a way to make her mother strong again. She sifted through the teachings she learned from Antiope, rites and cures handed to generations of women in her family directly from the healing goddess Kamrusepa. She and her mother both served as priestesses to the goddess, and though Briseis herself had not yet grown comfortable with the temple rites, her mother always expressed closeness to the goddess, especially in the temple. Until the last year, Antiope's life vibrated with Kamrusepa's presence. This illness was inexplicable.

Briseis noticed a twitch at her mother's temple, then nothing. She pushed off the bed, straightening to her full height, taller than most men.

"We will have to help her breathe." She turned to the doorway and saw Eurome's eyes brighten. For as long as Briseis could remember, her nursemaid Eurome had been part of her life—pampering, scolding, teasing, teaching—constantly chattering, but always reassuringly there.

"Eurome, we'll light the brazier. Mama hates foul smells, so I haven't used this cure before, but I don't care now. We're going to make a plaster of wax and spices to strengthen her breath. That's what she would do."

Eurome rushed downstairs for a coal from the hearth, agile despite her weight.

Briseis reached for her mother's satchel, full of healing materials, and laid out supplies on a table beside the bed. She measured mustard seed and sulfur into a mortar and ground them. She glanced at her brother, his narrow shoulders hunched forward.

Briseis passed Iatros the satchel. "Find the ball of beeswax and soften it on the brazier."

Eurome returned with a coal in a long-handled bronze cup and lit the kindling in the brazier. She put an empty pot on to warm and then rubbed one of Antiope's hands, the smoothness of the sick woman's hand contrasting with the wrinkles of age and work. "Take my strength, Lady Antiope, all you need."

Iatros worked the wax in the pot and then used the edge of his tunic to pull it off the fire. "It's ready."

Briseis nodded. "Mix while I pour this in. Careful. It will sting your eyes, but that's why it will awaken Mama and strengthen the intake of her breath."

"Shouldn't I do that?" asked Eurome.

Iatros shook his head. "It's my job."

When they'd blended the yellow powder into the soft wax, Briseis undid the braided tie at the neck of her mother's sleeping tunic and exposed a small area. She touched the frail, ashen skin and Briseis's breath caught—her strong, proud mother so diminished now. Despite the powerful fumes that made their eyes water as Briseis spread the plaster on her mother's chest, Antiope's breathing did not deepen. Her eyes, however, fluttered open and she wrinkled her nose in disgust.

Her mouth moved. Briseis bent close to hear the sighed fragments. "No more, daughter . . . The hardest lesson . . . is accepting death." Antiope's chest rose and fell softly as she caught her breath. "No more for me to do. Your training . . . as healing priestess . . . is complete."

Antiope paused. "My need . . . to escape this pain is greater than your need . . . family's need . . . for me. I served the goddess . . . . Now .

. . you, Briseis." She turned her head toward Iatros. "Son . . ." He took her hand in both of his and kissed it. "You and your sister help each other." The bones along Antiope's cheeks drew her skin to a fragile thinness, almost translucent.

"You've devoted yourself to Kamrusepa all your life," Briseis said. "Why won't she save you and take away the pain?" Briseis's fingers knotted tightly into the curly fleece covering the bed frame.

Antiope closed her eyes a moment. Then she opened them and looked at her daughter. Her throat rattled with the effort to draw in more air. "Even goddesses . . . must accept the death of mortals dear to them . . . but she is here with me."

Antiope raised her hand a little from the bed. "Your father? Brothers?"

"Father hasn't returned, nor Adamas and Bienor. I sent a messenger after them as you asked."

"Ah, well . . . ." Her mother's eyes closed, and she seemed to sink further into the bed.

Briseis slipped out of the room and stood at the top of the stairs, wanting to hear the noise of her father and brothers coming through the gate. She'd sent one of the menservants to tell them to come right away. In good weather it only took part of an afternoon to get from the walled city of Lyrnessos back to the estate, but with this storm . . . . When they left that morning, the sky was clear enough and her mother hadn't shown any alarming signs. They had no reason not to go, especially when the king needed her father's advice because of the rumors of Greek raids. Reports had come in of attacks on the towns north of their powerful ally Troy. Her father was the king's chief military advisor and he'd raised her two oldest brothers as warriors, so they had gone with him to the Council the king had called. But if they didn't get home soon, it would be too late.

Hearing nothing, Briseis turned back to her mother's room. When she held her fingers to her mother's mouth, she could barely feel the movement of breath. The burn of rage Briseis had felt for months flared hotter. Her mother had concealed her illness until she couldn't hide her pain any longer. They should have fought it together from the beginning. Her mother always said illness treated early was illness cured. When Antiope insisted they could do nothing, Briseis hunted for months for a cure among the clay tablets in her mother's library. While her mother had written, "Thus says Antiope" at the bottom of some of them, the tablets from past healers also filled the library. Briseis decided her mother hadn't had the strength to search through the records as she would have for any other ill person. But of the various teas and poultices Briseis tried, along with the many rites, none had improved Antiope's health.

Briseis believed her mother had given in to this illness, accepted defeat from the beginning. Illness generally came from the gods as punishment for violations against the gods' laws. In case her mother had neglected a sacrifice or some similar affront—any more serious sin seemed unlikely—Briseis performed a snake divination at the temple to ask Kamrusepa directly how they had offended the gods. But the swimming snakes had given only a muddled answer as they touched the words inscribed in the great basin. The snakes failed to identify anything Briseis could correct. Even before she'd tried the divination it had seemed impossible to Briseis that her mother could have sinned so greatly that Kamrusepa sent the illness, but giving in to the disease felt like a sin to Briseis. Her mother had resigned herself to death too easily, and the gods abandoned her because she did not love life enough—their gift to all. She needed to be dragged back to life.

Briseis had an idea. "You two stay with Mama. I need some supplies."

She ran downstairs to the back storerooms, the sound of the storm growing muted as she went deeper into the house with its thick walls. Once inside the library, the comforting odor of clay soothed her. Her mother, Briseis thought, was a mixture of lavender and earthy clay. She pulled tablets from the wooden pigeonholes, scanning the words formed with a reed stylus that her brothers said looked like bird tracks. She found it, "The Breath of Life Incantation." It hadn't made sense to her when she'd been required to copy it for practice three years ago, but it did now. Her heart felt light. She committed the rite to memory and tucked the palm-sized tablet back in its place.

She hurried through the megaron hall, the main room of the house with its two-storied ceiling and circular hearth, out to the main courtyard and into the kitchen opposite the stables. The wind-driven rain splattered under the portico's shelter.

The cook, a middle-aged woman with a kinder heart than her boney, hard face indicated, looked up in surprise from sorting lentils when Briseis appeared at the door.

"For Mama, hurry. I need honey, mint and sweet wine."

The cook quickly gathered everything on a tray, and Briseis carried it back upstairs. From the carved wooden chest next to the floor-to-ceiling loom in her mother's sitting room, she grabbed a sachet of lavender and a clay incantation jar shaped like a fig.

Iatros and Eurome looked up when she entered the sleeping chamber. She set down the tray on the table and leaned in close over her mother. Antiope's lips were parted, her eyes closed, their lids withered like fallen leaves in winter. The space between breaths felt impossibly long.

Iatros crouched by the bed, biting his upper lip, eyes fixed on his sister.

Briseis shifted her mother's legs aside and sat down. She closed her eyes and waited while the fear she felt emptied out with each breath she exhaled. The power of the ritual's words filled her mind. She called to Kamrusepa, praying for her to give power to this rite.

She opened her eyes and placed both hands on her mother's chest, then her head.

"Antiope, wife of Glaukos, mother of Bienor, Adamas, Iatros, and Briseis, you have heard death whisper in your ear. You have mistaken that whisper for the nurturing breath that flows in and out of every human being. You have gone after death. Return now. Hear the breath of life."

Briseis poured wine and honey into the fig jar, breathed into it, and then added the lavender and mint, crushing the leaves to release their scent as she held the jar close to her mother.

"Antiope, do you smell the spring? The time of new growth and blossoms? Remember the spring. Remember your children. Remember the sweetness of life. Remember that you love life. Take a strong breath."

Silently Briseis added, *Come back, Mama, I need you. Remember how much I love you.* Antiope sighed and her eyelids fluttered for a moment. Iatros cried out.

Briseis's heart leapt like a deer. "Mama!"

Daughter and son clung to their mother's hands. They waited for Antiope to open her eyes and reassure them that she would live. They listened for the slow rattle to quicken. Instead it faded, caught once, tangled in a last wisp of life, then fell silent.

Tears ran down Briseis's face, hot against her skin. Gradually her wet cheeks grew cold.

LATER—HOW much later Briseis wasn't sure—Eurome gently pulled Iatros and Briseis from their mother's side. The old woman gathered them into her arms and held them tight against her generous bosom. Iatros sobbed, but Briseis's tears had burned away in anger. She raged at her mother, Kamrusepa, and death itself. In spite of the storm, she needed to run outdoors into the fields and woods. Something vital would boil over inside her if she did not escape from this room with its stink of sulfur and the sight of her lifeless mother.

She broke free from her nurse, raced down the stairs and out into the courtyard. As soon as she left the protection of the portico, the rain and wind hit her full force. She ran across the courtyard toward the tall wooden gates that protected the house from raiders. The gate-keeper had thrown them open in the hope that Glaukos and his sons would soon return.

Briseis pushed against the rain, running fast along the path through the fields of her father's estate toward the creek. The storm surrounded her. The clouds lay so low they seemed to swallow the foothills of Mount Ida that fingered down into her father's land. Mist cloaked even the lowest terraces of orchards on the slopes, and the forests higher up had disappeared entirely. Soon her clothes clung to her in soggy, cold folds that she tugged out of her way. The wind pulled most of her coppery hair from its clasp, blowing it about her face and up like a wild crown. The icy spears of rain drove hard against her face, and she felt relief at focusing on her discomfort.

She wanted her mother. Antiope taught that the hardest lesson for a healer is accepting death, but Briseis had already lost patients. She had learned that lesson. Her mother's death wasn't a lesson. It was personal, a searing pain. She turned her palms and face into the hard-pounding rain.

The leather soles of her shoes slipped on the muddy path. She stumbled over a broken branch near the creek. Fallen limbs lay all about. She ignored the menace and headed for the place where a huge oak reached its branches over the creek. She had come here often as a small child with her nurse to look for watercress for the kitchen. Later she came alone on hot summer days to cool her feet, enjoying the sound of the creek and the tree's leafy shelter. Now she wanted to throw her arms around the trunk, an anchor against her loss.

As she peered through the rain, there, unmistakably, was the sharp bend in the creek, but instead of the tree she saw a strange emptiness. The gray sky glowered at her where once the oak's branches had offered shelter. The creek's bank looked like an angry god had ripped out a huge piece of it and flung down stone and mud in disgust. Upturned roots reached helplessly toward their old home. The tree sprawled across the creek, and the water boiled up behind it, creeping toward her as it overflowed its banks.

She retreated from the muddy surge. Her wet skirt tangled her legs, but she yanked it out of the way and climbed onto a boulder high on the creek's bank. Her tunic stuck to her back. Rain ran down her face. She shivered with cold, but she didn't want to leave the storm. Staring at the chaos around her, she felt a kindred soul in this violence. She wanted to break and tear until she rooted out the grief that filled her at the thought of her mother's lifeless body in the upstairs chamber.

She sat on the boulder above the churning creek and curled her arms around her knees into a tight ball, her head tucked. How would the days ahead feel without her mother's steady presence? She wanted her mother with her for one thing especially—her marriage to the king's son, Mynes. That day loomed close and filled her with dread. She feared Mynes. *Please let my fear be mistaken.*

Why hadn't Kamrusepa protected her mother? She wanted to demand an answer, but that might prove dangerous. She must not anger the goddess. As the city's only healing priestess—no longer in training, whatever she might wish—Briseis now held the well-being of Lyrnessos in her hands: the fertility of crops and women, their health. She would pray and sacrifice to Kamrusepa at the Spring Festival, and the goddess would either listen or not. She must do all she could to be beloved of the goddess the way her mother had been.

Her mother's whisper returned. "Even goddesses must accept the death of mortals dear to them." Briseis unfolded herself and stood. She gathered her sodden skirt and leapt from the boulder, throwing herself into the wind, feeling the strength of it course through her body. That strength could dash her against the stones and yet she felt it inside like blood flowing through her, sustaining her. Did her goddess understand her grief with equal pain and offer this strength? She ran with the wind's force along the edge of the swollen creek and saw the image of tears pouring down Kamrusepa's cheeks. Then from the stores of tales she had loved throughout her childhood came other grieving goddesses, bent in sorrow, flooding her imagination, providing her with strange comfort that they suffered as she did and yet endured.

Amongst these images, one goddess stood out. Thetis crouched over the body of her warrior son, clawing at her cheeks while she howled. From the bard's tale, Briseis recognized Achilles in the bloodied figure, the greatest of the Greeks, with his red-gold hair, piercing green eyes, and fluidity born of the sea—except this hero still lived. Why this image of his death? Then she remembered that his divine mother had tried to burn away her infant son's mortality, to spare herself this eternal grief, each night laying him in the magic embers and searing away a little more frailty, creating the most invincible warrior of all. Her husband Peleus, a mere man, saw her rite and misunderstood the flames. He snatched the baby from the fire and through his mistake doomed him to die. His love-inspired ignorance would also doom Thetis to suffer eternal sorrow once that dread moment Briseis had imagined finally came. Even a goddess could not escape grief, no matter how hard she tried. Forever this searing pain, like Briseis's. Perhaps, Briseis allowed, Thetis's pain would be worse—a child lost, unbearable, unnatural. Perhaps the gods should not love any mortal too dearly.

Briseis turned toward home, letting the rain, cold and hard, obliterate her tears. She stumbled back to the house, her limbs spent, slow going amidst the maelstrom's power.

2

BLOSSOMS AND A GROOM

Briseis trudged in from the storm. Ahead she saw her father and brothers hurrying in through the gates and ran to catch up. They stood in the megaron hall, wet and bewildered. None of the servants had greeted them. No one wanted to tell the sad news, she guessed. Her father turned when she entered. He always understood her. Seeing her drenched and drained, he pulled Briseis into a hug and then broke away to run upstairs to his wife's chamber without a word.

"Is it Mama?" Bienor asked.

She nodded. "She's gone. I'm sorry."

Her oldest brother had broad shoulders and muscular arms. He carried himself like the leader of warriors he had been raised to be, but at that moment he sank onto one of the mud-brick benches built into the back wall of the megaron hall. He had the same dark curls and soft brown eyes as Iatros, but even with his head bowed in grief, he retained a look of strength.

Bienor raised his head. "Did she go peacefully at the end?"

Briseis nodded, tears welling up. "She wanted to escape the pain. She was glad to go, but she asked for both of you. She wanted to see you, but... her strength didn't hold."

Adamas, the middle brother, shook his head. "How could she have gone so quickly? We came as fast as we could." His face flushed in anger. Briseis felt too exhausted to respond to his outburst and she could not soften his grief.

Adamas flung his wet cloak into a heap on the floor. His straight hair, lighter than his brothers', lay plastered against his head. His eyes, gray like Briseis's, darted around the big hall as if to find someone to contradict his sister's words.

"We ran through the rain to get here, but I didn't believe the messenger—that it was so desperate. She's been sick for so long. Why today?"

Briseis shrugged. She'd done everything she could to postpone her mother's death. "After you'd gone, her breathing grew labored. It was more sudden than I've ever witnessed." She touched her brother's arm. "I'm so sorry."

Adamas gave her a hug. "You're as wet as I am. I'm sorry. Did she say anything—a message for us?" Briseis shook her head and squeezed his arm.

A serving woman came in with linen towels. Briseis took one and passed through the megaron hall up the cedar stairs to her parents' sleeping quarters. The storm raged on and Briseis was grateful that her house, like the palace, had enough room for an inside staircase instead of the outside ladders most homes used.

Her father knelt by the bed where her mother lay, holding one of his wife's hands to his lips. His lean, tall body seemed too angular to embrace the fragile remnant of his beloved wife.

Briseis stood in the doorway, unwilling either to intrude on his grief or to desert him. His bent head had more gray than she remembered. It must be more visible now that his dark hair was wet—too soon for the shock of Antiope's death to turn it gray. His damp tunic dripped and she saw him shiver. She stepped forward and wrapped the towel around his shoulders, leaving her hand resting on his back, although the sobs she felt under her palm racked her as much as him.

BY THE NEXT MORNING, Eurome and the serving women had prepared Antiope's body, dressed her in the blue gown she wore as priestess on festival days, and laid her on a wooden bier before the family shrine in the megaron hall.

The storm cleared. The curtains over the doors of the upstairs sleeping chambers were pulled back; sunlight came down to the great hall through the windows of these rooms, which opened onto a balcony around the upper floor. This indirect light brightened the great hall's frescoed scenes of a bard singing to the accompaniment of his lyre and flowers growing among craggy rocks. To Briseis these familiar, cheerful surroundings seemed an incongruous place to lay out her mother's lifeless body.

As the servants and family gathered, the megaron hall, usually the heart of family life and the place for feasts and the bards' tales, was filled with grief. The serving women wailed in lamentation and raked their faces and necks with their nails. Briseis felt the scratches on her own face and smelled the sourness of her dried blood. Her father and brothers smeared ashes on their heads and arms.

Here, where the family's shrine held the spirits of their protective gods and ancestors, she must transfer her mother's spirit from the shell of her body into the object Briseis and her father had chosen— Antiope's satchel, which held her sacred healing materials. Briseis pressed the large satchel against her chest with both arms as if she could embrace her mother through it. If Briseis performed the rite correctly—and doubt about this haunted Briseis—then Antiope would watch over her family from the satchel that would reside forever in the shrine to receive their offerings. Later they would burn Antiope's body on the pyre and gather her bones and ashes, but this moment mattered most. Once again, her mother's fate rested on her. She had failed yesterday to save her mother. Now her mother's soul would find a peaceful place near her family or it wouldn't—dependent on Briseis's abilities as a priestess.

Briseis hadn't slept well. Each time she dozed, the hopeless finality of her mother's loss would penetrate and throw her wide awake as if someone had tossed her out of bed. Her body ached and her mind's grogginess frightened her. She wasn't ready. Her father and brothers, clustered near her, should have given her comfort, but they seemed lost in their grief.

At a moment when she most needed her mother, she was alone. Each time in the past when she'd had to do some important rite, her mother stood with her, even when her sickness had grown terrible. Briseis had never imagined being the only one alive in Lyrnessos who knew the rites and skills of a healing priestess, never weighed how heavy that privilege would sit upon her. Her mother had been sick for months, but that hadn't meant she would die, not to Briseis. Even now it seemed impossible that each day would go by without her. She felt crushed by an idea that kept insinuating itself into her thoughts —that her mother had chosen to abandon them. She wanted to shake her mother awake and immediately blamed herself for such a foolish thought.

Briseis stood in front of the shrine next to her mother's body and tried to put aside her anger. She knew from other rites she'd performed that she could empty her thoughts in order to allow the goddess to fill her mind, and an almost frightening clarity would take hold of her. She needed to make a similar space for her mother's spirit, but anger, if she let it, would demand to be heard. So she focused on the shrine, a place she held in awe throughout her child-hood. It sat on legs shaped like a stag's—Kamrusepa's sacred animal. Its broad doors, each as wide as Briseis's arm spread, swung on large bronze hinges. The polished wood, carved from ebony and cedar, shone black and burnt red against its ivory inlay. It had beauty and grace, a place in which her mother would happily reside and join the other ancestors who kept her family safe. Briseis felt a sharp pain pushing against her chest. The shrine's ivory designs swirled and danced before her tired eyes. Her mother's voice sounded softly in Briseis's ear, barely a sigh, without distinct words, but enough. She clasped the leather bag to her chest tighter and thanked her mother for this blessing.

Briseis opened the doors wide, revealing rows of small statues of their gods, mixed in with more humble objects like amulets, belts or daggers representing family members from past generations. She held the worn leather bag to her face, breathing in its smell, then kissed it and laid it on the shrine's middle shelf where Briseis had cleared a wide place for it.

Her father poured a libation into Antiope's silver cup and drank, passing the cup on to each of her brothers. His eyes were red and puffy, but as he held out the wine to her, one side of his mouth turned up in a lopsided, gentle sign that he loved her and knew how hard this was for her.

Briseis took the cup and sipped the wine, letting the sweetness on her tongue remind her of her mother. *Please let my prayers be strong enough.* Her hand felt slippery with sweat against the smooth wine cup.

She drew in a breath and let it out slowly before placing the cup next to the bag and beginning the prayers. "Let this be your spirit's pleasant home with food and wine among your family to protect us."

She took lavender from a handkerchief knotted to her belt and sprinkled the sweet blossoms over the satchel, crushing them between her fingers to release their perfume. She spoke the prayers for this rite, letting the rhythm of her recitation, rather than the words themselves, express her inner longing. When she completed the final cycle of prayers, she felt sure her mother had settled in this familiar place.

Before she closed the shrine, she leaned forward and kissed the bag once more. A tear fell among the dried blossoms.

FOLLOWING ANTIOPE'S DEATH, Briseis had to contend not only with the raw pain of losing her mother, but also with her new duties supervising the household. She settled quarrels between the servants, kept track of how many lambs or pigs should be slaughtered, how much goat's milk should go to producing cheeses, which serving women should be set to grinding grain and which to weaving, and a never-ending flow of other tasks. The constant decision-making overwhelmed her at times, but she had observed her mother do these things and had taken on some of them during the long months of illness. The servants now treated her with the same deference they had formerly given Antiope. She felt strange about that at first, but realized her transition from girlhood was complete—in all ways except marriage.

As Briseis took on the running of the household, Eurome gave her sound advice. Briseis had always loved her nursemaid, but instead of trying to escape her nurse's chatter and scoldings, she now discovered a steady common sense she had underestimated. She was glad that by tradition she would take Eurome with her when she married. It provided the one consolation each time she thought of her upcoming wedding.

She had been betrothed to King Euenos's son, Mynes, since they were infants. Her father grew up as Euenos's closest companion. In adulthood, he remained the king's strongest comrade in battles and counsel. The betrothal made everyone happy. As a little girl she'd liked the idea of becoming a princess when she married and living in the palace, which was grander and more beautiful than her family's home.

Then when she was ten, her mother brought her along to assist Queen Hatepa, who suffered from ill health. Hatepa endured frightening bouts of breathlessness. In the worst times, a strange blue color spread through the queen's fingers and face. A cough kept away sleep.

On this occasion, instead of observing her mother's cures, she secretly watched Mynes from a distance through a crack in the door curtain, curious to observe this person of such importance to her future. He and a slave child played knucklebones on the floor. When the slave's throw won the game and he gave a shout of glee, Mynes struck him so hard, his head slammed into the wall and he lay motionless on the floor. Briseis started toward the child but she stopped in shock, still shielded by the door curtain, when Mynes kicked the slave child in the belly. "Just remember who's going to be king."

Briseis retreated unseen, shaking in fear at his vicious power. That violent boy would be her husband.

On the way back from the palace as their cart bumped along, Briseis whispered what she'd seen to her mother. She had to know if such things were allowed for princes.

"No one," her mother said softly, "should ever strike out like that, especially not because they've lost a game and cannot bear such a minor disappointment. Mynes is young enough still, I suppose. He has time to learn to be gracious when he cannot have what he wants —as important a lesson for a ruler as for you, young lady. You and your brothers don't always remember that, either, you know." Her mother's voice sounded far more worried than usual, however.

Her mother had chewed the edge of a fingernail, an unladylike habit she scolded Briseis about whenever she caught her doing it.

"I'll speak to the queen about it," Antiope said, as much to herself as to her daughter. "Perhaps I'll have to ask your father to mention it to Euenos. I've seen it before, this temper in Mynes—" Her mother pulled Briseis close in a hug. "You shouldn't have to worry about such things."

The look on Mynes's face when he kicked the slave stayed with her, and she did worry. Duty required her to marry the prince. Her parents had no choice either, with such a longstanding betrothal.

A few days later, when Briseis and her mother were seated alone together, spinning wool by the hearth, Briseis asked if she'd spoken to Hatepa about it.

"Yes, I did." The small band of muscle running down her mother's neck went taut as it did whenever she was angry. This was one of the only outward signs her mother ever gave of her ire, along with a tenseness to her speech, a slight over emphasis on each word. "The queen replied that a future king should not be humiliated by his servants. I told her she misunderstood the importance of her son's actions. She changed the subject."

Antiope had closed her eyes. When she opened them and looked at Briseis, she wiped away a tear. "I'm sure there will be ways to guide Mynes once you're married." Briseis had taken comfort in the idea that her mother would know what to do when the time came and would give her advice about her husband. But now her mother was gone.

3

WARRIORS

The rules of modesty kept Briseis and Mynes apart in childhood, and after watching his violent temper, she didn't mind the distance. She admitted he was, even to her dubious eyes, a handsome man with a broad chest, dark wavy hair and dramatic eyes that seemed entirely black. They reminded her of a hawk's, which made her shudder a little. She knew boys grew and learned to control their tantrums; she had too, she admitted. She'd seen it often enough with her brothers—a wooden cup flung in anger, or a yelled, unkind word, but always taken back later. She hoped Mynes was maturing into a gentler man than the boy she had observed.

Sometimes she overheard her brothers when they returned from practice with the other young warriors, muttering about the dangers of getting too close to Mynes's sword if he was frustrated, and then the sharp bands would tighten around her forehead and the pain in her head would force her to lie down.

Almost two cycles of the moon had gone by since her mother's death. Soon King Euenos and her father would have to agree upon an actual day for the wedding. Spring was the preferred season, and spring had just begun to show its arrival. She wished she had more time—perhaps the marriage could be delayed somehow.

After Antiope's death, Briseis and her father continued their daily habit of walking through the fields, vineyards or pastures, wherever the activities of the estate were busiest. Briseis much preferred being outdoors. Now that her household duties had increased and kept her inside, she appreciated her father's old habit of consulting her about the estate. It provided a good excuse to escape.

She studied her father one morning on their walk. Glaukos wanted to check the vineyards nearest the cart road that went to Lyrnessos, so they headed along the path in that direction. Her father wasn't old, but his gait had slowed since Antiope's death. His lean body didn't have the same spring and the numbers of gray hairs amidst the black curls by his temples had increased.

Her parents had few shared characteristics. Her mother's connection to the goddess—the intimacy she felt with the unseen world of the divine and the power it gave her to heal others—had mystified her father; he preferred the feel of plowed soil in his fist or a well-shaped sword haft. Such differences hadn't prevented them from loving each other. They had relied on mutual advice, and during her childhood Briseis understood that their physical closeness provided them some essential reassurance, especially for her father. Now bereft of Antiope's presence—his wife's hand on his arm when bad news arrived—he sometimes plodded as if his feet weighed too much for him to lift.

Despite the lines of sadness around his eyes, his smile when he looked at his daughter walking by his side warmed her. They reached the first rows of grapevines, still leafless but ready to burst into green, and started walking over the clods of upturned soil where the workmen had dug the weeds between the vines.

He studied the budding plants, considering how much pruning back of branches would need to be done to provide the right sunlight for the grapes later. Briseis turned her eyes up to the slopes of Mount Ida. Her grandfather had cleared the pines and oaks from many of the surrounding slopes and built terraces with rough stone walls, which he planted with apricot, fig and pomegranate trees and with olive groves. The dense forest patches seemed to flow in green waves to the edge of the more widely spaced and grayer tones of the orchards, where many of the trees had not yet leafed out. She loved the mountain and its hidden places. She wondered how often she could walk in Ida's woods once she'd married and lived further away in the palace.

She wanted to overcome her shyness with her father on the subject of her marriage and ask him if it could be postponed. She could explain her need for delay without bringing up Mynes's temper. To admit that she feared Mynes would be too hard for her father to bear, although she knew he saw Mynes's faults. She should be having this conversation about her marriage with her mother, but now she would have to discuss it with her father as best she could. She rubbed her forehead and beside her eyes.

"Papa?"

He had bent down closer to the branches and now looked up at her with concern. Her voice must sound strained, at least to an astute listener who loved her.

She took a deep breath. "Do you think King Euenos and Mynes would be terribly upset if you asked them to postpone the wedding while I grieve? I know it's been two months and I don't want to cause trouble, but I'm struggling with so many new duties since Mama died. I can't imagine taking on the palace household when I'm only just learning this one without Mama's advice . . ."

Her father stood up. She saw him fighting tears. He pulled her against him for a moment and then started walking through the vineyard again while looking into the distance up the slopes of Mount Ida. She recognized this behavior. He found both her marriage and her mother's loss hard to talk about.

After a while he said, "King Euenos will be disappointed to postpone your marriage." At this her temples pressed tight. "But you are my daughter, too precious for placating even my old friend. I can tell him I've lost my wife and I can't lose my daughter so soon after. He needn't know *you* want the delay."

Relief loosened the bands around her forehead. "I will miss my mountain when I marry."

"*Your* mountain?" Her father laughed. "I guess it is yours, after all, in spirit if not in purchase. The mountain's woods and springs were your favorite places to play as you grew up, you and Iatros. Was that because you spent so much time looking for healing plants, or did Kamrusepa put this love inside you to draw you to her sacred places?"

She gazed up at the mountain. "I'm not sure. I always loved the woods."

He patted her arm. "As to your marriage, you'll be a fine queen for Lyrnessos. Don't worry about the palace household. Your mother did her best to prepare you and she succeeded. I haven't got any doubts about you, even if you are headstrong."

He looked into the distance again. The lines of worry returned to his brow. "Delaying the wedding will be good for Mynes also. Young men like Mynes need high spirits when they face their enemies in battle. We raise them to be fierce, but to listen, to control the temper —these qualities are also important."

He broke off a dead branch from one of the vines and tossed it to the ground. "Mynes needs some time to acquire these skills before he can rule well. Euenos thinks your marriage would stabilize Mynes— he talks of that often—but I'm happy to delay it until Euenos has had a chance to cultivate these virtues in his son. Your thought matches mine. Don't feel distressed to have asked me."

The clatter of a chariot and horse approaching the estate sounded on the nearby cart road, and they both looked up. "A summons for me from the king," said Glaukos. "I'd better go."

"There goes your day," said Briseis with sympathy. "I hope it's not anything too serious. I'm going into Mount Ida's woods. I'll restock the supply of horn bush for my healing work while I'm not needed in the house." She kissed her father's cheek and headed toward the trail leading up the slope.

A gentle warmth radiated up from the dirt path as she climbed through the orchards where her father's workmen cleared dead weeds from around the trees. As she slipped into the forest, the coolness of oaks and pines greeted her like an old friend. She breathed in the earthy scent of mulching leaves underfoot and the sharp tang of pine needles as she pulled them through her fingers in passing. She focused on her search for a horn bush. It should have tight purple buds this time of year.

Briseis enjoyed gathering the mountain's medicinal offerings, the gifts Kamrusepa had revealed to her healing priestesses. She found time for this task whenever she could, although both her grandmother and mother had left much of the locating of herbs, roots and bark to Maion, now the oldest servant on the estate. He had overseen the fields and orchards until age overtook him. When Maion was a boy, Briseis's grandmother had nurtured his instincts for finding plants and understanding their uses. Briseis had received her lessons in plant lore from him, with Iatros tagging along more often than not.

She sighed, remembering the temple duty for Kamrusepa that she should be attending to but had been dodging for weeks. As a healing priestess her duties differed from the priestesses who worked in the temple precinct. She travelled around to those who were sick, and she had no required duties on a daily basis in the temple, but she was expected to participate occasionally in the rites of the goddess's care and sacrifices. Briseis would never doubt her ability to serve her goddess if Kamrusepa only required her dedication here in the woods and, of course, in her work amongst those struck by illness or other disharmony with the gods. The temple rites, though, made her uneasy. She hadn't spent as much time learning them. She suspected her mother, for whom temple duties were a nurturing force, had never realized that they were something you had to study and grow accustomed to. Antiope had spent as much time as possible caring for Kamrusepa in her temple home, but she had preferred to make her devotions alone.

Briseis secretly thought Kamrusepa preferred her mountain haunts to the elegant sanctuary, but she'd never whispered such a sacrilegious idea to anyone. Unfortunately, now she had to assume her mother's role in the temple. Her excuse of a mourning period had gone stale a month ago, but she still avoided her responsibility. She hurried her steps and pulled aside the overgrowth, looking for her blooming quarry.

The Kamrusepa of the woods was also, in Briseis's mind, the Kamrusepa who brought Telipinu back to his home—a handsome, young warrior god whom Briseis felt was her special protective deity. The source of this belief remained mysterious to her. All the tales showed Telipinu loved the forest as much as she did, but that didn't account for her conviction. She even admired Telipinu's famous fury —he'd stood up to everyone with courage when he felt his honor had been insulted. This year at the Spring Festival she would be the one to recite the tale of how Kamrusepa soothed Telipinu's rage and returned him to his proper place, along with the fruitfulness of the fields and herds. This was the most important duty of the healing priestess each year. Her special bond with Telipinu had grown since her girlhood. He was her sheltering deity, even while Kamrusepa was the source of her healing skills and inspiration. She thought of her marriage and hoped she would not need Telipinu's divine protection.

Spying a horn bush peeking out from behind a scrubby juniper tree, she used her knife to clip some branches, tied the boughs to her sash and headed back to the orchard path.

At the edge of the woods, she knelt by one of the many springs that burbled up. Mount Ida's springs offered cool refreshment to shepherds and flocks throughout the range's peaks and valleys. The mountain separated Lyrnessos from their ally Troy, which lay on the other side of Ida, surrounded by a fruitful plain.

Soft leaves of watercress and spearmint edged this spring with fragrant abundance. Briseis recited the thanksgiving to Kamrusepa, the goddess of Mount Ida's springs, for the blessing of her water and filled the wooden cup that was kept there for any thirsty passerby. She took a long drink and felt the cooling strength of the mountain fill her.

THE PRESENCE of three Greek traders at the gate waiting to do business with her father shattered the sense of well-being she'd brought back from the mountain. Several of her father's workmen had gathered around, cautious about these strangers. They would protect her from these men in her father's absence, but that wasn't what worried Briseis.

As soon as she entered the courtyard, Eurome bustled to her side to chaperone, as modesty required in the presence of men. She tugged the veil of Briseis's cloak over her hair, giving her charge a scowl for forgetting these details. Three other serving women clustered around her.

Briseis could manage with these traders on her father's behalf, although they wouldn't expect to talk to a woman. Both Briseis and Eurome spoke Greek as fluently as they spoke the language native to Lyrnessos and Troy. Glaukos's family interacted with Greek traders and diplomats, and Eurome had been captured from a Greek fishing village by slave traders as a child. Besides, many of the bards sang in Greek, and Briseis never wanted to miss a tale.

The Greek traders bowed in courtesy. Their smudged tunics and workable but plain sword belts and scabbards showed that these weren't the most successful of merchants. Two of them had the squinty eyes and weathered, sun-darkened skin she'd noticed on men who made their living on the sea. One of these had arms like tree trunks and she could imagine him hoisting heavy sail canvas; the other seemed more agile than powerful. From their blank expressions she deduced that they were sailors, not captains, and she turned to the third man. He was the shortest of the men and the least sea-worn. His tunic had at one point been trimmed with yellow braid, but much of that had been worn down to shreds. He stepped forward as leader and asked for guest-rights from the household. He seemed annoyed to be speaking to a woman, and Briseis felt the burden of receiving them.

The household would provide a meal and probably shelter overnight. The rules of hospitality demanded that much. Her father, called to the palace, likely wouldn't return until late in the day. Her brothers, even Iatros for once, had gone off to the practice field to hone their fighting skills with the other young noblemen, so they would be gone all afternoon also. She would act as hostess alone with her servants, an awkward duty for an unmarried girl and a novel one for her, but she'd watched her mother in this sort of situation. She swallowed the sense of inadequacy that seemed to be growing as a lump in her throat. Eurome held her arm firmly and she gave an answering squeeze of thanks.

All of that was a worrisome nuisance, but more than that she wondered what these Greeks wanted to buy. Her father had traded with Greeks for years—his metalworking shop had a widespread reputation, overseen by a talented servant named Milos. From his days as a young apprentice to her grandfather's blacksmith, Milos had turned into such an excellent workman that her father had expanded both the space and the number of men he supervised, building several large workrooms onto the back of the original house, so that instead of filling only the household needs, the workshop now produced gold and silver jewelry and bronze weaponry. Traders came often to buy from Glaukos.

She'd have no worries if these men wanted to commission some jewelry. They'd be welcome to stay. However, she'd discussed with her father the rumors of Greek raiding parties that the gossip said might be part of a larger force. From north of Troy came word of this marauding along the coastline—no danger yet to her city, even if true —but it made her cautious of these men. Her father would not put his good swords into the hands of Greek warriors if they planned to raid any town near here. Lyrnessos owed her allegiance to the powerful city of Troy, as did all the towns and islands. In return, Troy kept them safe, and no one would be foolish enough to challenge Troy's mighty walls. Even so, if these traders had come to buy weapons, she guessed her father would prefer she send them on their way quickly. At least she thought that's what he'd want. She understood metalworking, having grown up shadowing Milos's fascinating labors. Milos could help her with questions of manufacture, but whether to do business with these men was a question for her father —now hers alone.

Briseis sent serving women to the kitchen to alert the cook to prepare a meal, bring wine to refresh the men and water to bathe their guests' feet. With the escort of her menservants, she welcomed the traders into the megaron hall, seated herself and Eurome on the women's side of the circular hearth in the middle of the room and indicated chairs on the men's side for the traders. The servants placed tables next to each, poured the wine and knelt to wash their dusty feet.

Until Briseis provided refreshment, the rules of hospitality did not permit her to inquire their names, much less the purpose of their visit. This custom protected travelers while they sought essential food and shelter, since once a household provided for them, the family was bound by the gods' sacred laws not to harm the visitors— whoever they turned out to be, even allies of old foes.

Briseis would have to wait. She twitched her foot in frustration. Even when she had fed these men as a young woman, there were limits to how appropriately she could discuss business. She chewed her lip. If they sought weapons, she wanted to send them away as soon as possible without causing offense. Every stage of hospitality increased her obligations toward them. Alienating traders was bad for business, and making enemies of Greeks seemed dangerous these days.

Four serving women came in with trays of flatbread baked with black cumin seed, sliced cucumbers, and wooden cups of chick pea soup, thick with yogurt and studded with fresh coriander leaves. *That ought to soften those sour looks.* Briseis noticed the servants had brought a small silver plate of dates stuffed with almonds. Dates were a delicacy from far away deserts and she wouldn't have wasted them on these men, but she figured the cook was throwing her support behind Briseis as best she could.

"I'm sorry Lord Glaukos won't be available to receive you," she said. She noted the disappointment on the face of the man who'd taken the lead. He shifted in his chair and looked around the room. He wanted someone to do business with right away. That he felt such pressure was interesting.

Instead of the questions she would have liked to ask, she sifted through the polite things her mother used to say that made everyone comfortable and easy.

"It's unseasonably warm today. The dust on the road from the harbor must have been choking." The two sailors nodded but did not interrupt shoveling their meal into their mouths.

"Yes, very dusty and hot," said the short man with the yellow trim, but then he lapsed unhelpfully into silence.

"Did you sail from a long distance?" Perhaps she could discover if they were working with the raiders to the north.

"Not too far."

Briseis sighed. She let them eat until the awkward silence made her desperate.

"I wonder in your travels among the Greek kings," Briseis said, using the only topic that came to mind, "have you ever seen Lord Achilles? The tales the bards sing about him seem impossible, an invincible warrior, half immortal."

She loved the bards' tales. The tale of Achilles had enthralled her the first time she heard it sung. Some versions even said an immortal centaur, Chiron—half horse, half man—had taught Achilles to be a healer, of all things. It seemed a pleasant topic to her, but the traders looked alarmed. She remembered that her mother had often warned her not to go on about the stories she loved—it was unladylike and wild. Look what she had done—made them uncomfortable with her inappropriate conversation.

The leader of the traders stared at her. A piece of bread, dripping chickpeas, stayed suspended half way to his mouth. The other two had also stopped stuffing themselves.

It occurred to her that their alarm wasn't about her rude manners. Did they, in fact, know about the Greek raids? Her mention of the most powerful of the Greek warriors was not a topic traders would want to focus on with her family if they knew of fighting—bad for business. Especially if they wanted weapons.

Briseis smiled at her guests. Maybe her wild conversation topic had been just right for the circumstances. A little surge of confidence made her sit up taller.

The three men looked at each other. The leader put his dripping bread back into the bowl. He cleared his throat.

"No, no, we've never seen Lord Achilles. Or King Agamemnon either." He quickly shoved in a bite of bread as if to shut himself up.

Agamemnon? Briseis's eyebrows shot up. *The powerful king of the Mycenaeans?* What a terrible, nervous liar this man was—bringing up what hadn't even been mentioned. He obviously had business with Agamemnon that he wanted to hide. Her doubts about what course to take with these men disappeared. She'd send them on their way once they'd finished their meal. Housing them for the night was out of the question. She'd avoid having her family antagonize these Greeks.

When the empty plates had been cleared and each had had his fill of wine, she rose from her chair and the servants drew up behind her.

"I am so sorry you have missed my father. I hope you will have better fortune on the next leg of your journey. I am sure you can understand that I am unable to assist you."

The Greeks rose in courtesy. The man with tattered yellow braid asked, "Your father's return isn't expected soon? We could wait. We'd like to discuss some trade with him. Profitable trade."

She tried to look apologetic. "No, I'm sorry. That won't be possible. However, it is fortunate that Lyrnessos's harbor is only a half-day's walk from here. You have not come too far out of your way. I am sure you will find good business elsewhere." She bowed them toward the door.

4

GOLD AND BLOOD

B riseis's three brothers arrived home late in the afternoon, but they stayed by the gate waiting for their father. From across the courtyard, Briseis watched them whispering together, full of some news. She went over to tell them about the traders' visit, but they fell silent when she got near.

Briseis crossed her arms over her chest. "What's so interesting that you don't want to tell me?"

"We should wait till Father gets home," her eldest brother Bienor said. "We don't really know anything for sure."

Now she was curious. She looked at Iatros to see if she could make him tell her. He pushed a pebble back and forth with his left foot, keeping his eyes on the ground.

They all looked up at the sound of Glaukos's chariot wheels and horse. He waved and they stepped back to let their father through the gates. He jumped down and tossed the reins to a groom.

"Since you're all waiting for me," Glaukos said, "I assume you have heard the news. A Greek army—a big one—has encamped before Troy." Briseis gasped. How had distant raids become an army at Troy?

"Will we fight?" Bienor asked.

"Probably not," Glaukos said, rubbing his fingers along his jaw line where the day's dark stubble showed against his olive skin. His expression was grim. "The Greeks have raided before. They fill their ships with treasure and slaves, whatever they find useful, and leave."

"I hope so," said Iatros. "They should go away soon."

"But won't we defend Troy?" Bienor looked surprised. He still had on the sword belt he'd worn to practice, slung across his chest. The gold lion inlaid into the bronze grip of his sword appeared to be running up toward his neck. As Glaukos's sons, both Bienor and Adamas had the best possible weapons from Milos's workshop. Briseis wondered how eager they were to use them in battle. She hoped they never got a chance. Iatros looked sick. He shared her feelings on this, apparently.

"Troy's walls will hold off the Greeks," said Glaukos. "They'll have to be content to prey on smaller towns nearby." His mouth turned down. "I'm so sorry, Briseis, they've already destroyed Sestos."

"Sestos!" Briseis had never been so far north, but Sestos mattered to her. A renowned healer from Sestos, named Henti, had stayed for several weeks with Antiope when Briseis was six. She remembered the piercing blue eyes that seemed to read her thoughts and the dusky voice that startled her coming from the tiny, birdlike woman. Henti had chosen to travel around the towns of the Troad to exchange knowledge with other healers. Antiope had revered her.

Glaukos put his arm around Briseis's shoulder. "I'm sorry. Sestos has been burned to the ground, the scouts say."

"What happened to the people? Is Henti safe? Do you know?" Briseis gripped her father's arm.

"We don't know about the women. Probably taken captive."

Briseis held tighter to her father. Her knees felt like they might give way. Then she understood what her father hadn't said—the men must all be dead. "But..."

"Why did Troy let that happen to Sestos?" Iatros looked close to tears.

Glaukos shook his head. "King Priam didn't have a choice. The Greeks brought a huge army this time, not the usual raiding party.

The king can't risk leaving Troy undefended by sending his warriors to fight somewhere else."

This didn't seem right, but there was no point arguing with her father. It hadn't been his decision to abandon Sestos, Briseis figured, but Priam should protect the small towns. Isn't that why they allied themselves to Troy?

Briseis guessed from the red flush of Adamas's face that he wanted to go straight to Troy to fight the Greeks. Her middle brother's coloring always revealed when he was upset or eager. Part of her sympathized when she remembered Henti. Bienor looked thoughtful though. He'd led skirmishes against the occasional small band of Greek raiders. Maybe he'd talk Adamas out of his enthusiasm.

She suddenly remembered the news she had been waiting to tell her father.

"Father, some Greek traders came while you were at the palace."

Her father looked at her in surprise. "They're still here? You should have told me when I entered."

"Oh no, I sent them on their way. They mentioned Agamemnon so I guessed they might be buying arms for the raiders you'd told me about. I hope I did the right thing. Your news—"

"Agamemnon? He's the king at the head of the army at Troy. If they have any business with him, you did exactly the right thing. Thank you."

Adamas tossed his head. "Mynes said Achilles is with them. There'll be some fighting for sure."

"Achilles?" Briseis felt odd saying his name now. Listening to the bards, even talking to the traders about the famous warrior, hadn't felt real. How could such a man walk the earth—born of a sea goddess who could take any form she liked, even water or fire? "They say Achilles is invincible. We should never let him be our foe."

Her father gave her an odd look.

"Mynes wants to fight him," said Bienor. Mynes's eagerness to fight didn't surprise Briseis.

Her father waved his hands to stop his sons. The lines on his forehead deepened. "The Trojans have their own warriors. You boys don't need to fight Achilles."

"Is it true," Adamas asked, "that a Trojan prince seduced a Greek queen named Helen? And they came to take her back?" He fiddled with the ties at his side that held his leather chest guard in place. She wished he'd take off those hot layers of leather, but neither brother seemed to want to unburden himself of his martial gear. She hoped this talk of Troy and armies would pass quickly.

Glaukos shrugged. "That scoundrel Paris did steal one of their queens. He'll have to pay recompense."

"Father, everyone's heard the tales about Achilles," Bienor said. "If the Greeks want that woman back, won't he knock down the walls and take her?"

Glaukos shook his head. "Troy's impregnable and has many allies. Not even a half-immortal hero can change that—if the stories are even true." Her father sat down on the brick bench built into the courtyard wall and indicated with his chin that they should also. She knew what would follow: one of his lessons. He always included her. She would rule as queen one day and needed to understand how the world beyond the household worked.

He told them it shouldn't surprise the Trojans to find angry Greeks at their doorstep. "The Trojans control the straits into the Black Sea—the only sea route for trade, and the Greeks are traders. The winds often keep Greek merchants trapped in Troy's harbor, and the Trojans take advantage of them by charging exorbitant fees: an amphora of wine for a bed to sleep in, a copper ingot for their meals. And they charge tariffs for the right to pass through. The Greeks resent this treatment."

"The Trojans' greed has gone too far," Glaukos said. "The Greeks are even greedier—especially Agamemnon, and he's in charge of this particular raid."

Glaukos stood. He shrugged. "Greed can be bought off and King Priam has plenty to pay with. He'll hand over enough to make the Greeks forget their grievances. They'll destroy another town or two and feel like a victorious army. Then they'll leave with their horde of gold."

Briseis hoped her father was right, but she wondered how much greedier a king like Agamemnon would become when he had an unconquerable hero fighting for him. The bards' songs said that Achilles had a burning inside him he could not control—left from when his mother, the sea goddess Thetis, attempted to make him immortal. This strange fire drove him to extraordinary feats in athletic competitions and mad killing frenzies on the battlefield. Just one time, Briseis would like to see this young warrior with hair like burnished bronze and fluid movements—on the practice field, not in battle—and then he could go back home and leave them alone.

Worries about the Greeks fled from Briseis's mind when a servant brought one of her father's herders into the hall, out of breath because he'd run from his hut on one of the slopes above their estate. He shifted his weight from side to side, his narrow shoulders swaying with worry. He had a shaggy beard and above it, deep lines fanning out from hazel eyes.

"I come home after rounding up the sheep. My wife's in tears. Our Nessa—you know our little girl, Lady Briseis—she's sick all day, nothing staying in." The herder's hands swung in awkward gestures and his eyes darted from one person to another. "Some evil spirit's gotten hold of her. Now she can't even stand and that little one don't never hold still. Please come quick, Lady."

Eurome had already brought Briseis's cloak and healing satchel. Iatros stood by, ready to go. Since Antiope's death Iatros frequently accompanied Briseis when she went out as healing priestess. The excuse at first had been to distract *his* grief, but in fact, they needed each other. With a reassuring pat or understanding nod, he filled the void each time Briseis felt tears threaten from some memory of her mother's guiding hand. Besides, compounding medicines and finding sources of illness suited him.

To her surprise, her father joined them as they hurried out. "It's close to nightfall. I'll come with you for protection." She shook her head, puzzled. *Protection on their estate? The Greeks aren't that close.*

They climbed the narrow sheep trail up to the herder's place—a one room mud and twig hut built into the hillside, along with pens for one of her father's herds and a small patch for vegetables.

The child lay damp with fever, limp with exhaustion. At the sound of visitors, the little girl opened her eyes. Two wide, impossibly big circles of fear looked up at Briseis. The mother had washed her body with wet cloths to cool her, but she still burned. Briseis tried to drip some wine mixed with water on her tongue, but after a few drops, Nessa whimpered and turned away her head.

Briseis glanced over at Iatros. He'd pulled out her mortar and pestle and was grinding a gray-green powder.

"Sion, willow bark and fennel," he said. She nodded. He made it into a paste with a dab of honey and knelt beside the child, smiling and cooing to the little one. He coaxed her into opening her mouth. With Briseis's long medicine spoon he slid the remedy onto the back of the child's tongue.

A faint smile crossed Nessa's face. "Sweet," she murmured.

Iatros worked in another taste and then a few drops of water. He and Briseis took turns slowly, waiting in between to make sure she held it down. Briseis relaxed. Her limbs felt heavy after the long day. She couldn't have managed this last part without Iatros.

Briseis asked the wife for an onion in order to drive off any spirits or cleanse the child of any sin she might have accidentally committed. She pulled off one layer after another, throwing each into the fire.

"Like this onion which I throw into the fire, that the flames may consume it entirely, so may any evil that has entered little Nessa be thrown into the fire and be burned away. Nessa is only a child. If she has offended any god with her childish ways because she has not yet learned what is permitted and what is not, may her error be burned up like this layer of onion. May all pollution be far from this child."

They sat with the child and gave her more to drink. When they saw she could keep this down and Briseis felt confident the girl would recover, she and Iatros set off for home with their father, who had stood in the doorway watching.

Glaukos put his hand on Iatros's shoulder. He was smiling. Briseis tried to remember when last she'd seen him smile so broadly.

"I watched you work beside your sister. The work of a healing priestess is not so different from that of the physician. King Euenos tried to entice another physician to live among us with the promise of a large estate, but no one has agreed, and a speedy apprenticeship of one of our own young men seems the only solution. You have more knowledge to start than anyone else—if you agree to it. The position brings honor as well as the estate."

"I would like that very much." Iatros embraced his father.

"You'll have to learn quickly," said Glaukos. "If our warriors go to Troy, they'll take a physician with them. Nowhere is a physician as necessary as the battlefield."

Briseis shook her head. Her father's decision made her happy, but she did not want the men of Lyrnessos fighting at Troy, and her brother would need time, even if he did know a lot already. He'd have to learn to bind wounds and reset broken limbs, which physicians handled, but not healing priestesses. She wondered if at some point she would be able to talk Iatros into showing her how to do those things. It wasn't ladylike to close up a bloody gash, but she'd like to try.

5

A GODDESS'S WILL

The next morning Briseis arose extra early. She couldn't put off a visit to the temple any longer. She had to assume her mother's responsibilities and build closeness to the goddess. The community's health and well-being rested on her ability to assure the goddess's protection of Lyrnessos.

She'd been so pleased the day before with her father's decision to let Iatros train as physician, but Glaukos's comment about needing two physicians because one would go to Troy undercut his assurances that Lyrnessos would not join the fight. Her duty as priestess had suddenly taken on a new urgency. Kamrusepa must protect their warriors—her father and brothers among them—when they fought at Troy. Only Briseis could gain that divine blessing for them.

She hoped her delay in attending on the goddess in her sanctuary had not caused concern among Kamrusepa's temple priestesses. They carried the burden of attending to the goddess's daily needs and sometimes viewed the higher status of the healing priestess with jealousy. Briseis understood that her training and healing skills gave her the ability to intercede with Kamrusepa on Lyrnessos's behalf, but the other priestesses did not always see that distinction as clearly. They had loved Antiope, but Briseis needed to maintain that same bond, and she had been remiss so far. Surely they understood how hard losing her mother had been?

So she pulled on the simple brown tunic and skirt that the priestesses wore for everyday practices in the temple, grabbed her cloak and went downstairs to see if the groom had harnessed a cart for her as she'd requested the night before.

The small donkey cart painted with yellow and red stripes stood waiting by the gate. The donkey twitched his ears to show his annoyance at being put to work so early. She slipped into the kitchen to find a quick breakfast.

"I heard them preparing the cart," said the cook, "so I gathered some of yesterday's flatbread and slices of the goat's cheese that you suggested I make with some thyme added in. It came out lovely. I thought it might cheer you along the way."

Briseis thanked the cook and took the bundle wrapped in a linen napkin. She wondered how the cook knew that she needed cheering up. She didn't want people to know how little she wanted to go to the temple. Probably Eurome and the cook had been talking. Briseis could never hide anything from Eurome.

She climbed up beside the groom onto the board running across the front that served as a seat, and the cart lurched forward so quickly she almost dropped her breakfast. She eyed the donkey with suspicion, but decided he was just energetic first thing in the morning. Their donkey had never before shown signs of being vengeful.

She uncovered a corner of bread and cheese and took a bite, enjoying the smell of the herbs with the briny cheese. She tried to focus her thoughts on the rites ahead. Her mother's death had loosened many of the anchors that held Briseis's world in place. In the household Eurome helped her, but Briseis faced her relationship with Kamrusepa alone. As long as her mother had been by her side, she had thought the right feelings would come with time and guidance. Now she had neither. Her city and family faced war, without Antiope's devotion to Kamrusepa to invoke protection.

The cold early morning air crept under her cloak and she pulled it closer with one hand while trying to balance the napkin of breakfast. They passed fields of wheat and barley, and vineyards, interspersed with pastureland and woods.

Part of her wished that her brothers hadn't told her that Achilles fought as part of the Greek army. Knowing they would face that particular warrior made the whole thing worse, and it was bad enough. The stories she had heard of the half-immortal Achilles troubled her. She felt disgusted with her previous delight in them. Any warrior born of a goddess would be formidable, but this man was born of Thetis, who had saved Zeus, the king of the Greek gods, when the other gods conspired to overthrow him. Briseis had noticed with interest that Thetis—female as she was—had the power to stand up to all the other gods. That had made Thetis so confident of her strength that she had dared to challenge her son's fate by burning away his mortality. She'd failed—the gods, as well as mortals, must yield to fate—but what sort of man had this goddess created? Briseis shuddered and wondered what standing near Achilles must feel like. Lyrnessos would need all of Kamrusepa's protection in the face of such a foe.

Because of her need to win Kamrusepa's goodwill, Briseis had decided to go extra early to the temple in order to bathe and dress the goddess, a statue the size of a three-year-old child, wooden but covered in shining silver. Generally, the resident priestesses performed this daily rite, but Antiope had viewed it as the strongest way to bond with the goddess. Performing this rite would prepare Briseis to beseech the goddess on behalf of Lyrnessos. Unfortunately, this ceremony, more than any other, made her uncomfortable.

"When I am bathing the goddess," her mother had once told her, "she speaks to me more clearly than at any other time. I can hear Kamrusepa's voice reaching into me." This closeness was what Briseis wanted to achieve, but she had heard nothing when she performed the intimate rite. Instead she felt impertinent, lifting and disrobing the figure, as if Kamrusepa were a helpless infant. Briseis hoped this time would be different.

Her stomach felt better now that she'd put something into it, but her shoulders and neck ached. She shook out the empty napkin and dropped it into the storage basket behind her on the floor of the cart. The sun was still too low to warm her. A dusting of frost whitened the twisting branches of the vineyard they were passing. It seemed too late in the year for even a light frost. She hunched down in her cloak and imagined the army camped before Troy. She hoped Achilles was cold and miserable. Maybe he'd go back to Greece and she'd have less to discuss with the goddess.

They had to wait at the city gates for the guards to pull open one side of the giant gates and let them through. She must be the first to enter the city that morning. Once inside the city walls they crossed the open marketplace. The stalls around the square lay empty at this hour. They bumped through winding streets of shops and crowded mud-brick homes. She held onto the seat as the cart climbed the hill to the temple. If the cart went all the way to the top instead of turning down the temple road, she would arrive at the palace, where it felt like Mynes lurked in every corner. That thought did nothing to settle her nerves. She squeezed shut her eyes and took a deep breath.

Her father's groom dropped her at the temple precinct gates. They towered above her head and even though she'd stood in this very place with her mother many times, she felt intimidated. She knocked for the temple gatekeeper to let her in. The stern-looking man, whose age she'd never been able to guess, peered out and opened the gate when he saw Antiope's daughter. She followed him past the stone carvings of processions of gods that flanked the entryway on either side. Kamrusepa marched with the others, but her head turned sideways and even when Briseis stopped for a moment to peer closely at the goddess's face, she received no divine reassurance of Kamrusepa's love.

They crossed the large courtyard that served all the gods and passed into a smaller area devoted to Kamrusepa. The walls of the goddess's courtyard were mud-brick on a foundation of large stones, decorated with red and green pilasters. The courtyard was large enough for royal assemblies to gather for worship. The gatekeeper left her at the heavy wooden door to the goddess's sanctuary, which was guarded by two life-sized stone lions.

A priestess on duty pulled open the door. Briseis entered the sanctuary with its soaring midnight blue columns trimmed in red, took a deep breath, and slipped behind a gold-plated door into the goddess's inner sanctum. Kamrusepa rested on a throne covered in tin, a precious metal brought by traders from a land far away. She had heard her father negotiating for it many times. Milos used tin in his workshop, mixing it with native copper to make bronze. The throne stood on a base of red stone carved as twin stags. The goddess wore a blue woolen robe with a tall, cylindrical hat decorated with lapis lazuli rosettes. A gold necklace set with precious stones hung from her neck. Briseis peered into her lapis eyes, but their deep blue wore a distant expression.

On the green nephrite altar, Briseis placed an ivory box of linen drying cloths and the golden basin for washing, then turned back to the goddess, bracing herself for the undressing. At the sound of the inner sanctum's door opening, she looked with relief as another priestess entered, bearing a pitcher of perfumed water for the sacred bath. She didn't know this woman's name, but she recognized her. The priestess had a lame foot, turned under in a way that must be painful, but Briseis had noticed how swift to volunteer for tasks this woman had been each time she'd seen her. A priestess like this devoted her life to serving the goddess. Briseis bowed her head in respectful greeting. The woman returned only the merest dip. Her lips formed a stern line. She held her thin, off-kilter body with stiff formality.

Briseis sighed and returned to her duties while the priestess stood to one side watching. The rose perfume filled her nose in a pleasant way as she poured water into the basin. She hoped the goddess enjoyed it. She dampened a linen cloth, caught by the iciness of the water, which came from a grotto underneath the goddess's courtyard. Her fingers ached from the cold as she wiped each part of the goddess's form as the rite required.

Briseis finished the bath, hoping Kamrusepa did not notice her trembling hands. The goddess's lips were pursed in a small, secret smile. What was she thinking? She dried the statue quickly, wanting desperately to be rid of the cold. Instead of dressing her in the same gown, Briseis searched through one of the chests at the side of the room and found the garment she herself had woven for Kamrusepa as an offering upon her initiation into the goddess's service six years earlier. She saw a look of annoyance on the priestess's face when Briseis brought it to the altar. Perhaps Kamrusepa had been wearing the priestess's own offering and now Briseis was putting it aside, but whether the woman liked the change of costume or not didn't matter. What mattered was Briseis's connection to the goddess. She hoped the goddess would give her a sign of approval.

The robe for the goddess had taken her the whole of a winter to make—the first fine thing she had made by herself. She had loved to weave from an early age, standing at the loom creating tapestries with her mother. The rich colors, fine wool and linen threads she'd spun, her increasing skill and her mother's praise, had combined to form the one inside activity she adored. The loom she shared with her mother stood in the upstairs women's hall. Its tall upper beams were braced against the ceiling and its feet rested on the floor two strides out from the wall. Stone weights suspended just above the ground held the warp threads in place, and the tapestry grew under her fingers, gradually being wound around the upper beam.

For Kamrusepa's gown, her father gave her sun disks hammered out of gold to sew on once she'd completed the weaving. She sewed all the disks he gave her onto five of the ten pleats and then asked for more to cover the rest. At the time she did not realize how extravagant her request was, but her father did not complain, instructing Milos to make more. Each sun looked as though it rose from a deep blue sea. She was glad her robe glistened with so many suns, the wool a soft caress to the skin. Briseis prayed skill and splendor would suffice to show the depth of her devotion.

She bowed to the goddess, her service complete. The priestess scowled and Briseis fell back a step.

The priestess stood at the altar, her expression pinched as if in pain. With precise movements she smoothed the damp linen cloths Briseis had used and set them to one side.

"Why did you come here?"

Briseis straightened to her full height. "What kind of question is that? You know why a healing priestess comes to serve Kamrusepa."

"I know why your mother came. She was beloved of the goddess. But you?"

This woman should not speak to her like this. "You're being insolent," Briseis said, "What gives you the right?"

"You may not have noticed me, the lame priestess. Who pays attention to a crippled servant? I am Zitha, and I have watched you with your mother. Today you are even worse. You do not understand the goddess. She does not speak to you. You assume your mother's place is yours. Now that Lady Antiope is gone, Queen Hatepa and the temple priestesses will determine who pleases the goddess enough to serve her. You did not even come to attend on the goddess for weeks. How could you keep away from Kamrusepa if you were devoted to her?"

Briseis's face flushed. How had this priestess understood Briseis's reaction to the rite when Briseis had worked to hide it from her own mother? It didn't matter. The priestess had no right to treat her with disrespect. Briseis had been seeing to her duties as healing priestess throughout Lyrnessos all these weeks. There was more than one way to show devotion.

"There have been conversations among the priestesses in the temple since your mother's death," Zitha went on. "You don't live here as we do. I have pointed out how young and inexperienced you are, though I have chosen not to mention that the goddess does not favor you... yet. Leave the goddess's rites to us." She brushed off the smooth green surface of the nephrite altar with a dismissive gesture.

Briseis confronted Zitha across the stone slab. "You have no right to keep me from worshipping Kamrusepa at the temple. How dare you suggest such things."

"I dare to speak the goddess's will," said Zitha. "I watched when you tried to read the snake signs in divination. You had no competency then either. You didn't find the answer you sought, did you?

How will you protect the well-being of Lyrnessos when you could not save your mother?"

A feeling like a knife pierced Briseis's chest. She shook off her dread, refusing to submit to this hatefulness.

"How can *you* take care of Lyrnessos?" Briseis said. "What do you know about healing? I am the healing priestess. My mother taught me every day. Who else can read the tablets and perform Kamrusepa's rites? You? Did your mother teach you?"

Zitha recoiled as though she had been struck. "My mother? She..." Her hands plucked at the stack of linen cloths as though they would save her from falling. "My mother abandoned me in the temple precinct..."

Then the arrogant glint in Zitha's eyes returned. "Kamrusepa is my mother. Antiope coddled you. You balk at even the simplest duties for the goddess. Kamrusepa is a stern but loving mother who taught me to serve. You think because you are going to marry the prince that you are important and deserve to be the goddess's priestess? You are an outsider here. You don't understand the goddess with your whole heart as I do. Have you ever scrubbed the floors of this temple or polished her silver ornaments? Have you waited with a hungry belly until her sacrificial meal fed you? You think you can serve her fully while you live in luxury on your father's estate or the palace. Only I love her enough for her to speak to me. Go read your tablets as your mother taught you and attend to the sick. Perhaps the goddess will have mercy on us and give your healing some strength. Leave the temple to those of us who understand the goddess's will."

Zitha turned and limped out of the inner sanctuary. Briseis let her go for now. Although she believed Kamrusepa loved her, Zitha's accusations had too much truth in them. She cringed at the idea that Zitha might speak of her doubts to her father or the royal family. She wouldn't give Mynes a reason to be angry at her if she could help it.

Briseis returned the golden basin, the pitcher and the linen cloths to their proper places. She pushed open the gold-plated door of Kamrusepa's inner room and looked around the main sanctuary to see who was there. No Zitha. The priests had gathered at the altar to assist Briseis with the sacrifice. Their faces revealed only polite attentiveness. She circled the altar with the basket of barley raised above her head and then cast a handful of the grain onto the lamb to be offered. She said the correct words in her plea to Kamrusepa, but she did not feel her whole being expressed in the prayers. As she held the silver bowl under the lamb's throat to catch the blood after the priest made the sacred slit, the hot scent of blood brought a sense of dread rather than the triumphant confirmation that the goddess would grant her protection. Was Zitha right about her incompetence as a priestess, or had Zitha's envy ruined her chance of connecting with the goddess?

On the way home from the temple, Briseis sat in the back of the cart on the floor instead of on the seat. She didn't want to look at the passing world or hold on when the road got bumpy. If only she could talk to her mother. She'd been so busy with running the household on her own that she hadn't had to confront the empty pit that gaped inside her. Zitha had forced her to feel the emptiness. Why in the months of her mother's illness hadn't she asked her mother how to overcome her difficulties at the temple? She hadn't wanted to confess those feelings, but the silence of the dead was worse. Maybe Zitha did know better how to approach the goddess. Maybe Briseis was too coddled and comfortable to connect to the suffering that she must pray to prevent.

It was terrible to miss her mother's advice so much and at the same time to be challenged by an older priestess who might very well be better prepared, even if she was only a temple servant. During the next couple of weeks tears overwhelmed Briseis every time she tried to think of a plan to silence Zitha's criticism or win her over. The only way she could prove to Zitha she did have a connection to the goddess was to perform rites at the temple in such a way that Zitha believed in her devotion. Except so far Zitha hadn't been persuaded by her bathing rite or her snake divination, and Briseis didn't think Zitha would ever believe in Briseis's devotion no matter what she saw. Going to the temple would cause a direct confrontation with Zitha.

The fear that most kept her from standing up to Zitha and

demanding an apology was the worry that Mynes would hear of Zitha's challenge and think Briseis was weak and vulnerable. She would do all she could not to appear to Mynes like that slave child he had beaten.

Patience was not a skill Briseis had, but she waited, unsure what change might repair this trouble, and chafing at the insult and worry. Each day she prayed at home and in the sacred places on the mountain, determined to build the bond she must have with the goddess to protect her family and city. Why couldn't the wretched woman have helped her instead of attacking her?

6

A WOLF CURSE

A couple weeks after her encounter with Zitha, a clattering of horses' hooves rang out in the courtyard, interrupting a busy morning on the estate. Briseis hurried outside to see a royal messenger reining in the two frothing horses harnessed to his chariot. Her father ran through the gates. Glaukos must have seen the chariot while coming from the fields where he had been supervising the plantings that came on the cusp of spring. Her father hailed the messenger with a wave of his arm.

"Kallu, you've worked your horses hard. What's happened?"

The messenger was a slender young man with beads of sweat running down his brow. "The king wants you and Briseis immediately."

"Both of us? Is the queen ill?"

"I heard the queen screaming, but I don't know what happened. Something to do with the priestess at the temple—the one called Zitha. They've dragged her off but no one knows why. Hurry. The king ordered me to bring both of you as fast as possible."

Briseis froze. *What has Zitha said? Am I going to be dragged off also?*

GLAUKOS CALLED over one of his grooms. "Harness a cart with horses for Briseis and me. And take care of these." He indicated the messenger's pair. He turned to the king's man. "We'll go ahead as fast as possible. You stay and let these fellows recover."

Glaukos then nodded to Briseis to run for her cloak. "You'd better bring your healing satchel, Briseis, in case this is about the queen's illness."

Briseis shook herself and went inside for her things. Why hadn't she warned her father of Zitha's threats? They would head straight into whatever was going on at the palace and he didn't know his daughter needed protecting. *The queen screaming and Zitha dragged off*? She couldn't make sense of this news.

She hadn't been called to the palace to care for the queen since before her mother's death—more than two months. Now she wondered if she should have visited anyway. Had Hatepa's health deteriorated? What did Zitha have to do with that?

They were soon rushing along the wagon road toward Lyrnessos in a cart drawn by two swift horses. Briseis considered telling her father about Zitha, but he focused on the horses and she couldn't get the words out. How could she admit to him Zitha thought she had failed the city and that Zitha might be right? Besides, they'd dragged the woman off—she seemed to be in the wrong. But did that mean Briseis was also in trouble?

The huge, bronze-reinforced city gates lay open for farmers and merchants bringing in produce and goods. The guards recognized her father and waved their wagon through without a stop. Briseis and Glaukos crossed the lower town and her father leaned forward with the effort of guiding the horses through streets made narrow by the overflow of displays from the shops. They climbed the hill toward the palace. The palace loomed above on the rocky outcropping surrounded with its own defensive walls, part royal home, part citadel. The walls' massive cut stones rose high overhead, topped with wooden towers.

Briseis said Zitha's name. Her father didn't look at her and she couldn't tell if he heard her. "I had a run in with Zitha a while back."

Glaukos risked a quick look at her and then turned back to the horses. "Did she harm you?"

"No—that's not it. She doesn't approve of me."

Glaukos shook his head. "She's a temple servant. Approve of *you*, Antiope's daughter?"

They had reached the final stretch of road to the palace gates. This last short piece narrowed and ran parallel to the walls and towers. The design forced attackers to come underneath a rain of arrows from soldiers on the towers. Briseis looked up nervously. There wasn't time to explain to her father. She wanted to tell him to shield her from whatever lay ahead, prevent her arrest, but she couldn't make him understand why in the moments they had.

"Whatever Zitha said to you can hardly matter," said Glaukos. Perhaps he was right.

A watchman announced their arrival and the lofty gates opened. As soon as they dismounted from their cart, a servant sped them through a crowded, working courtyard with stables and kitchens, then along the portico of a decorative courtyard and into the living quarters of the royal family.

The servant opened one of the double doors that led into the king's megaron hall where Euenos held court. At home on Glaukos's estate, Briseis and the servants used the megaron hall as an extension of the kitchen to chop vegetables or peel garlic, a space for carding or spinning wool, and countless other daily tasks. At the palace, the expansive frescoes, gold-plated furnishings and delicate, carved side tables of the megaron expressed Euenos's power. Here he conducted royal business. Discreetly off to one side, the scribes had space to store their styluses and clay to take down the court records and the king's decrees. Today the big room lay oddly empty of the king's staff and courtiers.

Briseis and Glaukos stepped into the silent hall. All she could feel was the pounding in her chest. She expected guards to grab her at any moment. Instead, King Euenos sat slumped in his throne, an ornately inlaid chair on a low platform. Briseis stared at him, undone by this peculiar scene.

His finely woven tunic of black linen glistened with gold embroidery worked into a winding leaf pattern. He wore his customary band of gold on his head. He was the same age as her father and still strongly built and in fighting form. But his posture and the deep lines around his eyes and mouth contradicted these signs of well-being. Even his long hair, turned white a number of years before, seemed to indicate frailty. He raised his head at the sound of their entrance and rose slowly from his throne.

At that moment Briseis noticed Mynes standing off to one side behind his father. His powerful chest and arms—usually attractive to her—felt like a threat in her panic. His black eyes, buried under his deep brow, flashed in her direction, and then he hunched his shoulders forward in what looked like fear. *Fear of what?* He wore both a leather kilt and chest guard as if ready for battle—or the practice field, she tried to tell herself. She gasped at a slash of red underneath until she realized it wasn't blood but the color of his tunic. She'd been nervous enough before she realized he was present, but she took a deep breath to settle herself and bowed her head to both father and son in modest greeting.

King Euenos stepped toward them, his face gray. "My friend Glaukos, and Briseis, keeper of Kamrusepa's divine healing. A curse has been cast upon the royal family."

"A curse?" Briseis stumbled forward until she could brace herself by gripping the back of a chair.

She glanced at her father. He'd gone pale. Euenos did not sound angry at her, quite the reverse, but a curse meant the worst sort of trouble. Curses could spread throughout a community. No poultice or mixture of herbs could relieve the suffering inflicted through such evil incantations. Only rites, carefully designed, could remove a curse —and such rites posed dangers to the healer. Curses rebounded onto the one removing them if the rite proved ineffective.

"What happened?" asked Briseis. She couldn't connect this news with what the messenger had said. She struggled to pull her knowledge as a healer into the forefront of her confused thoughts. Her life and the city's survival depended on those skills.

The king's hands shook. "A waking nightmare. This morning, Hatepa writhed as if a giant twisted her body. I tried to break this monstrous grip, but I couldn't stop her thrashing. She cried out, begging me to slay the wolves that lunged at her—to rid her of their bloody jaws, teeth, red eyes, and huge, filthy bodies. Wolves in our bedchamber! I saw nothing. How can I kill what I can't see? When they finally left her in peace, she told me Zitha had placed a curse upon her."

Now the messenger's words made sense, but nothing about this curse or Zitha's part in it did. Briseis's knuckles clenched white on the chair as she leaned on it. From the corner of her vision she saw Mynes take a fighting stance full of menace. He seemed prepared to attack the wolves or Zitha. She wished a sword would work.

"Zitha?" said Briseis.

"Yes, the temple priestess," Euenos said, stepping closer to Briseis. "You must know her, don't you? We had no idea what an evil woman she is." Briseis nodded. *Oh yes, I know her.*

"You must release Hatepa from this curse," the king said.

"Consider what you are asking of my daughter," Glaukos said. "She's very young for such a dangerous rite."

"Who else can help Hatepa?" Euenos said.

What had Zitha done? Haunted by wolves? She'd never heard of a curse like this. Curses caused people to wither gradually or struck them with illness of the bowels, barrenness, or other troubles. Wolves didn't make sense.

"I must know how it was placed on her," Briseis said.

"I have summoned the queen's maid. Start there. The less strain on Hatepa the better." Euenos glanced at the door as if expecting the maid to appear at any moment.

Briseis nodded. Mynes shifted uneasily—his discomfort at his mother's plight made sense, but Briseis wondered at the sour expression when his father recommended she speak to Hatepa's maid. Was the woman unreliable? That could prove fatal if Briseis designed the rite incorrectly. A clammy sweat dripped down between her breasts, spreading the sour odor of fear. She turned to Euenos, who had grasped her father's shoulder.

"I know I am putting your daughter in danger," Euenos said, "but she is all that stands between us and disaster. A royal curse will insinuate itself into all of Lyrnessos. We cannot be weak with the Greeks so close to our doorstep."

"I'll fight the Greeks. We're not weak," said Mynes. "This trouble brought on by a foolish priestess—that part Briseis can manage."

Euenos turned on him. "Silence! Where were you when your mother faced ravening wolves? Only the healing priestess can challenge these demons." His father's words seemed to strike Mynes like a blow. Fear for her future as a wife thrust up against her terror of this curse.

Glaukos edged closer to his daughter and took her hand. Tension had drawn the skin of his face and neck so tight that the bones of his lean face had shifted from their usual handsome definition to the painful sharpness of a corpse.

Glaukos leaned down and whispered, "Can you do this? Did Antiope teach you enough?" She squeezed his hand in a reassurance she didn't feel.

On one occasion, despite the danger, her mother had insisted she observe the removal of a curse. That time it had been a curse by a jealous woman against a nobleman's wife to make her barren. Briseis remembered with horror the pitch-black night, the pit dug near a spring deep in a cave on Mount Ida, the way her mother had locked the curse in the Underworld through that pit. If Briseis's rite did not seal the curse eternally in the dark realms below, it could attack her or anyone else. She had to prepare in haste. In order to ensure the queen's safety, she must perform the rite during the middle of this coming night.

Euenos slumped again onto his throne. His fingers thumped repetitively against the chair's arm. "Why would Zitha do such a thing? She has been sheltered in the temple almost since birth. Where did she learn sorcery? I ordered her locked into the farthest storage barn in the lower city. I'll keep that polluted bitch away from my household and our gods." He slammed his fist against the armrest. "I'll have her questioned. Who put this idea in her head? Are there Greek spies among us?"

Briseis pictured the invulnerable Achilles. He wouldn't need a curse against a foe. Maybe that greedy King Agamemnon would. She wished she were half immortal like Achilles. What had Chiron taught the young warrior about removing curses?

A striking serving woman, not much older than Briseis herself, appeared in the doorway of the hall. To Briseis's surprise Mynes stepped aside, hiding himself behind a pillar in shadow. Briseis turned her attention to Hatepa's maid, puzzled that the queen did not keep a trusted old servant to care for her, but maybe no one lasted that long. The woman's dignified carriage as she crossed the room reminded Briseis of her mother, and she wondered how long this woman had been a slave. Their eyes met and Briseis saw intelligence in the large brown eyes and beauty in the delicate features and glossy black hair smoothed into a braid. She also saw fear.

"Maira," said Euenos, "assist Lady Briseis." The woman bowed.

Briseis wondered where to start. "What contact has there been between Zitha and the queen?"

The brown eyes glanced toward the king. Briseis knew from supervising servants this woman would want to avoid being blamed for the queen's suffering. Did that mean she wouldn't tell the truth? Did she understand how important it was that Briseis find the correct source of the curse? Briseis shifted her shoulders to loosen the place where her sweat-dampened tunic clung to her back. Maira seemed to read the faces in the room and settled on Briseis's with a direct look.

"Zitha came to the palace," said Maira, "the day after Lady Antiope died. I remember because the queen was distraught over your mother's death. Queen Hatepa wondered what would become of her without Antiope's care. I worried also. If you were not mourning your mother, I would have sent a messenger to bring you here. No one invited Zitha. She came on her own." Maira clasped her small hands loosely in front of her, letting them fall into the folds of her rough woolen skirt.

Briseis nodded, feeling relieved at the servant's composure. It indicated honesty. "What happened that day?"

"Zitha didn't know much about healing, but she listened to Queen Hatepa's complaints, which soothed the queen. When the queen complained of pain and ordered me to fetch you, Zitha said she could perform the rite to take away pain. She did—with a mouse and green and red wool, which she first tied on the queen and then on the mouse. She sent away the mouse to carry off the pain. Your mother had used a similar rite except Zitha did not know the right things to say. Nonetheless, it pleased the queen, and Zitha performed it many times over the days that followed."

There was no way to form a curse in these actions, however inept, thought Briseis.

"Queen Hatepa's cough is the biggest problem," said Maira. "Zitha started making a warm drink for her that calmed it. Once Zitha began making the drink, Queen Hatepa stopped asking to send for you."

"What was in the drink?" Curses took form primarily from powerful words, not potions, but nonetheless Briseis felt a jolt at hearing about this cure.

"Warm goat's milk, wine and honey." Maira looked like she wanted to say something else, but she glanced at Euenos in silence and settled into her calm demeanor.

Briseis felt disappointed. "Those are harmless ingredients." Her mother often dealt with the cough by making Hatepa sleepy, which this drink would do. Zitha had had some healing sense. Maira's description gave her nothing to fight the curse.

Briseis guessed that Zitha had appeared so opportunely in order to worm her way into friendship with the queen. Just as Zitha drove Briseis out of the temple, so she must have been determined to influence the queen against her—tell her Briseis shouldn't serve in the temple and shouldn't be the queen's choice of priestess for the festivals. A soothing drink and a sympathetic ear would help her cause, but a curse? It made no sense.

"Why does the queen say Zitha placed the curse on her?"

"You must ask the queen," Maira said, with a respectful bow to King Euenos.

7

HANDKERCHIEFS, HERBS, AND SACRED TALES

B riseis looked at the king. Would he allow her to question the queen? She rubbed the soft indentation next to her left eye to relieve the throbbing that stabbed her there.

Euenos nodded at Briseis and rose from his throne. He started to lead her toward the doorway, but then turned back to Glaukos. "It's time to question Zitha. Take some of my men with you. Find out who is behind this. I cannot believe she has acted alone."

"Let me at her, Father!" shouted Mynes. He stepped forward from the shadows with his fists raised. "I'll get the truth of this Greek treachery from her. She'll talk and I'll make certain she never threatens us again." Despite her dislike of Zitha, Briseis shuddered at his words. Maira drew back and crossed her arms protectively across her chest.

Euenos waved a dismissive hand in Mynes's direction. "No, better that Glaukos handles this. It's too important." He turned back to his friend, his face still gray, although the shaking had stopped now that they had begun to take action. "Go to the storage barn where Zitha's being held. Find out whatever you can."

Euenos himself led Briseis and Maira upstairs to the women's quarters. He dismissed the two serving women sitting on stools in a corner. Hatepa lay limp in her bed. She had a pinched nose but bulging eyes that seemed too big for their sockets. Her dun-colored hair had broken loose from its braid and lay damply on the pillow. Sweat and thrashing had crumpled her white linen sleeping tunic.

Approaching the bed, Briseis found the stale, rank air of the room hard to breathe. When she sat down next to Hatepa, the queen whimpered and clung to her future daughter-in-law. Her sallow skin hung on her arms. Hatepa's breath came in irregular wheezes interrupted by coughing fits. Briseis sat quietly, holding the queen to settle her. Hatepa's bed had a much larger wooden frame than most and more generous cushioning of fleeces and pillows on the leather straps strung across it.

After a time, Briseis edged Hatepa upright against her pillows. "I will remove this curse, but I need your help, Queen Hatepa."

Briseis pulled her satchel off her shoulder and set it on the bed. She took out a mullein-leaf infusion and mixed it into some mead Maira brought her from a pitcher at the side of the room. Several wooden chests crowded the large sleeping chamber, filled, Briseis presumed, with Hatepa's robes, both sacred and royal. A queen had many duties to fulfill as the gods' royal servant, as well as sharing her husband's rule.

"Why did I let Zitha convince me not to send for you?" Hatepa reached out and clutched Briseis's free hand against her wheezing chest as though it were a talisman that would keep the convulsions and wolves at bay.

Briseis loosed her hand and encouraged the queen to sip the mead. She asked Maira to stir up the fire in a brazier in a corner of the room and to boil some water. Briseis then turned back to the queen.

"Can you tell me what Zitha did to make the curse?"

"Zitha is not a healer like your mother." Hatepa's mouth turned down at the corners in a pout. "She performed the rite to send away pain, but my pain never left for long. I don't know what I expected from a deformed cripple. Why did your mother have to die?" The queen's chest shook with sobs.

"Don't worry, Queen Hatepa. I will take care of you. You will be safe." Briseis bit back what she wanted to say and practiced the patience she'd learned by watching her mother handle Hatepa's difficulties. Her own life and the good of Lyrnessos depended on her getting the correct information from Hatepa. Something evil throbbed behind the quivering terror of this woman—evil that could just as well overtake Briseis.

She rose and sprinkled ground licorice into the pot of hot water on the brazier. The aromatic steam rose to her face. Maira watched and then began to stir the tea with a wooden spoon as it boiled. Briseis returned to Hatepa's side.

"Did Zitha ever take anything from you, something she could use for a curse?"

"Take from me?" Hatepa looked around the room with a glazed look. Then she drew her fingers to her mouth with a shrewd light in her eyes. "Ah, I remember now. That disgusting rat. The last day she took my handkerchief—a dirty one from one of my coughing fits."

Euenos stepped from the doorway to come close to his wife. His eyes focused on Briseis.

Hatepa coughed, caught her breath and continued. "Zitha tucked it into her basket—a filthy thing like that. She should have given it to my maid to wash—that's why I remember."

"Could that be it?" Euenos asked, resting his hand on his wife's shoulder.

"It's possible," said Briseis, while she weighed this idea. "Since she captured the queen's weakness in the handkerchief, she could use it for a curse. What made you realize it was Zitha who cursed you?"

Hatepa fidgeted with the yellow and green braided ribbon decorating the neckline of her sleeping tunic. "Zitha thought she was fooling me, but I figured out why she kept coming to visit. Fooling me!—she's the fool. I liked her company so I didn't let on. The temple had taught her manners and proper speech. I can't tolerate bumpkins around me. But I knew what she was up to. She thinks I'll choose her as Kamrusepa's priestess for the festivals if she's nice to me. She kept saying how she cares for our goddess's needs every day. What a stupid woman. What else would she do in the temple all her life? She even told me she knew how to recite the story of Telipinu at the Spring Festival—imagine that abandoned stray taking Antiope's place. Who could tolerate watching that limping cripple hobble up onto the platform above us all—above *me*? As if I would take that honor from my son's wife." Hatepa wheezed out the words, but in her anger she had lost her fearfulness.

"Yesterday, I lost patience with her boasting. I told her she was trying to steal her position from those above her. She was unsuitable to be a priestess and I would have her thrown out of the temple. I could see her fear then. That put an end to her ambitions. She left in a rush, barely saying a proper parting. I thought she was only an abandoned girl, left at the temple to serve us. I didn't dream she studied sorcery. Some in the temple have the knowledge, but who would have taught her such things? She must have created the curse last night. With my handkerchief—that's what she used."

The queen fell back against the pillows, struggling to breathe. She had given Zitha a reason to act, thought Briseis. She felt Zitha's terror at being cast out of her temple home, separated from Kamrusepa. Briseis resented the woman, but she didn't doubt her devotion to the goddess. After what the queen threatened she'd have nothing to lose, and the dirty handkerchief would have given her the opportunity to place a curse. Briseis squeezed her eyes shut for a moment and felt a slight release of tension. She felt stifled in this sour air and told Maira to pull open one of the shutters on the clerestory windows despite the queen's squawked objection.

"Fresh air is necessary for your health, Queen Hatepa," Briseis countered.

Euenos patted his wife's arm. "Rest. Zitha will be stopped. Briseis, you know what to do now?"

Briseis hesitated. The king was eager to proceed, but she wanted to be certain she had learned all she needed. "I should stay and settle the queen. Then I'll go home and use my mother's library to plan the correct rite."

"Of course," said the king. "I will order an escort if your father has not returned from questioning Zitha." He left the room.

Briseis poured licorice tea into a cup. "Try this, Queen Hatepa."

Hatepa tipped her head up and sniffed at the liquid. "Ah... like Antiope's teas." She sipped. "Not a horrible smell like Zitha's drink... not bitter."

Briseis startled. Milk, wine and honey? "What did Zitha put in that made it bitter?"

"Some herb," answered Hatepa. "She made a great show of hiding it, but I caught on, of course. It helped my cough. I didn't care about the taste since it worked. That's why I never sent for you." Briseis studied the queen, confused by this revelation and the queen's lack of concern about it.

Maira stepped closer to Briseis and held out a small pouch. "Lady Briseis, Zitha left this yesterday. She must have dropped it when she pulled on her cloak in her upset. Lucky, since I could make the drink last night when the queen could not stop coughing. I would have made another for her today, but—" *But the queen saw lunging wolves and the king sent for the real healer,* Briseis thought. *What had Zitha used?*

She opened the pouch and sniffed. A nauseating smell, not anything she recognized. "Queen Hatepa, couldn't this herb be what harms you?"

Hatepa looked surprised. "Oh no, Antiope used this herb for my cough before you were born. I could never forget that horrible taste. It's the same one. I don't know why she stopped—she must have forgotten about it—but if Antiope used it, I know it is not harmful."

Briseis knew her mother would not have forgotten a useful herb, but the queen had never seen wolves before, so how could the herb be the cause? The handkerchief provided a much better method of placing a curse, getting as it did to the source of the queen's weakness.

"Whatever it is, I should know about it. May I take some to study?" The queen nodded uncertainly. She would ask Maion if he recognized it. She put some of the green powder in an alabaster vial and tied it to her linen belt.

"Maira, please give me one of the queen's handkerchiefs to act as substitute in the rite, and then I must go."

Her father had not returned from questioning Zitha, so Briseis went home surrounded by six of the king's men. The crunch of the horses's hooves on the gravel road sounded strange to her, as though something pursued them. She wondered how the warriors sent to protect her would fight wolves they could not see.

Briseis sat in the courtyard on the bench by the kitchen door with a stack of tablets, catching the last of the day's light. The work of planning the rite had settled her. When she drew in breaths she no longer felt choked, although her heart still thrummed with a fear she'd had to push out of her thoughts.

Iatros sat nearby, helping her search the library's tablets as she planned the rite to remove the curse. Physicians, like healing priestesses, had to check the procedures for rites that had been recorded by their predecessors. Iatros didn't read as well as she did, since no one had formally taught him, but, like many things a physician needed to know, he'd picked it up at his sister's side, mimicking her practice with the clay and stylus, and now as an apprentice he used the skill regularly. He'd poured himself into the task of helping her find the needed pieces for this rite. Having him there had given her the strength to concentrate.

Antiope had taught Briseis to join ideas from several rites, to add as needed. Briseis still lacked one part—she must draw a god's presence into the rite with a story, a god who understood wolves and could make them leave Hatepa. Briseis felt desperate about finding this essential part, but neither she nor Iatros had come up with it.

The sun set, and Eurome brought out oil lamps, placing one on the bench and handing another to Iatros. Then she seated herself beside Briseis. She'd been horrified with the news that Briseis had to deal with a curse.

The old woman shook her head. Her gray hair had thinned, and the strands pulled into a wisp of a braid didn't cover her scalp. "Oh my stars and fishes, a curse? You'll be careful?" Briseis nodded. Eurome hugged her to her bosom. "My little Poppy. I wish your mother were here."

Briseis loosened herself. "Do you know a tale about a god and wolves? Neither Iatros nor I can find one in the library."

Her nursemaid sat up straight and folded her arms across her sizable belly. Iatros leaned closer to listen.

"Hmm . . . there's that one about the Sungod and the—no, that was a cow, not a wolf, and I think a fisherman and some snakes, but no—no wolves." Eurome closed her eyes for a moment. Briseis bit her lip to keep from scolding the old woman for wasting time.

"Let's see, sea monsters, magic sticks, birds. I can't think of no stories about gods and wolves." She sighed in disappointment. After a moment she brightened. "Wait. A long time ago, I heard a good story. Back when I was just a speck of a girl—I swear I don't know how I can remember it—not a tale about the gods of Lyrnessos, mind you, but a god, good enough. Maybe the god's name will come to me . . . . No, not yet, but I'll tell the tale and you see if it'll suit."

By the time Eurome finished her story, one of the oil lamps had gone out, but Briseis and Iatros smiled at each other. Properly focused, it would be perfect for the cleansing rite. If only she could perform the rite correctly and not endanger her own life.

8
———

VOICES

L ater that night her father returned home, along with the king,
who would stand in for his wife at the rite in the cave, since
Hatepa lay ill.

Briseis approached her father. "Zitha?"

He shook his head, "Nothing useful."

Briseis patted his arm, but Glaukos turned to his men and gave
the order to gather torches. Then they set out toward the cave on
Mount Ida where the curse could be buried in the Underworld.

Briseis had never found it so difficult to climb the mountain trail.
Her legs felt jittery and a forceful thumping in her chest set her off
balance. Only a small sliver of moon showed in the sky, making the
narrow path hard to see even with the torches the king's men carried,
made from mullein stalks dipped in mutton tallow. Briseis thought of
the mullein infusion she had given to the queen that day. Odd how
many uses one plant could have, while others were of no use, or
worse, harmful. She remembered the awful smelling herb. Even
though the sample she'd taken dangled from her belt, identifying it
had slipped her mind as she prepared for this rite.

Briseis carried a palhi vessel, the only safe way to lock away a
curse. The ceramic vessel was misshapen like a rough stone and

marked with black lines that crossed each other to keep the curse from escaping through its walls. The vessel filled her arms and balancing it in front of her blocked the view of the rough path, causing her to stumble on unseen stones. She worried she might fall and break the vessel, but at the same time she was glad for its solid feel against her forearms. She believed in its power to contain the curse.

They reached the upper part of the trail, and a cool breeze brushed against Briseis, carrying the scent of pines and the music of the unseen brook. This caress by her mountain reassured her. She formed a silent prayer of thanksgiving to Kamrusepa, sure her goddess sent the blessing.

She scrambled up a steep stretch, struggling with the palhi vessel in her arms, and one of the king's men steadied her. They arrived at a flat area on the trail, and she saw in front of her the greater darkness on the face of the mountain that indicated they'd reached their goal.

Briseis stepped in front of the men. The time had arrived. One way or the other, she'd have to go through with the rite she'd designed. At the mouth of the cave she prayed to Kamrusepa to keep her safe and then led them inside. The air turned chill and the darkness edged in around the torches' flares as if it were a living presence. The smell of dank mold surrounded them.

She felt certain they stood at an entrance to the world below. Its cold sank into her skin. The king's men worked on digging a deep pit next to the spring that rose inside the cave. Its waters would carry away the curse when she buried it there inside the palhi vessel.

The digging took a long time, and standing with nothing to do but hold the empty vessel, Briseis grew more nervous until finally it was time for her to recite the sacred tale to draw the wolf god into the cave. She placed the vessel in the pit and stepped into the dim light of the torches held in a circle around her. She raised her arms in prayer to the gods. She was shaking hard and looked around at the faces lit by the flickering light to see if anyone noticed. Tension strained them all. Then she closed her eyes and let Eurome's tale unfold before her in her imagination as she spoke.

"On a hot day a young man hunted. Exhausted, he stretched out by a sparkling brook to drink and saw a beautiful maiden's face reflected in the water. How he yearned to touch her hair, soft as robin's down, to gaze into her eyes, the deep green of the forest. He burned with love despite the cool water on his lips. He turned to embrace her, but the startled nymph—for she was no mortal —ran away.

"He chased after her. Three times she rejected him. Armed with beauty and his lyre, he sang to her, but she stopped her ears. He brought her the sweetest flowers of the woods, and she cast them aside. He offered tender kisses, but she fled in horror.

"Desolate, he wandered so far he grew thin. His hair grew long and grey. His teeth hung over his lips. His nose grew into a muzzle, his hands and feet shaggy paws. He ran on four legs. He yearned so much for the beautiful nymph, the immortals took pity on him and transformed him into a god, but he kept the form of a wolf and still sings love songs during the long nights."

Briseis opened her eyes. She again saw the dank cave, replacing the world she'd felt deep inside her: the sunny woods and the dark nights on the steppes, full of lovesick wandering. She raised her arms higher and beseeched him to enter the cave, this shaggy god who now lived inside her.

"Please, god of the broken heart and rough coat, cleanse Hatepa of those vicious wolves, so unlike your own lovelorn self. Will you do this for her, for me? I will remember your story all my life and tell it to my children and grandchildren, and in this way grant you a second immortality, undying fame among mankind. Please, come into this cave and free Queen Hatepa."

A glance at Euenos and her father told her they also sensed a benign power around them. Their expressions were intent but exultant. The taut fear they'd worn had melted from the faces around her.

She removed the handkerchief from a linen sack tied at her waist, balled it up and trapped it between her palms, walking around the cave three times in one direction and seven times in the other. Her steps felt steady and strong even on the rough ground with its slippery patches where the spring left perpetual moisture. She approached the pit and dropped the handkerchief into the palhi vessel. The king and one of his men crouched down and sealed it tight with a lid of lead. The thud of soil echoed against the close walls as the men refilled the pit over the vessel. Briseis let out a deep sigh. She'd overcome the danger.

She finished with the last words of the rite as the pit grew level with the cave floor once more. "I bury this cloth. I send this curse down to the Gods of the Underworld to lock away. Scrap of linen, I have found you out. Release Hatepa, Queen of Lyrnessos. The vile sorceress Zitha has tricked you. She has sung dark incantations of evil. Hatepa's breath, fly back to the queen! Be gone, wolves which cannot be seen, into the dark realms of the earth forever."

THE MOON HAD SET, but a soft glow to the east meant dawn had arrived as Briseis, Glaukos, King Euenos and his men made their way down the mountain.

As they arrived about midway on the trail, Briseis recognized in the distance the huge trees of Lyrnessos's sacred grove, a dark mass against the lightening sky. At the center of the grove, the priests and townspeople, on the appointed days, conducted the city's festivals in a meadow that held the circle of stones representing each of the gods.

Kamrusepa held honor with the oldest stele, the carvings worn and darkened by the libations each generation poured over it. As Briseis pictured the stele, she felt drawn to it. With her need to grow closer to the goddess, she dared not ignore this sensation. She hoped Kamrusepa had helped her in the cave, but she didn't feel sure of the goddess's presence—only the support of her wolf god felt certain to her.

"Father, I would like to spend some time alone in the sacred grove —by Kamrusepa's stone. I know the way home from there."

Her father turned to her in surprise. "I can't leave you alone in the forest, especially not today. If you need to commune with Kamrusepa, I can wait outside the grove. Your mother often needed time with the goddess." Glaukos's shoulders sagged. The dark circles under his eyes made them look bruised.

Euenos took Briseis's hands. He looked less bleary-eyed than her father, but he had not regained his usual color, and his sallowness echoed his wife's complexion. "You have great courage and presence, Briseis. On behalf of my wife, I thank you."

The royal group went on alone. Briseis knew her desire to spend time in Kamrusepa's grove was not like her mother's. Despite the goddess's healing powers that Briseis had seen first hand, she had not yet found her mother's intimacy with the goddess. Tonight, however, the wolf god had allowed her into his heart—she could feel it. Perhaps now Kamrusepa would do the same. She could outgrow the confusion she felt with the goddess, find comfort from her presence. She'd always loved telling stories, but now she had discovered the recital of sacred tales was her gift as a priestess. At the Spring Festival she would be able to tell Telipinu's story—her own protective god— with the same conviction she'd had tonight and make the crops and herds flourish as they had when her mother told it. She had not felt such a lightness of heart since her mother died. She didn't have to be her mother: she could be herself.

Gradually the trees grew larger as she walked with her father through the sacred grove to the meadow where the gods' altar stones stood. The gray light fluttered in the upper branches of the huge pillars of pine and oak, yet the path was easy to follow, soft underfoot with fallen pine needles and dried leaves. Briseis heard the awakening birds calling to each other.

At the meadow's edge, her father sat down and leaned against a tree trunk. His eyes closed even before she walked on.

The meadow glowed with a saffron radiance as though all the light that could not break through the trees had settled in this one unobstructed expanse. She walked into the center of it, her heart rising with the brightness around her. In her mind she could hear the prayers of each seasonal festival, the rhythms she'd absorbed over and over, a myriad of voices to a pantheon of gods. Aloud in the meadow, she joined in until gradually the others faded and hers alone recited Kamrusepa's prayers. Her own voice, clear and confident.

She understood. Kamrusepa did not speak directly, but her own voice connected her to the goddess's. Kamrusepa had been in her voice, her stories, her prayers all of her life. If her mother's place to hear the goddess had been the temple, hers was the grove on Mount Ida.

Briseis knelt and embraced Kamrusepa's ancient stele. She let the rough stone press into her forehead and the flesh on the inside of her arms, a tangible connection with the goddess. Perhaps the stele absorbed the heat of her body, but it seemed to share with her a warmth of its own.

She kissed the stele and walked back to her father.

He snored softly, his head tilted back against the trunk. She sat down next to him and let her nearness wake him.

"Ready?" he said.

She nodded.

In the early morning light they took a shortcut down to the highest of the orchards on the estate.

Within sight of the house, she noticed Maion, the old servant who had taught her plant lore, climbing toward the orchards, out to greet the morning in the company of his trees. He used a stick to steady himself, and his back, bent with age, caused his head to tilt downwards so that when he wanted to look up the slope ahead, he had to turn his neck to the side a little. He looked frail, with his almost bald head speckled with irregular splotches and his hands and joints knobby, but he still had skill with the pruning hook amidst his fruit and olive trees. He could be heard chatting with them as if they were human friends. This morning he wore a torn, old tunic with mysterious smudges staining it that made Briseis shake her head. She'd woven a soft replacement for him, but he had yet to decide he needed a new one. No one's knowledge of medicinal plants matched his now that her mother was gone.

"I have a question for Maion. Zitha gave Hatepa an herb I don't recognize, but the queen said Mama used it awhile ago." Her father nodded, and they joined the old man on a bench among the olive trees.

Briseis pulled the alabaster vial that held the sample from her belt. She offered it to Maion. "Do you know what this is?"

The old man sniffed and drew back his head with a wrinkled nose. "Not a smell a man can forget. Henbane. That's what that is." He glanced at Glaukos. "A priestess like our Briseis is maybe allowed to have it, but henbane isn't never meant to be used outside the temple." He put his hand on Briseis's arm. "Sacred to the Stormgod—that's what your grandmother told me years ago."

"My grandmother? Did you ever speak to my mother about it?"

"Back before you were born, Lady Antiope asked me about henbane. I told her that in her mother's day, people still used it for healing."

"Why did my mother ask you about it?"

Maion hesitated. "Your mama was fearful about some things not sitting right with her, and she come to me even though some of it were temple rites I had no business with. If you're tangling with henbane, I'd best tell you, now that she can't. I—" He looked at Glaukos for approval. A sliver of worry worked into the well-being Briseis had brought down from the sacred meadow.

Her father nodded. "Antiope told me a little about this—that she didn't like henbane. Briseis needs to know anything you can tell her."

Maion shifted uneasily on the bench and rested his stick against the plank they sat on so he could gesture with his hands. "Lady Antiope weren't but about your age when those priests at the temple talked her into being what they called 'the servant of the Stormgod's voice.' That all meant, they burn some of that." He pointed to the alabaster vial with a gnarled finger. "The whole leaves, though, not ground like that." He held his thumb and index finger apart a little to indicate the size of leaf he meant.

"They made Lady Antiope breathe in the smoke. A fearful thing, if you ask me. She was afeared, all right. Then when she's taken in the henbane smoke, they ask their questions and whatever she says back is the god's answer."

His frown deepened. "Antiope come to me, weeping and saying she couldn't no more hear the goddess's voice after breathing that henbane. I tried my best to calm her. Told her what her mama said about the healing henbane can do for a cough or a pain. She'd be herself when it passed. The next time those priests called on her, she said no. She was Lady Kamrusepa's priestess and wouldn't serve no other god."

Maion rubbed the palm of one wrinkled hand with the crippled fingers of the other. Briseis sifted what he'd told her. There seemed to be some sense in Zitha's use of henbane if it healed a cough, but her mother's fear unsettled her.

"Mind you," Maion added, "while that henbane has some gentle uses, your grandma told some old stories of priestesses who breathed in too much and it killed them dead away."

Briseis looked from Maion to her father in alarm.

"Your mama said now they only use a priestess who hears the voice with a little henbane so that won't never happen, but even so. I can see why they went stopping others from using it, gentle uses or no."

"Did my grandmother say how the priestesses had died, in those old stories?"

"No, and that weren't my place to ask."

Briseis twisted the alabaster vial back and forth between her fingers and watched the green powder shift and fall with the movement. What secret did it hide?

Maion hesitated. "I'd best tell you one more thing. A good deal later Lady Antiope asked me to say all I knew from her mama about using henbane for a cough." Briseis looked up from the vial and gazed at Maion intently.

"The queen was sickly, over sickly, and cranky about her cough. Worried about Her Majesty, Lady Antiope asked permission for henbane of the Stormgod's priest. Protecting the queen was protecting the whole city, she told me, and the priest agreed. Only for a time, though. Then he got afeared the god would be angry and made her stop. I don't think she minded. Better the queen's fussing than that herb. She hated that herb."

Briseis let out her breath. She hadn't realized she'd been holding it. Her mother had used this on the queen in an open fashion and left off for good reason. Whatever darkness this powder might hide, it did not overshadow her mother.

Maion shook his head and patted Briseis's arm. "Don't you let those priests talk you into being the Stormgod's voice. You stand up to them like your mama. Stand up tall."

Briseis laughed. "I don't have much choice, do I? I always stand up tall." Her brothers teased her about being too tall for a girl.

"Don't ever be the Stormgod's voice. It scared your mama."

"I won't. I like my own voice." That *was* true, but despite her experience in the grove, she didn't feel confident anymore. Zitha had given the queen a dangerous herb; Zitha, who didn't have her mother's knowledge about how much was safe and all the ways a medicine could go wrong. Was this green powder the source of the queen's terrors? Briseis didn't know what to do except to put all the queen's supply of henbane back in the temple where it belonged.

9

CONSEQUENCES

Briseis gathered up her healing satchel for attending to the queen, and Glaukos gave orders to the grooms to harness a horse and cart. They headed toward the palace on the wagon road into Lyrnessos that passed by her father's wheat fields and then went through a neighboring estate's land. They talked about what Maion had said. Glaukos was convinced that his daughter had banished the terror however Zitha had caused it. In these difficult times they should not bother Euenos with complications. Briseis wasn't so sure, but she said nothing. Euenos liked certainty. Exhaustion made it hard to think with any clarity.

Briseis sat in the cart beside her father and wondered. Where did all this leave Zitha? The woman had been hostile toward her, but she'd also been right about Briseis's discomfort with Kamrusepa. Even the henbane might have been meant only as a cure. Briseis stomped her foot in frustration against the floor of the cart.

Her father looked at her in surprise. "What is it?"

"Papa, what did you learn from Zitha last night? Did she admit placing a curse?"

Her father looked away. "She denied it—through it all she denied it."

"What do you mean, 'through it all'?"

Glaukos evaded her eyes. He shifted the reins from one hand to the other and back again and cleared his throat. "When I came into that barn, I was frightened for you, Briseis. I demanded to know how she'd placed the curse. When Zitha said she hadn't cursed anyone, I let the men . . . hurt her . . . . Then she began to say hateful things about you—you had always had everything, you had no right to be a priestess, the goddess loved only her, Zitha . . ." He looked down at the reins wrapped around his hands. "The men stopped her saying those things. Still she denied making a curse. She said she'd done nothing but try to help the queen. She begged to be allowed to serve the goddess—she would scrub the temple floors forever if we would let her return. We finally left, knowing nothing useful."

"Then why did you think she'd placed the curse?"

"Who else? This is Zitha's fault, however she caused it. Let it be, Briseis."

The air had turned colder and gray clouds gathered behind Mount Ida. Briseis pulled her cloak close. They passed through the city gates. Somewhere over to her right must be the storage barn where they had locked up Zitha.

She turned to her father. "I want to know what Zitha did. Take me to her. She might talk to me, especially now that I know about the henbane."

"Absolutely not."

"Why not?"

"Don't insist. We're going to the palace."

Briseis laid her hand on her father's arm. He rarely said no to her. "If I don't know what caused the danger, then it can turn against me. Do you want that?"

Her father glared at her. "All right. I'll take you." He slowed the horse and then turned off the main road down a smaller lane.

They came to a long, low storage barn with mud-brick walls in need of repair. The outer mud plaster had worn away leaving exposed bricks to melt under the force of rain and wind. The logs and branches supporting the roof had bleached to a gray brittleness.

"I'll speak to her alone," Briseis said.

"I am sure she doesn't want to see me again." Glaukos jumped from the cart, gave Briseis a hand down and spoke to the two guards leaning against the wall by the door. They pulled back the heavy bar.

The only light inside came from the open door. A musty smell rose from the dirt floor and crumbling walls. The ceiling was lost in darkness. In a far corner Briseis saw a huddled form. It moved. Briseis walked toward it. "Zitha?"

Zitha's head rose from the floor. She raised a hand to shield her face. "Lady Briseis?"

Briseis approached. "I know you gave the queen henbane from the temple."

Zitha moaned. "Only to help her. I used some cast off by the priests. I serve as the Stormgod's voice. I know how soothing henbane can be."

Briseis's eyes grew accustomed to the gloom, revealing Zitha's swollen face, misshapen and covered with patches of dried blood. No wonder her father didn't want her to see this woman.

Zitha dragged herself upright. "It did help her. I was right. She liked it. Until she threatened to throw me out of the temple. Where would I go? I was terrified."

"Is that why you placed a curse on her?" Fragments of old chaff and mouse droppings littered the floor.

"No! Your father and those men kept asking me about a curse. I don't know how to make a curse. All I could do was weep."

Briseis pulled out her satchel. "Your wounds need attention. May I tend to them? Kamrusepa would wish it." Zitha nodded.

Briseis looked around for water and saw a pitcher and cup set in a corner by the door. They'd left water too far away for Zitha to find in the dark. Briseis pressed her lips tightly together as she brought it over and poured some for Zitha to drink. "Are you sure you didn't retaliate? I would have."

Zitha coughed as she drank, fresh blood dribbling from her mouth where a tooth was missing. "You have the power to do so. How could I change the queen's mind or make her regret her cruelty to me?"

"Didn't you take the queen's handkerchief to use in a curse? That gave you power." She dampened some linen and began washing Zitha's wounds.

Zitha gasped in pain. Briseis softened her touch and Zitha asked, "Handkerchief? I don't understand."

"You took it the last day you visited her."

"The dirty handkerchief?" Zitha frowned. "I put it in the basket I'd brought with me. I do the laundry in the temple. I would have washed it and brought it back. How could I make a curse from dirty laundry?"

Zitha sounded genuinely puzzled.

"Are there wounds or hurts that I can't see? Do you feel pain here?" Briseis touched Zitha's chest. The smooth wool of her brown priestess's robe had been torn at the shoulder.

"When I move or take a deep breath, it hurts here by my side."

Briseis gently felt where Zitha indicated. "That sort of hurt heals with time if you rest." *And if the king lets you live long enough.*

Briseis shook her head. "I don't understand. If you did not curse the queen, why did she thrash and see wolves attacking her?"

Fear shot across Zitha's battered face. "What? Is that why they beat me?"

Briseis nodded.

In a tiny voice Zitha said, "The old ones in the temple tell some tales about priestesses of the Stormgod who died screaming about wolves and beasts. To scare us, I thought. It could be the henbane. I will be blamed, executed."

Briseis refilled Zitha's cup and encouraged her to drink. "You meant no harm, however much you've done. Perhaps I can persuade the king to let you live." Somehow the dilapidated storage barn chosen for Zitha's prison, with its filthy floor and smell of decay, didn't offer much hope of that.

"Why would you? I said those awful things to you in the temple, and I did try to win the queen's support. I feared that only I was dedicated enough to Kamrusepa to keep the city safe. I didn't see devotion in your actions as I had always seen in your mother. Forgive me. I thought I spoke for the goddess, but the will of the gods is difficult to understand, and they have little regard for mortals' feelings. You can't save me now."

"I'll try. I must go to the palace for the rest of the henbane."

"Thank you. Thank your father for me, also. If he had not been here yesterday, those men would have beaten me to death, yet he had the greatest reason to fear me. If I had really made a curse, your life would have been at stake."

Briseis squeezed Zitha's hand. "Will the dark frighten you when I close the door?"

"It isn't the dark that I fear."

THE QUEEN'S SCREAMS, when Briseis and Glaukos arrived at the palace, reverberated far from her rooms. Father and daughter ran behind a panicked servant toward Hatepa. At the door of the queen's chamber, Briseis pushed through several servants yelling and clinging to each other. Hatepa thrashed on the floor. Her limbs and torso jerked.

"Aieee! Help! Their teeth, their teeth . . ."

The high-pitched wails knifed into Briseis. She clutched her head. Each shriek pummeled Briseis like storm surge. She was so tired. Her communion with Kamrusepa felt lost. If henbane alone caused these visions, what of her wolf god? Hadn't his benign power filled her?

"They tear my arm. Blood dripping from their mouths—Ayy!— everywhere—Husband, kill them! Where are my guards? Help—they come at my neck . . ."

Euenos brandished his sword above his wife.

"Appear, you demons. Are you afraid to face me? Cowards! Threaten me, not this defenseless woman!"

One of Hatepa's legs struck the floor in spasmodic blows.

Briseis put her hands over her ears. Amidst the flailing and screaming, only Maira sat silent, couching the queen's head and shoulders in her lap, shielding them from the stone floor. The slave woman sensed Briseis's presence and raised her head. On her face Briseis saw no fear or panic. Maira gave a slight nod. Briseis dropped her hands and stepped toward the seated figure. In Maira's calm, Briseis saw her wolf god's benign presence. She felt Kamrusepa's sacred stele giving off soothing warmth into this chaos. Here was the clear and confident voice Briseis had found in the meadow, expressed in stillness. She found her own voice in Maira's strength.

"Stop," Briseis shouted. "No wolves haunt this room. Look! Maira holds the queen and no wolf attacks her. An herb, not a curse, causes these visions. Father, Maira, help me lift the queen to the bed."

Exhaustion's fog burned away. Briseis grabbed Hatepa's hips and helped her father and Maira raise the queen from the floor. Lifting Hatepa to the bed's shelter had as dramatic an effect as Briseis's words. Quiet fell on the room. The king put up his sword.

"You," said Briseis to the cowering servants in the door, "bring a large pitcher of cool water—quickly." She had no patience with their fear.

She climbed onto the sprawling bed and braced Hatepa's face in her hands. "Hatepa, no danger threatens you. No wolves—no matter what your eyes tell you. Look at me."

The queen's eyes showed no understanding. Her bulging eyeballs, looking even more exposed than usual, lolled from side to side without seeming to be under the queen's control. Their circles of muddy green-brown with huge black centers seemed both sightless and disconnected from a human being. Briseis waved her hand before the queen's face. The eyes did not focus. Perhaps they never would.

Briseis sat back and turned to the king. "Her flesh is whole. No bloody harm comes to her. Do you see?"

A servant crept forward with a pitcher and cup. Briseis said to Maira, "Help me get the queen to drink this water. I hope she can swallow. We must wash out the henbane. It's too late to make her throw it up and she seems so weak. Retching would do more harm than good, I fear."

Water dribbled down the queen's chin, but she drank. Briseis and Maira worked sip after sip into the queen. It took patience. Gradually Hatepa seemed to gain more control over her limbs. Her eyes sometimes followed Briseis's movements. After a long effort, they let her lie back and sleep. Briseis slumped down onto a stool and prayed the visions had made their final visit.

Briseis felt as if she floated somewhere outside her own body in an exhaustion she had never known before. Assisting Antiope with long labors had brought her close, especially when the mother or infant remained in danger for hours, but nothing like this. She needed sleep. She wanted to hold onto the elation she felt about Kamrusepa, but her fatigue clouded it.

"Is she safe?" asked Euenos.

Briseis nodded. "I think so."

"You are brave. How could you face those unseen demons?"

Briseis shrugged. "There are no demons here."

"What did you mean about an herb?"

Briseis explained to him. She took the remaining henbane from the queen. Now she could give Euenos certainty about the source of the visions. He refused to decide what to do about Zitha, saying it would be up to the Stormgod's priest. That seemed enough to Briseis. Zitha must have friends in the temple.

Euenos proclaimed her bravery and declared that such a woman was more than ready for marriage.

"Why delay the wedding any longer? Your mother's death was tragic, but certainly you've had enough time since that loss. And today you were so brave. You have the courage to face anything."

Briseis backed away from Euenos and reached for her father. She couldn't understand why the king brought up the marriage now. She shuddered. Even the king thought courage was the necessary quality for marriage to his son.

Glaukos interrupted the king's urging and said Briseis and he both needed to return home to rest after the strain and sleeplessness of the last two days.

"You are right," said Euenos, dipping his head in apology. "I owe everything to Briseis today. She deserves a long rest. We can discuss marriage another time."

Glaukos put his arm around her shoulders. Briseis leaned against her father in gratitude as he guided her slowly to the outer courtyard where their cart and horse still stood abandoned from their panicked rush. A bewildered groom stroked their horse's neck, unsure whether to stable the beast or not, and perhaps needing reassurance as much as his charge after the unnatural shrieking.

SEVERAL DAYS later Euenos made good on his promise to discuss the marriage, although he did more than talk. He sent Mynes on a courtship visit.

10

VISIONS AND SWEET, SEDUCTIVE FLAMES

A messenger had come the day before to announce the prince's impending visit. In preparation, Eurome dressed Briseis in her best dark russet skirt, the pleats picked out with multicolored braid, and a cream linen veil to cover her bright hair. Briseis stood flanked by her father and nursemaid in the megaron hall. Antiope's absence stung like a reopened wound.

A retinue of the king's servants entered and laid out the bride-price gifts. Behind them in the doorway Mynes stood with his legs braced, his eyes darting like a hawk seeking prey. Briseis pulled Eurome's arm closer. Her father placed his hand on Briseis's shoulder. One by one the servants placed the gifts on the plank table: a necklace and earrings of gold rosettes and garnets, then a set of makeup jars carved from a rainbow of exotic stones fitted with gold and filled with kohl, ochre rouge and perfumes.

Mynes stepped forward when the slaves completed the gift offering. Briseis's father's hand slipped from her shoulder. She remembered to lower her head in modesty. Glaukos welcomed Mynes and thanked him for the gifts on behalf of Briseis, then led Mynes to a place of honor near the hearth.

Seated across from her, Mynes stammered a few conventional

greetings and fell silent. She peeked at his powerful limbs and his square chest, clothed in dark purple wool worked with gold threads. He drew his lips tight in a nervous line and tapped his foot repetitively. Over his long, dark hair he wore a thin, gold band, a detail she'd never seen on him before—perhaps Euenos's reminder to them of the importance of this marriage. She folded her hands in her lap to conceal their shaking and tried to think of some topic of interest to him.

"My brothers say you are training hard in case we must send warriors to Troy."

"Every day." Mynes sat up and his foot went quiet. "I hope the Trojans don't drive off the Greeks too soon. I want to fight, but Father keeps insisting we wait. For what? All the glory to be taken before we get there?" His full lips turned down.

"Perhaps your father wishes to protect the young men of Lyrnessos. Men die in battle no matter how brave they are." She hoped she didn't sound like an old woman. Her father nodded as she spoke, but he did not interrupt the two young people.

"I will fight Achilles and kill him. Him and that Patroklos."

"Patroklos?"

Mynes looked directly at her for the first time. His black eyes glinted. "They say Achilles is a great warrior, but he never goes into battle without his companion, Patroklos, at his side to protect him. The tales make out that Patroklos is there to dampen the immortal flames his mother put inside Achilles—sounds like some drunken sot made that story up—otherwise, the gossip says, Achilles could not control his battle rage. Ha! What a ridiculous way to hide the fact that he's too big a coward to go into battle without his friend's help. The Greeks hope we don't figure out what a frightened child Achilles is, but I'll be the one to strip off his armor. You'll see."

Briseis was silent. Her brothers bragged about their fighting prowess, but not like this. Mynes was boasting. She hated fighting. Euenos was wise to keep his son far from Troy. She only wished he had as strong a desire to keep his son from the wedding chamber.

In her imagination a giant warrior in golden armor raced toward

Mynes, sliding his spear with agile grace under the protection of his opponent's shield and piercing his armor with deadly precision. Then, under Mynes's helmet she saw only terror in those black eyes. She closed her own eyes, and when she opened them a moment later, Mynes was looking at her with a strange expression on his face. She shivered with a sudden chill, although the fire in the hearth gave off a pleasant heat.

AT THE FIRST crack of the Stormgod's thunder, the priests declared the time had arrived for the Spring Festival. The orchard trees had leafed out fully. Crocus and iris dappled Mount Ida's meadows with bright hues.

On the appointed day, Briseis rose before dawn to make the needed preparations at the temple. Her discomfort had lessened—doing each rite precisely pleased the gods and seemed enough. Her voice would join with Kamrusepa's on the mountain, if the goddess willed it. Zitha had been allowed back, and she had gone out of her way to assist Briseis.

After the temple rites, the procession to the sacred grove formed. Taking her place for the first time in the procession felt daunting, but the other priestesses around her gossiped and enjoyed the celebratory day, and she relaxed. This had always been her favorite Festival. Briseis peered around the priests and sacred litters to watch the royal family.

The king and queen walked at the head, of course. Euenos carried a ceremonial axe in one hand and a sun disc on a golden staff in the other. Hatepa wore a gown of red-purple trimmed in gold braid. Antiope had once noted to Briseis that the queen never shirked her religious obligations—she attended all the festivals throughout the year without regard to her health. Briseis thought it unlikely that Hatepa would ever miss being the center of the show and pomp.

The king's bodyguard marched on all sides around the king and queen. These noblemen wore their bronze armor, polished to its brightest, as they would in war, the leather guards they used in practice put away for this festive day. Colored plumes cascaded from their helmets and caught the wind. Mynes marched at their forefront, his gold embossed breastplate catching the sunlight. Briseis watched him strut before his men as he ordered them into their places. She turned away.

Behind the royal family, she admired the aged Stormgod's priest in his long gray robe. Despite his advanced years, he held aloft the heavy golden standard that represented the Stormgod as a golden bull. In front of him, the divine statue of the Stormgod as King rose above the priests, supported on the powerful shoulders of four honored men. Their chief god was dressed in his finest robes and seated upon a throne of crouching lions.

Briseis walked with the other priestesses behind the litter that carried Kamrusepa. She smiled at the others, but couldn't join in their conversations. With so much at stake for Lyrnessos, she must succeed in bringing the gods' goodwill to her people. She hoped the sureness she'd felt on the mountain by Kamrusepa's stele would return. A fluttering in her stomach when she dressed that morning had made her skip breakfast, but her nerves gave her a heightened energy. She hoped it would be enough to bring the goddess's presence.

Like her goddess, Briseis wore a deep blue gown decorated with golden sun disks, and with each step she shook her sistrum—a square rattle on a staff surmounted with Kamrusepa's silver stag. The thin metal strips strung on the cross pieces made a silvery rustle. Briseis loved being adorned like her goddess. These sacred garments would draw the goddess's identity into her and her voice would fill with Kamrusepa's power as she told Telipinu's tale later that day.

Behind her followed the singers and players of drums, cymbals and horns. Jugglers and acrobats leapt and twirled as they progressed toward the grove—a less dignified part of the procession, but important. Briseis knew it was wise to entice the gods with entertainment so they would give the town blessings. She preferred the songs of the bards, but most people liked the acrobats and jugglers along with the instrumental music, so the gods must also.

The temple servants walked behind the performers, carrying offerings. Baskets of breads in every shape: circles and twists, even birds and hands. Pitchers of wine and beer. Barley to scatter on the sacrificial animals. Bowls, baskets, and trays carefully loaded up with all manner of food. Also the sheep, cattle, and goats to be sacrificed, each animal washed and garlanded. Briseis glanced back. Poor things, the animals were already frightened by the noise and crowds. It took all the skill of the herdsmen to keep them from bolting. Everyone knew their part from long practice, and eventually the distressed cries of the animals went quiet and even they fell under the spell of this day with its combination of solemnity and joyous celebration. The citizens of Lyrnessos brought up the end of the procession.

Briseis shook her sistrum and felt comfort in this familiar process—now as one of the celebrants, fulfilling her mother's role for the community. She closed her eyes for a moment and prayed to her mother's spirit for success. *Please, don't let me bring suffering and ill-health on Lyrnessos because I am not as devoted as you were, Mama.*

The procession fell silent as they entered the grove and followed the path to the meadow. The ancient carved stones, representing each of the gods, stood shoulder high in a semi-circle in the middle, surrounding the platform upon which Briseis would stand when she told Telipinu's tale.

Briseis watched the men place the gods' statues on thrones next to each stone. She marched over to where the meadow rose up in a gentle curve on the right side and she joined the royal family and the other priests and priestesses in their places of honor. The central area around the stones was kept clear for the sacrifices and entertainments. Curving around the left side of the meadow, the nobles, her father and brothers included, sat on benches and the rest of the townspeople filled in behind, stretching out as far as Briseis could see. The whole community thus formed a circle around the ancient stones. Her people would listen and watch as she told the sacred story. Briseis switched the sistrum to her other hand and surreptitiously wiped her sweaty palm on a fold of her skirt so she could hold the instrument without it slipping.

Kamrusepa's prayers and sacrifices came at the end of the daylong rites, and Briseis had only a minor role before then. Occasionally she partook of a libation or added her cry of assent to a prayer, but primarily she turned inward, preparing herself as best she could to speak for Kamrusepa.

During the offerings to the Lord of the Sun, the sound of shouting caught Briseis's attention. Who disturbed these sacrifices?

The noise came from a cluster of nobles standing next to the royal bodyguards. She saw Mynes strike another young man once, then again. The other man stepped back rather than return the blows, but when Mynes hit him a third time and angrily insulted him, the other man struck back. The men standing around them froze in horror. Then Bienor cut through the crowd, his head above the others. He threw himself in front of Mynes and caught the future king by the shoulders. He said something which caused Mynes to drop his arms and unclench his angry fists. Bienor called to the men standing near, who quickly led the other man away. Her brother put an arm on Mynes's shoulder and guided him to the edge of the crowd, out of her sight.

What had caused this fight? The king's son, of all people, should know better, but she had already seen his temper. As a boy, he hadn't needed much to make him lash out. A fight in the middle of the Spring Festival could drive away the gods they had worked so hard to entice here. How could Mynes have so little thought for the well-being of his people, especially with half-immortal enemies like Achilles threatening? The flustered people refocused their attention on the Sungod, the giver of light and life, hoping their gods still attended to the offerings.

The final cycle of prayers—those to Kamrusepa—began. As Briseis lifted the goddess's silver libation cup, shaped like a kneeling stag, and recited the hymn of thanksgiving, she felt the presence of the whole gathering in her voice, their hopes and needs. She scattered barley over the sheep and goat to be sacrificed. An assisting priest cut their throats, let their blood drain away, and while everyone waited, the priests who were trained in ritual butchering prepared them for the fire. The townspeople would partake along with the goddess of the roasted meat, so they could be patient.

Later, as the smell of the roasting meat enticed Kamrusepa to be present with the people, Briseis climbed on the stone platform to recite Telipinu's story. She tried to sooth the nervous twitch in her stomach with thoughts of the goddess. Instead of Kamrusepa's image, her mother's face came to mind, smiling and calm. Briseis took it as a good omen.

She looked out at the people of Lyrnessos gathered in the ancient grove—except that instead of the trees, it seemed to her she saw a great hall, bigger and grander than Euenos's, and the townspeople of Lyrnessos had disappeared, replaced by others all regal in dress and carriage, and seated on golden thrones. A wondrous awe filled her, the very air seemed clearer, her vision sharper.

At the center she saw a young man, so handsome he seemed to glow. Of course. It is Telipinu, seated next to his father the Stormgod. Something is wrong—he is angry. Thunder and lightning crash and spark across the huge room.

The assembly of the gods has taken something from him—his honor. He will not tolerate the insult. He lifts his sword and races from the gods' assembly. She follows him, hovering above the ground. All the fields and houses burn as he passes. The great river dries up, withdrawing from its banks, now blasted and blackened. She tries to call out and tell him to stop, but she has no voice. She hears only a buzzing when she speaks.

She realizes she is the tiny bee Kamrusepa sent to sting Telipinu so he remembers who he is and what he must do. Then she must comfort him and bring him back. She flies, hunting for him throughout the burnt landscape until she sees him blending into the moor. She stings the handsome god's feet and hands. She must stop his rage. She soothes the stings with her wax, then rubs more wax on his shoulders and chest to calm him, but he burns it away. She flies around him over and over, seven times seven. The flames begin to damp down and amber fluid pours from the wax, down his face and chest, coating him in a glistening shimmer of sweetness. Now she can hear her words, "I burn away your anger, I sweeten your heart."

She is no longer a bee, but herself again. He looks into her eyes, lays down his sword and touches her face. Under his fingers, her hair bursts into flames, but she is unhurt. She hands him a cup of honey-sweet wine and his hand wraps around hers. They share the drink. Flames dance along their arms. A delicious sensation fills her. He laughs and pulls her into his arms. The sweetness of his lips shimmers through her like stepping into the warmth of the sun. His hands slide over her body. Together they float as if in water. She enfolds him into herself. A wave of delight undulates through her, golden and luscious, lingering, reverberating as she lies next to the god. She reaches for him, but he is insubstantial now, as fingers passing through the tips of flames or trickling water.

Briseis blinked. She saw the sacred grove around her again. Why was everyone so quiet? What had she done? Were they waiting for her to speak? Their faces shone with contentment. The Stormgod's priest smiled and bowed to her.

"The story has never been told with such life before," he said. "Truly you brought the goddess here amongst us. Kamrusepa and Telipinu will fill our land with abundance."

BRISEIS GROUND some astragalos root with her pestle. The solidity of stone meeting stone felt comforting against her hand after the visionary experience at the Spring Festival the day before. The experience puzzled her. She'd asked Iatros what he thought of the day—even with him she couldn't be more direct about the intimacy she'd felt with the god. He only referred to Mynes's fight as a problem and described her performance as different from their mother's but luminous and inspiring.

Her vision had filled her body with such intense sensation and yet it had not really happened—at least no one else had seen what she had, thank the gods. At the time she didn't think she had spoken out loud, but she must have because the priest congratulated her. No one thought anything was out of order. The community shared her euphoria.

On the trip down the mountain from the sacred grove, the townspeople exchanged joyous wishes for a fruitful year. They congratulated Briseis. She didn't understand the experience, but she knew she had indeed become the priestess of Kamrusepa and Telipinu—a priestess of the sacred grove and the voice that rose from that place. The intimate connection she shared with Telipinu in her vision confirmed that he acted as her protective god.

Only Mynes's fight marred her memory of the day. When she asked Bienor about it, he said the fight had been over some insult Mynes felt from the son of a farmer who had recently been training with the nobles, one of many whom Euenos had provided with armor so that they could serve as henchmen to his warriors. The Greek army at Troy had already shifted their lives in many ways. Mynes's inability to control his temper when most needed filled her with foreboding. How long could she hold off her marriage?

Telipinu did not wait for the next festival to visit her with more visions. She had heard tales about gods loving mortal women. She supposed this might be how such things happened—through dreams. Gradually she became less embarrassed by her dreams, filled with her golden god, and they became more vivid. She could not refuse a divine gift.

The moments before waking grew sweeter. He leaned over her and a shower of his red-gold hair caressed her cheek. "You are mine," he whispered "and I am yours." His sweet breath filled her with warmth. She reached up with both hands, following the margins of his sea-green eyes with her fingertips, down the straight nose, and the fullness of his lips. She pulled his face down to hers into a kiss and felt herself melt into him. His tongue explored the hollow of her neck, the aureoles of her nipples, and then, drawn by desire, glided lower until she lost herself in fiery waves of an ancient sea that radiated from her center through her limbs.

She lingered in the warmth and aftereffect of her dream, and hoped that tomorrow would bring another.

HER VISION at the Spring Festival had one other result.

A few days later, returning one afternoon from treating a man with inflamed eyes, Briseis crossed the portico opening into their megaron hall. Through the open door she saw Euenos seated by the circular hearth and her father pacing in front of him. Her father must have come in directly from supervising in the fields. His plain brown tunic was stained with sweat under his arms and across the back. The king, however, had dressed royally in a cream-colored tunic with gemstones embroidered into a crescent design on the front.

The king was speaking. "—seductive. You wouldn't see. You're her father. Mynes thinks of nothing else. He—" Euenos noticed Briseis and stopped.

She came into the room. His face reddened. He turned his attention to the cup of wine he held. Usually the king held his broad chest and compact limbs at ease, but he held his back stiff, leaning forward, and his elbows didn't relax against the carved armrests.

Briseis looked from him to her father.

"You're back." Her father was not in the habit of stating the obvious.

"Good to see you, Briseis," said the king. She bowed and sat in her chair by the hearth. The men would have liked her to leave the room —that was clear—but they were talking about her and she would stay.

"We were settling on a date for your marriage to Mynes," said Euenos.

A date? She glanced at her father. He looked as unsettled as she now felt.

"A speedy marriage is for everyone's good," said Euenos. "The war threatens to draw us in. Let us celebrate this happy occasion in proper form while all of us are still present."

Briseis felt her breath seize in her chest. The struggle with her mother's loss hurt enough. She imagined her wedding ceremony if she lost her father in the battles that threatened. What if she didn't have his advice either?

"And Mynes pushes for it constantly," said Euenos.

Mynes wanted her—that was an interesting change and a source of strength if she needed it. So the 'seductive' did refer to her. When had he grown attracted to her? She realized when and blushed. How—

Her father spoke. "A young man's...eagerness should not determine a matter as important as this." Glaukos returned to pacing. "Briseis did well stepping into her mother's place so young. I'm proud of her, but not surprised. She's never done anything with only part of her soul. Always shown spirit." He stopped, placing his hand on her shoulder.

The king sat opposite them. He had put down the wine cup. His neck muscles stretched taut. Briseis saw anger in his eyes. Briseis had never seen Euenos like this, but her father ignored the threat.

"However, that doesn't mean she's ready for marriage," Glaukos said. "Let experience temper her spirit without more responsibility resting on her." He bowed slightly to Euenos. "Mynes will benefit from tempering also."

Euenos shook his head. "Marriage will steady them both. I am seeing to it that Mynes gains some tempering. He needs it. He showed poor judgment at the Festival. Just the day before I'd told him I'd appoint him commander of the city guard if he thought he could handle it, but after that fistfight, I took the honor away. We'll hope his disappointment teaches him something."

Glaukos raised his eyebrows. "That isn't what I had in mind. But let's give the children some more time. There's no harm in that, is there?"

Watching Euenos, Briseis knew her father hadn't persuaded the king.

Euenos rose, his arms crossed and clamped hard against his chest. "Do not oppose me, Glaukos." He took a deep breath and seemed to collect himself. "What do you gain from quarreling with me about this? Don't we have enough enemies right now?" He sank into his chair. "Marriage will settle Mynes."

Briseis saw resignation in her father's expression. She was going to lose her delay. She couldn't force him further. He'd agreed to the marriage long ago. He'd never been willing to anger the king before.

Glaukos reached out his right hand to the king in agreement. Euenos rose and embraced him.

Glaukos turned to his daughter and laid his hands on her head in blessing. "May it be a happy marriage.

11

VEILED WEDDING

"Get up, my Poppy. Last day of girlhood. Better have slept well. There'll be little sleep for you tonight." Eurome laughed and bent down to kiss Briseis. "No dallying this morning. Up, up, you lazy girl. To the bride bath."

Briseis allowed her nursemaid to tease her—all part of the day. Young brides were supposed to be tardy in their steps toward the marriage bed. Was she reluctant? She pictured Mynes lifting her veil in the marriage chamber. Part of her worried, but the last few weeks had been encouraging. As she enjoyed the warm summer days, her sense of hope grew.

During the final courtship, when Mynes visited with still more bride gifts, he came now with a courteous demeanor. He complimented her beauty and talked about life in the palace. His words stumbled on occasion but he was trying to please her. Once as he went down on one knee to present her with a necklace of amber beads, he put his free hand on her thigh and whispered in a husky voice, "I dream about you every night." He looked up at her and she saw desire so hungry it stopped her breath.

A river of sensation flowed from his hand up into her. Her blood rose and her face felt hot. She thought of her own dreams. All well and good to be loved in her sleep by a god with fiery hair like her own, but this raven-haired, powerfully built man at her knee was real. She wanted the waking caresses his nearness promised.

Off the courtyard in the cluster of rooms used for bathing, Eurome filled the stone tub with hot water and oil scented with roses. Briseis lowered herself into its perfumed steam, watching the glistening beads of oil form first on her legs then gradually creep along her belly.

Briseis luxuriated in the warmth and soothing attentions as her nursemaid scrubbed her limbs, then helped her out of the tub and toweled her off. Eurome wrapped Briseis in a linen sheet, and they turned to the stone boxes and jars containing her cosmetics, all part of her bride gift. Briseis pivoted open the lid of a hematite jar on its golden peg and swiveled it back and forth a couple times, delighting in the fineness of the work. Tiny cylinders carved into the stone held black eye paint. Another jar of a deep mustard shade held ochre rouge. Eurome smoothed on the colors to highlight her cheeks and drew the black outlines around her eyes. Briseis studied her face in the mirror Milos had made from a wide, flat dish with shallow sides. The silver had been blackened so that when filled with water it caught her reflection. She smiled.

The sounds of arriving guests drifted in. The courtyard and great hall would barely contain the ceremony and feasting. Briseis shrugged her shoulders up and down to loosen the tension gathering there.

She put on her linen tunic and swirling skirt, bleached a brilliant white and rubbed with an oiled stone until the fabric glistened. Eurome reached underneath the pleated skirt to pull the tunic snugly over her breasts so that the fabric curved and swelled around her body. Briseis ran her hand over the smoothness of the tunic and then spun in a circle to feel the heavy skirt fly out. Eurome laughed and then made her hold still while she tied on a linen belt decorated with gold sun discs. Briseis slid on the matched bracelets that Antiope had received from Glaukos for her wedding day—two wide bands of gold set with cornelian.

Eurome brushed Briseis's hair until it glowed, a long red-gold cascade. She wove the front strands into a crown and attached the diadem Milos had fashioned of golden sprays of lilies intertwined with tiny pomegranates. Traceries of flowers and leaves wound down from it, gleaming against the deeper gold of Briseis's hair. Eurome clasped a matching necklace around Briseis's neck.

As Eurome lifted the saffron-colored veil out of its chest, they heard the king, queen and Mynes announced and her father's greeting.

"Your husband is here to claim you. Lucky we're almost ready," said Eurome. The breath caught in Briseis's chest.

Eurome covered her from head to toe in the translucent veil, holding it in place with a golden pin shaped like Kamrusepa's bee and arranging it so the delicate fabric clung to Briseis's form and suggested the beauty that it only partially concealed. Her hair, the jewels and shimmering fabrics glinted through the golden cloud surrounding her.

Her old nurse stood back to admire her with a contented sigh, speechless for once. Briseis leaned against Eurome for a moment before they left the privacy of the bathing rooms.

At the megaron's doorway her father came forward to walk her to her groom, who stood with both families in front of the shrine. Her three brothers waited at the right of the shrine. Bienor and Adamas towered a head or more over the other men. She saw Iatros swipe his eye. Not working with him each day would be hard. She pressed her lips together to keep away tears.

Briseis turned to her father and as they walked forward, she studied the familiar room—odd to see it full of people. She looked at the shrine and her mother's presence. She thought of spinning wool next to her mother by this hearth, playing with Iatros, gathering the family in the evening to listen to an itinerant bard sing the tales she loved—especially tales of Achilles's feats, though her feelings about that hero had shifted now that he had stepped from the realm of stories onto the shores of Troy. She caught sight of Mynes. He watched her intently. She felt her father's hand on her lower back as he guided her toward the shrine.

Mynes's eyes moved slowly down her veiled form. Briseis only partially listened to the prayers and offerings the priests made. Mynes's eyes were hooded by deep brows, his lips full with a slight downward tilt. He went clean shaven as most men did, but she could see the shadow of black hair on his jaw and imagined what his cheek would feel like under her fingers, how that would contrast with the smooth skin of his brow or his shoulder.

As they reached the final part of the ceremony, one of the priests nodded to them. Mynes reached for her right hand and breathed in sharply as his hand touched hers. His hold tightened. Her long fingers suddenly looked small inside his powerful hand. He spoke the traditional words that sealed their marriage. "You will be my wife. I shall be your husband."

When Mynes helped her into her chair for the feast, his hand brushed down her back as she turned to sit. She felt herself blushing and lowered her head so that she did not look into his face, which she felt above her. He did not move to his own seat. A low groan startled her, and she looked up in concern. He lowered his head so that his lips brushed hers. She did not understand how she could feel that touch in so many parts of her body.

Through the feasting and performances by dancers and jugglers, Briseis could only nibble at her food. She kept reaching up to her lips, remembering that kiss.

Finally, the time came to leave for the palace. Mynes handed Briseis up into a cart decorated with flowers and climbed in beside her, his thigh pressed against hers. A procession of carts and people on foot accompanied the bride to her new home. The loud crowd trailed around and behind the couple. Musicians played horns and drums. Guests made bawdy jokes and threw figs and almonds to bring the couple a sweet and fertile marriage. Briseis's heart pounded and she kept her head down. She couldn't look at Mynes, but the heat where their thighs touched seemed to speak for both of them.

At the palace the huge gates stood open. Men in armor with

upright spears flanked the area inside the gate. A loud hurrah went up from them as the cart carrying Briseis and Mynes came through. A guard offered Briseis a hand down. Hatepa stepped forward and signaled for Briseis to follow her to the bridal chamber. Behind her, Briseis heard Mynes respond to the teasing crowd, "No more waiting for my prize—she's mine now."

THE BRIGHTNESS SLIPPING through the cracks around the shutters told Briseis morning had come, but she didn't care. The darkness she had sensed as a little girl watching Mynes beat another child had proved to be her husband's true self.

At a knock on the doorframe, Briseis shuddered. She clutched the covers close around her in this strange bed.

"May I come in?" Eurome called.

"Yes," Briseis answered, but the word came out hoarse and strangled. She watched Eurome through half-opened eyes.

Eurome pushed aside the door curtain, peeked in the bedchamber and entered, carrying an elaborate breakfast tray. A wide smile creased her face. She placed the tray on a chest and approached the bed as though expecting her Poppy to say something, but Briseis stayed silent, unable to speak, even with Eurome.

"I'm sure you're hungry. Here's a fine breakfast. No, it's more than that, a wedding feast for the morning. Fresh boiled eggs—maybe there'll be some new little chicks 'round here soon— almonds, sweet honey cakes and sweet mead—you can never have too much sweetness at a time like this and—" The old woman stopped. Her smile faded.

Her eyes swept the room. "Oh my, oh my," Eurome muttered under her breath.

She lifted Briseis's wedding tunic, snagged on the corner of a chest, and folded it. Briseis heard her gasp. Eurome stooped and picked up a fragment of gold. The bee pin lay on her palm, smashed flat. She sat on the edge of the bed and brushed some strands of hair from Briseis's brow.

Briseis turned away and drew her knees toward her chest. The movement sharpened the pain between her legs and increased the warm stickiness of her blood. She shifted her knee from where it rested on the other thigh to keep it from pressing a place where her flesh felt raw. She had no energy; only murky fog where her thoughts should be.

Eurome looked at the remains of the bee in her hand. "So it's like that, is it?" She sighed. "Oh, my sweet girl, who should be prized beyond measure."

Briseis knew what Eurome had expected to find—two entwined bodies, bashful at the intrusion of a quickly left tray. Mynes and she had not entwined last night—what he had done to her had no kinship with the images of love that she had expected. When the agony of his grunting thrusts and the stench of his panting breath had stopped, he had left. Eurome's knock had made her fearful he was back—and even her presence was no protection if he returned. Her servant could easily be sent away by the man who would be king.

Tears ran from Briseis's eyes. She pulled a hand from under the covers to wipe them away. Eurome leaned in and pulled Briseis into her arms even though Briseis went rigid. "There, there, my little Poppy. There, there." Eurome rocked her back and forth.

After a time Eurome said, "A bit of food'll give you strength."

"I'm not hungry."

"Then drink the sweet mead I brung."

Eurome silently fed her little bites and sips. Her nurse tugged a clean handkerchief from her belt. Briseis wiped her tears and blew her nose, smearing it with the makeup Eurome had put on her for the wedding. Had that been only yesterday?

The dirty handkerchief made her think of Hatepa whose rooms lay nearby. She cringed at the thought that Hatepa might have heard her cries. "Eurome, have you seen Queen Hatepa this morning?"

"No, but I talked to that pretty maid of hers, Maira. She said the queen is wore out from all the carrying-ons yesterday, and she gave her a draught to help her sleep. The queen is sleeping still. She'll never ask for you today—I'm sure. Not when she'll think that son of hers is with you. Maira will manage and no need for you."

Eurome seemed to have misunderstood her question. Briseis certainly hadn't been thinking of attending on the queen. "Yes, you're right. I only wondered if..."

Eurome looked at her. "A sleeping draught—Maira said Hatepa slept like a stone. She said that particular."

Eurome put the plate and cup on the tray to carry to the kitchen. "It's hard for you to believe, but you'll come through this. Rough treatment by men is nothing new to women. I just never would ha' thought you'd ever know such as this. I'll do my best by you but I wish your mother was here. She's what you need most, I'm afeared. She'd be the one to tame that beast they call a prince." Eurome looked over her shoulder at the doorway as if worried someone might overhear. Briseis didn't blame her—for the worry or the insult.

When Eurome left, Briseis lay back. Her mother. If her mother were alive, would she have the courage to talk to her about any of this? She had seen tenderness between her parents countless times. Last night had started well enough, giving her hope that her fears were groundless. After Hatepa brought her to the bridal chamber and Mynes came in, he had treated her gently. He seemed shy. Certainly she felt that way. He hadn't said anything when he sat next to her and lifted her veil from her face. He had kissed her lips and tentatively touched her breasts. They'd both laughed in embarrassment.

She'd felt a shadow fall upon her when he tugged away her veil, but it was fine stuff, easily tangled and the little bee got caught in the linen fibers. She cried out when he stomped the bee flat, but he seemed startled at his anger and kissed her as if to erase his outburst.

He pulled at the tie around her tunic's neck, and she had giggled, embarrassed at the thought of her nakedness.

"Wait, let me untie it," she had said.

He yanked at it then, so hard she could still feel the burn on her neck. Had he thought she was laughing at him? Once he pulled the tunic off and exposed her body, he pushed her hard onto the bed. He spread her legs roughly and leered at her while he tore off his own clothes. She sat up, reaching out a hand to calm him, but he flung himself on top of her, shoved her legs apart again and thrust himself into her. She screamed in pain but he smashed his hand against her mouth and hissed, "Silence, or I'll beat you." She writhed and kicked under him trying to escape, but it made him angrier. She lay still, hoping for an end to the pain and humiliation.

Eurome was right. She'd mend somehow, but she felt like the little bee—smashed beyond repair. The smith would have to melt down the gold and start over. How could she re-form herself? What fire would she need—and how could she endure it?

Eurome returned. Maira slipped in behind her, her eyes downcast.

"I've brung Maira so you won't go worrying about the queen," said Eurome.

Maira said, "There's no need for you to attend the queen today." She added in a murmur barely loud enough to hear, "I remember your courage when you faced Hatepa's demons, Lady Briseis. You remember also." She looked directly at Briseis, her eyes full of understanding. Maira, who always slept by the queen's bedside, had not taken a sleeping draught. She bowed and left the room.

Eurome bustled around unpacking Briseis's possessions. "Most of the household is thinking Mynes is here in your chambers—I surely did—but when I found he wasn't, I wanted to know where he'd gone. I found some of his menservants gossiping outside the stables. Mynes ordered them to gather hunting spears and the dogs—and supplies for sleeping overnight in the forest."

Briseis lifted her head as Eurome continued. "Mynes called out the best of his fighting men—servants, not none of his noble friends —to go after a boar causing trouble in some fields far from the town. He claimed it was a duty for a prince, but oh my stars and fishes, the servants found it mighty odd on this day and they were full of talk." Eurome patted Briseis's arm. "He's safe away for two days at least."

Briseis felt the fear release its grip on her insides. Two days.

12

WOOL

Two days of sleeping and resting in solitude restored Briseis's determination if not her happiness. During those days, Eurome kept the palace staff at bay and wrapped her shielding of Briseis in her genial chatter. If the servants wondered whether Briseis's stay in her room was a sign of trouble—they had witnessed Mynes's violence often enough—no one gossiped loudly enough for Eurome to hear. The palace was accustomed to Hatepa, who regularly stayed in her royal bedchamber all day.

Briseis had no intention of letting Mynes find her moping in bed whenever he returned. She arose and dressed, well before his predicted arrival. Eurome arranged her hair in a low, wide twist to hide the raw cut on her neck where Mynes had ripped at her tunic. She had to go out into her new household. When she had arisen each day at her father's, she knew what tasks lay ahead, felt love surrounding her and feared no one. She did not know how to live this new life, but she would figure it out. The more independently of her husband the better.

Hatepa's room lay first in her path, a dreary thought, although she might learn something useful about Mynes. Understanding would help her prevent those dangerous flashes of anger. The queen was not a perceptive person, but his mother must have some insight.

As Briseis walked down the hall, she heard Hatepa's voice complaining. "You must send for her. Certainly my son can spare her for a little while. He should come to visit me also."

Briseis knocked on the doorframe. "It is Briseis. May I come in?"

"Why has it taken you so long to come to me?"

Hatepa lay in her huge bed, propped against pillows. The deep, creases on either side of her mouth accentuated the sour mood permanently inscribed on her gaunt face. Her bulging eyes gave her a startled, unsettled look. Briseis worked a smile onto her face.

She placed her hand on Hatepa's cheek and listened to her breathing. "You look well today, Queen Hatepa. Your color is good—bright roses blooming in your cheeks. Maira must be taking excellent care of you." She turned to look directly at Hatepa's servant. "Thank you, Maira, for all your care."

Maira dipped her head.

"My son has not come to see me since the wedding," said Hatepa, picking at a rough bit of skin on her arm. "His desire to spend time with you must not distract him from his duty to his mother."

Briseis held in the answer that first came to her lips. "I am told the prince has gone to hunt a boar that has become dangerous to his people. I am sure when he returns he will visit his dear mother before he comes to see me."

"No one told me he was attending to his duties as prince." Hatepa turned to her maid. "Why didn't you tell me that? How annoying you are. How can I run the palace household without knowing everything that happens?"

Briseis interceded. "Queen Hatepa, I believe only his menservants knew your son's plan. You understand his habits best of anyone. A new wife knows so little. Perhaps you can tell me if this is customary for him?"

Hatepa opened her mouth and then abruptly shut it again. "If the prince is attending to his duties, that is all you need to know."

Briseis searched for some safe topic to fill her visit since Hatepa offered nothing useful about Mynes. She remembered a question she wanted to ask. She had not decided yet whether to bring to the palace the loom she and her mother had used together. She had a strange feeling that if she removed it from her mother's hall, all the memories of weaving on it together would also tumble down—or the emptiness would break her father's heart.

"Queen Hatepa, I have always loved to weave, but I am not sure if there is a loom for me to use here."

"You may use the one in the women's hall. A virtuous activity for a young bride like you. I'm too ill for it. That loom belonged to Euenos's mother."

"I will start on a tapestry. Shall I brew you some licorice tea or are you feeling strong enough without it?"

"Don't you have some stronger medicine? My cough will return."

"Licorice will soothe you." Although anxious to get away from the woman, Briseis stirred the ground root into a pot of boiling water Maira had ready for her and made herself wait until the tangy scent rising from it told her the tea was ready.

Hatepa sniffed, her nose twitching like a rodent's. "That smells good. Always sweeter when you make it. I have slept soundly these past two nights because I knew you were near. I feel safe now." Briseis met Maira's eyes across Hatepa's bed.

"I am glad to find you well, Hatepa. I will leave you to rest now but will visit again later."

Briseis pushed through the curtained doorway and walked toward the staircase. Her legs felt unsteady. How could she live in this household? How had her mother taken such patient care of that woman through the years? Angrily, she brushed away some tears. She didn't want servants seeing her cry.

She spent the rest of the afternoon in the women's megaron. She opened the shutters of its clerestory windows and ordered the hearth lit, driving off its abandoned look.

The loom leaned against the west wall, its beams marvelously carved with figures of people and animals, the wood rich in tone, deepened by time. Piled beside the loom sat a basket filled with balls of wool yarns the colors of gemstones. Briseis knelt down and picked through them. They had been spun thin and fine, for detailed work. An idea bloomed in her mind: a tapestry of the medicinal herbs and flowers. She would record them all in a weaving.

She went upstairs and retrieved her basket of weaving supplies and settled into the job. She enjoyed the familiar repetitions of setting up a warp and the oily, earthy smell of wool running between her fingers.

As she was absorbed in her work, Euenos entered. He wore a gray tunic edged in red braid, much finer than her father would have worn for every day. He greeted her with a kiss on the cheek.

"It's been a long time since the women's hall has been used," he said. "Hatepa prefers her chamber upstairs. When I was a child, this was one of my favorite rooms in the palace. Let's sit and visit." He indicated the small central hearth with its the grouping of three chairs made of cedar inlaid with ivory and ebony. The feet of the chairs were shaped like lion's paws as if they might pad silently out of the room.

They sat together, discussing palace life, the staff she would supervise and her duties running the royal household—Hatepa could do so little, the steward would be glad of Briseis's help. She saw a place for herself that had nothing to do with Mynes.

The king apologized for Mynes's sudden departure. His son did not always think before he acted, but Euenos promised to reprimand him. She could not confess how relieved Mynes's absence made her —nor did protecting the farmers from a boar seem a great sin. The king's willingness to find fault with his son when he did not seek to understand his son's actions bothered Briseis. She could almost have felt sympathy for Mynes if he'd been kind to her.

Euenos invited her to join his Council, the group of nobles who advised the king, as the Queen of Lyrnessos traditionally did. Her father held the chief advisory role there, although he did not always attend when the needs of his estate occupied him. Euenos assured her that her experience as healing priestess would bring a useful perspective, despite her youth, and she needed to learn statecraft by observation. Hatepa had not fulfilled this role, as had always been done before her reign—her health, of course, prevented that—but Briseis should follow the more active model of traditional queens. This challenge appealed to her, although she suspected the son did not share his father's vision of her role. She could not see that vicious beast consulting her at the Council.

Euenos stood. "I'll leave you now. You have everything you need?"

She nodded. She couldn't, after all, ask for a longer reprieve from her husband.

WHEN EUENOS LEFT, Briseis returned to her loom and picked up a bobbin. Leaning in close to the threads, she worked the purple wool into tiny flowers shaped like clusters of beads, crowding a stalk of sage. How to create the gray down that formed a hazy cloud on each bloom, softening but not hiding the deep tone below? She stood back to examine her work and heard heavy footsteps. Her stomach clenched, but she willed away her fear. She turned and saw Mynes in the doorway with a small bundle in his hand. He still wore dusty hunting gear—leather kilt and chest guard over a thick wool tunic of olive green.

"May I come in?"

He sounded apologetic. She nodded.

He came a little way into the room and glanced around as if unsure of his surroundings. His head and shoulders hunched forward, reminding her of a dog's posture when it fears a beating. Did Mynes feel apprehensive of her? She remembered his father's misdirected criticism of Mynes. She supposed he had grown accustomed to his parents feeling disappointed in him. He certainly shouldn't expect her to feel glad to see him.

Mynes looked up at the open windows still catching the last of the day's light.

"You're weaving on my grandmother's loom," he said, with wonder in his voice. "Perhaps this present won't offend you. I didn't choose it—a farmer's wife gave it to me. It's some of her wool, the first clippings, which she said are especially soft and would serve as a blessing for our wedding. She had set this aside from her new lambs this past spring and hadn't spun it yet with all the outdoor work of summer on her hands. It's just white wool, but..." He stopped and took a step closer. His dark eyes pleaded. He was asking forgiveness. She could see that and wondered if she could ever grant it.

"After I killed the boar, we were packing up our camp and had food left over. One of my men suggested we give it to the farmer. His wife gave me this in return. I didn't ask for it, but she had tears in her eyes and said the food meant her little boy would eat well. She said you'd delivered the boy safely with the gods' blessings so she wanted to give you a blessing in return."

He put it to his cheek and then held it out to her. "The wool is soft."

She put down her bobbin and went to him. She put the wool against her cheek just as he had. "It is soft. Thank you."

He looked down at his dirty clothing and dusty feet. "I have to go wash up—from the hunt...before dinner." He stood stiffly, his weight carried equally on both legs. When she said nothing, he turned toward the door and his shoulders slumped.

"Would you like to have dinner here with me—after you wash?" asked Briseis.

His "Yes" came out in a kind of gasp. He turned back toward her for a moment and then left.

Eurome served them lamb stew and lentils cooked with leeks in the women's hall. They ate in silence. Mynes tapped his foot repeatedly, the annoying habit she'd seen in his early courting. Briseis wished he would say something. She didn't have the energy to carry the conversation for both of them.

They were both startled when a log crumbled suddenly into the hot coals, releasing some inner reserve of sap that ignited with a furious spitting noise.

Briseis stirred herself. "Tell me about the boar hunt."

Mynes jumped into a description of how hard it had been to kill the boar, even though they'd tracked it to its lair. He and his men could only wound it. It charged directly at them. The others jumped back, leaving him to make the killing blow. Mynes described how he had thrown his spear directly into the beast's neck, jumping away just in time to avoid its tusks. His face lit with excitement.

A serving woman appeared in the doorway. Hatepa wished to see Mynes.

Mynes offered her his arm before they climbed the stairs. She drew in her breath but managed to put her hand on his arm, covering her discomfort by talking.

"Your mother will be happy to see you. She was worried that you might spend less time with her now that we are married. She was feeling a little cross with me."

"My mother would never be cross with you—she thinks everything of you. It's me she finds fault with." His shoulders hunched forward as he said this, the fierce boar hunter gone.

Mynes knocked on the doorframe and they went in. Maira quickly left the room, murmuring she had to go down to the kitchen for some supplies.

Ignoring Briseis, Hatepa chastised Mynes for not coming to see her as soon as he got back. He sat down on the edge of her bed, quieting her fussing by reminding her of the dangerous hunt he'd been on. He started telling the details of it. As he described the blow to the charging boar, Hatepa looked alarmed. She interrupted him.

"You should be more careful. Place the other men in front. That is why your father keeps trained hunters. You are the future king."

Mynes objected. "Mother, I am a better fighter than our servants. No one else could kill the boar."

Hatepa shushed him. "They are only servants. It doesn't matter if they get hurt. You must lead by giving orders from a distance."

Briseis heard Mynes mumble, "That isn't how Father leads in battle."

But he turned to Hatepa and said loudly, "Yes, Mother."

For the first time that evening Briseis heard anger in his voice—the voice of her wedding night. She watched his face. It was oddly stiff, as though gradually turning to stone.

A serving girl came in with wood for the brazier. Hatepa ordered her to send Maira back.

As the conversation between mother and son wound down, Briseis felt panic. In a moment she would be outside her rooms with her husband. What would he expect from her? Mynes glanced at her. To her surprise a look of pain flashed across his face. Had he understood her thoughts?

Maira returned. Mynes stood. "Mother, now that your maid is here to take care of you, I must say good night." He leaned over and kissed his mother's cheek.

He and Briseis left Hatepa's room. They walked toward the stairs that divided the hallway joining the queen's room and hers. No servants passed by. They were alone. Mynes stopped.

"May I kiss you? I won't..."

She nodded and he embraced her, letting out a strangled sound. His hands moved hungrily over her body and his lips found hers—she tried to think of the moment when he had put his hand on her thigh during one of the betrothal visits and wished for the response she had felt then—but she could not. She stood stiffly. He released his arms.

"Good night, Briseis," he said, and rushed down the stairs.

13

PLOWING AND FIGHTING

The months passed and autumn colors came and went, but the difficulties of her marriage remained. Each time Mynes came to her room—blessedly he kept away more often than not—she retreated inside herself. She recognized Mynes's hunger for her body, but she felt no desire for him. It was like an illness. He had caused it, and neither of them had a cure. She guessed his awareness of this kept his visits few and short. Outside her room, she learned to engage him in conversations he found interesting and to show him the deference he found agreeable. She prayed to Kamrusepa to bring her husband calmness and so far the goddess had granted her this—or at least Mynes directed his violent eruptions at others.

One part of her life was less trying than she had dreaded—caring for Hatepa. Maira learned each healing procedure Briseis used, and she was far more patient with the queen than anyone should be. This puzzled Briseis. Maira showed quick thinking and a liveliness at odds with her subdued life at Hatepa's side. Briseis heard tales of previous maids who lost their tempers with Hatepa and ended up grinding wheat, the lowliest household chore. Maira had, for a time, served the king in the main hall, a privileged assignment reserved for the most graceful servants. Maira had requested to serve Hatepa instead.

This much Briseis had gleaned from servants' gossip reported by Eurome, but not why. An uneasy suspicion she wanted to ignore hovered at the edge of her thoughts. She'd noticed that Maira always left Hatepa's room if Mynes entered. She recalled how after her wedding night, Maira had told her to remember her courage—Maira who had been close enough to hear what Mynes had done. Maira acted as her ally and support. Briseis accepted her silent loyalty and returned it, but hoped she was wrong about another bond they might share.

As healing priestess she escaped from the palace regularly, although Mynes grumbled at her absences. He questioned her in detail, especially when she attended on men. The long hours of delivering a child infuriated him when he wanted her company. She pretended to sympathize while relishing her work even more than before her marriage.

Occasionally she assisted Iatros as he accompanied the physician —some illnesses required both priestess and physician, and she felt the old happiness of family and shared enthusiasm. With winter's cold weather came increased illnesses and she and Iatros crossed paths more often—a hidden blessing to offset the increased worry of treating her people's ailments.

The physician said Iatros's apprenticeship progressed with all the speed Euenos could hope for. Iatros took to healing as if he had always done it. Briseis suspected he had absorbed more as a child than he realized, listening in while Antiope taught Briseis. She envied his expanding range of knowledge, but with her palace duties, it was all she could do to fulfill her responsibilities as healing priestess. She didn't ask Iatros to teach her any of his new skills.

One evening while she was eating dinner with the royal family in the great hall, a messenger called for her to deliver a child. She rose immediately and turned to tell Eurome to go for her cloak and satchel.

Mynes put down his wine cup. "My wife shouldn't be dragged out into the darkness like some common servant. You should stay here where you belong. It's too cold and stormy outside. I won't have this."

Hatepa murmured in agreement and patted his hand. The rings she wore, so large and heavy with gemstones, clattered against each other on her bony fingers.

Briseis clenched her hands into fists, hidden by the folds of her skirt. "A healing priestess is not a common servant. I serve our goddess Kamrusepa. What I do is sacred. Do you care so little for your people that you would let a woman and child go without my help because she happened to labor in the hours of darkness? Are you mad?"

She turned to Euenos for help, glad he witnessed Mynes's outburst and might curb his son's increasing annoyance with her necessary work.

"Now, now, Briseis," said Euenos. "Don't be so upset. Mynes is only concerned for your welfare."

"Is he? Then while I'm gone you can help him be concerned also for the welfare of his people. He is their future king, after all." She knew she should not have let her anger speak, but she didn't have time to apologize now. Eurome arrived with her cloak.

She started toward the door, but her fear of Mynes turned her back. She forced herself to speak. "I'm sorry, Mynes, I spoke so sharply. A wife should not address her husband like that. I only meant I cannot neglect the responsibilities the goddess has given me. She brings on the time of a child's entrance into the world, and I must obey her summons. Even your wife, I'm sure you agree, must listen to the will of the gods." Mynes grunted. She took it as assent and left.

She did not return until the next morning. Exhausted, she wanted only to go up to her room and rest. She answered the palace steward's few questions so the palace day would go smoothly and then started up the stairs. Mynes came storming in and grabbed her arm. She flinched away from him and he dug his fingers into her skin so hard she cried out.

"How dare you stay out all night and not come in to greet me! The worm of a steward gets your time, but not me." He dragged her off the stair and forced her arm behind her back, pushing her against the railing. He pressed his mouth hard against hers, forcing in his tongue.

He kept his face pressed in close, his stale breath making her gag. "The men in the barracks jest about their wives—that an unplowed field grows no wheat. A proper wife welcomes her husband every night. You'll start acting like my wife. I'll be digging deep furrows every night with my plow."

He let go of her, laughing. She stumbled up the stairs, praying he wouldn't follow.

LATER THAT DAY, Briseis slipped outside to the royal family's court-yard despite the frost that made the cobblestones slippery—not as restoring as a walk on Mount Ida, but all she could manage in the palace. As she returned inside to the small connecting hallway, she overheard two servants gossiping while they scrubbed the great hall's floor, and she realized someone among the serving women must have witnessed that horrible scene with Mynes.

"—hates him, I'd say. Not surprising, the way he treats her."

"He's handsome enough if you ignore them eyes of his, but I'm glad he won't take a grab at the likes of me, only beauties like Maira or poor Lady Briseis. Not easy for Lady Briseis to get him out of her bed—no one's like her. Only Maira is close. She'll have to choose—Hatepa or Mynes. And which is worse? Maira can't keep both enter-tained, not unless she took on both at the same time."

"Wouldn't the queen love that!" They laughed. Briseis felt sick. The servants' gossip confirmed her suspicions. She knew why Maira chose to live in Hatepa's sickroom—the one place Mynes couldn't get at her.

UNLESS SHE WAS out of the palace tending to the ill or delivering babies, Briseis never missed a meeting of the king's Council. At first, she only spoke up when they discussed something directly related to her work as healing priestess. Gradually, as talk of war with the Greeks increased, she realized she could contribute to this topic also.

The war showed no signs of ending. The Greeks couldn't prevent supply ships from entering Troy's main harbor and restocking the city, although they attacked during the unloading and caused losses of men and supplies. Equally, the Trojans couldn't starve out the Greeks because the Greeks had taken control of a fort that guarded a small harbor to the south of the city and they too could supply their army.

Although the young men were eager to go fight at Troy and end this stalemate, the Council was made up of men with sons to lose and they sought ways to postpone. The Council understood much better than did the young men that Lyrnessos's warriors would not shift the balance enough to end the war. When Briseis proposed they offer King Priam weapons instead of warriors, they listened. Many of Troy's allies could supply men, but there was an acute shortage of arms. Her father's workshop with Milos in charge could fill that void if the other nobles assisted in providing the ore from the mines up in the Taurus Mountains. The Council dispatched wagons and slaves to the mines. A delegation traveled to Troy. For months this arrangement kept Lyrnessos out of the war, and the nobles' coffers grew richer from the trade. Her father's weapons bought the lives of Lyrnessos's men even while they were used to kill others.

The Council could be tedious. Some of the king's advisors spoke as much to hear themselves as to solve problems, but she appreciated her growing understanding of Lyrnessos. Fortunately, Mynes considered training with the young warriors more important, so he rarely attended. When he did, his irritation at her presence showed. He interrupted and contradicted her when she spoke, especially if she discussed ways to keep Lyrnessos's warriors out of the war. He did not share Euenos's view of her role as future queen. An invalid like Hatepa would have pleased him more, but she gained the respect of the others. Her knowledge of metalworking did not disgust them as it did her husband. For now, she let the value she held in others' eyes sustain her and soften the pain of her husband's repugnance.

ONE MORNING, when Briseis had been delayed by her household

responsibilities, she entered the Council after the king and his advisors had already begun. A larger number of men than usual had gathered—twenty or more, including her father. The lines around his eyes had deepened in a way that no longer originated from laughter.

The noblemen sat in a semicircle in wooden chairs facing Euenos's throne, which stood on its platform framed with a fresco of two griffins behind it. The regal beasts spread their wings on either side of the throne and bowed their heads to the king. Something about the attentive posture of the men that morning mimicked the beasts' special deference, and she wondered what event they knew about that she had missed.

Some of the Council were men in their prime with bodies well-muscled by training for battle. Others showed their age with bent backs and white hair. The tension in the air warned her that these men expected something significant to occur.

Mynes sat beside his father. Irritation twisted his face when he saw her. She took her seat slightly apart from the group. Her father glanced at her briefly, but she couldn't read his thoughts.

The king stood and lifted his scepter from the table next to him. "I have called all of you here to witness my announcement of war."

Briseis's heart dropped.

"I have had enough of waiting while the Greeks batter Troy. We must fulfill our treaty obligations to Priam. Glaukos's weapons production gave us valuable time to prepare, but we can no longer put off our duty." He nodded toward her father in thanks. "The winter weather will make transporting our warriors and supplies more difficult—we are close enough to manage, though. Troy suffers in this cold, harsh season, and our succor now will be of greatest benefit. The Greeks will not expect the arrival of new allies at this time of year. I will lead our warriors to Troy within the week, with Glaukos as my second in command."

Without thinking, Briseis rose from her chair. "No! Let us hold off a little longer. Perhaps the Greeks will leave. King Priam knows how valuable we are as a supplier of weapons. We—"

"Silence!" roared Mynes, leaping from his seat. "What right do you have to contradict my father? It is time to fight! We are not cowards who skulk at home like frightened women! I will go to Troy and slaughter Achilles. The Trojans need real warriors."

Euenos put his free hand on Mynes's arm, but turned toward her. "Briseis, this is a Council of war. I understand your concern for our men's lives—your help has been invaluable—but you do not have a place in this decision."

He faced his son. "No one doubts your willingness to challenge Achilles. Troy has need of heroes like you. But you must serve Lyrnessos. Who will protect our city while I am gone? Who will rule in my absence? You must stay here. Our soldiers need experienced commanders at Troy."

Mynes lunged at his father and Briseis feared for a moment he would strike Euenos. "Stay here? I am the one who trains our warriors every day. I am going to Troy! Are you afraid that my deeds on the battlefield will outdo yours? You've had your time. You stay and rule. I'm going to fight!"

Euenos folded his arms across his chest. Briseis watched him conquer his anger in the shifting lines of tension around his mouth and across his shoulders. He dropped his arms to his sides and stepped closer to his son. When Mynes's expression did not soften, Euenos placed his hand on Mynes's arm.

"You don't mean what you say. There will be battles enough for you in the future. You will understand this after you've had a chance to settle yourself. Stay in Lyrnessos where you are needed. I have decided. There will be no more discussion."

Mynes ripped his arm from his father's grip and raced from the room. Briseis watched Euenos close his eyes for a moment. He returned to his throne and looked around the Council. "Every noble household must provide at least one warrior of fighting age and his equipment. Those of you with greater obligations know what you must supply. Spread the word. I have ordered the ships prepared in the harbor. At the rising of the sun five days hence, we sail to Troy. You know your duty."

Mynes had shot her a poisonous look as he stormed out. Her neck and shoulders felt as taut as an archer's bow. Every young man in Lyrnessos wanted to fight at Troy, but Mynes more than any. He could not take out his disappointment on his father. She had chosen the worst moment to speak up. Mynes would turn his fury against her.

SHE ATE ALONE in her own hall that evening and went upstairs. Eurome was combing her hair. Mynes entered with his arms crossed, his face hard.

He waived dismissively at Eurome. "Get out!" Eurome gave her a frightened look. Briseis nodded and her nurse went.

Mynes circled her. She could see he savored the anticipation of his revenge for her interference. Fury rose up in her throat—she had only been protecting her people. She breathed slowly to hold back the words. Her outbreak in the Council only offered an excuse.

"I'm sorry your father wishes you to stay here," she said, "but I know the people will be glad to have your protection and guidance." He envied the way the people loved her for her healing work, so she hoped this lie would calm him.

"Take off your clothes," he said.

"What, now?"

"Yes, now."

With trembling fingers, she took off her tunic and skirt, her underclothes. She fought back the shame and tears she would not allow him to see, hating her helplessness. She could do nothing against him, doubly so since he was both her husband and the ruler. She stood naked and refused to drop her eyes.

Perhaps he saw the hatred and it added fuel to his wrath. With a blow he sent her crashing into a wooden chest. She hit her shoulder and fell to the floor. She bit her lip as pain shot across her torso. He walked over to her, pulling up his tunic and shoving his loincloth to one side.

He yanked her up by the hair, threw her facedown over the chest. She felt the edges dig into her hips and breasts. He thrust himself inside her.

"Like this" he grunted, "I'll drive my spear into Achilles's guts." He grabbed her hair again and pulled her head backwards so that her face was close to his. "I'll make you feel it. You don't want me to be the hero—you want a husband who hides at home. So take Achilles's deathblow." She cried out in pain. He laughed. "You feel it now, don't you?" He slapped her face. "Don't you?"

She nodded and closed her eyes.

14

HURRIED PREPARATIONS AND DIVINE SILENCE

The next morning Briseis dragged herself out of bed. Everyone around her except Eurome ignored her bruises and misery. The household whirled with the work needed to ready the expedition. The king had given them only four days. At sunrise on the fifth day, the warriors would set out for Troy. Organizing these efforts absorbed Briseis's attention and for a portion of the day she buried herself in it to forget what her life had become. Her loathing of her husband's nightly visits turned to a terror that seeped into her limbs and seized her chest.

The fading light at the day's end increased her panic—it would not be long before he came to her room. Then Eurome brought the news that Mynes had been sent to guard the loading of the ships at the harbor. He'd stay there until they sailed. Even with this short respite, she felt only an icy chill, a foreboding that the worst had not yet struck her. She tried to pray to Kamrusepa, to find some solace at her loom, but nothing fended off her fear. She stumbled through each of the busy days.

All Lyrnessos focused on preparations: armor, weapons, food-stuffs, cooking pots and tripods, amphorae of wine, the slaves needed to run the camp, along with readying the ships themselves. Euenos had laid the groundwork for this expedition many months ago, but the final ingathering posed a huge task. The frantic pace seemed to her one more reason to delay the departure, but the rest of the community did not share her worries. Once the king announced his decision, Lyrnessos caught the young men's enthusiasm for war.

She wondered, if she were a man, would she have been as eager to fight in this war? What if she had been born in Troy and had no choice? She wondered how her brothers felt. Euenos had granted her father's request that they stay. She knew, though her father would never speak of it with her, that they stayed to protect her—a hopeless task. Were they upset about staying home, not the way Mynes was, but still disappointed?

She made private prayers to Kamrusepa and Telipinu during these days. She also entreated them to safeguard the warriors setting out for Troy and the town that was being left without their protection. She overheard men talking of the gods' enthusiasm, boasting that the Stormgod and Telipinu would run in front of the king in battle, but her prayers received no response and she feared that the soldiers would not have the gods' support.

To safeguard them she planned a snake divination at the temple to find out if the gods held Lyrnessos responsible for some offense against them. She must identify what offering could be made to soften the divine anger. She would not send Euenos and her father into battle without placating the gods.

Briseis entered the main sanctuary of the Stormgod with its high ceiling supported by brightly painted columns. The air felt even colder inside than out and she pulled her cloak around her. At least the wind no longer whipped at her face. In one corner stood a large ceramic basin, wider than she was tall, filled with water into which the snakes would be released for the divination. Painted on the outside of the waist high wall were dancing women holding snakes. Through the water Briseis could see the words carved into the sides, bottom and stone slabs that protruded irregularly around the basin.

The goddess's answer would come through the snakes when they touched the words in response to Briseis's questions: "life," "temple," "sin," "prison," "oath," "child and mother," "house," "bloody deed" and so on. Some words were favorable, some unfavorable, a form of yes and no.

The priest stepped to the edge of the basin and tipped the tall bowl filled with water and snakes. The first snake's head appeared in the bowl's channel. For a moment it resisted following the water that flowed into the basin. Its green eyes stared at Briseis. Then it glided along with the water. The other snakes followed.

"Kamrusepa, goddess of our safety and well-being, you know all our misdeeds and sins. Has Lyrnessos offended the gods in some way?" Briseis searched for possible misdeeds she could ask about so she could receive a clear answer. "Have we deprived the Stormgod of his proper offerings in our haste to prepare our soldiers?"

Briseis observed the snakes. All but one were out of sight behind or under the stone slabs. She saw the glint of green eyes as one snake swam toward the symbol for "hearth." Favorable. No, their chief god's offerings had not been neglected.

She continued her questions for a long time, never able to identify a sin to remedy. Finally, the attending priest cleared his throat and murmured, "Perhaps you should not look for a sin when none has been committed. Why do you fear for our warriors?"

She could not tell the priest that she personally heard only silence where she had once felt the presence of two gods— Kamrusepa and Telipinu. He, apparently, did not feel this discomfort and he must be praying for the king and his warriors also. She gave up and declared the divination showed the gods found no fault with Lyrnessos and would support their warriors in the upcoming war. But perhaps Mynes's violence had made her deaf to anything else. That felt true.

It also felt likely that Kamrusepa, the goddess of childbirth and renewal of the earth, had turned her eyes away from Lyrnessos now that the king had embraced war, but that didn't explain Telipinu's withdrawal from her. He savored war and thrived on the battlefield. He had reappeared in her dreams soon after her wedding night and she had found these visions a soothing refuge from her husband's violence. Now he had disappeared.

The only dream she did have terrified her and left her trembling in bed. The dream contained a warning, but she couldn't decide what it meant.

In her dream she saw Iatros lifting a sword in the air. She hid behind him, or was it behind something—a thicket? A low wall of some sort? Why did she hide when her brother was in danger? He defended her from something coming toward them. A huge boar with blood-drenched tusks charged him. Then the boar became a man—bigger than any man she'd ever seen. When he swooped down on Iatros, flames consumed both her brother and the warrior. She realized she hid behind a well. She must get water to douse the flames, but she found no bucket, no rope to bring it up. Before she could act, they disappeared and left her alone. The flames returned and burned closer.

What a strange and frightening dream. Iatros never hunted, certainly not boar. More importantly, Iatros and her other two brothers, thank the gods, would stay safe at home. She had few blessings, but she had that.

BRISEIS PAUSED inside the doorway of the great hall. A servant had delivered the king's summons to speak with him in his megaron hall. As she watched, the king bent his head toward a bearded man with dark skin whom she recognized as the trader charged with preparing the ships. In addition to the warships which the king had built, Euenos had commandeered merchant ships from unlucky traders who had been in the harbor at the wrong moment—and many had chosen their quiet harbor for sheltering out the winter. Their vessels would be returned to them, but only after transporting the king's supplies in their deep holds, designed to carry long rows of shoulder-high amphorae of oil, wine or grain, stacks of copper ingots and herds of cattle or sheep.

"We can hope no winter storms will prevent our departure—or

worse, force us off course on our way, but we must keep careful watch as we sail," the trader said. "I've received word that Achilles and his marauders have attacked towns on the island of Lesbos in recent days. That puts them dangerously close to our course as we head toward Troy."

"Lesbos?" said the king. "They spread their destruction ever further, the insolent whelps—Achilles most of all. Yet that means, if they've already raided towns there, they'll be sailing back north to Troy with their spoils—ahead of us, out of our way." Euenos discussed the fleet's readiness with the trader.

Achilles! That name again. She heard Mynes's hateful words and closed her eyes. Mynes wished to fight Achilles and kill him, but the reverse was more likely. She put her hands to her temples. She would not think such things. She couldn't believe she'd ever thought of Achilles the way the bards had described him: the lost young hero, filled with a burning rage left by his mother's immortal flames, finding peace through the healing skills his teacher Chiron gave him. Now violence and horror followed in the wake of that name.

She leaned against the wall. The island of Lesbos lay not so far away. How could Achilles have come so close?

Achilles's renown had grown as his destruction spread among the small towns. Briseis wondered what it felt like to be in his presence. Two of the bards' tales about him actually spoke of Achilles's mother, Thetis. One described how she had freed Zeus, the king of the Greek gods, when the other immortals tried to overthrow him. Achilles's mother could withstand the force of all the other gods combined. The second tale said Zeus and his brother Poseidon had vied to marry Thetis, driven by lust for her, but they had instead forced her to marry a mortal man because oracles said she would have a son greater than his father. Neither Zeus nor Poseidon wanted a son who would overthrow them. Perhaps the half-mortal Achilles could not conquer the king of the gods, but now that he fought as Lyrnessos's foe, Briseis dreaded the strength born into him from such a mother.

"I still think it would be wiser to send some small scouting ships," said the trader.

"That won't be necessary." Euenos dismissed the trader with an abrupt wave of his hand.

Briseis stepped forward.

The corners of the king's mouth sagged. He no longer held himself as straight and his ruddy complexion had gone pale. He motioned to Briseis to draw a stool close to him.

"Will you pray for us?" he said. "Will you come to the shore tomorrow to bless the warriors and ask Kamrusepa to keep them safe?"

Of course she would. This would be her last chance to be with her father until the fighters returned—if they did.

So, the next morning, just as the sun's light began to glow in the eastern sky, Briseis accompanied the warriors down to the fleet. She had made this journey with her father many times before when he went to inspect traders' goods. The cart road wound up and over one of Mount Ida's foothills through pine forests and then down a deep ravine to a small harbor protected from Aegean storms by a narrow bay.

The early morning air cut through her cloak with its chill. She'd bundled up with several layers, but she didn't envy the men who would be exposed for days to this cold on the sea. And what when they got to Troy? She hoped the city would have room for them inside as Euenos insisted. Building a camp would be hard in this weather.

The king led in his chariot at the front of the large group going to the harbor. Glaukos had already sent his one chariot and pair of battle horses ahead to be loaded on the ships, so Briseis and her father walked. Slow carts drawn by oxen followed at the back with the last of the supplies to be loaded aboard. When she glanced behind, she saw steam rising from the noses of the hardworking beasts, giving them an odd appearance.

Briseis didn't speak for fear of letting loose the tears she could barely contain. The road came over the top of the ridge, and she could see a band of blue sea in the distance. The smell of pine trees mixed with a salty breeze. She was grateful to share one more walk with her father.

Mynes supervised the ships. Euenos had finally appointed him commander of the city guard as they protected the fleet during the last four days. She hoped it made him feel important enough to soften the blow of being left behind. Mynes would rule as king once his father left, so Euenos's gesture seemed as empty as she felt.

She could hear the waterfall before they reached the ravine. When she was little and the weather was considerably warmer, her father had lifted her to his shoulders and climbed close to the falls, letting its spray mist them and showing her the rainbows that arced in glistening brilliance against the steep rock face. Now, as they both looked at the falls, Glaukos rested his hand on her shoulder. Sadness filled his eyes. What did fate hold for them?

"Keep yourself safe, my daughter."

She hugged him. "You too, Papa."

They arrived at the ships with their bows drawn up on the shore and saw grooms loading the horses. Only the richest men in Lyrnessos would fight with the advantage of a chariot, but those who did needed their warhorses. The men had to coax them up wide planks into the recesses of the ships.

Her father was called away and Briseis stood watching the loading of his pair of horses. The big gray cooperated but the black one, always temperamental, snorted and tossed his head, backing away from the plank. She hurried toward him when she recognized her old friend.

"Stand back, Lady Briseis," cried one of the men. "This horse is a brute."

"I've known this fellow since he was a colt," said Briseis. She called his name. "Easy there, Diokles." She put her hand on his withers. He rolled his eye to look at her. "You'll be fine, big fellow." He quieted and let her stroke his neck. She scratched behind his ears and watched the alarm soften in his dark eyes. "That's it, Diokles. You have an important job to do—keep my father safe. Now come along with me. I know this plank looks frightening, but you're a warhorse.

You've seen worse, so let's not get in a muddle about a piece of wood." She took the halter. "One step and then another. That's it." Two men followed the horse down into the hull to a place where straw had been laid between wooden crates—a sort of stall.

"Treat him well," she told them. "My father will need him in good health."

The men bowed. "Yes, Lady Briseis."

As she climbed out, she heard one of the king's servants call out. Euenos was going to speak.

She stood beside her father and Euenos on the prow of the king's ship as he addressed the men gathered on the shore, more than two hundred strong. An offshore wind blew back her veil and caught her hair. They'd have good sailing. She heard the king's voice but not the words as she looked out at the faces below her. How many would not return?

When the king finished, the priests performed the sacrifices on the shore and she said a prayer for the warrior's safety. Then her father and she walked toward Glaukos's ship. They stood in the shadow of the black hull. He brushed some of her unruly hair out of her eyes, then hugged and kissed her. "Goodbye, Briseis."

"Stay well, Papa."

He climbed onto his ship. She watched as men shoved the hulls into the water and maneuvered with the oars away from the shore. The foremost ships hoisted their sails, and gradually the fleet glided up the bay. Somewhere out there, she thought, Achilles was sailing around. *Please do not let him cross this fleet's path.*

She watched her father standing on the foredeck of his ship, his arms moving as he issued commands. She thought he looked back at her once. His ship gained speed as the sails billowed out, and she could no longer distinguish people on deck.

She looked around her, at the channels the hulls had cut into the beach of rounded stones and at the men harnessing oxen to now-empty wagons. She turned back to the sea. "Kamrusepa, you may not like this expedition, but please, for the sake of my mother's devoted service, keep my father safe and bring him home soon."

15

ATTACK

B riseis kept to her duties as healing priestess, endured what she
had to from her husband's visits, and left Mynes to rule as he
would. Through the palace steward's reports and Eurome's eaves-
dropping, she heard about the difficulties Mynes's decisions caused,
but said nothing. Even when he ignored the advice of those
remaining in Lyrnessos who now formed the Council, she kept silent.
She could not pay the price of contradicting him, nor could she have
influenced him to change his mind.

Fortunately for the running of the state, Mynes spent most of his
time training the city guards, not interfering with the Council's work.
The guard, a group made up of younger sons of peasants with no
land to work, did not fight like the noble warriors. They were not
trained in hand-to-hand battle with shield and sword as were the
men who had gone to Troy. They didn't need to be. When the guard
was placed strategically on Lyrnessos's sturdy walls and armed with
the spears and bows they had learned to use as boys to hunt for food,
they could hold off a strong force if the city were attacked. Since
Euenos's departure, Mynes had developed grand notions of what he
could train the guard to do, and Briseis let this ambition occupy him

as the winter months crept by and spring once again arrived in the outside world if not in Briseis's heart.

One day Briseis was called outside the city to attend on a farmer's wife in labor. The farmer came in after a time and said that her brother waited outside to speak to her when she was available.

Bienor had come to tell her about a scene with Mynes earlier that day—and to warn her. Mynes had stored up a fierce resentment against Bienor and Adamas, and it had boiled over that morning. Mynes had insinuated that they had arranged to be left home out of fear, and somehow Mynes decided to blame them for his being kept from Troy. Briseis's heart sank. She worried her brother, who could do nothing for her, would guess that Mynes included her in that blame.

Mynes, Bienor told her, had screamed at Adamas and him that morning in front of the city guard, calling them cowards, frightened women, too terrified to go into battle. Screeching that he would show them what battle felt like, he drew his sword and lunged at them. Bienor told her they avoided a fight by fleeing. No doubt Mynes was boasting he'd run them off. Briseis saw the sting of this accusation of cowardice in Bienor's eyes.

"We won't be able to come to the palace to visit you any more," said Bienor. "It will infuriate Mynes and I'm not sure I could stop myself from fighting back next time."

"You can't let Mynes insult you like this."

Bienor shrugged. "I've watched Mynes work himself up before— never this far, it's true—but he'll keep choosing fights until he finally starts to calm down. It's never a good idea to be in one of the fights he picks. I've learned. Step back and wait. Things will get better eventually. Adamas and I will have to take the insults for a time, but he'll want our friendship later and he'll make it right. He's the king. What else can we do? Briseis, you need to be careful while he's like this. Has he been upset around you?"

She couldn't look her brother in the eye when she lied. "I'll be fine."

She suspected he didn't believe her, but what could he do? Stand guard at her bedroom door and deny her husband access? All they could do was try to avoid direct confrontation that would increase Mynes's fury.

Bienor's warning ate at her. Was Mynes growing even more violent? She felt like she teetered on a cliff edge. Bienor believed Mynes's behavior would settle with time. She cast about for some way to escape until then. Her father had left her brothers behind to protect her, but Mynes had separated her from them. They couldn't come to the palace, but perhaps she could retreat to her father's estate.

Mynes grumbled constantly about the need to arm the city guards with proper swords. In his complaints Briseis saw an excuse to stay for a time at her father's house. Milos had always been the most skilled blacksmith, and now he was the only one left in Lyrnessos, since the others had gone with the king to maintain their arms.

At dinner that evening with Mynes, Briseis pretended to express her sympathy with the guards' lack of noble weapons. She suggested she consult Milos about making some to fill this need. Mynes would never admit it aloud, but even he understood that Briseis knew far more about metalworking than he did. She thanked the gods for Mynes's ignorance about the quantity of ore that would be needed. No such supplies remained in her father's storerooms, but Milos could get started with a small quantity and pacify her husband. In her conversation with Mynes about arranging the manufacture of weapons, she never mentioned her brothers. She emphasized she would need several days to plan the work with Milos—difficult without her father's expertise, but she'd do her best. Mynes gave her seven days. Her duties running the palace household could be left in Hatepa's hands for that long, he allowed.

Briseis spent the days at her father's estate feeling like she could breathe again. She could feel the renewal of spring when she walked on Mount Ida's familiar paths. Milos agreed to reuse some bronze they had and make a few swords to please Mynes. On one of the days, she went with Iatros to take care of a sick family. It turned out to be bad meat they'd eaten—an easy cure—but the children needed care, and she loved watching Iatros nurse them. She felt alive again. She enjoyed sitting around the familiar hearth, listening to her brothers tease each other. She stayed silent with them more than she used to —too many hurts she could not share. The restraint saddened her, but the time away restored her.

After the seven days she had to return. She hoped Bienor was right and Mynes's madness would have calmed. Eurome and she walked slowly back to the palace, escorted by three menservants. Briseis had turned down the offer of a cart. She was in no hurry. The sun fell softly on her face. A wind made the woods alive with movement and filled the air with the scent of the wildflowers dotting the meadows. If only she could stay forever outside among the mountains.

As they drew near the city walls, guards rushed out. "Lady Briseis, come inside." They hurried her along, almost carrying her in their haste. "Reports of Greeks nearby. The prince has ordered the men to prepare for battle."

"Battle? Why aren't you taking your positions on the walls? Close the gates! Defend Lyrnessos!"

"Lord Mynes commanded us to arm for battle outside the Great Gate." Briseis drew back from him. He must have misunderstood the orders. Euenos had trained the city guards to defend the walls. Then she understood what Mynes's training sessions with the guard and his desire for swords meant. He intended to confront the Greeks head-on. He was really that foolish. She had to stop him.

She ran through the gates but halted almost immediately, blocked by the chaotic crowd already gathered in the marketplace square. Men and women poured down each street and alley, and Briseis realized the rumor of the Greeks must have spread. Voices shouted questions, screamed in panic. Children cried. Frightened family members clung to each other. No one understood what was happening. Why leave the gates open? Why didn't the guards take their posts on the walls?

A war cry cut through the noise. Briseis looked up the hill toward the palace. Mynes in his chariot dashed down the main road and the crowd scrambled to get out of his way. Behind him ran more guards, trying to keep up.

Briseis held her ground before the city gates, her arms outstretched toward her husband. Mynes raced at her. He raised the whip and lashed the horses, making no attempt to avoid her.

"Lord Mynes," she shouted. "This is madness. Command your men from the walls. Follow your father's plan."

He held his course straight at her. What words to persuade? No time for flattery and false deference. Despite him, the horses slowed and shied sideways to avoid her. She grabbed the leads, pulling hard to stop the horses, her feet skidding out from under her.

"Get out of my way, you bitch. I won't hide like a woman behind walls."

She held on, struggling to think of something to say to him that would keep the guard inside the city. Mynes slashed his whip across her face and chest, knocking her to the ground. The crowd gasped. Hands pulled her out of the way as the chariot lunged forward. Mynes screamed another war cry. His men flooded after him. Euenos's decision to leave Mynes behind bore this deadly fruit.

Blood ran into her eyes from the gash the whip had cut. She pressed it with the upper edge of her cloak and turned to the palace steward who had run to her aid. He stared at her, dumbfounded.

The steward helped her up. "How could Lord Mynes—even he..."

Eurome pushed her way through the crowd and clutched Briseis's arm.

"That doesn't matter," said Briseis. "We must protect the city as best we can."

"How? When herdsmen came to warn Lord Mynes that Greeks, led by Achilles himself, stole herds and moved this direction, Mynes ordered all of the guard to arm for battle. The palace commander tried to reason with him, but..."

"All of the guard? He left none to protect the palace citadel?" The steward shook his head. Eurome groaned. Briseis felt desperate. The last refuge of her people, now stripped of its strength. The palace storerooms held the people's grain. Even if the women avoided slaughter or capture, they would starve.

They had been doomed by the shepherd's mention of Achilles. Of course Mynes had insisted on a direct attack. He must deliver Achilles's deathblow.

She saw Mynes in the open space below the city walls, shouting orders from his chariot. She turned to her steward. "We must use what we have to protect the city if Mynes is not victorious."

"Perhaps the Greeks took the herds to their ships and left."

She shook her head and pointed to the wooded hillside that fell away from the city. In the distance she saw the movement of men. Mynes had better hurry his guard into formation. He had the advantage of being at the top of the hill, but the Greeks already climbed the slopes.

As Mynes's chariot raced back and forth organizing his men, the sun glinted off the gold on his helmet. She saw an answering gleam flash from the trees. Which Greek would wear brilliant armor if not Achilles? How had the bards described him—burning with fury like the sun? Their greatest foe had arrived.

Briseis climbed onto a stone plinth dedicated to the gods of the city. She called out to her panicked people. "Together we must defend our city if the worst befalls and Lord Mynes is not victorious." She pointed to a group of men, nearby shopkeepers standing in a worried huddle. "Close and bar the Great Gate. Every man and boy old enough to shoot a bow and throw a spear, bring your weapons and climb the walls. Defend your city. Our walls will protect us."

The crowd cheered her. The huge wooden gates, reinforced with sheets of bronze, swung closed and the wooden bar shot home under the force of four men's strength. Briseis looked at the terrified faces stretching across the marketplace plaza.

"To the walls! Women, provide assistance to our fighters and pray to the gods." She jumped down from the plinth and spoke to her steward. "We must defend the palace."

A group of nobles too old to have gone to Troy entered the marketplace. The unaccustomed weight of their armor made their steps unsteady. Their bows bobbed on their shoulders like broken limbs. One nobleman cried out, "We have defended our city before. May the mighty Stormgod breathe strength into our limbs to keep Lyrnessos safe once more." He climbed the ladder to the tower by the gate.

A few men, Briseis knew, could hold off many because to reach the gate the attackers had to charge up a ramp that ran underneath the defensive towers. Above them would be those aged archers. Perhaps their experience would count, if their eyesight was still sharp enough to find a target. The elderly nobleman had prayed to the Stormgod. As she ran to the palace, Briseis begged Kamrusepa, protector of their city, to keep her people safe.

When the steward, Eurome and she reached the palace, they gathered the few men servants who had not fled to their families and sent them up ladders to the citadel walls. Briseis counted seventeen, some more boys than men, too few to man the gates of the palace, not to mention the towers and stretches of walls in between. Once the Greeks realized how few men guarded the walls, they would send men up on ladders at the unguarded places. The steward had been right—removing the palace guard left the citadel defenseless. But for the sake of the people's grain, she had to try.

"We'll also place the women servants on the walls to sound the alert when they see Greeks scaling them."

The steward nodded. "Tell them to bring heavy pots. They can slow the attackers by flinging them down."

That's what it's come to, she thought, women defending the palace with cooking pots. *Lady Goddess, Kamrusepa, strike down the Greeks with dire sickness. Weaken them so that they cannot hold their spears but crumple under the blows of all who fight to protect Lyrnessos.* She reached up to the burning places on her cheek and chest where Mynes's whip had struck her.

She sent Eurome to warn Maira. She would need to prepare Hatepa, though they would keep what was happening from the queen for now. Then she started up the ladder to a defense tower.

A tremendous crack rang out and the ground shook beneath her.

It felt like a lightning strike, dangerously close, but the sky was clear blue. What had happened? She climbed to the top and looked toward the Great Gate of the city. Where the wooden beams and stone supports should have been, a cloud of dust and debris arose.

What force could have pulled down the massive gate in so little time? The men, few as they were, could harry the attackers from above the gate, inflicting enemy losses so great most leaders would choose to withdraw.

She saw a huge warrior standing on the rubble, his sword held high, the morning light reflecting fiery gold off his full-length shield. She knew then. Mynes was dead. Nothing stood between Achilles and Lyrnessos.

She raced down the ladder.

As she reached the ground she yelled to the servants hurrying to their posts. "The Great Gate is down. We must gather everyone and escape from the city and head to the sheep camps. No point defending the palace. Achilles knocked down the city gate as if it were a pile of kindling."

Servants ran to call the others from the walls. Briseis hurried inside to get Eurome, Maira and Hatepa. She tried to appear calm. The less frantic Hatepa became, the faster they could escape.

Maira stood at the top of the stairs outside the queen's chamber. "I heard a crash."

"The city is taken. We're leaving. I'll help you with Hatepa."

"Lord Mynes—?"

Briseis looked up at Maira's intelligent face. "The warrior Achilles has battered down the Great Gate. Some of the guard may have run in retreat ready to regroup later, or perhaps been taken prisoner, but Mynes lacked neither courage nor recklessness. I think he would not have given up the fight until he was killed." Maira nodded. She turned back toward Hatepa's room.

Briseis pushed aside the door curtain. "Lady Hatepa, your son has asked you to come with me quickly outside the city."

The queen fidgeted in her chair. "My son? Outside the city? What are you saying? What is that noise I heard? What is that cut on your face?"

"Your son is fighting the Greeks. I am sure he will soon drive them off, but he commanded me to take you to safety." They pulled the queen to her feet, ignoring her protests. Eurome handed Briseis her healing satchel.

Hatepa began to cough. "I must sit down. Why are you dragging me around?" She batted at Maira and Eurome.

Eurome looked the queen in the eye. "Queen Hatepa, unless you wish to be skewered by a Greek spear, you'd better walk. There are no servants left in the palace. Come with us or stay alone to greet the Greeks."

Hatepa's eyes bulged wider than usual. Her mouth opened and closed like a fish stranded on the shore. For a moment Briseis wondered if she was unable to breathe, but then she squawked, "How dare you—"

"Eurome is right, Queen Hatepa," Briseis interrupted. "We wish no disrespect, but you can come now or be left behind. We cannot endanger others to suit you." Hatepa stopped resisting.

Outside in the main courtyard, the remainder of the household staff had gathered, men and women with some children. Such a large group would have trouble getting through streets jammed with fleeing townspeople. She could hear screams rising from the lower city. They had to get out. Greek warriors could be climbing the hill toward the palace right now. Everyone looked at her.

"We must leave the city. Go from the back of the palace away from the fighting that is centered on the Great Gate. We'll escape the other way, out the Stag Gate, and head up into the hills for the sheep camps."

She hoped that by starting their journey on the steep backside of the palace hill, well above the packed neighborhoods, they could avoid both Greeks and crowds. By the time they dropped into the populated area, they would be near the Stag Gate where they could leave the city.

The menservants had knives, clubs and other weapons snatched from the work sheds or kitchens, but she said a prayer that enough of the guard had survived to keep the Greeks busy so that her household and the townspeople could escape without a fight. The shrieks from the battle kept increasing. Had the fighting spread this far? As they unbarred the gate, Briseis held her breath.

The street lay empty. They hurried along the road that hugged the back of the palace. The children held tight to their mothers and moved silently with the adults. All went well until they reached a side road with houses and shops on either side.

Other fleeing people crowded in so that she lost sight of the servants at the front of her group. Family groups trying to stay together got pushed to the sides by faster moving men. Some women, carrying children in their arms or on their hips, shoved others out of their way in desperation to get through. Briseis glanced behind and saw Hatepa stumbling forward, her eyes wide with terror.

Maira walked next to the queen, holding her arm, but Briseis couldn't find Eurome. She tried to go back to look for her, but the flow of the crowd made it impossible, and in the confusion her old nurse could have passed her. Briseis pressed on, fighting back tears.

Other paths and alleys led to the gate, but she stayed on the main road, hoping her household and Eurome had also. The crowd pushed her faster, and she could no longer see Maira. A few of her servants ran near her. Two of the men, armed with a club and a butchering knife, stayed on either side of her. How had they clung to her when she had lost both Eurome and Maira?

Suddenly she heard screams. The crowd in front turned back, driven by something. The serving man with the knife took her arm. "Down this alley."

She ran up several stone steps and into a narrow passage between the buildings. Some of her serving women ran after her in single file, the men behind them. She heard a man bellow in agony and looked back. The man with the club was on the ground. Close behind she saw the horsehair plume of a Greek helmet. As the other manservant sprinted forward, terror flashed in his eyes.

She raced faster, the serving women screaming behind her. The alley widened, but it was stacked on either side with piles of wooden crates. She turned and beckoned to her servants. As they scrambled past Briseis, one of the women knocked Briseis sideways. Her head struck the corner of a mud-brick house and she plunged to the ground.

16

ASH, FIRE AND ARMS

Briseis opened her eyes and saw a grayish blur. Where was she? On the ground. Sitting up caused a wave of dizziness. With her hand she steadied herself and grasped splintery wood. Something wet ran down her forehead. She reached up. Her fingers came back bloody. She saw again Mynes's whip lashing out. Was she bleeding from that? Her vision cleared. She sat behind a pile of weathered crates. Leaning forward, she peeked out.

One of her serving women sprawled close by. The woman's arm had been cut off, and the bloodied fingers of her severed arm brushed the cheek of a palace serving man in a grotesque caress. The Greeks chasing them—it came back to her—this was the servant who had tried to protect her, but now he had a gaping wound in his side. Briseis wanted to curl up and stay behind the protection of the crates, but she crawled forward to check for signs of breath. None, only the overwhelming stink of spilled blood. How long had she lain there?

She was rising on one knee when she heard a man groan and another speak in Greek. "Help is coming."

She scurried back into her wooden cave. Through a crack she could see the men further up the alley. One lay propped against a wall, his chest armor removed. The other held fabric against the wounded man's shoulder. Blood seeped out.

The wounded man's eyes drooped closed, and the other man was turned away from her. She started to creep out.

The metallic footsteps of bronze-nailed soldiers' boots rang out. She dropped back behind the crate.

"He's over here." Three men ran past her hiding place to the injured man and his comrade.

"Let's see this slash. Next time dodge the knife, my friend." A towering man, encased in the most magnificent armor she had ever seen, knelt down and expertly pressed the wound. He had tossed his shield on the ground beside him—the same shield she had seen raised above the fallen gate. Achilles.

He turned and she saw his face. She gasped. Even wearing a helmet, she could see enough to recognize him. Why? Why did he look like the god she had first seen in her vision during the Spring Festival and in her dreams ever since? Why did Achilles look like her Telipinu? Those same sea green eyes.

"Patroklos, hand me the wound kit."

Briseis remembered that name—Achilles's great friend. As Patroklos pulled the supplies from a leather bag, Achilles reached for them. At the sight of those hands that knew her body so intimately, had given her such pleasure, Briseis shivered. Nothing made sense.

Achilles crushed a dark root in his palm and pressed it into the cut. The wounded man's face relaxed as the pain subsided. Achilles wrapped a linen bandage across the shoulder and around the chest to hold it in place. Watching Achilles lit a quiver low inside her. She had to grip the wooden crate to keep herself from going toward him.

Achilles lifted the injured man to his feet and supported him. Heads taller than his patient, he bore him up as easily as a mother guides her child learning to walk. Even in armor he moved with fluid grace—exactly as Telipinu did.

The others followed him toward the main street.

She looked down the empty alley. Her confusion felt like the kind that comes in a dream, but the rough cobblestones refused to dissolve under her fingertips. Had she brought Achilles to Lyrnessos through her dreams? Had her protective god betrayed her?

Perhaps Telipinu had taken Achilles's form in her dream, but had truly been the god. The gods could take any form they liked. Had Telipinu envied this man's beauty and taken it for his own?

It didn't make any difference. Her city lay dead around her, and she had been helpless even to slow its destruction. The smell of fires already filled the air. She pulled herself up and looked down the way Achilles had gone. She saw only the bodies of her dead servants. She walked in the opposite direction.

Her head ached and a dizzy nausea made her unsteady, but she pulled herself straight and took a deep breath. She had to do something useful. She could no longer help the palace household escape —*let Eurome and Maira be safe*. She would tend the wounded—the Greeks must have left many—snatch every life she could from the jaws of this monstrous attack. If Achilles could care for his injured, she would match his skill. She felt the healing satchel at her side and walked faster.

She thought of Iatros. Perhaps he helped the wounded somewhere in the city. Adamas and Bienor should be safe—unless they had seen the Greeks moving down from the mountain pastures with the stolen herds. If they had seen the Greeks, they would have joined the fight.

Briseis worked her way toward the neighborhoods nearest the marketplace by the Great Gate where the Greeks had burst through. Many of the wounded would lie there. Smoke darkened the sky above her and she hurried her pace. She couldn't leave those incapacitated by wounds stranded to burn.

Houses had their doors battered in. Bodies lay piled like sacks of grain. She knelt by men with sword wounds only to find them already gone. These fallen did not wear the leather armor of the guard. The Greek warriors had cut down her townsmen as they fled. Few women lay among the dead.

The Greeks appeared to have attacked her people from all directions. Leaving the palace, she had imagined the Greeks sweeping through the Great Gate, the townspeople fleeing in front of them toward the Stag Gate. More Greeks must have been waiting on the other side of the Stag Gate, and when the Lyrnessans opened the gate to escape, the enemy entered.

Suddenly she heard a sound and rushed behind a door. She panted in panic. The destroyed city felt so abandoned she'd foolishly forgotten to keep watch. A group of Greek soldiers trudged past carrying plunder: wine cups, platters and other objects of silver and gold, quantities of foodstuffs. One soldier walked bent over like an old man with a full-size amphora of wine on his back.

Two soldiers carried a chest loaded so full that the lid did not close, and a strange assortment of silver cups, bronze tools and wheels of cheese poked out, but their words turned her stomach.

"We'll take back a lot more 'n cattle from this raid. With all the women we've captured, even an ugly sot like you will finally get some flesh for your bed."

"Ugly is the word for what we'll get. Agamemnon skims off all the beauties for himself and the commanders."

"We won't be back to the camp at Troy for days. Those bitches have to bed down somewhere, don't they?" They both laughed in a way that reminded her of Mynes.

Fragments of ash blew in chaotic patterns on waves of hot air, making her choke and cough. Taking a strip of linen from her satchel, she tied it over her mouth and nose.

The fires did not appear to have spread to the palace, but the wealth there would draw the Greeks like crows to a newly seeded field. She avoided the streets leading up the hill and aimed for the area from which she had heard the cries of her people.

In a neighborhood of potters and other artisans, humble dwellings lined a street with broken-down doors. The Greeks had rejected the modest belongings of these residents, but not before they ransacked them. Plain wooden chests, earthenware dishes, rough tunics and cooking tools lay strewn in the street.

Her anger compelled her to look inside one of the shops. The family had not left in time. A man lay dead amidst a pile of broken pots—his trade. Huddled in a corner, three children had been run through with swords; their blood formed a pool around them. A baby had been swung against a wall, its head crushed. The mother must have been dragged off. The Greeks left only the dead. Briseis fell to her knees. She ripped away the linen covering her mouth and threw up, then pulled herself up.

Blinded by smoke, she ran down into the next street, her throat so dry she was desperate for water. Her head throbbed. She hated feeling so helpless.

From the marketplace square she heard voices shouting orders in Greek. They must be gathering their loot there by the Great Gate. No escape that way. The picture returned of Achilles tending his wounded soldier. His men had smashed a baby's head and run their swords through children. Yet he had carelessly tossed aside that extraordinary shield the moment he had seen one of his men hurt. Who was Achilles, and why did he look like one of her gods? She shook herself.

In the streets approaching the marketplace square, she saw dead guardsmen. She'd hoped to find Iatros working among the injured, but the smoke grew thicker and she heard the crackle of fire. She guided her steps by running a hand along the rough plaster of the buildings and when she came to a corner, she looked around it.

Two soldiers carried a litter. Though she could barely see through the ash in the air, their helmets looked Lyrnessan with downward ribbons, not horsehair plumes. She ran but they disappeared in the smoke. Then she caught sight of them again. She hurried forward but tripped as her skirt caught her legs. Yanking it, she followed fast, but she lost them again. She climbed a pile of rubble.

At the end of the alley a door closed.

She hurried to it and listened—no sounds. Greeks wouldn't go inside a workshop. She knocked. The door opened a crack. She saw the glint of a sword blade. Two powerful hands grabbed her. She screamed. Both she and the man who had seized her fell to the floor inside and someone else slammed the door shut.

"Lady Briseis! I apologize, I didn't recognize you."

Her name! The man withdrew. Her heart pounded from the shock, but hearing her name—she hadn't been captured by Greeks. Someone knew her. She wasn't alone.

"When I saw a woman outside, I just pulled you in as fast as I could."

"Who are you?" Briseis asked. "My eyes are full of ash. I can't see."

Then she heard a voice and as quickly as she recognized it, she felt his arms around her. Iatros, her brother, at last.

17

BROTHERLY LOSS

B riseis and Iatros clung to each other. "Bris, I'm glad to see you, but why are you here? It isn't safe."

"I got separated from the palace household as we fled, so instead of leaving the city, I looked for our wounded—but with all the ash I can barely see. Are Bienor and Adamas with you?"

"Let me bathe your eyes." He stood. Something in his voice chilled her heart.

"Where are they?"

"Tip your head sideways." She felt the cool water and blinked. "Now the other way." She did as he asked. "How did you get this gouge on your cheek? And there's dried blood in your hair. Is your head injured?"

"Yes, but I'm fine. You know how any cut on the head bleeds."

She reached for his hand. "Have Bienor and Adamas been wounded?"

He looked away and she knew. Iatros groaned and hung his head. "They're gone—killed in the battle outside the city."

Brother and sister held each other.

People moved in the room. Her eyes cleared and she looked around. In spite of the dim light she knew where she was. She recognized the smell of a leather shop she had visited with her father. Racks against one wall held tanned skins. The craftsman had arranged his tools on bronze nails in neat rows. Behind the shop she could see into the rooms where the family lived. Now injured men lay on the mud-brick worktables. Two soldiers attended the wounded.

She took Iatros's hand. "Tell me what happened."

He looked exhausted. His eyes had sunk in their sockets and the skin underneath looked bruised. "Not long after you left the house this morning, Bienor went out to the fields. He saw movement on Ida and came back for his armor. We went to investigate—Greeks. Too many for us alone, so we raced to the city to warn them to close the gates. Instead, Mynes was organizing the guardsmen outside the city wall. He screamed that he would not let cowards near his men and ordered us away. We slipped into the ranks where Mynes would not notice us. The men welcomed our help.

"You know the guards aren't trained warriors. Some threw their spears before the Greeks came into range, and they didn't have the skills to defend themselves. They fell before the Greeks like wheat before the farmer's scythe." He shuddered.

She looked at him. "Mynes?"

"He fought with courage. He raced his chariot directly toward their leader—a giant man who must be Achilles, the warrior we heard about. I've never seen anyone so terrifying, but Mynes didn't stop, even when the huge man threw his spear. He dodged, but the spear flew fast and true through his chest, and he fell into the dust."

Mynes was dead. She had grown to hate him. He had humiliated and hurt her, but the picture came to her of Mynes hesitating in her doorway holding the soft wool he had brought as a gift.

"Bienor and Adamas?" she whispered.

"Bienor saw Mynes fall and took command. He and Adamas rallied the men, and the Greeks fell back." He spoke with fierce pride. For a moment Briseis even imagined that the story would turn out differently.

"Bienor and Adamas said a healer was too important to risk being killed, and I should stay back." He looked at her. "I felt relief when they said that. I am a coward." The look in his eyes tore at Briseis's heart. "But I paid for it." His voice broke.

"I heard Bienor's war cry. He came face to face with the huge warrior who had killed Mynes. They had their spears raised. Bienor threw true—it pierced the warrior's shield, but the giant somehow eluded the point and in the same moment threw his spear. It pierced Bienor just below the ribs. He fell to the ground.

"I ran toward him, but Adamas reached him before I did. With his legs straddled over Bienor's body, he swung his sword. The Greek withdrew as if to let Adamas pull Bienor's body out of the fray, so I ran faster. But as the warrior turned away, Adamas, seeing his advantage, dove in with a sword thrust." Iatros's voice had dropped to a whisper.

"As if he had a sixth sense, the Greek avoided Adamas's blow and turned, driving his sword into Adamas." He looked at her, tears streaming down his face. "I did nothing to defend them." He turned away from her, shaking with sobs.

She reached for him. "You would only have been killed. I thank the gods you are alive. This work takes courage." She indicated the wounded.

"We should get back to the men," he said. "Word spread among the survivors to bring the wounded here. Once I'd patched them up, the men went back out to fight, though they shouldn't have. They've stopped coming. All dead, I fear." She nodded.

They checked on the men laid out on the worktables. One man, his face drained white, had a chest wound that Iatros had compressed with a linen bandage. Iatros had bound strips of leather around the man's chest to keep the bandage in place. Briseis thought the leather must increase the pain of the wound. The man's unfocused eyes lolled in a sort of trance.

"I've run out of linen," said Iatros with a shrug when he saw her studying the leather straps. "He bled so profusely. Without pressure, he'd bleed to death."

She nodded. She studied the binding. She didn't know much about wounds like this. As healing priestess, rather than a physician like Iatros, no one had taught her to mend a wound. Men's work. She had linen in her satchel, but under the circumstances the leather had a better chance of holding and restraining the bleeding if they had to leave this shelter. That would matter more than the pain.

"Briseis, how bad is it out there?"

"The fires are spreading. I don't think we can stay here much longer."

"Then we should get these men ready if we can. This man has a sword cut in his calf. As long as he lies still, the bleeding has stopped. Without linen bandages, I left it unbound." She peered at the long gash and pulled her supply of linen out—at least she could offer that even if she weren't skilled at closing it up. They'd need to bind him up before he could move.

The man lying on his stomach turned his head and smiled gamely at her. "Lady Briseis, it's no great cut." The cut extended the length of his calf and must have hurt terribly, but she appreciated the man's spirit. As Iatros bound the wound, he needed a second pair of hands. Working side by side comforted Briseis. Iatros taught her how to tie the linen in a crossing pattern to hold it tight against the leg.

She glanced up when she heard someone at the door softly call out the guards' greeting. One of the men unbarred the door and helped an injured man as he slumped against the wall by the door. Iatros went over to see to his bloody arm and shoulder.

She went to another of the men lying on a worktable. His face was white, eyes staring. She leaned close to check. He was gone.

She looked at his boyish face and felt a pang when she recognized him. She had gone with her mother when he fell out of a tree and broke his leg. The physician had set the leg, but the family wanted him restored to harmony with the gods, so Antiope had cast stones on the divining board and revealed he had offended Telipinu. Who had cut him down today—Achilles?

The man who had come in spoke up. "I don't think it's safe here. The fires are spreading rapidly, but I don't know what we should do." As if to emphasize his words, they heard a dull crash, sounding nearby even through the thick walls. She looked at Iatros. His body sagged.

Briseis looked past him. Could the wounded men walk? The men with the chest wound and injured leg should be carried on litters, but they'd never get through the debris with litters. She jumped at another crash of collapsing buildings close by.

She turned to Iatros. "We'll aim for the Stag Gate. By now perhaps the Greeks have abandoned that part of the city. Tie linen over your noses and mouths to keep out the ash. Is there any wood for walking sticks to support the wounded?" Iatros cut lengths of bandage for each of them. The others stirred into action.

She knelt close to the man with the calf wound and asked softly, "Do you think you can walk?"

"It's that or burn to death, isn't it? Only a leg wound. Who needs a leg to walk?" He gave her a wry smile. "You look to the others, Lady Briseis. Give me a stick to hobble on, and I'll be as fine as you are." He tipped his chin at her bloody cheek and head.

"You're a brave man."

Iatros helped the man with the bandaged chest get to his feet, although from her brother's shaky movements, his own strength seemed drained. One of the guards came from the back rooms with a stout pole. Bits of wool were tied to one end. He must have broken it off a loom. She thought of her own loom with the tapestry of medicinal plants on it, almost finished—probably in flames by now.

The skin by Iatros's left eye twitched and the lively warmth of his eyes had worn to a deadened blear. *Mama*, she prayed, *I don't think the gods care what happens to us anymore, so you must watch over us, your only remaining children. Bring us safely from this burning city to the mountain pastures, which have nurtured our flocks and are now our only shelter.*

They gathered by the door and a guard pulled it open. Ash rained down and smoke assailed them. The linen masks created weird disfigurements as if the men had lost their mouths.

They stumbled along the narrow lane, but when they came to the main road where they should have turned toward the far side of the city, flames and unbearable heat sidetracked them, forcing them back toward the marketplace. She thought they would still be able to reach the Stag Gate, but they would have to climb up the palace hill and go down the back way. With the Greeks gathering their loot at the Great Gate, she could think of no other choice.

The man with the chest wound struggled and his pace was slowest, even with Iatros and another man supporting him. Briseis stayed next to her brother.

She wondered, as they started up the hill, if the palace remained intact. With all the smoke, she could not see the top, but as they ascended, the sound of the firestorm lessened and the air became more breathable. She hoped the Greeks had finished pillaging.

As they climbed, she listened to the heavy breathing of the man with the calf injury a few steps in front of her. Next to her Iatros stopped. Blood dribbled through the linen covering the mouth of the man with the chest injury. Iatros and the guardsman caught the man as he collapsed. Why had they thought this man could walk?

They would have to make a litter. She saw a nearby gate ajar, opening into the courtyard of a large home.

"Let's bring him in here." She helped her brother and the other two guardsmen carry the injured man inside. They laid him by the well.

"We'll need something to make a litter," Iatros said.

Briseis pulled off her cloak. "If you can find some stakes to tie my cloak to, that should work." The men scattered to search the stable and storerooms that opened onto the courtyard. The man with the calf injury started to limp away. She stopped him. "Rest now." He lowered himself onto the low wall surrounding the well.

She drew some water and Iatros washed the face and mouth of the man with the chest injury. His eyes were closed, but he breathed. She turned toward the gate.

"We should close the gate so no Greeks will find—" She stopped. A shadow had fallen across the opening.

The guardsman sitting on the well drew his sword. Iatros pushed her down so she was hidden behind the well and drew his sword. She heard the sounds as bronze-nailed footsteps rushed. Swords clashed. A man fell.

Then a voice called out in Greek, "Lord Achilles, come over—" There was a grunt, a thud. The voice fell silent. A Greek warrior lay against the well. His hand loosened its grip on his sword.

She lifted her head to see over the well. Iatros stared at his bloody sword and the dead Greek. The man with the leg wound was on the ground, his sword arm still outstretched, but his innards poured out onto the hard dirt.

Other guardsmen came out of the stables, but it did not matter, for the gate filled with a huge form, and Achilles plunged toward Iatros. Her brother lifted his sword to meet the oncoming stroke. A rage rose up in her; the sound of a hundred bees filled her head. In one motion she swept the dead Greek's sword off the ground and leapt from behind the well. Achilles's blade flashed in the air above her. She saw his hands grasping the hilt and sensed their power, then saw his look of astonishment as she raised her blade against the blow aimed at her brother. A new, invincible strength coursed through her arms. The desire to strike—raw and terrifying—drove out her helplessness. Her blade met his. A bolt shot through her, and she reeled from the force. Achilles jerked his chest backwards even as the momentum of his swing carried him forward. Achilles's sword cut through the unprotected joint of her brother's armor between the neck and shoulder. Iatros's head fell to the side. As the weight of Iatros's body carried her to the ground, she heard an anguished cry and could not tell if it was hers or Achilles's.

18

WANDERING IN THE SHADOWS
OF DEATH

The Greeks built their base camp near the burnt-out city, in a wide space where a storm had washed out the sloping banks of the stream. The place felt raw—exposed soil and boulders—a wound in the landscape, despite the trees that had withstood the onslaught. A dozen or so injured soldiers rested near the main fire pit. The mild spring weather made caring for the injured in the open air workable. When the other thirty or so men weren't loading wagons with the spoils from Lyrnessos to haul to their ships, they ate or rolled out their blankets near the fire.

The women formed a group apart and had their own cook fire. Many captive women had already been taken down to the ships. Among the women still here, only Briseis could not rise from her makeshift bed.

She heard sounds, voices maybe, but the effort of listening seemed too great. If she could open her eyes and look—but that was too hard. She drifted.

"My Poppy. Oh my stars and fishes. Come back to me, my little Poppy."

Eurome. She heard Eurome's voice. Relief pulled her from the darkness. She opened her eyes. Eurome cried out in delight. Briseis attempted a smile and reached toward her nurse, but the pain struck as soon as she lifted her head. She raised Eurome's hand to her lips and kissed the worn palm. One dear person left to her, so dear. Everyone else gone.

Tears ran down Eurome's cheeks. "Thank the gods, you're awake, but lie quiet now, my girl. That Achilles said you must rest. He made a drink I'm to get into you, but I couldn't see how with you lying almost dead like that. Thank the gods, you're back."

Briseis drifted into the darkness.

THE SMELL OF SMOKE. Her eyes flew open in panic. Her body lifted in fear, but it was only a cook fire. Briseis heard the familiar slap of hands making flatbread and saw Eurome throwing dough onto a stone set on the coals. Another woman pulled the baked breads off with tongs. Other women gazed empty-eyed into the fire, their cheeks scratched from grieving and their hair gray with ashes they had thrown on their heads.

She turned slightly to study the activity around the men's fire pit. She didn't see Achilles anywhere. Patroklos knelt by a pallet and helped one of the injured men drink from a cup, then quietly went from one to another, attending their needs. His gentle movements gave healing. He had a round, open face framed by brown wavy hair tied back with a strip of leather. His limbs had a compact agility completely different from Achilles's flowing strength.

How wrong Mynes had been about this man. In contrast to Achilles's explosive nature, Patroklos brought a soothing calm with him as he worked. Achilles had no need for Patroklos's protection in battle. The peace Patroklos offered formed the bond between them. She knew that from watching him. Just as she had sensed in her dreams, just as Telipinu yearned for a calm he could not achieve by himself, so all the tales about Achilles said he hungered for cooling water—Patroklos. She had loved Telipinu for this vulnerability, a god who needed her. Achilles was not a god though, but a killer.

A soldier approached the women's fire. He glanced at the women with their hollow looks and turned to Eurome, who must have taken on the role of communicating for the other women, not all of whom knew Greek. "Thank you. Fresh bread is a welcome luxury to men who've been sailing and fighting."

Eurome glared at him. "Then you should ha' stayed home where you can get your bread easy." Her hand supported her back as she straightened slowly and walked away from him. Briseis appreciated Eurome's retort, but she felt alarm at how the soldier might react.

He grabbed Eurome's shoulder. "You've a sharp tongue, old woman. You remind me of my old nurse, so I'll let you be. You've got the spark of life left in you. If you can help the others to come through this—their husbands are gone. The city's burnt. There's nothing left for them but to make the best of it as servants to a Greek lord."

"Servants and bedmates, y' mean. Why should I help 'em face that?"

"Because that's all there is for them, unless you would rather leave them dead in the streets. You've been a servant all your life, I imagine, or taken slave early on, and you know well enough it's not all sorrow and grief."

Eurome shrugged. "They don't want to hear no such things now."

The soldier turned away, carrying the basket of bread. Briseis looked around at the seven women sitting on the ground near the fire. They slumped in torn, dirty clothes. Most of them hadn't looked up as the soldier came near. They'd lost interest in what fate still held for them.

Eurome returned to the circle around the fire. She sat next to a woman and took her hand.

Patroklos walked toward the group with a bowl of cheese. He stopped, and Briseis saw him glance at the top of the washed-out riverbank. The late afternoon sun cast long shadows from the willows, oaks and tamarisks that grew by the stream. Dark fingers crept up the steep bank.

Patroklos looked intently down the path. Briseis found the place he watched. A flash of red-gold caught the sun's rays. A moment later

Achilles dipped into the shadows as he came down to the camp. The dagger in her head jabbed behind her eyes. She remembered Achilles standing on top of Lyrnessos's fallen gate, his gold shield reflecting the morning light. By then he had already killed Mynes, Bienor, and Adamas. She wished she still had a sword.

He saw Patroklos and waved.

"How are the injured recovering?" The two men embraced.

Briseis studied Achilles. Even in the afternoon shadows he exuded a shimmer like sun on moving water. She did not trust her eyes. Despite the marvel, she hated him.

"Faster than we'd thought," said Patroklos, "even with all the smoke they breathed in. It's dangerous when a city catches fire so quickly. If we raid again, we'll need to control the men."

"You're the one to teach control, not I. Let's hope there's no more raiding. I've done Agamemnon's bidding enough. Men can't fight without meat in their bellies and wine in their hearts, and that greedy heart-of-a-doe knows I'll always provide for the men. For the gods' sake let's take Troy and be done with this."

Achilles looked toward the women. His eyes fell on Briseis. Her breath seized. "How is she?"

"I don't think she's any better. Her nurse says she doesn't eat or drink."

Achilles walked toward her. As he drew closer, she saw the two leather satchels over his shoulder—hers and Iatros's.

Eurome hurried to her side and let out a cry when she saw the satchels.

"You recognize these?" Achilles asked.

Eurome lost her voice. She stood frozen, her hands at her mouth.

Achilles crouched beside Briseis and extended the satchels to her. In spite of the racking pain whenever she moved, she reached for them, but when her hand brushed his, she recoiled as from a searing heat. The severing of Iatros's neck flashed before her. She wanted the satchels desperately, but she wouldn't take anything from this man's hands.

Achilles's sea-green eyes flared into flame. The muscles of his neck and arms contracted. He seemed suspended in the moment before action. A rushing sound of waves reverberated in Briseis's head. Perhaps her vision faltered, because he wavered in and out of her sight like the ebb and flow of the sea. Then he leaned back on his heels and placed the satchels on the edge of her blanket.

"One of my soldiers saved these," he said in a voice that held the same sounds of the sea and a storm restrained with struggle. "He stood by when—when you suffered injury, and he stole them, thinking they held treasures. He was disappointed at what he saw inside, but when they came to me, I saw their worth, though they did not shimmer." A strip of linen bandage had come loose and trailed out of her satchel. He folded it into a neat square and placed it inside.

"How did they come to you?" she asked, her voice hoarse.

"The soldier brought them to me, suspecting I might want them because your fame is already well established among my men—they tell your tale over their wine cups at night like a warrior's glory. I'm accustomed to their exaggerated stories of my deeds, but my sword knows your sheer courage, and that they cannot overstate."

She gazed at the satchels in silence. She didn't want his admiration.

He turned to Eurome. "Have you been giving her sips of the mixture I brought you this morning?"

"I've tried and tried, but she drunk no more than a drop each time. As you says this morning, her stomach is unsteady, though why a head wound causes that, I don't follow, but I see it's true."

"Start with small sips. She'll heal when she eats." Briseis noted what she had to do to get better. She would eat despite the nausea. "Work at it with patience, as I'm sure you've done many times before."

Eurome nodded. "That I have, many a time since the day she was born."

Achilles looked over at Briseis. He had moved away as he spoke to Eurome, and she felt able to breathe more freely now that he wasn't so close. "These satchels hold healing supplies. You are a healer, and the man also? Is that why you leapt to his defense? Healers always share a close bond."

Even from this distance her heart pounded when she saw his hands, the same hands on the hilt of the sword that had cut through her brother's neck; the same hands from her dreams. She closed her eyes.

He spoke to Eurome. "Why did you cry out when you saw these satchels?"

"One of them is my lady's. The other, her brother's. The pain to see that one—" She pointed to Iatros's. "And know—" She stopped.

Achilles waited.

"I knew he were gone when you says to me what my Briseis done with that sword. Who else would she ha' done it for? But to see both of them satchels—." Eurome groaned. Briseis looked up.

The old woman wrapped her arms around her torso and swayed. "They weren't never happier than working side by side. Lady Antiope, their mother, she were a great healer, and teaching Briseis since she were only a tiny girl. See here—" Eurome pointed to the embossed design on Briseis's satchel. "The same pattern as her mama's and Iatros's too. They asked special for that to honor their mama."

"I wish I had not caused his death," said Achilles. "Healers are sacred to the gods, and if I had realized, I would not have struck. But he stole the life of one of my men, and my only satisfaction comes through vengeance. If Patroklos had stood with me, he would have soothed my battle rage, as he always does, and I might not have acted so rashly. The lives a healer has saved tilt the scales in his defense. Indeed, when your lady mistress rose up like an avenging fury, I struggled to withdraw my blow, but that was not fated."

He bowed his head to Briseis before turning back to Eurome. "Try to get her to eat and drink tonight. Sustenance will do more good than anything. She needs her strength to regain her breath. Be sure to bathe her wounds with the seawater and ground root I brought you. Boil them together."

Achilles's gaze lingered on Briseis and then he pivoted quickly and strode across the camp, except that his movement made no sound on the gravel and the brightness around Briseis and Eurome diminished as soon as he moved away.

BRISEIS TURNED her head from side to side. The pain had receded. She had eaten and drunk as much as she could yesterday evening. She did not want to be an invalid like Hatepa. She breathed in the crisp morning air, but sensed the gentleness of the breeze promised a warm day. She pushed herself up to sit. Her body, stiff from lying in one place for so long, ached all over.

From a willow tree, a bird with a blue chest and a bright yellow neck peeked down at her. Her father called these birds bee-eaters. She had seen them catch bees and bang them against a branch until the stinger fell out and then they'd eat the insect. A large colony of them lived here where the steep stream banks provided a good place to make their homes, digging holes to lay their eggs. She and Iatros used to watch them kicking out the dirt, their tail feathers poking out amidst the flying rubble.

How could the day offer such beauty when her brothers had been killed? And her husband, she tried to add, but she could not mourn him. She had felt something sad when Iatros described his slaughter, but Mynes had brought on his own death and caused the death of countless others through his rash desire. The gods would forgive her for being unable to mourn the man who had made her suffer in humiliating helplessness.

Her heart ached as she pictured the scene Iatros had described of her brothers' deaths. Bienor leading the men, although he must have known the battle was doomed, ill-chosen. His spear hitting its mark, but failing to stop Achilles nonetheless. Adamas standing over his fallen brother, sword threatening, so formidable in his loyal defense that Achilles had stood back. Even that had not been enough to save Adamas. It was something, she supposed, that they had died in a way they would be proud of, but she wanted them here, even in this wretched camp. All of them gone. And Iatros.

The dream had forewarned of his death, but the warning hadn't been enough to save him. None of the dreams the gods—or demons —had sent her had done any good. They seemed malicious tricks now, designed to make her a traitor to her people by using her to draw their greatest foe to Lyrnessos. She could not understand the language of the gods, if indeed the gods were speaking to her through her dreams. It was no use being Antiope's daughter. Listening to her dreams was like lifting a shell to her ear.

19

KINDNESS AND A PYRE

The women awakened around her. Their subdued motions spoke of their shared despair. Now that Briseis could look steadily without feeling dizzy, she recognized some of them—daughters of noble families she had grown up with, wives of farmers and shopkeepers whom she'd healed or bought things from. As she studied one dejected face, the woman noticed Briseis and smiled.

"Lady Briseis, it does my heart good to see you sitting up."

A smile and kind words—Briseis felt a momentary lightness. She smiled back and voiced her thanks.

Briseis remembered her as the stonecutter's wife, a motherly woman with round hips and bosom and striking blue eyes. Her husband, a strong, handsome man, had fetched Briseis when his apprentice was injured, and she'd seen his wife in the doorway of the living quarters behind the open-air work area, surrounded by three small children. She had lost her family, and yet this woman found the strength to speak a kind word.

Briseis stood. She touched her head, fingering the bandage.

She took a few steps then leaned against a willow tree to catch her breath. How could so little effort make her short of breath? She saw

Eurome coming from the stream with a large water jug. Eurome set down the jug near the banked fire and hurried toward her.

"Careful now. Not steady on your legs, by the look of it." Eurome supported her around the waist. "You ate and drank, and see what good that did you. That's what I always say. Food and drink is what a body needs no matter how bad the body feels. You remember that, Poppy—a little food and drink no matter what."

Eurome helped Briseis sit on a blanket. "I'll stir this fire and make some porridge for you and the rest."

Other women gathered. Briseis noticed that some helped Eurome, but others stared without seeing.

Next to her, on a plank of wood used as a worktable, someone had put out a wine pitcher and cups, a bronze grater, a mortar and pestle, and a square of cheese. The mortar was filled with toasted barley. Someone—Achilles?—had given them the materials needed for the restorative mixture her mother used to make when her father felt exhausted.

Her father—did he still live, fighting at Troy, unaware for now of the disaster that had befallen his family? The gods might have taken him also, striking him down as he led the men of Lyrnessos into battle. Even if he were alive, she doubted she would ever see him again. She would be slave to some Greek lord.

Briseis looked at the women's ashen faces and felt guilty for her self-pity. She was not the only one who had suffered a loss. If the stonecutter's wife could offer strength to her, she must find a way to support these women. She was their healer.

She lifted the stopper from the pitcher and sniffed—sweet wine. She poured it into the cups. While she grated some cheese into each of them, a slender, young woman sitting near said, "Let me help," and took the mortar and pestle to grind the barley.

Together they sprinkled the barley into the cups and passed them to the women. One left the cup untouched on the ground in front of her. Her gaunt face looked dead.

Briseis went to her, and bending carefully, she pressed the woman's hands around the cup and guided it to her lips.

Briseis noticed movement at the far end of the camp. Achilles, accompanied by Patroklos, carried a covered litter out of sight behind a stand of tamarisk. She turned her attention back to the woman next to her.

One of the others said, "Do you think they'll take us down to their ships today?"

"Waiting for the injured to mend, is what I heard that Patroklos fellow say," said Eurome. "And then they was saying the hurt soldiers was patched up. So seems like might be so."

"I don't know if it'll be worse or better," said another woman, "to be taken away from what we know. I remember washing clothes here by the stream with my sisters. Will it hurt less not to see what I remember?" Her hair, like that of all the other women, was uncombed, and its frizzy curls had matted into a dark mass around her head.

Eurome, despite her plumpness, squatted comfortably by the fire and stirred the pot of porridge she had set in the coals.

Briseis set out bowls. "Did any of you see Queen Hatepa among the women they took to the ships—and her maid Maira?"

The stonecutter's wife said, "I saw the queen, and there was a girl with her—tall, black haired. I don't know if her name was Maira. The queen wasn't nice to her. Acted like the young woman had caused all her troubles. Later, I didn't see the girl. They held the queen alone."

"Did you see her, Eurome?"

Eurome shook her head. "No, not Maira, nor I didn't see Queen Hatepa neither. I've had 'nough to worry about with you, Poppy. I haven't never given the queen a thought." She laughed. "And I'm acertain she hasn't never thought of me." Then she frowned. "I do hope for the girl."

The women fell back into silence.

They ate. Briseis lay down again. She heard a man clear his throat and saw Achilles standing a few paces away. He approached. She had the sensation of a current pulling her along a river.

"You slept well? From the look of you, there's been a sea change since yesterday. I'm pleased you are recovering."

She frowned at him.

"I worried that you would slip away from the daylight. You have reason enough to desire Lethe's oblivion." He stopped, watching her. She wished he would leave her alone. What was Lethe? She thought she remembered it from one of the bards' tales as a river the Greeks said flowed around the Underworld and made you forget your grief if you drank from it. She didn't want to forget.

"Leave me alone." She turned away.

"You have every right to scorn me. I killed your brother." His tone held a hurt that the words denied.

She turned back to glare at him and wavered for a moment, seeing the tautness of his muscles, the storm that brewed just underneath his courtesy.

Let him be angry at her scorn. He could at least know the full extent of the harm he had done to her. "My brother? Yes, you killed one of my brothers in that courtyard, but that is not all. In front of Lyrnessos's walls you cut down my other two brothers. They were brave warriors defending their home and family and you struck them down."

Achilles sat down and looked directly at her. That strange rushing sound of waves reverberated in her head again. "I am sorry that you have lost so many, and that I am responsible. We cannot shift our natures. Only with you have I desired to. I wish I had not been a warrior on that day, but at the same time you must recognize that your brothers and I had more in common than your grief is willing to concede. Your family is noble, that is clear, and therefore your brothers were born to be warriors just as I was, and the same loyalties drove them as drive me. With a slight twist of fate, we could have been on the same side. I wish we had been, but fate did not allow it. I am not sure which of the men I fought in front of Lyrnessos were your brothers, but you tell me they were brave warriors, and having witnessed your bravery, I do not doubt that. Can you accept that I had no choice but to slay them because they, great warriors as you say, would have slain me if I had not taken sword and spear against them? Their courage and loyalty to their men matched mine and locked us in a fatal fight. For that I give them my sincerest respect. For you I shed tears for their deaths."

Achilles waited, but she stayed silent, not able to acknowledge out loud the truth of what he said. It didn't matter. Her brothers were dead. He had killed them. Why should she accept this odd apology? He couldn't know what he had meant to her—or some delusion that appeared in his form. She wanted nothing to do with him. Through her dreams, he had betrayed her even before he'd attacked her city, though she would never tell him that.

"I have grown disillusioned with Agamemnon," Achilles said. She wondered why he felt so driven to talk with her, to explain himself, and hoped it did not mean he felt drawn to her. She wanted to shout, *Go away*.

"He leads the Greeks in this war and his greed will not stop until he feeds on Troy's riches, but that does not mean that I can abandon the other warriors. I wish this war would stop, but the only way to accomplish that now is to vanquish Troy. I will strain every measure of my strength toward that goal for the sake of my men. Your brothers would have done the same. On that ill-fated day when I sacked your city, it was to provide for my men both food and the treasure that their fighting courage merits. Only when Troy falls can they return home with their hard-earned bounty to their wives, their aged fathers and mothers. I fight out of loyalty to them and the honor that battle brings us. Isn't that what drove your brothers? Couldn't we have fought side by side if fate had not brought us together as enemies?"

She didn't want to, but she nodded.

"Fate has given you a cruel portion by my hand. I would change it if I could."

His green eyes spoke of a troubled sea within. "Are we ever able to choose our actions to suit ourselves? As it is, we live only for a short time, and then we pass away, barely noticed, as snow melts into the soil. I cannot suffer your grief in your place, but I understand your sorrow. We can only honor the dead with proper service. This morning I went through the ruins of the city and found your brother's body and brought him to this camp. Patroklos and I washed him

and laid him out for you to perform what burial rites you hold dearest. I did not know of your other brothers. Perhaps this one burial can
give honor to all three."

He paused. Briseis could not speak. Then he said, "Shall I help
you walk to the place we have laid him?"

She shook her head. He walked away and said something to
Eurome.

Why did he care about her feelings and allow her to give Iatros
this last honor? Why did he remind her so much of the god of her
dreams even while she hated him? She turned her face into the
makeshift pillow Eurome had made.

Eurome came to her and helped her walk to her brother's body,
muttering something under her breath all the while that Briseis
didn't absorb. Laid on a tapestry of deep-hued blues and reds, Iatros's
limbs were arranged as though in quiet sleep. A wide band of linen
wrapped his neck.

She knelt by Iatros's body. Eurome sat on the ground a few steps
back. Despite the warm sunshine, Briseis felt cold. She shook. The
flesh on Iatros's face had sunk inwards, revealing the bones underneath. He looked old. She ran her nails down her cheeks, digging into
her flesh, as her keening writhed from her burned lungs.

Through a blur of tears, she saw his stony white skin. The blood
had been washed away. He was dressed in a clean tunic. Only in his
dark curls could she see mats of blood.

She brushed her fingertips against his smooth cheek and a hard
knot formed in her chest. How embarrassed he'd been never to
have scraped a beard at his age. A small thing, one of many, he
would never do. The violence of his death was so unlike his nature.
She couldn't accept it. Her fingertips had left a tinge of red on his
cheek. She thought of the animals sacrificed to give the dead
strength for their final journey. *Let the blood of my grief be your sacrifice, Iatros.*

She grasped his hand, stiff and unresponsive, and remembered
how this morning she had wanted to hold her brothers. Was there
comfort in this clasp? The bodies of her older brothers and husband

must lie in nightmarish piles or abandoned as they fell on the battlefield.

She turned to Eurome. "How can we mourn only for Iatros, when so many others lie dead, unhonored? How will we find the means to do a proper rite even for him?"

Eurome came close and put her arm around her. "My little Poppy, we'll do what we can. Lord Achilles told me they'd made a proper pyre down by the city walls. You know the prayers—make them do for all our poor lost menfolk."

She could not perform all the traditional duties for the dead. What had Achilles said—those she held dearest? She could place Iatros's spirit in his satchel as she had done for her mother. Instead of the family shrine, she would take it with her on a Greek ship to Troy and someday, she supposed, to far away Greece.

She asked Eurome to bring her both the satchels and some wine for a libation. When Eurome returned, all the women were with her. Why had she brought them here? Weren't they burdened enough with grief of their own?

The stonecutter's wife stepped forward. "Lady Briseis, may we help in the burial rites for Lord Iatros? If we share your grief, it will help us with our own."

Briseis bowed her head. "I am honored. I will pray for all of our dead. Our city served as their funeral pyre."

Briseis raised Iatros's satchel and called to his spirit. She kissed the satchel and put the strap over her shoulder and held it close to her side. "Stay with me wherever I go, protecting and comforting me."

The women had gathered around her. One by one, they lifted up tokens to serve as shelter for their dead, small objects they could carry with them in their exile: simple rings or amulets they had on them when captured, small leather pouches tied to their belts, hand-kerchiefs, smooth stones from the riverbed. Even the women who had gazed blank-eyed this morning joined in.

Briseis held out a humble wooden cup. The stonecutter's wife filled it with wine. Briseis took a drink and passed the cup on. As she recited the traditional prayers for the dead, each of the women drank from the libation cup. Briseis had to stop to catch her breath. The women waited each time and listened for the familiar words. She poured more wine to the spirits of all their loved ones and to the Sungoddess of the earth below, to honor them, to accept these rites as complete for all the dead of Lyrnessos.

When she finished these prayers, without words or plan, four of the women lifted the litter onto their shoulders. They waited for Briseis to lead the procession, Eurome at her side supporting her. The other women followed. Both their sorrow and their strength flowed into Briseis.

At the pyre the women lifted the litter onto the logs. Briseis wanted to climb up and cling to Iatros one last time, but she held herself back—the other women could not take comfort in that way, so she would not either. A small fire burned near the pyre. With a trembling hand, Briseis took a branch from a nearby pile and lit it in the coals. Each of the women followed suit.

Briseis stepped back from the heat. The flames licked at the tapestry Achilles had laid her brother on, a beautiful one of great value. She couldn't watch the flames reach Iatros's body and turned away.

Ox wagons stood on the road. Achilles and some other men stood waiting. Briseis understood. It was time to leave Lyrnessos.

Most of the way to the harbor, she slept, huddled against Eurome. To her surprise only one ship remained. The others must have been sent on ahead to Troy as soon as they filled. The soldiers unloaded chests and bundles from the wagons and stowed them on board. The women got down and followed the soldiers' directions to climb onto the ship.

Briseis leaned on Eurome as they walked down the rocky shore. Gusts worked the sea into foam-tipped waves. Surges pitched the ship back and forth, causing the boarding plank to shift along the beach. She hated to feel so weak. She had never been afraid of losing her balance until now. Eurome, on the other hand, hadn't even liked looking down from the upstairs balcony. This passage would petrify her, and Briseis could not even offer her a confident hand. She could feel Eurome quivering.

One of the women in front of them hesitated, and a soldier took her by the hand and led her up behind him. Briseis hoped that would be enough for them also, but her legs felt shaky and the smoke from the pyre had taken away her breath.

She stared at the plank. Achilles and Patroklos approached.

Patroklos held out a hand to Eurome. "You've been working hard caring for your young lady. I worry you might be too tired for this steep walkway. May I help you?"

Eurome looked at Briseis, clearly not wanting to abandon her. Briseis let go of her nurse's arm and pushed her forward. She watched as Patroklos braced Eurome firmly in front of him with both hands. He commented on the beauty of the white puffy clouds above them and drew Eurome's gaze upward while he guided her steps.

Briseis's turn came. Certainly she could walk up a plank. She didn't glance at Achilles who stood next to her. She climbed part way up. Her shortness of breath made her head spin. She willed her foot to take another step but tipped backwards. A strong hand steadied her.

"May I carry you up?" she heard Achilles ask, a searing undercurrent crackling in his voice. "It takes time for balance to return after a head injury."

She nodded. She would fall if he didn't. He lifted her effortlessly as though he were not balancing on a plank barely wide enough for one. Her face rested against his chest and she breathed in the fresh saltiness of an ocean breeze. When she lifted away her head, she lost this pleasing scent. It emanated from his skin, as if he exuded a share of his mother's seaborne immortality. She had not been carried in the shelter of arms since she was a little girl.

Achilles carried her past the rowing benches on the main deck and placed her at the bow of the ship facing the bay. "You should rest here on the deck where the sea air will allow you to breathe freely." He wrapped a length of stout rope around two pegs fixed on the side of the deck. "Have you sailed before?"

She shook her head.

"Some people feel ill when they sail, but you won't."

How did he know that? He headed toward the stern to help the men take away the props and push the ship free of the shore. She noticed the other women were clustered in the center of the ship below the main deck, seated on a platform over the cargo.

She felt the change underneath her as the men used their oars to work the ship out into the bay. She had often imagined what sailing would feel like.

She looked at the shore. The foothills of Mount Ida rose from the beach. On the other side, out of sight, lay a valley rich with wheat and barley fields, orchards, and good pasturage. In the center of that valley was a hill, girdled by strong walls. The city those walls had once guarded lay in ashes. Below the walls, beside an abandoned camp, one last fire burned. She clutched the two satchels and turned toward the sea.

20

JOINED BY FIRE

Achilles's men set the sail, hauling high a wide crosspiece to which they had attached the heavy canvas. One group, their legs braced for the effort, grasped side ropes. At a shout from Achilles, they heaved, and the square sail unfolded. A moment later the rowers pulled in the oars. As the sail filled, Briseis felt the motion change to a gliding rhythm and the ship came alive, moving through the waves.

From the foredeck, Briseis viewed the gulf and coastline. Their course through the lapis lazuli sea held close to the shore. Mount Ida's steep slopes tumbled down to the rocky shoreline, a patchwork of granite outcroppings and tree clad heights. A steady breeze blew them toward the open Aegean beyond the gulf. She felt the wind rise up from the familiar landscape of home, carrying her away.

The sea air bathed her lungs. She pictured each breath cleansing away the smoke, as salt water mends a wound. Achilles understood her—sailing did suit her.

Briseis looked up the slopes of Mount Ida. She had never seen this side of her beloved mountain range: It was rockier, the trees shorter and scattered further apart. The mountain's massive size reassured her; even Achilles looked small in its shadow. Lyrnessos was gone, but the Greeks had not touched the forests and crags. Kamrusepa's sacred mountain stayed inviolate even though her temple had burned. The goddess would reside in her mountain haunts, content with the company of the mighty stags and refreshed by the libations of her springs, until someone remembered and made her offerings again.

Sometime after midday Patroklos walked to her from where he was sitting with Achilles, past the rowing benches that filled much of the main deck. Since the wind did the work today, the men sprawled on the benches, relaxing. From supplies he had laid out on the deck by Achilles, he carried two wooden cups to her, one filled with fresh water, the other with cheese and olives.

"It isn't much," he said. "We won't eat a proper meal until we camp on shore late in the day."

She thanked him. "And the others?" She looked toward the women sitting together below the main deck. Unlike her they could not see above the sides of the ship.

"They have food and fresh water, although some are seasick and not hungry. It will pass when we are back on land for the night. Your Eurome does not enjoy the sea as you do, but I assured her I would take care of you."

"She's sick?" Briseis started to get up.

Patroklos stopped her. "Don't worry. She fell asleep once I told her you were fine."

Briseis nodded. She watched Patroklos jump down from the raised foredeck and join Achilles on a rower's bench where he lolled against the side of the ship, his long legs stretched in front of him. As Patroklos sat down, Achilles bent one leg so Patroklos could lean on it while they ate. With one hand Patroklos reached for cheese and olives, with the other he stroked the inner part of Achilles's thigh. She had never seen this level of intimacy between two men. She knew from the women's gossip that Achilles chose one of the captives as his bedmate each night. Patroklos did also. This friendship intrigued her with its many facets. Once she'd noticed Patroklos's caress, she could not keep her eyes from straying to that smooth stretch of Achilles's powerful thigh. She clenched her hand into a fist and forced herself instead to watch the cool blue water parting with a white furl as the ship cut through.

Achilles stood up and stretched, looking out to sea. Suddenly he cried in delight and pointed. Briseis saw what caught Achilles's attention: dolphins swimming together. They leapt into the air and chirped their songs.

Achilles smiled up at her. "My mother sends a sweet omen." Briseis did not know what to think. When the bards sang of Thetis, she had had no trouble believing his mother was immortal, but now, seeing Achilles before her, it seemed utterly strange. She remembered the scent of the sea that arose from his flesh. Not so strange, perhaps.

When the sun hung low on the horizon, the wind died and men with burly arms brought down the sail. Oarsmen maneuvered the ship so that its stern faced a narrow strip of beach. Achilles and Patroklos jumped ashore first, both with bow and quiver. Two others jumped down, caught the stern lines thrown to them and secured them to boulders and trees. Then they dropped a gangplank so that they could unload the sheep and camp supplies for the night. Briseis thought there would be little pasturage or watering for the sheep on this rocky shore until she noticed a cleft in the slopes so filled with green there must be a creek. The Greeks apparently knew how to pick their night's berth. She wondered how many times they had done this.

The unloading of the sheep distracted her, and she almost missed the flash of movement in the narrow canyon and Achilles's swift response. Had it been a deer? Patroklos raced after his friend. The men cheered, hoping for a venison feast.

Her breath came freely as she moved to the rear of the ship and greeted Eurome.

"How are you feeling?"

Eurome groaned and held her stomach. "Oh my stars and fishes, if we was meant for seagoing, the gods would gave us fins and scales."

Briseis put her arm around Eurome. "You'll feel better on the land."

"I was afeared this cursed sailing would do you more harm," said Eurome, "but Lord Patroklos promised you was doing as well as a fish in the sea. I told him I didn't want to hear a word about any sea, not even to hear my Poppy's fine. I must say you was a grand sight sitting on that deck high up, like a queen on a throne, your hair blowing around your head all golden in the sun. You were a sight, yes you were."

"Sailing agrees with me. It's washed the smoke out of my breath."

They climbed down, and as Briseis gathered firewood, Patroklos returned alone and declared to no one in particular, "I lost him. I can never keep up. He's after a huge stag. We'll have a feast if he can catch it."

A man laughed. "When did any creature known to mortals outrun Lord Achilles?"

After being alone all day on the foredeck, Briseis listened eagerly to the women's talk. She squatted by one of the fires, and as she'd seen her cook do, she mixed some of yesterday's dough, flour, salt and water together into a workable dough for the night's bread.

"—I couldn't have borne it so soon," the stonecutter's wife said. Her name, Briseis had learned, was Sumiri.

"Well, some be all too happy to bear it," said a short woman with close-set eyes and lips that formed a thin line. She smirked knowingly at a pretty girl sitting next to Briseis. Sumiri shook her head to interrupt the direction of this conversation but the short woman ignored her. "Not just her—a lot of them think bedding down with those swine will make their lives easier. Witless fools."

"Hush. They've no choice, Nisa. None of us do. At least the men turn to those who seem more willing. They care that much for our feelings. Think about it, you owe those women thanks. If not for them, the men might have come after you or me."

"That'll come soon enough. They'll hand us over like so many sheep. They don't care nothing about your feelings, Sumiri."

Briseis slapped a piece of dough into a flat circle and tossed it onto the stone they had heated in the coals. "If you think about it," she said, "they have been strangely considerate of our feelings. First they destroy our lives, and then they ask us whether we are comfortable or hungry. It doesn't make sense." Briseis had wondered why Achilles singled her out for kindness, but it occurred to her that the rest of the captives, while not receiving the degree of deference she had, had not been roughly treated.

The short woman named Nisa snorted. "Considerate! Ha! Don't you be a fool also, Lady. That's their way to get us in their beds and doing their work without a fuss—make you think y' owe it them cause they've been kind. Kind? They're killers, that's what they are. You best remember."

"Many men fight in war," Sumiri responded, her blue eyes narrowing in rebuke of Nisa. She pulled a finished bread off the stone with some tongs. Briseis threw another on. "They can't be cruel all the time. Remember that good men from Lyrnessos trained as warriors. There are brutes among these men, but some of them see our grief and try to help—even though they made our sorrow to begin with."

Nisa shook her head. "These men love fighting. Do y' know they'd already taken another city before they come upon us—and it weren't enough. The Greeks are thieving wolves," she said, looking over her shoulder to make sure she wasn't overheard. She leaned closer to Briseis and Sumiri. "I'll tell you something. Women like that one—" she tossed her chin in the direction of the pretty girl whom she had implied was happy to be bedded by some Greek soldier, "—at least catch good gossip, especially if they know that Greek jabber, what with their families doing trade with the swine." Briseis laid her hand on Nisa's arm to quiet her. The woman Nisa meant had flushed deeply and her hands pressed hard against each other in her lap.

Nisa patted Briseis's hand but continued with her gossip. "Anyways, I heard from her the swine never meant to raid Lyrnessos. It were all an accident. They'd filled most of their ships from the other city they took, but it weren't enough to fill their bellies. That wolf Achilles wanted more cattle and he saw our pastures on the mountain."

"If there's an army to feed," said Sumiri, "they need meat. I wish they had only stolen our livestock and left our men and children alive."

"Them stop at livestock?" scoffed Nisa. "When they saw our city, they couldn't stop their greed."

The younger woman sitting next to Briseis faced Nisa angrily. "You're wrong. Lord Achilles hates King Agamemnon's greed. He doesn't mind stealing cattle and sheep to feed the men—like Sumiri said—but he's tired of sacking cities which haven't done any harm to him or his men."

"Oh, nonsense," retorted Nisa. She stabbed her finger at the young woman. "That man's good looks been knocking the sense right out of you. Don't you remember what he did to us, Asdu? If he's so tired of taking cities, why Lyrnessos? Agamemnon wouldn't never know if they left us in peace."

"Nisa, we've had enough misery without fighting among ourselves," said Briseis. Yet, she asked herself, why *did* Achilles choose to destroy us? Our flocks weren't enough? Was it greed? Habit? Or was it Mynes riding out with his men to confront Achilles?

Asdu's face turned a deeper red. She tossed her sandy-colored hair away from her face in a defiant gesture. "If you like gossip so much, Nisa, surely you've heard the men complaining of Agamemnon's greed and all the cities they've sacked for him with little to show for their work. Achilles told me he *was* going after our herds, but when he saw Lyrnessos from high on Mount Ida—with its fertile fields and great walls that promised wealth inside—he thought its plunder would silence Agamemnon's greed until they could take Troy. Achilles only sacked Lyrnessos because he hoped he and his men would have no need for more raids, and they could finally finish the fight at Troy and go home."

Briseis noticed Asdu's willingness to defend Achilles and his men. "If they are tired of raids," she couldn't help saying, "why don't they leave? They aren't chained to the plains of Troy."

Sumiri leaned forward. "You know men. These Greek kings no doubt boasted about destroying Troy, and they brought big armies with them. They are men, so they are chained by their pride. Our city's burnt and gone, so I'm not sure it makes much difference now whether Agamemnon's greedy or Achilles, but it may matter when we arrive at the Greek camp and they select whose servant each of us will be."

That comment silenced the group.

What Sumiri said ran through Briseis's mind as she tossed dough onto the stone. Which Greek would take her? She considered how different the life of the slaves in Euenos's palace had been from slave life on her father's estate. Eurome had been loved and respected. Briseis knew she didn't have Maira's inner restraint to bite back her words and deal patiently with insult.

Did Achilles's unwelcome deference mean he would claim her? She had welcomed him in her dreams as a lover, and even now, his presence ignited feelings she didn't want to own. Achilles meant slaughter and betrayal to her. She had never had a protective god— only a delusion. Asdu said the flocks and Lyrnessos's wealth drew Achilles to her city, but Briseis blamed herself, even if the waking Achilles never knew that he'd appeared in her dreams. The gods worked through dreams in incomprehensible ways. She did not understand how it had happened, but her guilt felt like poison flowing through her body.

By the time the bread was done and the coals for the meat were burnt down to a good level, Achilles returned, the stag draped over his shoulders. No other man could have carried the beast alone. Achilles directed his men to prepare the innards, some thigh meat and fat to offer to Lord Zeus, father of the gods.

"Can you tell me," Achilles asked the huddle of women, "since you are native born to this area, what goddess or nymph claims as her sacred place the mountain and the spring which feeds this creek? I chased the stag up to the creek's source. After my arrow struck down the buck, I noticed a nearby stone carved with a goddess standing on a stag for her throne. The markings are worn smooth by lichen and water, but her power emanates from it even so. She must be a strong goddess. When I make my offering to Lord Zeus, I would like to sanctify an offering to her in thanks for this gift from her forest, but I do not know her name or what she will find pleasing."

The women around the fire, alert but shy, looked at Briseis.

Eurome spoke first, proud to identify Briseis's role. "My Lady Briseis is the priestess of Kamrusepa. That's the goddess you mean if she were standing on a stag."

Achilles turned to Briseis. "A healer and a priestess." He bowed to her. "Your goddess must be sorrowing for her people, longing for offerings. I know how deeply a goddess mourns when mortals dear to her have lost what brief life was bestowed on them. Will you assist me in an offering?"

Briseis could not deny Kamrusepa an offering, much as she wanted to stay away from Achilles. She prepared for the rite, hoping for one of those sustaining moments of clarity that the goddess had given her in the past, but she felt heavy with Achilles's nearness. She didn't think Kamrusepa would hear her.

The main cook fire of their camp would serve as sacrificial altar for the burnt offerings. She and Achilles stood before it. She lifted her hands, recited an invocation for the well-being of the captive women, and scattered the barley Achilles had given her on the fire. By custom both the priestess and the king drank from the libation cup. After a moment of hesitation, she gave the cup to Achilles. The firelight reflected like dancing flames against their arms joined by the cup. The image from her vision at the Spring Festival was realized here, harmless flames dancing up and down her arm—she almost expected to taste the sweetness of his lips—except that neither of them laughed and her heart felt despair rather than delight. She poured the dark wine onto the ground and hoped the libation would serve as an offering not only to Kamrusepa but to her dead as well, that they might forgive her for having welcomed their killer into her dreams.

The ritual completed, the men laid spits of meat on the fire. One of Achilles's men called him to the ship about some problem Briseis did not understand. She brought more firewood to add to the supply of coals under the roasting venison. She'd have to get used to that now, carrying firewood, hauling water. Once they arrived, no telling what they'd have her do.

The wine the men had broken out made them boastful as they minded the spits. "—Lord Achilles charged them and before they could gather their wits, he'd killed all seven brothers in one charge— that's a commander you can follow with confidence."

Seven brothers lost at once, thought Briseis with a pang. Nisa gave her a look as if to say, what else do you expect from these men?

Briseis addressed the man who'd spoken. "Who were the seven your Lord Achilles slew?"

The man took a drink and wiped his mouth with the back of his hand. "Interested in the prowess of Lord Achilles, are you? The seven he killed, almost in one blow, were the sons of King Eetion—whose daughter became a princess of Troy, married to Hector, the deadliest of our enemy. Lord Achilles will have knocked all the joy from her lofty marriage. Maybe Hector will stay off the battlefield to dry his wife's tears."

The men around the fire grunted in appreciation. The man laughed. "The old man, King Eetion, didn't have to suffer over losing his sons. He'd already been killed."

"How considerate of your commander. I assume by Lord Achilles?"

The bitterness in her tone finally penetrated the man's awareness. He scowled at her.

"Of course it was Lord Achilles. Who else could kill a warrior like King Eetion?"

Sumiri's brows knitted in concern, and Briseis suspected that Sumiri's worry was for her—for provoking this soldier unwisely.

Briseis broke a branch over her knee. On the other side of the fire,

186 | JUDITH STARKSTON

Patroklos rose. He had heard what she said. *Now I've gotten myself in trouble.*

Her courage dimmed as he approached her. He raised his hand. She flinched as she remembered Mynes's blows.

He pointed to the water's edge. "May I speak with you? Away from the others."

21

WARRIORS AT TROY

Briseis did not wish to be dragged, so she walked quickly to where the waves caught slivers of moonlight. She pulled herself to her full height as she turned to face Patroklos.

He leaned toward her, pointing at the soldiers around the fire. "Achilles's men boast of his prowess because his skill as a warrior keeps them safe, but they do not understand what it costs him."

Briseis drew back in surprise. "What do you mean—what it costs him?" She realized the tension in the set of his shoulders did not come from anger.

"Back there, as I listened by the fire, I could not bear to let the men's boasts stand without trying to explain. Some battles a warrior chooses with a willing heart. Put Hector on the field and Achilles will arm with enthusiasm, but sacking towns grows grim unless you are very greedy. It must offend you to hear me complain about this since you have lost everything at our hands, but it's true. Some men enjoy these raids. Achilles and I do not. But Achilles cannot go halfhearted into these attacks. His nature knows no control or limit—in this he is like his divine mother. Besides, devoting his whole strength to the fight brings the surest safety to his men, and his loyalty is always for them. It's even more the case when we meet up against warriors the like of Eetion and his sons."

That was what he wanted to tell her? To defend his friend?

His eyes did not leave hers. "You hate him, don't you?" Sorrow darkened his expression. "I don't blame you—neither does he. But you have no idea the agony your hate causes him."

"Agony I cause *him*?" She took a few steps away to where the waves unfurled softly against the sand. She needed distance from this man whose words felt like a cruel affront, even though he delivered them with gentleness in his voice and carriage. He wanted something from her, but the energy he exerted had no threat behind it, only a disappointment that she could relieve if she chose.

"Forgive me. Nothing could be as painful as losing your brothers and husband, your home and all the familiar places of your childhood. What he feels seems trivial to you, but that is because you do not know him. Nothing is small or manageable about Achilles."

"Isn't being a good killer what makes him a hero? Isn't that what you love about him? Does he grieve for all those he's slaughtered or destroyed on these raids?" She had a bitter taste in her mouth. She leaned down, picked up a pebble and tossed it as far out as she could.

Turning back, she was startled to see the moonlight shine on a tear running down Patroklos's cheek. He shook his head. "No warrior can grieve for all the harm he's done in life—that would be a madness no god could relieve. All this sickens him, but you cause him a singular agony—though you deny this power."

"I am a slave woman. I have no power." She knew as she said it, this wasn't true. She'd felt her power when she lifted the sword. No one could take that from her.

Patroklos tipped back his head. "Achilles has never treated you as a slave. From the moment you defended your brother with a sword, you have held a place in Achilles's heart. You have the courage of a warrior. I thought he expressed his love with all the signs of respect he has given you since." Patroklos studied her face. She felt uncomfortable under his scrutiny. "He has taken your distaste for speaking to him to heart, but didn't you notice his actions—even tonight restoring you to your role as priestess?"

She had. And now she knew Achilles acknowledged her courage and loved her for it. She recognized the spark she felt on hearing that and disowned it. She avoided Patroklos's eyes, looking down at the sand, refusing to be tricked into feeling guilty about hating her brothers' killer.

"Even in your anger, haven't you noticed how well you are suited? When you straightened tall as you faced me after I called you here, your gesture mirrored his exactly."

She turned to him in surprise. What now?

"If he could withdraw that day's fate when he sacked Lyrnessos, he would, but fate can never be undone or avoided. Agamemnon's demands have sunk him into despair, and you overflow with grief. Each of you holds the comfort the other most needs. You are meant for each other. Even the men see that: your height, your hair color and the divine poise you share. I see more than that. I see inside you: the same gifts, the same fire. Only you can heal each other. I have always been the one who brings him peace, but his anguish lately has been beyond my power to mend. I give way to you—you have a fire whose strength can quiet his fire. Imagine. Fire dampened by fire. You two should cause a conflagration. I do not understand it, but I accept it. Only you can calm his storms."

For the second time that evening she thought of her vision at the Spring Festival—flames that brought her pleasure as they danced upon her arms and blended into an embrace. But what if she did not want to restrain Achilles's fire or soften his storms? What if she longed to plunge headlong into a fiery maelstrom and whip it into greater force? What would happen to his friend then?

"On that day he found you, Achilles swore an oath that he would make you his wedded wife. If you are willing, when this hateful war ends, Achilles will take you back to Phthia, to his father's palace. He will bring you before Peleus, bent by old age and the too-long absence of his dear son. 'Here is my bride, my lawful wife,' Achilles will say, and Peleus will welcome you."

Tears came to her eyes. For a moment she could feel the loving acceptance, the family she would again have. Did the dreams sent by Kamrusepa have a gentle purpose, to make her long for Achilles before his actions could set her against him? She did not see how she could wed the man who had slaughtered her brothers. She turned away from the illusion.

Patroklos must have sensed her refusal to accept Achilles's offer. He sighed and walked back to the fire where the men were enjoying the spitted venison. Briseis stayed by the shore alone until hunger drew her back and she sat with the women.

THEY REACHED their destination early in the afternoon the next day. Briseis, alerted by a shout from the man at the tiller, climbed on the thick wooden box that housed and supported the mast, grasped the mast for balance, and looked out.

She knew the Greeks used a small harbor south of Troy. She looked out at an unimpressive bay guarded by a fort built on the rocky headland. She tried to glimpse Troy, but either the cliffs or the distance hid the city.

Achilles ordered the men to lower the sail. As they maneuvered the ship into the bay with their oars, she waited with the anxious women.

After her strange conversation with Patroklos, Briseis avoided Achilles. He did not seek her out. She was tempted to pour out her confusion to Eurome, but much as she loved and admired the brave old woman, she was afraid her nurse would not understand. Achilles's and Patroklos's courtesy had charmed Eurome. She would tell her to make the best of these circumstances by marrying Achilles. Dear as Iatros, Bienor, and Adamas had been to Eurome, she would not understand the guilt that clutched at Briseis when she remembered the caresses Achilles had given her in her dreams —she could never tell Eurome about those. It didn't matter that even the scent of the man lighted desire in her body. She had found Mynes attractive before her wedding—look how mistaken she had been. What would her father think—if he still lived—to hear she had accepted the man who had destroyed their family and city?

Perhaps Eurome would know best. They both lived as slaves now. What had happened to Eurome's dreams of marriage when she became a slave? It had never occurred to Briseis to consider Eurome's life beyond being her nurse. What if Eurome's experience provided a wiser guide than her own confusion?

Briseis saw wagons appear on a road cut into the hill surrounding the bay. Scruffy gray-green shrubs and trees dotted the rough white stone of the hillside. The men herded the sheep toward the gangplank and off the ship. The frightened animals bleated and skittered, and the soldiers cursed and shoved them. Next, on shoulders glistening with sweat, they carried the chests filled with treasure to the wagons that would carry them up to the Greek camp. Finally, a soldier signaled the huddled women to disembark.

Their feet touched the beach and Eurome said, "Soil under my feet. I don't never want to step on a ship again." She sat on a large rock while Briseis walked a ways to work off the rocking feeling.

Briseis lifted her hand to block the sun's glare while studying the fort.

"It feels good to stretch your legs after being shut up at sea, doesn't it?" said Achilles, startling her. How had he slipped near her unnoticed? His face shone in the sunlight, his green eyes calm, his smile relaxed.

She stammered a yes and looked around for the safety of the other women, but she had walked a long way without realizing it.

He had put on his armor and sword belt—bringing images of the destructive warrior he had been in Lyrnessos. The huge ash spear balanced easily in his right hand, as if he'd picked up a stick from the beach. The muscles along his arm swelled and glided as he swayed the great weight of the spear back and forth without noticing. She remembered the sensation of power she had felt when she took up sword against him.

"So close to Troy, it's wise to be secure," he said, indicating his armor and sword. "Our camp has been safe till now, but we can't chance a Trojan ambush on the road."

Despite her resolve against talking to Achilles, her curiosity overcame her. "How close are we to Troy? I've been told it is a beautiful city."

"Troy is majestic. We Greeks have been close to it for a long time and yet immeasurably distant. I sometimes think the omens deceived us when they showed we would seize Troy." His gaze had gone far away, but he returned and smiled at her. "It's that direction." He pointed, leaning closer to her. "Farther up the coast."

She looked where he pointed, but saw only the turquoise sea, the narrow strip of pebbly beach and the headland covered in tough, wind-beaten shrubs. She liked the dreamy quality of his voice when he spoke of Troy.

He seemed to enjoy this chance at conversation with her. "Troy lies opposite our camp on a sizable bay that opens onto the narrow strait of water we call the Hellespont. From the camp you can look across to the city's mighty walls. Sailing through the Hellespont is often impossible because of strong winds. This small harbor is easier for us." Briseis remembered her father had told her that much of the Trojan wealth came from payments the merchants had to make while their ships waited for the winds to change.

"Before our long siege reduced her glory, the splendor of Troy surpassed anything I had ever seen. Troy's beauty spread out from her citadel in all directions. As you approached, wide wheat and barley fields stretched from the lower flanks of Ida to the shore of the sea. The Scamander and Simoeis rivers flowed down, embracing Troy on either side. The golden wealth of grain fed Priam's people and his mighty stock of horses. The city itself still rises in two parts. A stout ditch and stone wall surmounted by a wooden palisade surround the lower city where people have their homes and, until we came, made their livelihoods." His voice had dropped into a mournful register. "The grandeur of the palace citadel sits like a crown upon the whole —huge stone walls rise up to protect it, and room after room of golden splendor lies within—or so I'm told."

A bitterness in these last words made Briseis look at him in surprise. "No wonder," he said, "that we cannot draw ourselves away even while we destroy ourselves by staying." She felt pulled under a spell by the beauty of the images he described.

His attention focused on her again. Their eyes met. The spark of that meeting made her hear an echo of Patroklos's phrase "the same fire." She looked down and wanted to flee, but once again Achilles had been kind to her. He had told her so much more than she had asked—things she wanted to hear. She could be polite in return.

"I can picture Troy from your words. Thank you."

His face lit with a broad smile. She smiled back in spite of herself.

He cleared his throat. "The wagon is ready." He pointed the way.

As Briseis settled onto the floor of the wagon, she shuffled closer to the woman next to her to make room for the other captives climbing in. What would happen next? She held her arms tightly around her knees to stop the quivering. The faces grouped around her showed the same fear.

The oxen made their slow way. As Achilles had described, behind her rose Mount Ida and from the foothills came a line of trees marking the course of one of the two rivers. The wheat and barley fields lay fallow now. No spring planting had occurred. No farmer could plow or reap in the midst of this prolonged war.

As the road climbed, Troy came into view across the plain and her breath caught. The massive walls glowed gold in the afternoon sun as though the city were made of that precious metal, worth, to some, the grief this war had caused. Even the frightened women sitting around her in the wagon exclaimed softly among themselves when they saw the city's walls.

The broad sweep of Troy's bay lay ahead of them. The road brought them near the river where it flowed into the bay.

"Look! That must be the Scamander River," exclaimed Asdu. Briseis contemplated how Asdu had collected all her information, but she noted which river was called Scamander.

The road followed the edge of the bay furthest from Troy. The shore inclined gently up to a ridge. In one place the ridge dipped low and the sea twinkled beyond it. They must be on a peninsula bounded by the sea and bay on either side.

Soon she saw what looked like a city of ships terraced in row upon row around the sloping shore of the bay. A mighty force— greater than she had imagined. In the midst of the ships, propped with long timbers to keep them upright on the land, the Greeks had built wooden shelters, some larger than the farmers' homes on her father's land. These structures spoke of a determined permanence. This huge army would only leave when it chose to. Troy was doomed. Her own city had had no chance in the face of such power.

Around her in the wagon, Briseis felt the women's anxiety grow in equal measure to her own as they approached this intimidating camp where a distribution would determine their fates as captives.

22

THE CHOICE

The wagons stopped near an open area where feet had turned the grass to mud in what seemed to be a meeting place for the army. Many soldiers had gathered and more were arriving. She heard the heralds' shouts, calling them to an assembly of the army.

The first load of women climbed down from their wagon. The soldiers doing the unloading told them to wait at the far side of the field. The assembled men, when they caught sight of the captives, began heckling them about the roundness of their breasts, their youth or age, their desirability.

From her wagon, Briseis saw a larger group of women being herded by soldiers. Seeing familiar faces, she realized these women had come from Lyrnessos on the earlier ships. She scanned the crowd for Maira, but a soldier ordered her out of the wagon. She jumped down and turned to help Eurome.

As Briseis crossed the field of assembly, the men's heckling grew quieter and they stared at her. They jostled each other to get a better look and she heard comments, "red-gold hair like Lord Achilles" and "tall as an Amazon."

"It's true. She looks like Aphrodite."

"When has any goddess ever appeared to you?"

"If she had, that's what she'd look like."

"I'll take a woman who won't plunge a sword into me. I'll do the plunging." Coarse laughter. She glared at the men. They fell silent.

Achilles appeared among the crowd. He had removed his armor and wore a cloak the color of lapis-lazuli, pulled back from his shoulders. His hair captured the sunlight so that his head seemed surrounded by flames. He stepped onto a speakers' mound and raised his hand in greeting. The men cheered wildly.

A commotion revealed a group of Greek lords hastening to the speakers' mound. One man carried a gold scepter and wore a gold-trimmed cloak held in place by an enormous clasp studded with precious stones. He had a chest like an ox's, but Achilles towered over him. He scowled at Achilles and tried unsuccessfully to use the group of men around him to push Achilles aside. This must be Agamemnon, thought Briseis, the most powerful of the kings, the one the men called greedy. He seemed angry that Achilles had gotten here before him and had been cheered while he was not. Even in her fear for herself and the women, she thought how similar this vying for positions was to the tensions among nobles that she'd sometimes witnessed in Euenos's court.

Agamemnon raised the scepter to silence the crowd. "We must welcome back Achilles and his men." The men cheered enthusiastically and Agamemnon's expression grew sour. Finally, he could continue. "The herds of sheep and cattle you have seen as they went to the holding pastures. The captives, beautiful delights for men, are there." As he pointed, Briseis and the other women shrank back. "The wealth of Thebes and Lyrnessos is heaped by my ships ready for distribution."

The men shouted, "Achilles! Achilles! Achilles!" He bowed to them and they roared with delight. Achilles reached for the scepter. Agamemnon released it with a frown.

Achilles spoke with the roar of the waves in his voice. "My men and I have brought riches and an abundance of food back for you, sons of the Achaians, fierce fighters from all the lands of Greece. Now, through your might, we will bring down the walls of Troy and take these treasures to our homes far across the sea. To our victory." He raised the scepter high, the bare skin of his arm shimmering more than the gold.

The tumult rose ever louder like the great wind of a storm at sea. Achilles's eagerness to sack Troy sent an icy cold through Briseis. How these men love him! He fights for them; he feeds them. What would they do if they lost him? Patroklos was right. There was no restraint or limit either in Achilles or the reactions he caused in those around him. He frightened and thrilled her.

Agamemnon took back the scepter, but it was a long time before he could be heard. "Sons of the Achaians, shall I distribute this wealth to the forty kings who are your leaders, as I see fit, each according to his honor and the size of his fighting force so that they in turn may hand out what is needed to each of you?"

The men shouted their assent. Agamemnon continued, "I will be first to take what pleases me and brings me honor, as is my right, since I brought the most ships—one hundred in all—and hold the greatest power among the Achaians." He spoke to four of his heralds who waited at the foot of the speaker's mound. As the heralds dispersed toward the different areas of loot, Agamemnon's henchmen prepared to carry their king's portion to his shelters.

Briseis held her breath as one of the heralds came toward the group of women. He scanned the women and pointed to a fair-haired girl Briseis did not recognize.

The herald continued pointing, a second and third time. He acted with such speed that Briseis assumed the choices must have been agreed upon in advance of the assembly. Beautiful women stepped forward.

He pointed again, this time far back into the group of women. The others made way for this fourth choice. The tall figure moved slowly, her head held high, her dark hair glistening down her back. Like most of the captives, who had no cloaks with which to veil themselves, her head was bare. Briseis gasped as she recognized Maira. Maira caught Briseis's eye. Her expression spoke of fear but also fierceness. Briseis tried to give her an encouraging look in return.

Briseis wondered if she too would be included in Agamemnon's portion. She would be near Maira; she would escape Achilles, but even so, she hoped not. She looked at Agamemnon and imagined living in the glare of those eagle eyes. Her breath stopped at the thought of being crushed under his powerful girth.

Nine more women followed Agamemnon's henchmen, and then his herald turned away and walked back toward the speakers' mound. She felt her breath return.

The assembly waited while Agamemnon's men finished removing quantities of treasures, amphorae of wine and grain, and many other things which Briseis did not attend to. She focused on Achilles. Would his choice be next?

Agamemnon turned to Achilles. "As the leader of this raid, I give to you the right to select next. You know the quantities I have allotted you."

Achilles spoke to the crowd, his body turned away from Agamemnon. "My men and I seized these riches with our own hands from the cities of Thebes and Lyrnessos. Now from the store we won through hard fighting, I will receive my gifts, bestowed by the sons of the Achaians."

He laid emphasis on his final words. It was not quite an open insult, Briseis thought, to interpret in this way the assent Agamemnon had received from the men—that Achilles received his portion from them and not from the king. But Agamemnon missed none of the force of the insult. His face went red. When one of his men came up a moment later to ask him a question, he struck the man and walked off in anger. She was glad she would never be his slave, even if it meant she had to face Achilles every day.

Achilles's herald studied the women's faces and said Asdu's name. She blushed. The herald named three other lovely women. She noticed Achilles had chosen delicate beauties more suited for bed companions than camp work.

Next the herald came to Eurome. There were cries of derision from the men—an old woman.

Then he turned to go. Briseis felt her face flush with humiliation.

So Achilles did not intend to claim her, he preferred those other women—but did he mean to punish her by separating her from her trusted companion? She had thought she did not want to go with Achilles, but now—whose slave would she be? She hugged her beloved nurse to her, but Eurome had to follow the herald.

Briseis thought of the men's comments as she walked through the assembly. They would know she had been rejected. But she didn't want Achilles—did she? Stricken, her face burning with shame, Briseis kept her eyes down, so she did not see Achilles leave the speakers' mound and walk toward her, the men parting to make way. Only when he stood in front of her, did she feel him and look up. A wave of sensation struck her. He reached for her hand. Only as they walked back to his ships did she realize she had reached back.

Briseis could see Eurome and the other women with Achilles's herald up ahead, but Achilles seemed in no hurry. He told her about the men who lived in each grouping of ships: the name of their king and which city in Greece he ruled over. The number of ships revealed each leader's relative power.

Achilles did not release her hand. She did not try to take it back. Even as he told her about these kings dwelling all around them— names she had heard and wondered about, now brought to life— their joined hands never left her awareness, that point of contact, warm, alive, and gentle.

His ships, he told her, lay at the far end of the camp—nearest the Hellespont. He did not need to hide behind others for protection. She noticed Agamemnon's huge contingent in the center, well protected. The terraced rows of ships and thatched shelters had seemed impressive from a distance. Now, in the midst of them, she saw the squalor. They walked around piles of rotted food scraps and worse that she did not want to identify. The stench of too many men living in close quarters assaulted her nose.

The camp splayed out with no plan to accommodate daily life for all these men. The Greeks had anticipated an easy victory, not a prolonged stay. Briseis knew that Troy held out only by means of her many allies.

"Let's go the rest of the way on the summit of the ridge," Achilles said. "At least there you breathe sea air." He shrugged in apology. "I'd like to say you'll grow accustomed to the smell, but you won't. I never have. It's even worse in the winter when the rains turn everything to mud. The spring has dried us out a little."

They climbed a grassy slope above the camp. At the crest of the ridge, the dazzling blue of the sea spread out below. She took a deep breath. The sun hung low over the water, spinning gold and silver onto the rippling surface. The beauty of it made her ache inside, and her grief rose up and burst the hold she had tried to maintain. A tear ran down her cheek and she brushed it away, but more tears followed. She crumpled to the ground, taking her hand away from Achilles's. She pulled her knees up to her chest and buried her face.

After a while he sat next to her and said softly, "The grace of the sea's shimmer can make life's sorrows insufferable."

She lifted her head in surprise. "What do you mean?"

"It makes us too aware of the distance between our mortal world that daily brings loss and that shining unchanging world of immortality—even as the sea moves and sways, those changes are only on the surface. Tomorrow I will wake up and gaze on the same vast sea, which is like my mother, who can change form but remains unalterable. To be human is too painful in the face of this."

"I'm not sure I understand, but I know my life is full of grief and pain—and the sea's beauty has undone me."

"I recognize your sadness. Perhaps it doesn't always have to be thus. You have lost so much, but you are alive, and even in the midst of sorrow, simple joys bring healing if you let them. The beauty of the sea can also bring elation."

His words seemed to cast a kind of spell again, but she shook her head. "How can I enjoy anything when my family and my city have been destroyed? How can I betray them?"

"Are you sure your brother would feel betrayed if you felt joy?"

Briseis buried her face again. "I don't know. Sometimes I feel the grief lighten—but then I remember." She looked at him. "I do not want to forget the people and places I have lost."

"You are right to remember. Memory is our only immortality. At the same time, we pay a heavy price in pain when we remember our lost. I have seen many good men sacrifice their lives. I understand some of the weight you feel. Perhaps my advice was too simple, and you cannot yet remember the good things in life while the dead demand your attention."

Briseis half rose, pulling forward onto her knees. "How could my goddess have abandoned the city that worshipped her? Why didn't she prevent our destruction? Someone said you had not planned to raid Lyrnessos. How hard would it have been to keep her people safe? We made all the proper sacrifices."

"The gods and goddesses can do many things as suits them, but they cannot alter fate. Goddesses must bow before fate no matter how much it grieves them."

Should she blame fate for Lyrnessos's destruction, not her goddess, or worse, her dreams? Who else among men understood fate better? Briseis thought of his divine mother who had tried so hard to change his fate and make him deathless. If an immortal mother could not save her own child, why had she expected Kamrusepa to save her city? She thumped back onto the ground.

"What is it like to talk to your mother?"

He gave her a bemused look and leaned back on his elbows, sprawling his long legs in front of him. "It is like speaking to anyone else, except that she loves me beyond measure, and when I feel that love and the sadness that is the essential part of it, I feel a longing that I know will never be fulfilled. Did you know she tried to burn away my mortality so that I would never die?"

Briseis nodded.

"When I was a boy, I could still feel the searing that went through me when my father pulled me from those strange flames. Then Patroklos came. He became my closest friend. He had his own wound —he'd killed a friend accidentally in a fit of rage, a tragedy that haunted him. From the horror of the death he'd caused, he learned to control his passions, but he remained scarred by sadness for his friend's loss. Our friendship cured his sorrow and he brings me back from the pain those flames left, the anger and confusion—I've never learned to control it on my own. He is like cool water on the flames that forever torment me."

Patroklos's description had been similar. She wrapped her arms around her knees, hoping he would continue. He pushed himself up to sit cross-legged, and she had to tip her head up to watch his face. Even seated he felt towering.

"As for speaking with my mother—her feelings are not different from mortal mothers, just more dangerous. Even the other gods and goddesses shuddered so at her strength they coerced her to marry a mortal. Any immortal child of hers would be so unseasonably great that the balance of power among the gods would be endangered."

He looked at the sea. Briseis wondered about the mortal child of Thetis—what was the nature of his greatness? How powerful were his storms and that inner fire that never died? His beauty and strength did not feel mortal to her. When her father brought her down to the shore, she had seen places where the tides created whirlpools that pulled into their center anything that came near. She felt herself swirling in the whirlpool that his strength generated.

Achilles turned to her. "When my mother visits me, no one else can see her. We sit apart on our own shore."

Briseis marveled at this intimacy. She had envied her mother's closeness to Kamrusepa, but he described something she could not grasp. To love a goddess as your mother.

Briseis studied him. She remembered the intimacy and delight of her dreams. Images of happiness with him beckoned to her, but to accept Achilles's love ignored the weight that pressed upon her. The dead demanded her attention. He had said that himself.

23

A BARD'S TALE

Achilles seemed to read Briseis's thoughts and dropped the conversation. His lips turned down with a look of resignation. He glanced across the bay toward Troy and then down to the camp below them.

"Shall I show you where you will live? Patroklos will have reassured Eurome, but she will be waiting."

"I don't want her to worry."

Before they started back down, she studied the distant view of Troy. Her father resided somewhere out there, if he had not been killed in battle.

She turned to Achilles. "Several months ago my father, Lord Glaukos, arrived at Troy with King Euenos of Lyrnessos and our other warriors. Do you know if he still lives, or have you heard of his death in some battle?"

"During the attack on Lyrnessos your father was here at Troy?"

She nodded, watching his face for bad news.

"I have never been challenged by a warrior named Glaukos, nor have I heard of his death." Her shoulders dropped in relief.

He shook his head. "No, nothing worrisome comes to mind, but I will listen on the battlefield with care. You would be surprised at how much information we warriors exchange while trying to kill each other."

She looked at him in surprise, struggling to imagine warriors conversing on the battlefield. They started walking down the ridge toward the camp.

"Can you describe his armor? I will avoid him on the battlefield. Not for anything would I spill more of your family's blood."

She held off the tears that she felt rising up by pressing her tongue hard against the top of her mouth. When she dared, she pulled in a deep breath and described her father's armor in great detail.

Achilles's eyebrows rose in astonishment. "A woman who knows armor. How is this possible?"

She told him about her father's workshop, the metalworking she had grown up observing.

He replied, "I will remember what you have described. It is good that I know to avoid him, otherwise such fine armor would in itself have made him a worthy target."

This comment would have been more reassuring if so many other Greeks wouldn't seek to kill her father in order to take Milos's workmanship for themselves, but as they climbed down the path, she concentrated on the likelihood that her father remained unharmed.

ACHILLES'S MEN had built him a shelter from hewn pine-timbers, and with close-set stakes they had enclosed a courtyard spacious enough to assemble his fighting troops, called the Myrmidons. His shelter, with its thatched roof and covered porch, stood at the center of the courtyard, and the women allotted to him had a hut to the side. Scattered among the Myrmidon ships, his men had built their own shelters. Some were not much more than the lean-to sheds she had seen in the sheep camps. Others would have made most farmers' wives jealous.

Inside the women's hut she found Eurome, Asdu and the three others settling in. Against the walls the women had placed several pallets cushioned with fleeces. A small hearth in the center provided warmth. The only other light came from the door and the smoke hole in the roof. Eurome had already set up Briseis's bed.

Achilles's captives told them that their main job was to cook for his men, but the soldiers saw to their own butchering and roasting of the meat by their shelters, so they had only to grind grain and make the bread, stews, porridges, and other foods. They also did mending and washing.

Eurome brimmed with news she had ferreted out in her brief time in Achilles's camp. She pulled Briseis outside to a bench at the side of their shelter.

"There's one of the captives that's older like me—the one with the gray hair and squinty eyes—she told me 'bout Agamemnon—I knew as you'd be wondering for Maira's sake. They say he's got so many women they don't never work overmuch—and for bedmates, well, he goes after small, fair-haired girls, poor things. Just keeps the others for show."

"Maira's not what he goes after. Good," Briseis said, though she thought with a pang of the pale, delicate blonde who had been Agamemnon's first choice. She looked barely more than a child.

"Yes, that's one blessing for us to count. Seems Maira'll be safer than some. Agamemnon's men might want to go after her, but they'll be afeared to offend Agamemnon."

Briseis had seen how easily the king got offended.

"I almost forgot," said Eurome after a moment. "I found out what happened to Hatepa. The crews on the other ships I hear were rougher, and Hatepa got herself the worst of it what with all her complaining. They stuck her down in the hold, next to the smelly sheep. How that must ha' made her cough and wheeze. I never liked that mean, foolish woman, still..." Eurome shook her head.

"Appears she climbed out. When the other women tried to hold her to stop trouble coming on 'em all, she hit out at 'em—not as frail as she let on, I guess. Made her lose her balance, it did, and she went right over the side. Under the water and gone. She might be breathing like you and me if she'd been able to think of someone other than herself."

Briseis nodded. Hatepa had been oblivious to any needs but her own, but the thought of sinking below the cold water made Briseis shudder. The women couldn't even prepare her body for the pyre or perform the rite to give her soul a place to rest. Briseis scolded herself —she'd made Iatros's rite apply to all their dead back at Lyrnessos. She supposed she should come up with some prayer for Hatepa's journey in death.

While Eurome and Briseis talked, the chatter of women had grown louder as they worked nearby in the part of the courtyard that served as kitchen with a lean-to and cook fire.

"We should go help, Eurome."

Briseis observed two pretty women carrying dishes into Achilles's shelter. From their demeanor she guessed they viewed this as a privileged task. They were welcome to it.

Briseis got up from the bench and walked over to the work area. A slender, curly haired young woman poured wine from an amphora. It started to slip from the woman's grasp. Briseis leapt over and helped her place it safely back on the ground.

The woman smiled her thanks. "My name is Iphis."

Briseis introduced herself. Iphis laughed. "I know. Everyone knows who you are." Despite the words, her tone was friendly and her eyes gentle. "Will you help me carry this cup to Achilles? I can't manage both the full pitcher and his cup in one trip." Briseis hesitated, then nodded. She liked this cheerful woman.

Briseis saw Asdu slip out of the shadows, pick up a tray of wine cups and join them on the way to the open door of Achilles's shelter.

Inside, six men sat in chairs around the hearth, four other warriors besides Achilles and Patroklos. Achilles's presence dominated the room.

As soon as they crossed the threshold, Briseis felt the men's eyes turn toward her. They looked with curiosity and either admiration or wariness, Briseis couldn't tell which. Achilles's look puzzled her most of all—his face was filled with light, despite the shadowy room.

Patroklos sat on one side of Achilles. On the other side was an old man past his best fighting days. From the porch Briseis had heard Achilles call him Phoenix. He patted Achilles's arm with affectionate familiarity, more like a father than a comrade. Briseis didn't catch the names of the two others, but the fourth, across from Achilles, was called Aias. His fame as a warrior, like Achilles's, had reached Lyrnessos. She had heard him called the bulwark of the Achaians—a name that suited him given his bulk. He would have been the largest man in any other gathering, but unlike Achilles, who moved with a fluid grace, he carried his size like a stone wall.

When Achilles beckoned to them, Briseis followed Iphis. He thanked Briseis as he reached for the cup. She noticed it for the first time. The cup portrayed dolphins swimming beside a goddess as she rose from the waves. Milos, for all his skill, had never fashioned so real a scene. She could feel the rhythm of the waves and the splash as the dolphins leapt in the water.

"Do you see the waves dancing?" he asked her. She nodded. "Not everyone does—the skill of Hephaistos is too fine for some eyes. He gave it to my mother as a wedding gift. See how he's shown her rising from her father's kingdom under the sea? When I came to Troy, she told me to bring it. Mothers have their ways of spying on their sons. Sometimes I think she really is watching me from it, but I suppose she has no need for tricks like that." Briseis studied the face. His goddess mother depicted by an immortal—that must be what her face truly looked like. For a moment it felt as if Thetis stared straight into her heart.

Achilles drew another chair close to him. "Sit here by the fire. You are still recovering and should rest. Do you mind enduring our rough talk of this cursed war? I would enjoy your company." She noticed surprised looks on the faces around the fire, but they nodded graciously to Achilles's suggestion, however unusual.

Briseis was about to shake her head, when over Achilles's shoulder she saw Asdu's face contorted in a sour expression. Achilles smiled, holding the chair. She sank into it, murmuring her thanks. To refuse would be rude, but she knew that wasn't the reason she sat.

Briseis felt jealous. Asdu was attracted to Achilles—lovesick over the man who had ruined their lives. Asdu had been his bedmate; he had shared with her the names of rivers... *I am jealous over a man I have said I want nothing to do with. I was mean enough to cause Asdu to feel jealous in return.* Briseis sank lower into the chair.

Three other young women came in with trays of food. Iphis poured wine for the men, and when she reached Patroklos, she lingered over him, her lips brushing his as she leaned down to fill his cup, and after he had taken a drink, she wiped a drop from the side of his mouth and then raised her wine-stained finger to her lips. Briseis blushed at this intimacy. She had never seen a woman behave like that in open company with men. She lowered her head and looked down into her lap.

When Asdu left, carrying an empty tray, her head was bent low, and Briseis thought she saw a tear glisten on her cheek. She felt bad for Asdu—for all of them in this newfound captivity whose rules and cruelties they would have to learn. She would try not to hurt her again.

The six warriors seated around the hearth discussed the battles that occurred during Achilles's absence—an endless ebb and flow on the plain of Troy. Apparently the Trojans had pushed the Greeks toward the banks of the Scamander nearer to the camp. These men discussed the cataclysms of war as casually as her father and brothers had discussed crops and the possibility of a frost. Had they been fighting so long that they had become habituated to the horrors? She didn't want to hear their talk of battles against her people.

They laid plans for tomorrow's renewed attack. Now that Achilles had returned, they could shift the battle back toward the city. Troy's massive walls had a weak point where an older section joined a newer part—the men referred to it as "the place of the fig tree." They had aimed at this spot before without breaking through, but Achilles said they would succeed now because they had worn down the Trojan forces during the months of fighting. Briseis wondered if Achilles's certainty arose more from his impatience with the war than the state of the Trojan army. It seemed odd to her that the huge Greek army depended so heavily on one man. Only his presence on the battlefield drove back the Trojans. She remembered Achilles's remark about the danger any immortal child of Thetis would pose to the balance of power among the gods.

Briseis felt uneasy sitting amidst the men. At home, she would have sat on the women's side of the hearth. Here all sides belonged to men. As a girl, she had disliked her separation from the men, where all the interesting conversations took place. Now she hunched her shoulders and pulled her feet close up under the chair.

Despite her discomfort she ate hungrily and tried not to think about the closeness of the strange men around her or being singled out again for special treatment. At least Iphis and one of the serving women stayed through the meal, refilling food and wine as needed. When the rest of the young women reappeared to clear away the meal, Asdu took Achilles's plate and received a polite smile. As they carried away the dirty dishes, Briseis saw Asdu turn her head and gaze at Achilles before she went out, but Achilles was listening to something Patroklos said, and if he noticed her, he showed no sign of it.

Patroklos rose and went to some chests at the back of the big room, returning with a silver lyre.

"As you requested," he said to Achilles, "I saved this from the greedy doe's clutches. I buried it under some cheeses that had started to mold." The men around the fire laughed at this, although Briseis sensed their unease with the open disrespect toward Agamemnon.

"When Agamemnon's henchmen reported back to him about the treasures he should tell his heralds to take away, they didn't know it existed. When one of them saw me carrying it and complained that he'd be in trouble for missing such a valuable item, I told him it was far too fine an instrument for the riff-raff Agamemnon finds to sing his praises." Patroklos bowed to Achilles and handed him the lyre. "An instrument fit for a king."

Phoenix called out, "A song, Achilles, sing a good tale for us. We've missed your company in more ways than one." This request surprised Briseis. Achilles was a bard? How could that be?

Achilles held the lyre reverently in his hands. He tried the strings. The sound was as silvery as the lyre itself. Despite the beauty of the instrument and the trueness of its sound, he wore a sad expression.

"You can't find fault with this lyre," said Patroklos.

"No, the instrument is flawless. I will have to choose my song carefully to do honor to it. Yet I cannot help but mourn for whoever in Thebes had such musical skill that they owned so fine an instrument." Briseis had never heard of a great bard in Thebes, but she liked the tribute the anonymous man received.

Achilles plucked the strings with the plectrum, and she heard the familiar rhythm of bardic songs. She felt the thrill that always struck her heart when a tale began—greater this time because this unlikely bard piqued her curiosity. What sort of story would he tell? For a time, he played the lyre without singing, stopping to tune the strings occasionally until they suited him. He had turned in his chair so that he gazed in her direction, but his mind seemed to rove, searching for a tale to sing.

Then he smiled as if he had thought of something that pleased him and his eyes looked into hers. "Up on the ridge, you asked about my mother, and many know the story of how my father wooed her on a rocky outcropping while the waves crashed on either side—no easy courtship, as she changed from lion to serpent to fire and then tried to slip away as water. He held on through it all and won her love. But before the gods chose my lady mother, Thetis, as his bride, Peleus loved another, the daughter of King Eurytion. By winning her heart he also won a kingdom, for Eurytion ruled in Phthia, where now my father reigns. Together Eurytion and Peleus performed many heroic deeds worthy of song, but tonight I will sing about the Calydonian Boar Hunt—where Peleus won great fame, but the gods demanded too much in return."

His expression took on a faraway look as Achilles sang of the famous hunt for the monstrous boar that ravaged Calydon. Briseis had heard this song before but not this piece of the story. Achilles described how the boar charged Peleus like lightning from the sky. The hero threw his spear but did not notice Eurytion standing behind the boar's rocky lair. Peleus's cast overshot the noxious beast and struck his father-in-law instead. Achilles told of a fateful spear cast that the hero would give anything to withdraw. She knew he spoke to her.

The song told of further sorrow. With heavy heart Peleus buried Eurytion, giving him all the honors due a king. Briseis thought of the pyre which she had left burning by the fallen gates of Lyrnessos.

The rules of death—no matter how accidental—could not be gainsaid. Peleus faced a year's exile and purification by another king before he could go home to Phthia and his grieving wife. Without the comforting words and embraces of her husband's presence, his wife could not forgive. Her abyss of grief, Achilles sang, drew to itself a greater darkness. She found fault with her husband no matter how his messages pled. She even believed a false rumor of a new love her husband had found. Though Peleus's arms ached to hold her and offer solace, she hanged herself and walked below in shadows far from the sunlight's comfort. Peleus grew inconsolable at the pain he had caused.

Briseis heard yearning in the song and knew Achilles meant it for her.

Achilles had come to her in visions and dreams, spoken through her voice during the Spring Festival, and here, at last, Briseis heard his own song, his warning and his offering. She felt her understanding of him growing, along with her confusion.

At a pause in Achilles's song, Aias spoke up, his broad forehead creased in bewilderment. "I know you are inspired by the Muses, Achilles, but I've never heard the story of the Calydonian Boar told this way."

Briseis understood his perplexity. When the bards had sung this tale in her father's home, they had emphasized entirely different aspects.

"Didn't Meleager slay the boar and protect the city of Calydon?" asked Aias. "Isn't that what matters? Your father is a fine hero—no one blamed him for a misthrown spear. It could have happened to anyone, and the gods gave him Thetis soon after. What's this about being inconsolable? You know that our fathers, brothers that they are, fought many battles together. They didn't have time for brooding." Briseis smiled in sympathy. He'd told the standard version. She liked Aias's blunt honesty, but the purpose of Achilles's tale escaped him.

Achilles laughed. "How right you are, my trustworthy Aias. You always see the short path where I see the winding one. Let me mend my tale. Meleager killed the boar and won the glory that day."

Achilles stood and the other men rose. Under his breath she heard Patroklos say, "And then more strife broke out over the trophy of the boar's hide, so that Meleager killed his uncles and even his mother wished him dead. That's another winding path."

Briseis frowned at this. He saw her look and shrugged in apology.

24

OFFERING OF LOVE

As the men bid one another goodnight, Briseis slipped out. She was unsure whether Achilles intended for her to stay or not, but she knew she wanted to escape. Aias had been confused, but she understood the truth of the song: that love should not be rejected even in the midst of sorrow and that forgiveness brings back joy. Yet as Patroklos had just reminded her, even stories of love have conflict hidden along the path. She could not cast aside the darkness of grief that swirled around her and the voices of her family, even if only one might still be living.

By the dying light of the cook fire, she could see that most of the women had retired for the night. Those left were the prettiest who, Briseis guessed, might be expected to serve in one other duty for the night. She headed toward the women's hut. Instead of going inside, she sat on the bench facing Achilles's porch. No one looking out from there would see her in the dark, but she could watch who came and went, lit by the firelight coming through his open door.

The warriors came out onto the porch with Achilles and Patroklos. She heard them reviewing where each king would deploy his forces. When they stepped off the porch, Aias shouted, "To the fig tree!" She smiled at first at how ridiculous a goal that sounded—even if it was the weak place in Troy's walls. Then she pictured the Trojan women watching as the enemy burst their city's defenses just as she had done such a short time ago. How could these men make such things the daily business of their lives? The warriors walked off toward the gate. Aias's bulk overshadowed the others, and Phoenix had an uneven gait, caused, she guessed, by aging joints or an old injury grown worse with the troubles of time.

Patroklos and Achilles remained on the porch. Achilles's size dwarfed Patroklos, but the greater contrast showed between Achilles's restless motion, even when nothing remained to be done, and Patroklos's comfortable stillness. Achilles stretched his arms and then looked around as if he'd lost something. He put his arm around Patroklos's shoulder and sagged against his friend. Patroklos wrapped his arms around him and supported him. It looked strange to see the smaller man sustaining the colossus. She thought of the word from his song—"inconsolable."

Patroklos had said that she could cure Achilles's despair. She wondered. Did she want to? Achilles had described how their friendship had healed Patroklos's grief and given Achilles the restraint he lacked on his own. If she had her arms around Achilles as Patroklos did now, would the despair leave him and would the weight of her own grief lessen? Her arms, traitors to her brothers, longed to feel Achilles's smooth, muscled body in their embrace.

She thought too of Peleus holding tight to Thetis through all her transformations, even when she burned him as fire. He had found the strength to love again, to hold on through scorching flames. How to follow Peleus's lead? How could she embrace a man who had burned up everything she loved? She also remembered the flames that had brought her pleasure in her vision. Which flames would Achilles bring to her?

Achilles and Patroklos stepped out from under the porch roof and looked up at the stars.

"Perhaps tomorrow will be the day we take Troy," said Achilles. "At least we're back here where we can finish this war."

He glanced over at the kitchen fire and called a name Briseis did not recognize. A woman rose and Iphis joined her. They followed the two men into Achilles's shelter.

Briseis watched as Achilles pushed shut the wooden door, leaving the world around her in darkness.

WHEN SHE FOUND HER BED, she didn't sleep well. The few times she drifted off, she had restless dreams, which stayed just beyond her memory when she awakened in the dark. Deep into the night she finally fell into a sound sleep.

The heralds' call-to-arms jolted her from this oblivion. She pulled on the same dirty tunic and skirt she'd been wearing for days and went outside.

The courtyard buzzed with organized commotion. The women served breakfast to hurried men. Grooms prepared chariots. Other men sharpened blades and finished the small daily repairs to armor that constant warfare required.

Achilles's henchmen laughed and joked as they fastened their leg greaves and chest corselets. She shuddered at the ordinariness with which they viewed arming for battle. From outside the courtyard came a groundswell of noise: the Greek army preparing for battle.

Achilles strode through the courtyard. Across his shoulder he had slung his silver-studded sword and massive shield, thick with leather and bronze layers and faced with blinding gold. His bronze-and-silver greaves formed to his legs as if part of his flesh. His gleaming helmet and its horsehair crest towered above all the other men in the courtyard. Across his chest a skilled craftsman, surely divine, had scattered the starry heavens on his corselet. This is how he had looked when she first saw him astride the fallen Great Gate in Lyrnessos—a god of war bringing destruction to all she loved. She shrank back into the doorway of the women's hut.

She watched as, despite the weight of his armor, Achilles leapt lightly in beside his charioteer, and saw his horses toss their heads when they felt his presence. She heard his war cry and the cheers that echoed as he drove through the Myrmidon camp, gathering his men behind him like a towering wave that threatened to crash upon Troy. She felt the ground shake as the thousands marched to Scamander's plain below the walls of Troy.

As a storm recedes and the thunder wanes, so the courtyard gradually fell into dusty quiet, with the rumble of two armies still a distant backdrop. The men left on guard duty shut the gates and struggled to pull across the timber that barred them. Briseis felt hollow, as though she had been a drum in which all that clamor and menace had reverberated.

She saw Eurome by the cook fire.

"Good morning. Let me fetch you something to eat," her nurse said cheerfully. "What a busy place this morning." How differently Eurome responded to the camp's activities.

Her nurse put before her some cheese, a bit of onion and flatbread. Briseis looked at it without eating.

"Feeling lost?" asked Eurome, pushing a piece of the bread into Briseis's hand.

"All those Greek soldiers readying for battle made me feel terrified all over again—too many reminders of Lyrnessos's destruction."

Eurome nodded. "We've seen sorrows, we certainly have. My poor Poppy. Eat up, anyway. It'll do you good, sad or not. You need a distraction from all this, not reminders, I'll say that."

It seemed unlikely that she'd find a distraction from the war around her, although perhaps she'd grow accustomed to it as the soldiers had. How could anyone ignore the looming violence that thrived and mounted in intensity all around them even before the army left camp? The sounds of fighting filtered to her, less thunderous but disturbing even so. At times she could make out individual shouts and distinct clashes of bronze against bronze.

She thought of the view from the ridge. Across the bay the Trojan warriors confronted that horde she had watched arming, and somewhere in their midst, her father fought. She listened intently to the cries muffled by distance. Was that exultant war cry her father's voice? Or was that shriek his death agony? She couldn't think this way. She'd go mad.

She tried to eat.

Eurome poured some water into a kettle suspended on a tripod over the coals, then she poked at the fire to waken it. "Chamomile tea, that'll settle you. I always say, chamomile for whatever troubles you."

Briseis smiled. Eurome and her chamomile tea. The homely reminder made her feel better. How good to be near Eurome. Her home wasn't a place anymore, but she still had one.

Eurome's bustling around made her think of Maira somehow, and Briseis wondered how she fared. Maira had maintained a quiet reserve at the palace, but Briseis guessed that wasn't her chosen nature. Maybe escaping Hatepa and ending up in the Greek camp would be better for her. Mynes had forced her to make a stifling choice. They were both free of him. They'd never spoken of the bond they shared, but Briseis felt it deeply.

Briseis looked around her and an idea started forming. She remembered the layout of the camp as Achilles had shown it to her. If she could get someone to unbar the courtyard gate, perhaps she could go through the camp and find Maira. She'd have to think of a way to convince Agamemnon's guards to let her inside his stockade. If she brought her healing satchel, she could claim she was seeing to Maira's health. Eurome wanted a distraction for her. This sounded like a good one. The hollowness began to fill with something solidly familiar.

"Eurome, I think I should go make sure Maira's all right."

"Maira? Oh my stars and fishes, what are you saying? You can't go willy nilly where you please. You're... you're forgetting." She shook her head. "Drink your tea. There'll be work to get onto in a bit. I knowed this weren't going to be easy for you."

"I'll be back in plenty of time to help."

Briseis studied the guards sitting by the gate, eating their breakfast. If Iphis had known who she was, probably these soldiers did too. Even the lords around Achilles's fire had seemed wary of her. She thought the guards might obey her if she told them to open the gate for her—that she had some brief business elsewhere in camp. It was worth a try.

Eurome looked like she was going to launch into one of her scoldings, but Briseis gave her a kiss. "Don't worry. I may get no further than that gate."

She brushed the crumbs from her clothes, though there wasn't much point. Her tunic and skirt were a mess. Eurome, bless her, had found some clothes to replace the ones singed by fire and soaked in Iatros's blood—rough clothes and even dirtier now after days of wearing them. Difficult to look commanding in such rags, but they'd have to do. First she retrieved her satchel from the women's hut and then headed to the gate.

The men scrambled to their feet as she approached—a good sign. She pulled herself tall as she had on the beach with Patroklos and made her request. The soldiers looked at each other. She gave them her most imperious expression. "Well?"

One cleared his throat. "You'd return directly here?"

"Of course. I have duties here that I must attend to." She wasn't quite sure what those duties might be, but as Eurome had said, there'd be work in a bit. The men leaned into the task of unbarring the gate.

She set off on a garbage-strewn path she hoped would lead toward Agamemnon's ships. It occurred to her too late that walking alone in a camp of soldiers could prove dangerous. Fortunately, as she made her way, the camp appeared empty. The two soldiers she did see, both obviously wounded, paid no attention to her. Eventually she reached the huge group of ships that she recognized as Agamemnon's. Winding her way among the propped hulls, she looked for a stockade similar to Achilles's. When she noticed smoke rising above the ships and realized that it must come from cook fires, she hurried forward.

She soon ran into a wall of timbers much sturdier than Achilles's stockade and followed it around until she came to a broad, open gate. Peeking through she saw a huge shelter surrounded by several small huts that looked similar to the one she had slept in. Clustered near the huts, she saw a large number of women, working at various tasks.

A guard yelled at her. "What are you skulking about, woman? Where do you belong?"

Briseis stepped out of the shadow of the gate and marched up to the guard. She was shivering inside but it wouldn't do to show fear to this rude soldier. She saw the moment in which he recognized her. Some of her shivering quieted when he stepped back.

She patted the healing satchel at her side. "I need to attend to one of Agamemnon's captives. I am a healer." The soldier didn't look persuaded, but Briseis continued on toward the women.

Fortunately, Maira had noticed her and hurried over. "Lady Briseis, you've come." Maira took her by the arm and led her to the women's area.

Briseis resisted the urge to look back at the soldier's reaction. She whispered. "I told the guard I came to see to one of Agamemnon's captives."

Maira nodded. "I guessed that when you patted your satchel. The captives don't move about the camp. That guard shouldn't have let you in, but it seems like you managed it. No one else could." She smiled at Briseis. "It's good to see you. I'm so glad you dared."

"It's wonderful to see you."

They stood awkwardly for a while and then sat on a bench away from the others. After their initial greetings, they remained in silence. Their connection had always been unspoken.

Then Briseis leaned over and hugged Maira. "Everything's different now, isn't it?"

Maira nodded.

Briseis looked around. "Agamemnon's camp has far more huts for women and his shelter—it's a palace almost."

Maira shrugged. "He likes to look like the king of the whole army, not just his warriors from Mycenae. And he likes to have lots of captives. He has to house them somewhere. How many women's huts does Achilles have?"

"Just one. It's rather full, but our pallets do fit in one." Briseis counted six huts for Agamemnon. She remembered the much larger number of women he'd taken at the distribution than Achilles had been granted.

Maira hesitated. "I'm glad you came, but didn't it seem dangerous? I mean..." She shook her head. "You're not used to being—" She waved her hand to indicate the other captives.

"The soldiers left me alone," said Briseis. Maira laughed.

Briseis realized she'd never heard Maira laugh before—she liked the sound. "What?"

"You may be the only woman who can walk wherever you please —no wonder the guard let you in. They're all afraid you'll go after them with a sword. You have more courage than any of them and they know it. You fought against Achilles and lived."

Briseis shrugged. "I guess you heard about that. What I did wasn't so great, whatever the soldiers think. It was useless. Achilles still killed Iatros. I feel sick remembering it."

Maira put her hand on Briseis's arm. "You did everything you could to save your brother. To defend a sibling—that's not useless. It's love."

She'd acted from love, true, but also from something darker, a violent strength hidden inside her. "When I think about it, it felt good to fight back even if I didn't save Iatros."

"I understand," said Maira. "It's hard to be strong and yet powerless to take action."

Briseis grasped her hand. "You do understand. I'm only beginning to."

They sat, their silence companionable.

Briseis turned to her. "Do you ever wish you could have taken a sword to Mynes?"

Maira drew back in surprise. Briseis regretted her question— Maira's sympathy didn't mean she wanted to take up swords.

"I'm sorry," Briseis said. "I shouldn't have said that."

Maira shook her head. "It isn't that." She sat looking off in the distance. Then she turned to Briseis. "A knife, not a sword. That's what I always imagined."

They looked at each other and started laughing so hard the other women turned and stared at them.

"I don't know what made me say that, Lady Briseis," Maira sputtered.

"I do, and I agree with you. He's dead anyway, and I can't mourn him. I tried. And I'm not Lady Briseis anymore. We're two captives. Maybe less captive than we were in the palace?"

Not wanting to upset the guards by staying too long, Briseis said goodbye. She'd visit again. She returned to Achilles's camp where she worked with Eurome and the others in the lean-to kitchen through the morning and then asked them if she could rest. Smoke made her short of breath.

She went into their hut and closed the door. The only light came from the smoke hole. She was alone and grateful for that. She picked her way to her pallet, stepping around the other bedding and possessions. At her own bed, she started back in fear. Someone lay there, rolled up in a blanket.

Collecting herself, she touched the sleeping figure. It wasn't a soldier or one of the other women, mistakenly sleeping on her bed. Her hand grasped a tapestry, rolled in such a way it looked human in the dimness. She squatted down next to it and unrolled a portion with shaking hands. It was her tapestry—her tapestry of medicinal plants. Someone must have slipped it in here after she had gotten up that morning.

She spread it out to examine the healing plants and flowers scattered over its surface like a spring meadow. Even in the poor light, they appeared as fresh as the day she had last worked on it. No soot dimmed their colors. She ran her hands over its surface, feeling the variations of weave as her fingers moved over different flowers and leaves. Then she clutched it up in an embrace and wrapped it around her body. She had almost finished it when Lyrnessos had been taken. How had it ended up here, placed like an offering on an altar? Why hadn't it been burned with the rest of Lyrnessos? An unfinished tapestry was of no value.

Briseis untangled it from around her and examined the unfinished top. Someone had carefully cut it from the loom and tied each warp thread so it would not unravel. Who had taken such pains with a partially formed tapestry of medicinal plants? There was only one answer—only another healer would have cared so much, one who also had an eye for beauty. She remembered Achilles's delight in the fineness of his wine cup. A healer whose eye had been trained by the immortals. And he brought it to her.

25

THE RHYTHMS OF LIFE AND DEATH

B riseis lived amidst the constant noise of war from morning till sunset: bronze clashing, men shrieking, and horses—their death screams made her feel hollow. Each day she watched the two sides face off in battle, fighting like the stags on Mount Ida, their magnificent antlers locked together, pressing against each other but incapable of breaking off or overpowering one another. Each night brought her horrible dreams of wounded men, smashed babies and her brothers bleeding to death where she couldn't reach them.

By chance she found a routine that brought her a measure of inner stillness and helped her live with this turbulence. At dawn, before the battle started, she made several trips to the spring on the lower slope of the ridge, carrying a large pitcher. One by one she filled the storage amphorae and replenished the water supply in Achilles's camp. Most of the captive women feared the soldiers and did not wish to venture beyond the courtyard, but Briseis enjoyed the freedom and the soldiers gave her no trouble. At the spring, she could look out at the plain before it filled with warriors and death. She could breathe the silent air.

By the time she finished her last journey to the spring each morning, tired-eyed women had come out of the sleeping hut to start their chores, leaving it empty. She unrolled her tapestry in the sunlight by the doorway. She was left to herself, but she wasn't alone.

Looking at her tapestry, the memories unfolded: Mount Ida's meadows and flowers, the smell of pine and oak, the luxuriant green wherever a spring blessed the land. She could hear Maion explaining where to find a particular plant and feel Iatros holding her hand as they explored the woods. She could see her father breaking an olive between his fingers to test its ripeness and Bienor and Adamas standing in the wheat fields, the ripe grains waist high, as they helped their father oversee the harvest. She could smell the fragrant dried herbs in Antiope's workroom and the sharp scents of the teas and poultices. She found strength.

LATER, toward the evening on the day she found the tapestry, she had seen Achilles on his porch and hurried to thank him before her hesitation to speak to him overcame her gratitude. He must have just finished washing away the grime of battle because his skin was still damp, the fresh tunic clinging to his chest.

"Thank you for my tapestry."

His face broke into a smile. "I hope it brings you some happiness," he said, warmth in his voice. "If I had not discovered that work in the hall of a mortal princess—one whom I knew nothing about then but have since come to esteem—I would have assumed that, like the cup we studied together, an immortal hand had fashioned it. I could not bear to relinquish it to the flames, but I did not know how glad I would be that I saved it."

"I am pleased to have it, although you exaggerate its skill. I made it to remember the plants I use as a healer, but this morning it helped me remember everything." She felt tears threaten.

"That is good. You wanted to remember."

She had nodded and left the porch.

IN CONTRAST to the war the men waged, which kept her on edge, the women's tasks soothed with their repetitiveness. Chores which would have made her restless before, grinding grain, kneading dough, washing the soldier's tunics, now helped her feel calm and sturdy. Briseis enjoyed their communal life. Even simple activities, such as getting clean over buckets of water in the cramped confines of their hut, became enjoyable as the women worked through them together. After all the violence, the womanly touch of washing each other's hair helped mend their sorrowing hearts. They were allowed to take simple fabrics from the goods brought back from raids and created enough clothing to keep themselves decent and clean.

The chatter of women accompanied all their tasks. These women's conversations were new to Briseis. With her older brothers she had listened to their male adventures; with Iatros she told stories; with her mother and even Eurome, she had listened and questioned in order to learn; to her servants, she had commanded. These women talked to fill the hours. Briseis liked the relaxed purposelessness of it. To her surprise she had a place among these women, and they gave her the shelter she needed.

In return, she found that she could heal the women through her mother's rituals, designed to mend sorrow and restore harmony. For materials, she mixed herbs and roots, polished bits of wood, made clay forms and tugged colored wools from the upper row of her tapestry. As the months unfolded through the spring and into the heat of summer, familiar words, actions and scents brought healing and renewal to the other women and to herself.

EUROME HAD BECOME the errand runner. Any task too lowly for Achilles's heralds became Eurome's, and she carried around her neck an official token marked on a piece of leather so she could enter and leave the various stockades without trouble. For reasons different from Briseis's, she had decided she did not need to fear the soldiers— her old age precluded anything but insults, and Eurome's love of gathering gossip soon outweighed her concerns.

One afternoon in midsummer, she pulled Briseis aside in a rush.

"Oh, little Poppy, sit down and listen to what I heard. Some soldiers was going on about what they'd done in Lyrnessos. I been listening after anything about home, of course. Most of it ugly stuff I wished I could wash out of my ears, but there's one tale you'd care to hear, even though it's sad enough." Briseis felt her throat tighten. She had left behind so many unknown fates in Lyrnessos.

"In the temple. That's where those soldiers was, near as I could tell from what they were saying. Today as they went on about it, they were still grumbling about how they'd been told by their betters not to take the gods' statues or such like so as they wouldn't have the gods angry with them. Lord Achilles's orders, they said, and no one dares go against him. There was lots of things they could steal anyways, so they were busy at it and killing all the priests as the poor souls tried to protect their temple. I'm sorry to remind you of the priests dying. You went there often and must have knowed them. Strange to say, though, it weren't a priest that scared those big louts. It were a priestess. A priestess they come across in a little room with a silver goddess wearing a golden necklace."

"Kamrusepa." Briseis said, with a sinking heart.

"That's what I were thinking," said Eurome. "That necklace were too much for them. They'd been told not to touch any such like things, as I said, but it were too much. All that gold finery and them just rough men, not lords or anything. They'd never have a chance for such a treasure any other way and no one else around to see them at it—or so they thought. One man reached out for it, egged on, I can imagine, by the others. Then, like the angry goddess herself, a priestess rose from behind the altar—I'm guessing she were hiding there from the scoundrels like I would ha'—she rose up, as I say, and scared the daylight out of that man, what with raising her arms in the air like she were calling down all the gods on the man's head. I can see it myself, and that man were afeared right out of his wits."

Briseis felt a shiver run down her back. "Zitha!"

Eurome nodded. "Who else could it be? And you'll see from the rest that's who it were sure enough. Even with her rising up like that, the man still snatched the necklace, so the priestess screamed curses at him about wolves ripping out his insides since he'd ripped away the goddess's necklace. The man dropped it and ran. Can't you see it happening? Afeared out of his wits, I tell you. Zitha turned out to be a wild one after all, didn't she? I knowed she caused you a lot of trouble with that henbane and the queen before you made up as friends. She done too much this time, I'm sorry to say. Those men killed her to put a stop to that cursing."

"She was a brave woman," said Briseis. "She would have chosen to die at the feet of her goddess, I think."

Eurome patted her hand. "There's another bit that's downright satisfying, if I say so. Zitha might ha' gotten back a mite from them louts. The man who grabbed the necklace, well, he up and died sudden-like here in the camp. That's why them soldiers was talking about it. Everyone's saying how it were the curse that killed that man, the wolf curse, they call it. You told me there weren't no such curse, but it were satisfying to me to think it might ha' been Zitha's doing. A bit of revenge, I'm saying, whether it were or no."

"Perhaps she did," said Briseis. "I like that idea, too." She put her arm around Eurome. A healing goddess could kill with illness even if there wasn't a curse. Zitha had been brave to defend her goddess and to think of the wolf curse when she'd been beaten for it before. Her heroism was no less than that shown by her brothers as Lyrnessos fell.

EARLY ONE MORNING as Briseis brought the last of the day's water, she noticed Achilles talking with another warrior—a king, she judged, by the way he carried himself and the richness of the warm cloak he wore against the autumn chill. The man's head came only midway up Achilles's chest and he was somewhat bandy-legged, but he still exuded a smooth confidence that marked him as important.

Achilles looked at him as though the man gave off a noxious odor.

Why was that? Curious, Briseis lugged her pitcher of water over toward the large storage amphora that sat next to Achilles's porch. She had already almost filled it with water, but there was room for one more pitcher-full. From there she'd be able to overhear them. She set down the pitcher to warm her hands against her body under the length of rough wool she'd made into a cloak.

"Agamemnon would be in your debt," said the warrior. "He isn't asking for this without dire need. Food supplies are low again."

"You can tell the greedy swine," said Achilles, "to sell off some of his piles of treasure to buy food for his army. I will not go on another raid for him, Odysseus. You know that already. In my debt? The only debts Agamemnon recognizes are those he holds against others."

Briseis looked with greater interest. So this was Odysseus, the Greek with the silvery tongue—a different voice for each listener. That was the phrase Asdu had repeated—she'd overheard it from Achilles and shared it with the women when they were seated around the fire after dinner. The captives liked filling out the picture of the different Greek kings they'd first started back at home. In Lyrnessos they'd heard of Odysseus because he seemed the only Greek interested in negotiating a way out of the war. For that, her father had admired Odysseus, although he'd never met the man. Achilles didn't seem to share her father's approval of this king.

"The men need this, Achilles," Odysseus said. "How can they fight without meat in their bellies?"

Achilles snorted a bitter laugh. "How many times have you heard those words from my mouth, Odysseus? Did you think I would forget that they are mine? Your silver tongue is slipping. I can't be persuaded with such transparent tricks. True enough words, but tell the greedy sow to fill his men's bellies out of his own stores. Otherwise he may find himself buried underneath his stockpiles when they tumble down upon him."

Achilles made a dismissive gesture. Odysseus bowed respectfully, although Briseis thought he must be burning from the insult.

"I will relay to Agamemnon your eagerness to remain in the battles here, Achilles." Then Odysseus walked calmly away. The man had remarkable control. Briseis wanted to laugh at the way he'd turned that last parting into something positive. She wished she could hold her tongue so commendably.

Achilles took all the steps of his porch in one of his extraordinary strides so that he landed quite close to her. She realized he'd known she was listening in.

He smiled at her. "Never believe anything that man says without looking very carefully at who is to gain."

She nodded, somewhat startled by this odd confidence. "I will remember that, Lord Achilles."

They had talked together a few times since she'd thanked him for the tapestry, but only briefly. He usually greeted her with the solemnity appropriate to a court ceremony, but their conversations felt awkward and ended quickly. This peculiar meeting seemed even more strained than their previous ones. She pulled her cloak more tightly around her.

He never asked her to serve meals with the other young women. It relieved her not to have to be near him. The liquid movements of his limbs and his vigor stirred a response in her whether she wanted it to or not. She recognized his kindnesses and how well he understood her nature, but she could not forget her brother's bloody death. Achilles's presence threatened to tear her in two.

Achilles tipped his head sideways and he seemed to study her. She lowered her head.

"The war creates a great need for healers," he said.

She looked up. This topic interested her. Maybe he would ask her to help, although she'd never been taught how to treat a wound. She wouldn't be much use. She fought back the lump in her throat when she remembered wanting Iatros to show her. Without her dear brother, she couldn't imagine learning these skills.

She had seen the injured brought back and tended to by the healers in the camp, not only Achilles and Patroklos, but also two others, Machaon and Podaleirios, who were said to be the sons of a healing god named Asclepios. These divinely instructed men wouldn't value her skills.

"You are a healer from a family of healers," said Achilles. "Your mother before you and your brother, Iatros. I remember your matching satchels. I wonder—"

She balled her hands into fists. Hearing Iatros's name from his lips felt like a desecration. "Don't speak of him."

She couldn't betray Iatros, couldn't talk to this man about her brother. Bands tightened at her temples as her fury grew and threatened to boil over.

. Achilles's face flushed and his hands also turned into fists. His eyes burned into hers, disorienting her. Crashing waves reverberated inside her. He turned away abruptly and left. She swayed on her feet and grabbed the porch upright to steady herself.

Her anger at the too-familiar pain of her brother's death had flared quickly. She regretted her curtness, but she knew where it came from. She'd even mistreated Eurome when her nursemaid had gone on about Iatros. It was too painful to talk about her brother, and with Achilles, of all people, unbearable. She understood her response and yet this surge of emotion also felt foreign. She shook her head in confusion.

He disappeared into his shelter. She'd never know what he meant to say. She had embarrassed him, and besides, she had to admit he always showed respect for her grief. He wouldn't intrude if he thought he'd caused her distress.

AFTER A DAY that had gone badly for the Greeks—they'd suffered great losses, especially among the rank and file, something about a retreat that had gone wrong—the men returned to camp in a vicious mood. Nothing the women could do was right. The same bread they baked each evening was now too burnt or underdone. They were told their ugly faces were an offense, although usually the men bantered with them in a bawdy way, respectful of their commander's property but willing to enjoy a little harmless flirting with some pretty captives when he wasn't around. They'd been beaten and they were looking for someone to take it out on. A camp full of men who behaved like Mynes, thought Briseis.

She finished her tasks with relief. Most of the women retreated to their dark hut, but the sun's last light still glowed dimly on the horizon and Briseis wanted fresh air despite the chilliness that crept in as soon as the sun went down. She took advantage of the freedom she had won with that Greek's sword. She walked down to the shore of the bay where the breezes might bring her a breath of less fetid-smelling air.

She stretched her tired back and shook out her legs, stiff from crouching by the cook fire, then walked along the edge of the water in quick strides, enjoying her solitude. After a time, to her annoyance, she saw another person ahead of her, someone who frequently came to the sea, although whether for the breezes or because he was born of a sea goddess, she didn't know. She wished he hadn't chosen this evening. Quickly she slipped behind a ship hull until he had outpaced her far enough not to notice if she also took a walk.

She had come almost to the midpoint of the shoreline the camp occupied when she heard a loud exclamation. "Let go of me!" That was Maira's voice. Scuffling, blows. Briseis ran in the direction of the sounds. Dimly she saw two figures struggling. A man dragged Maira toward the open doorway of a hut.

"Leave me alone or I'll tell Agamemnon."

"I saved the winesack's life today, though you won't hear him tell the tale."

The man yanked Maira through the doorway. "He can share his women with one of his henchman today whether he wants to or not. I dare you to tell him."

Briseis ran. As she got to the doorway, the soldier flung Maira to the ground, his back to Briseis. Maira kicked out at him, but before she could scramble up, he kicked her in the belly, making her gasp for air, then dropped down and clamped both her hands against the ground over her head with one of his. Seeing Maira pinned like that, stretched out and exposed, enraged Briseis. He was ripping at Maira's clothes and yanking his own out of the way with his free hand. Maira screamed and he slapped her face and jammed his knee into her middle. Here was Mynes all over again. Briseis needed something to stop the soldier. A dribble of blood ran from Maira's nose and her struggling stopped.

Briseis scanned the meager fire in the middle of the hut and the cooking implements scattered around it. He was a soldier. There must be a weapon. Somewhere.

"That's more like it, bitch. Quiet now, like a good girl. I like a regular hole to plug and you're it." Maira tried to kick him, but she couldn't get free and he hit her again with even more force.

He leaned in over her face. "You tell Agamemnon and he'll have you killed. He won't share, but he won't take it out on a man who keeps the swords from his belly on the battlefield. I plan to cram you full every night."

Briseis leaned down toward the fire. Not again. Not to anyone she cared about. Her fingers grasped a filthy butchering knife partially buried in the ash.

He'd bared most of Maira's body and was intent on spreading her legs with his knees while keeping her hands pinned.

Briseis lifted the knife. She aimed for the soft area below the ribs and drove it in with her whole weight and fury.

The man bellowed like an ox. Briseis yanked out the knife, shoving him over on his back with her foot, off Maira. She silenced him with the knife in the hollow of his throat. Blood went everywhere and the man lay dead. She shivered, but at the same time burning heat lifted her.

Maira scrambled away from her. Briseis had to explain, to make that shocked look soften. "Mynes used to laugh, 'I'm going to plow you every night.' When Mynes was forced to stay behind, when he was so angry at me and everyone for losing out on the chance to kill some Greeks, he took all his rage out on me. I wasn't going to let this filth do that to you. He's probably the same monster who threw babies against the wall when they destroyed Lyrnessos. I saw that. Now maybe I won't keep seeing it in my nightmares every night."

Movement in the doorway made her turn with a start. Achilles stood there. Maira gasped. Briseis helped her up. Maira pulled her torn clothes around her body, her arms wrapped tightly around herself.

Achilles glanced at the dead man, at Maira, at the blood splattered on Briseis. He nodded as if they'd explained what had happened.

"I'll drag this corpse to where the rest of the day's dead are still piled, waiting for burial. Only the princely dead received honors today. One more will never be noticed, and this offal less than most."

He looked at Maira. "Hide what happened here, for her sake—" he indicated Briseis, "—and for yours. Go now."

Maira nodded. She looked at Briseis and started to reach for her, but her tunic slipped and she clutched it again. She bowed her head to Briseis and slipped out of the hut.

26

STRONG LOVE

Achilles turned to Briseis. "Wait for me here while I—" He indicated the body. "You must not be seen like that." She looked down at her blood-drenched clothes, nodded and dropped the knife. Achilles hoisted the body and left.

She shook uncontrollably, but she didn't regret killing the man. She didn't feel repulsed by what she'd done, but exhilarated. She'd never liked attending while the priests sacrificed the sheep and cattle, hating the blood flooding into the sacred bowls, but this drenching made her feel strong. This must be how warriors felt in battle.

She held up her blood-soaked hands. They looked like Achilles's hands covered in her brother's blood. A dam gave way inside her and a flood washed away the aversion to Achilles that had held her tighter each time she remembered her brother's death. Iatros's loss did not grow less painful, but she couldn't condemn Achilles any longer for having the same inner urge, as a warrior, that she had discovered in herself. She'd attacked twice—no aberration born only of a single moment, but a part of her true self. This time she'd killed a man. With relief, she no longer felt torn in two when she considered Achilles's nature. She understood it. She knelt and washed her hands with a pitcher of water.

Achilles returned to the hut. He watched her and she looked him in the eye. A fire kindled within his sea-green gaze. "You really are a warrior. A fierce one." He looked around the hut. "Did you know that woman?"

She nodded and stood up. She wondered how to describe who Maira was to her—long ago she had ceased to be a servant. Circumstances and understanding had created a bond as close as the one she had shared with Iatros. "She is like a sister to me."

"Then you had no choice."

The final knot let go inside her. He understood.

He stepped closer to her, moving around the fire pit in the center of the hut. "When I am on the battlefield, it's the same. Every man around me is my brother." He put his hands on her shoulders. He hadn't touched her since he took her hand at the assembly. Awareness of each of his fingers and the powerful palms pressed into her, rippling through her. "Can you forgive me?"

She knew what he meant. He'd had no more choice when he'd killed her brother than she had when she lifted the sword, when she plunged the knife. And she understood rash acts.

He didn't wait for her to answer. He leaned down and pressed his lips onto hers. His hands slid from her shoulders to her lower back, pulling her against his body, melding them together. For a moment she remembered the blood, and then it didn't matter.

His hands sent hot waves through her. She needed his skin against hers and pulled at his clothes. He smiled at her eagerness and lifted his sword belt and tunic over his head, and she untied his underclothes, letting them drop to the ground. She shivered at his beauty and ran her lips down his chest, softly undulating over the muscles and contours.

"Off with yours, please," he said.

She smiled up at him and undid her belt, tossed off her dreadful clothes.

He embraced her so powerfully that she was lifted off the ground and wrapped her legs around him. Her arms braced against his shoulders as he slid inside of her, moving her body in a rhythm that submerged them both in an oblivion of heat.

When he released her gently to the ground, she began to tremble again. Achilles wrapped his cloak tightly around her.

"It's the aftermath," he said. "When the battle madness passes. Every warrior with a heart goes through it—you can't quite take in what you've done. There is a necessary horror. Let it shake you. You are strong."

He pulled on his clothes and his sword belt, then tied her clothes into a bundle. "You'll need another skirt and tunic. These belong in the sea." He looked at her. "Can you walk or shall I carry you?"

She felt herself blush. He read her thought. "We might never get out of this wretched hut," he said, laughing. "Walk, then."

On the way back, they walked down to the shore where the ripple of waves curled against the pebbles and dragged them with a soft rumble. He flung the bundle of bloodied clothes far out into the bay and suggested they take advantage of the dark cover of night and the sea water to rinse themselves off. She shivered at the idea of being wet on this cool autumn evening, but the desire to be rid of the blood won out.

The sea actually felt warmer than the cold air, and the sensation of floating next to Achilles brought back her vision during the Spring Festival. She reached for him and enjoyed a watery embrace. When they left the water, Achilles bundled her in his thick, warm cloak and, without drawing anyone's notice, she followed as he entered the courtyard and slipped into his shelter. She stood inside, unsure what to do about her nakedness under the cloak and her lost clothes, but he went to a chest in one corner and searched. He came back to her with a folded pile of rich fabrics.

"See if any of these suits you. They are yours in some way in any case. Loot from the towns surrounding Troy. Your father gave you an eye for fine armor. My mother taught me a taste for fine weaving. Remember?"

She took the beautiful garments and chose the least showy. Still, with its pleated, forest green skirt with crimson and lapis lazuli colored braid and matching tunic and belt, she wondered how the other women would react. Standing there holding her new clothes, she felt shy about revealing her nakedness again. He leaned down and tipped her face up to his, kissing her lightly.

"You've been through a great deal tonight. Sleep in your accustomed place with Eurome to care for you." He smiled. "She'll raise an alarm if you don't get back soon."

He turned away and busied himself in the back of his shelter while she quickly slipped into her clean clothes, enjoying their feel even while she felt guilty at the luxury. How was she going to explain them to Eurome?

As soon as she had brought the water in the morning, she told Eurome she was going to visit Maira before the rest of the chores began. She had already told Eurome that Achilles had given her the clothes and been annoyed at Eurome's knowing little smile. The tumult of last night left her confused. The feeling of exultation had worn off, and she both longed for it to return and feared it. She didn't need any comments from Eurome.

Maira had taken several hard blows last night. Briseis worried about her. With her healing satchel on her shoulder, Briseis received permission from the guard on duty at Agamemnon's camp and entered the women's area, but Maira wasn't there. She walked around the cook fires, checking for her in the lean-to.

"Looking for Maira?" one of the women asked. Briseis nodded. She had visited Maira often enough to be recognized, and the occasional healing work she'd done for Agamemnon's other captives gave the guards good reason to allow her visits. They never challenged her at the gate anymore.

The woman looked concerned. "Said she weren't feeling well and stayed abed. There's plenty here to do the work. She does more than her share most times, so we haven't let on to them." The woman tossed her head toward a group of soldiers bent over some armor they were repairing. "That hut, over there on the far side of the kitchen fires. Good thing you come today."

Briseis thanked her and went into the hut where Maira lay on a pallet not far from the door. Briseis left the door partly open for some light. As Briseis sat down next to her, Maira opened her eyes and smiled at Briseis.

"How are you? Do you feel badly hurt?" asked Briseis, kneeling by her.

"Sore, but not too bad." Maira's voice was low but she sounded like herself. "I'll mend. Bruised—but not where it shows. Easy to pretend I'm just sick."

Briseis nodded. "You didn't have trouble getting back inside the stockade?"

"No, the gates were open. Agamemnon was expected back, I suppose. That's how that swine got hold of me—I was fetching wood from the pile by the gate. He hauled me out and dragged me down to his hut."

Briseis thought of something else. "I better sew up your clothes as well as take care of you."

Maira nodded and pulled out a basket of sewing things. "Thank you—for everything. I couldn't have . . ." Maira shrugged.

Briseis understood. She found it hard herself to believe she'd stabbed a man. She was glad Maira didn't know what came after— that had confused her even more. Achilles had said something about battle madness, and what they had done felt like a madness.

"I'd been lucky so far," said Maira. "Agamemnon's left me alone."

Briseis looked carefully at Maira's bruises. She began to lay poultices on the worst of them to speed the healing. "Let's hope you stay lucky. He's repulsive."

Maira shuddered. "True. I feel sorry for the unlucky. Do you see a small girl huddled by one of the fires—blonde and tinier than the others?"

Briseis pushed the door open a little wider. She recognized the fair-haired girl first chosen by Agamemnon's herald at the assembly.

"That's who he takes to bed?" Maira nodded. "She seems more a child than a woman."

"I think that's the point," said Maira, her tone grim. "Agamemnon likes his women timid and childlike. That poor girl isn't strong like you and me."

Briseis finished checking Maira's hurts, relieved that Maira could move without causing herself sharp pain. She threaded a bone needle to repair Maira's clothes.

"Who is she?" Briseis asked. "I noticed her at the assembly. She was dressed like a girl of royal birth."

"Not quite royal. Her name is Chryseis. Her father is a priest whom King Eetion of Thebes held in great esteem. Chryseis's mother died when she was five, so the king invited her to live at court. I keep hoping Agamemnon will tire of her and choose another bedmate. Many of the women find the status they receive recompense enough, but they are the sturdy ones, used to hardening themselves to circumstances."

Briseis handed her the repaired tunic. "That's lovely," said Maira. "You made the repair look like decoration—like it was meant to be there."

"Mmm, it did come out well, didn't it? The skirt's a bigger job."

Maira seemed about to say something, but she stopped. Briseis kept her eyes on her sewing. She hoped Maira didn't ask her about her own beautiful clothes.

Instead Maira said, "Your poultices are soothing. Talking with you has helped also. You're a good friend. I felt bewildered when I returned last night. You've put my feet back on the ground."

Briseis glanced at her. It was an odd expression, but she knew what Maira meant. For Briseis also, their conversation had returned her sense of stability. She wondered if her feet would stay on the ground when she saw Achilles again.

She sewed while Maira rested, her eyes closed. When Briseis finished the mending, she laid it next to Maira and whispered a good-bye.

Maira nodded and mumbled a sleepy farewell.

Briseis walked back toward Achilles's camp. Strong—Maira's word echoed Achilles's—and she and Maira were strong. She'd prefer to think of her actions last night as strong, not bloodthirsty. She'd built strength all her life—from her healing work and from her family. Her new strength—being a warrior able to protect—felt akin to her previous experiences. She'd felt so trapped by Mynes, caught in a sticky cobweb of the fear he caused, that she'd lost this sureness somewhere. As a little girl she'd had it. She welcomed its return.

She thought about the ordeal Chryseis had to endure. The girl seemed so frail by nature—of all the women, the cruelest choice for Agamemnon to make. She wondered why Chryseis did not have the inner strength she and Maira had found. They'd had similar noble upbringings. Briseis considered Antiope's exacting expectations of her as she prepared her to be a healing priestess, her brothers' reliance on her, the casual way her father had consulted her as they walked together about the estate: all these relationships grounded so firmly in love. She fought back tears. She missed them, but they were with her every day. She held them inside as fully as a honeycomb holds its sweet nectar.

Briseis hurried along. She'd been gone a long stretch. Nonetheless, she stopped when a vine with yellowish fruit caught her eye, growing in a sloped area off the path. She stooped and gathered the fruits—colocynth, a strong purgative. Adding to her store of medicines was nearly impossible in the camp and she wouldn't miss this opportunity.

The army had not mustered for battle. She saw soldiers building pyres along the shore and surmised the two sides must have declared a truce for burials. It had happened before. She shuddered at the thought of one of the corpses that would burn—one who had not died on the battlefield but by her own hand. She kept away from the shore.

The gates to Achilles's courtyard were open as his men came and went. She thought her return would go unnoticed, but as she scooted across the courtyard toward the women's area, juggling the colocynth in her arms, Achilles stepped out of the blacksmith's

lean-to into her path. He was pulling a long leather strap through a
bronze loop and knotting it. She moved to the side to avoid
running into him. He saw her and his face lit up. Her heart
pounded.

He held up the bronze loop. "A repair for my chariot." He looked
at her armful of fruits. "What have you got there?"

"Colocynth. I'll dry it and grind it."

He nodded. "Strong medicine. Careful how you use that. I hadn't
noticed it. Was it growing in the camp?"

"On a kind of rough hillock by the path that goes through the
middle of the camp."

"Oh, I always walk by the shore—or up on the ridge." He smiled.
"I'm about to go check on some of the men who were wounded
yesterday. Why don't you come with me? If the Trojans keep this up,
we'll need another healer."

Now her heart leapt—to work fully as a healer again! Then she
frowned when she remembered how little she knew about wounds.
She saw Achilles's face fall.

"I don't know how to care for wounds," she said in a hurry, so he
wouldn't think he'd made her angry bringing healing up again.

He looked confused.

"I'd like to learn," she said. If she didn't learn how to mend battle
wounds, she'd have almost no healing to do here and she needed her
work. It was part of her. Iatros would forgive because he would
understand.

"I would like to teach you."

She smiled. They each gathered their healing materials and went
into the camp.

As soon as Achilles knelt beside the pallet of the first wounded man,
concern filled his face and his eyes burned with a fiery light. She
wondered if he were angry at himself or someone else for the
soldier's obvious downturn. The man's feverish flush worried her.
Without thinking, she reached into her satchel for pounded willow

bark and asked one of the nearby soldiers for boiling water. Achilles glanced at her and nodded.

He lifted off what remained of a blood-soaked linen bandage. The man had knocked most of it off in his delirium. The bloody, angry gash across his thigh made her stomach roil, but she willed it quiet. Some birthings had been worse. The flesh that needed to close the wound gaped open. It would never heal like that. Achilles touched the wound as he checked for festering. The man's groans mounted to screams.

Achilles looked at her. "We'll wash the wound again and try to seal this with better bandaging." Achilles looked over his shoulder at the soldiers who shared the man's hut. "You must keep him still when the fever makes him thrash. The bandage has to hold shut the wound."

Achilles showed her how to wash the wound with warm water. He ground a small root to dust between his palms and placed it into the gash, quieting both the man's screams and the bleeding.

"What is that root?" she asked.

"One of Chiron's immortal herbs. I don't know if men have a name for it. Most physicians use astragalos root."

She nodded. She had some of that in her satchel. It had many uses around blood.

Achilles added, "Both slow the blood, but only Chiron's takes away the pain. Did you know a sword can wound the gods? They cannot die, of course, but they do not bear pain with patience, hence Chiron's skillful cure. I have enough of my mother in me to work it."

"Astragalos for me, then," she said. He shrugged in apology and nodded.

Achilles took out a roll of fresh linen. He showed her how to bandage with thin strips crisscrossing the wound and tied together behind the leg.

She realized why the man's movement had loosened the bandage and caused the wound to gape again. Achilles had bound the wound firmly, but the linen could be shifted sideways too easily.

"May I try strengthening the bind with some sewing?"

Achilles's eyebrows shot up in surprise, but he nodded. Briseis thought of the pattern of supporting pieces Milos used to hold together the bands of metal in chest armor. She folded linen into tight narrow strips several layers thick and stitched them into a firm support that she sewed along each side of the crisscrossing bandage. When she had added several bands under the man's leg connecting these two supporting strips, she was able, with Achilles's help, to pull the wound more tightly closed and keep it in place with her stitches on the bandaging.

They both leaned back from their work. A lightness filled Briseis's chest. She reached out and tucked under a bit of the bandage's linen so that it wouldn't catch on anything.

Achilles took her hands and lifted them to his lips. "Stitches? That's the trick?" He laughed. "No wonder we men never figured it out. Your sewing looks like the pattern on some chest armor. That's what you copied, isn't it?"

She nodded, feeling proud but a little shy.

"The stitching warrior. My fierce stitching warrior." His face glowed. Then he sighed. "On to the next wound. Let's hope this is the only man who's sickened like this. It's a bad sign."

They stood up and he spoke to the men standing behind them in the hut. "Keep him still. And give him more sips of this willow bark around nightfall." Achilles clasped her hand tightly as they left the hut.

27

A TOO-BRIEF FEAST OF FIRE

Achilles and Briseis traveled around the camp taking care of men with a disorienting array of wounds. Each one posed a new challenge, a puzzle of body and linen and suffering. The intense work absorbed her completely. She forgot her awkwardness around Achilles.

"Will you feast with me and my friends around my fire this evening?" His question took her off guard despite their long day working side by side. Soon after dinner came bed. She remembered his naked beauty. He was giving her a choice if she could bring herself to refuse him.

"I shall sing you another story."

She smiled. He understood her well.

Briseis helped Iphis and the other women bring in and serve the meal. She knew she held a different status than the others, but she did not want to be separated from the women.

While Achilles and she ate, Briseis described the medicinal herbs that grew by Mount Ida's springs, and he told her about plants from his home in Phthia. They found many in common. The other men around the fire talked little, but from their pleased expressions, she guessed they had been waiting for her return. These men loved

Achilles and wanted him to have whatever he wished in his life. She wondered if any of his friends understood why Achilles had waited for her to choose him when he could have taken her by force. She barely did herself, although his delight in her strength as a warrior, as a healer—this respect could not countenance force. He gave her the honor he demanded for himself, sweet nectar for her soul.

After dinner, Achilles took up his lyre and sang the tale of Peleus and Thetis. She remembered how it had stirred deep inside her when she first heard the bards sing it. Achilles had been part of her life even at her father's hearth. This time her spirit rose up to meet the song. His version emphasized his father's persistence and then Thetis' delight when she accepted his love.

Achilles stood after his song and the others rose to go. He took her hand and brought her onto the porch as he said goodbye to the men.

"Will you walk with me?" he asked when they were gone. "The stars and moon are bright and I need the fresh air of the sea. I like the crisp chill of autumn nights."

She nodded, blushing at the thought of their nocturnal swim the night before. He reached inside for two of his cloaks, wrapped one of them around her shoulders, threw the other over his own and led them toward the trail onto the ridge. Even by moonlight the path was shadowy, but he had no trouble climbing and held her hand so that she would not stumble.

They reached the top and the sea spread out below them, glistening in the moonlight. They walked to a spot where the rocky spine of the ridge formed a crescent. Inside this sheltered bowl the grasses flourished, creating a soft mat. He spread his cloak on the ground and seated her on it with a little bow as if she were a queen.

He sat behind her, his legs and chest becoming her throne. She leaned back against his body, her arms resting on his thighs. She felt his face relax into her hair, heard an intake of breath and his moan of desire as he took in the scent of her. He kissed her ear, then her neck and wrapped his arms around her, pulling her close. She entwined her arms around his. A tingling rose from deep within. He rested his chin softly on her shoulder, and they both looked at the shimmering water.

"I feared after the battle lust had waned, you might withdraw from me again. You haven't, have you?"

She shook her head and kissed his arm.

"The sea is as filled with light as I am at this moment," he said. "I would have waited longer for you, but restraint—I struggle with it. Giving myself to you completely is far easier than waiting."

"Are you mine completely?"

"Yes. I have no ability to hold any part of me back now that I have started." He drew in a sharp breath. "Not all of my nature is easy to hold onto."

"Not all of mine is either."

He laughed gently. "That much I understand, but I promise to hold on anyway."

"And I to you," she said without reserve, although she knew she had agreed to hold onto fire.

She tipped her face up and his mouth found hers, hungry, devouring her as she remembered from her dreams. She turned her body so she could run her fingers through the cascades of his hair showering her face. Offspring of the sea, his movements, his body, even his hair, were fluid, balancing precariously between ocean and earth.

He reached for her waist and she felt her skirt loosen. She sought his mouth, sweet as honey. Under her tunic, the lightest touch up her belly, a pause and then his hands caressed her breasts. A delicious sensation surged through her and she forgot everything else in the delirium. Whose moan of pleasure was that?

He pulled off his tunic. His chest shone in the moonlight. She kissed the hollow of his neck and moved down his chest. She wanted to feel her skin against his and slipped her own tunic over her head. While her arms were raised, he caught one of her breasts in his mouth and she lost herself again.

He laid back. She tugged the last of her skirt off with one foot and spread herself over him. Heat vibrated off his body. He was made of fire and water. When they joined together, she was filled with feelings far beyond the capacity of her spirit and body to contain—pleasure and delight, pain and despair also, fiercest bonding, radiating out from her in dancing flames.

Satiated, they lay back together. She watched his chest rise and fall with his breath. She felt his need for her as tangibly as she felt the heat where their bodies touched.

They lay there until the cool night air made her shiver. Achilles reached for his cloak to cover her, and she sat up so he could wrap it around her, but she was overwhelmed with dizziness. Achilles cradled her against his chest.

"When I hold you," he said, "I feel quiet. Most of the time the sea waves crash around me. I am torn and lonely. In the midst of that, you bring a stillness and I feel peaceful. How can you do that? No wonder you are unsteady from it."

"How can I bring you steadiness?" she asked and held him tighter. Tears poured out. In this time together she had felt flooded with emotions, far from the calmness he described. If these ups and downs she felt, which he called sea waves, had passed from him to her, she did not mind. Her loneliness and sorrow had also washed away. Achilles rocked her until the tears stopped flowing and her breath grew even.

He kissed her. "I told you not all of my nature is easy to hold onto."

She laughed. "Parts of you are very pleasant to hold onto."

ACHILLES AND BRISEIS returned from the ridge to his hut. She slept by his side and had no nightmares, awaking from what seemed at first one of the delicious dreams when Telipinu had come to her. Now he was real, coaxing her awake with caresses until the fire in both of them burned so hot that she floated in an updraft of pleasure.

When they lay still, she savored this flesh and blood man and her own eager body. To endure her marriage she had left her body behind. Achilles's touch brought it back to her. But morning had arrived. She embraced Achilles, gently pushed aside his answering caresses, dressed and went out to bring the day's water to the women.

Returning with the first jug, she watched the women's reactions and was relieved at their usual cheerful greetings. She didn't want her friendships with them to change. When Eurome saw her, she smiled happily. By her last trip to the spring, fresh bread lay fragrant in baskets, and she took one into Achilles's hut.

He smiled as she came in. She handed the bread to Patroklos who had turned from the spits of meat he was tending on the fire to watch Achilles's reaction to her entrance. He nodded as if his friend's happy expression settled some doubt he had harbored.

She bent over Achilles to give him a kiss and see what he was doing. He held one of his leg greaves, inspecting the silver links that joined the front and back pieces at the ankle.

"A few days ago Hector had a lucky throw," he said, "and his spear nicked my left greave." Briseis pictured the deadly spearhead so nearly missing Achilles's calf and had to lean against his chair. Achilles pulled her onto his knee. "See here—the link twisted a little but I can't see any other damage. The armor Hephaistos made for my father has served me well again."

"It's your father's armor? How is it that it fits you? Are you the same size?"

"No. He was a great warrior, but no one matches my size. That came from my mother, whose forms are boundless."

"Then how can you wear his armor?"

"Hephaistos's immortal armor fits each warrior who wears it, although I sense when I lay my hands on it, that it must find a fire in the heart of the warrior that responds to the immortal flames in which it was forged. Perhaps if a coward like Agamemnon put it on, it would rattle about him like an oversized cage."

Patroklos laughed. "Or squeeze the life out of him in disgust."

She took the greave from Achilles and felt its weight in her hand. "What is it like to fight each day?"

"Each day? Not so different from a single fight against the mightiest Greek warrior in defense of one's brother—" He dropped his voice. "—or against the worst of the Greeks." He squeezed her against him. "It is both exhilarating and dreadful. I'm not sure I can explain what fills me when I fight. I think you have felt it—a fire and a strength that I yearn for. It's only afterward when I'm cleansing a comrade's wound or carrying the fallen off the field that I realize that I have taken men's lives, and I shudder. But if I did not ward off death from my friends in battle, I could not live with myself."

Patroklos nodded as if he understood. The individual confrontation made sense to her, but not this willingness to carry on the war month after month.

"The men talk about your fighting as if you alone could drive back the Trojans—win the war all by yourself. That seems true. The other day I watched as you entered the battle—your golden armor and chariot are easy enough to pick out from the masses—and the Trojans scattered before you like rabbits when a fox enters a meadow. If your strength and fighting prowess so far surpass all others, why does the war drag on so long?"

"What you cannot see are the gods fighting on the battlefield. Each time I reach for Troy's citadel—there are moments when I can almost feel its stones crumbling under my hand—I feel the arm of Apollo or one of the other gods who favor Troy pulling me back. It is not fated that I should take Troy. Another will do that. So my mother tells me, although she says the glory of my brief life will be never-ending."

Briseis twisted to face him. The immortal greave slipped from her hand and crashed to the floor.

"What do you mean?" And then she didn't need him to explain—didn't *want* him to. He would die before the walls of Troy—that was what he meant. A searing pain tore into her chest as if one of those same gods who pulled him back had struck her with his immortal fist. She panted in agony and saw her sorrow reflected in his eyes.

"If I left Troy and abandoned my men—my brothers—I might live longer, but I can't, even for you." He shrugged—he could do nothing about fate, his shoulders seem to say. She closed her eyes.

She had promised to hold onto him, but fate would not grant them long for their love.

Achilles wrapped his arms gently around her. They sat in silence like that until after a time he spoke. "I have little to offer you during this wretched war except my love, but I promise when finally Troy falls, you will return to Phthia as my wife and you will be welcomed by my father Peleus and honored in his household as a princess."

He kissed her hands and then her lips, and as she kissed him back, she felt the shadow that lay between them—a shadow he needed her to understand. He had not said he would bring her to Phthia, only that she would go there.

Patroklos was taking the spits off the fire, and with a sigh, she rose to help him place the meat on platters and tried to shake off her melancholy. She wanted to be happy in her new love.

As Achilles and Patroklos ate with the necessary enthusiasm of two men who will fight all day, she pictured her brothers, whose appetites had similarly amazed her. The familiar gripping at her heart that held in her grief whenever she thought of her lost family did not come. Some force opened the wellsprings of memory and she traveled through vivid scenes, sensing her brothers as if they were alive with her. She felt dizzy and closed her eyes to quiet her mind.

These feelings were like the deluge of emotion she had gone through yesterday—Achilles's storms. The wild outpouring overwhelmed her at first but also felt healing. She welcomed it. She liked the intense images in her mind and she discovered she wanted to ride out the storm. Last night Achilles told her she brought him inner quiet. Perhaps Patroklos had been right—only she could heal Achilles now. Achilles gave her the power to weather her grief and she gave him peace. This was her place now.

When she opened her eyes, Patroklos was studying her. Achilles strapped on his greaves and then his breastplate. He reached to catch the shoulder strap of his armor. She stood on tiptoe and tied it for him.

With an eerie sensation she watched him transform from her lover into a warrior god. She touched the stars that glowed on the breastplate, studied the bronze layers topped with gold that seemed to meld to the contours of his chest. The workmanship mystified her.

He slid his sword belt over his head and across his chest, then grasped the silver-encrusted hilt to adjust the height to the correct angle. The bronze blade slid against its scabbard as he partly withdrew it, making a scraping sound that filled her mind with blood and her tongue with a metallic burn.

Achilles touched her cheek. "My beloved who admires armor. Is there some way in which you are not the perfect wife for me?"

"Hephaistos makes extraordinary armor, and I wish I could understand how he constructs such things, but its beauty does not lessen its terror," she said.

Sadness shadowed his eyes. "I forgot. This is how I looked when I killed your brother." He cradled her face in his hands. "This too is who I am."

She kissed his lips.

He put on his helmet, which Hephaistos had also plated in shining gold. Achilles's long hair flowed out below the helmet, covering his neck and shoulders, the lighter sheen of hard gold against his fluid gleam, reminding Briseis of both his unyielding strength and the deadly, immortal flame that even he could not contain.

He took his ash spear up from where it rested against the wall by the door and then shrugged and moved his torso and limbs to settle everything into place, the weight and heft of all of it, a second skin. He smiled at the feel of it and turned to her.

"I will introduce you to Xanthos and Balios."

She looked up, puzzled. "Xanthos and Balios?"

He took her by the hand. "My horses."

They went outside, and she saw a groom trying to yoke two elegant horses to Achilles's chariot, one white, one tawny gold. They stamped, snorted and then reared in unison. The groom jumped out of the way. He saw Achilles and bowed.

"I'm sorry, Lord Achilles. They are usually cooperative, but today—"

Achilles walked up to them, Briseis close behind. The horses stood alertly looking at her. Their eyes were strange—almost human. Achilles chuckled and gave each of them a rub on their faces.

"I'm sorry for the trouble," he told the groom. "I suspect they didn't wish to be yoked when they met Lady Briseis. I can't blame them. It's best to have all your resources available when you first encounter her."

He turned to her. "Lady Briseis, this is Xanthos, and this is Balios." The horses lowered their heads until their streaming manes brushed the ground.

She found herself bowing in return. They raised their heads, and she saw pity and unspeakable sadness in their eyes. She stepped back, startled.

"They are immortal," said Achilles softly. "They know my fate and pity you your love for me." Xanthos laid his golden head over her shoulder and Balios nuzzled her hand. "They like you. I knew they would. Now under the yoke, my friends."

His fate. Her chest ached again. She had lived in his love for such a short time and already she had been forewarned twice of his fate. How could she bear to love this man when fate would soon intervene? Why did death follow her every step?

Achilles laid his spear on the ground and walked to the other side of the chariot to adjust the horses' head straps and thread the reins through the rings on the yoke.

She felt a hand on her shoulder and turned to see Patroklos. "Do not despair. With Achilles you must live as much as possible as though he were an ordinary man. The immortals have special knowledge, but we cannot live with that awareness of the future always in our minds. Not even he can manage that. Uncertainty and hope are as essential to man as breath." Patroklos took her by both shoulders and they stood silently for a moment. The grooms had brought out Patroklos's horses and chariot. He turned from her and swung up behind his driver.

Achilles pulled a last strap tight by Balios's shoulder and returned to Briseis's side. He lifted her high into the air.

"Wish me well," he said.

She looked down into his face, surrounded and intersected by the bronze helmet. She placed her hand on his armor. "Guard my love well, armor of Hephaistos." Then she put her fingertips to his lips.

He placed her back on the earth and leaned close. "I will be thinking of tonight when I'm not wearing any armor." Then he swept his ash spear from the ground and leapt into his chariot.

His charioteer held the horses with difficulty. Briseis watched the magnificent creatures. *Xanthos and Balios cast aside their sorrow and leap toward the battle—how else can one live with Achilles?*

As she joined the women working in the kitchen area, she thought about fate and living with immortal knowledge. Her mother and she had performed divinations to gain that divine understanding, and it had brought them no good. Her mother had died. Briseis's divinations on behalf of Lyrnessos had failed to save her city—or her brothers. Immortal knowledge only brought sorrow.

Briseis felt heavy with these thoughts, and she wanted to be joyous in her newfound love. She slipped away from Achilles's camp to visit Maira. It was difficult to find the words, even with the bonds they shared, but she described her attachment to Achilles, his respect for her, his offer to bring her home as his wife and the bewildering emotions that had thundered through her—a storm she savored. Maira listened but said little. Her gleaming eyes told Briseis she understood.

28

FREEDOM AND FETTERS

That evening Achilles returned, gladdened by his victories on the battlefield and joyous to see her. He removed his armor and let her douse him with buckets of water to wash off the slaughter of battle until, wet and naked, he laughingly beseeched her for his clothes, or better yet, their bed.

Later, the friends Achilles most valued gathered to eat together: Patroklos, Aias, and Phoenix. Aias said little, as usual, but Phoenix charmed her with stories about the infant Achilles. Because Phoenix could have no children, he had devoted himself to the little tyke. Briseis smiled at this expression applied to Achilles, but she guessed at what lay unspoken in Phoenix's affectionate stories: that Thetis had returned to the sea when she had failed to make her son immortal. Her grief at knowing she would someday lose her son had prevented her from enjoying his childhood. Phoenix cared for the lonely baby like a mother. He regaled them with stories of Achilles's tantrums when anyone but Phoenix tried to feed him and how he burped on his shoulder. Achilles finally quieted the old man's reminiscences with an arm around him and a promise not to burp on his shoulder. They all laughed.

As the discussion moved on to a review of the day's fighting, she felt impatience at the continuing stalemate; then, with a sick feeling, she realized what the war's end would mean—Achilles's death, the fate his mother foretold. She felt Achilles's intolerable bind: He fought for Troy's fall, but with it, he would bring his sure death.

She shook off this thought. "Please sing a tale."

He lifted her hand to his lips, and his eyes lit with a mischievous flicker.

His song celebrated Prometheus's clever stratagems on behalf of man over Zeus, the selfish king of the gods. Briseis had never heard this story. The Greek bards in her father's hall had sung of mortal heroes for the most part, since their gods differed from hers.

Achilles's Zeus became tricked by his own greed, picking the sacrifice of barren bones wrapped deceptively in juicy fat. No one missed the reference to Agamemnon. Achilles, the half-immortal, described a comic scene of gods and goddesses jostling each other to better sniff the offering. Even while Briseis laughed, she trembled at the familiarity her lover felt in the world of gods, his ability to insult them without fear of reprisal. Her telling of sacred tales, even when visions filled her, had been bound by mortal limitations that Achilles could never understand.

The tale shifted to Prometheus's courage against Zeus's cruelty—when he lay chained to a mountain while eagles ate his innards. Was that how Achilles felt when he acceded to Agamemnon's demands? Briseis froze with tension until at last Achilles described Prometheus breaking free with Heracles' help.

After the feast ended, Briseis and Achilles sat talking by the fire.

"Prometheus freed himself of Zeus's shackles," Briseis said. "Can't you refuse to follow Agamemnon when he acts only from greed?"

Achilles let out a rumble like waves crashing against rocks. "If only I could. It isn't that simple." He pressed his face into his hands as if pushing back his emotions.

He sat up straight and looked at her with a far away expression. "If I faced Agamemnon alone—this war and all the men fighting in it no longer existed, the other kings gone—then I would crush him with my bare hands and feel peace." She clasped her hands over his.

He shook himself. "We are brother kings, two among many. I cannot be disloyal to a brother, even one I hate. He brought far and away the greatest number of ships and men, and because of that he believes that he holds sway over the rest of us. By all men's reckoning, he does. Only my immortal strength tips the balance—and only if I forget the responsibilities that I hold as a king. I cannot, will not forget—those duties serve as the shield that protects all my men."

He stood and paced the room. "If I refused to fight, I would be letting down my fellow warriors, true brothers. Unlike Agamemnon, I claim them as brothers not by right of rule but by shared courage and danger on the battlefield. For them most of all, I swallow my disgust when Agamemnon struts like a cock claiming more authority and honor than his deeds have ever earned. He bought his power with his wealth from Mycenae, and now he forces all of us to serve him and swell his mounds of treasure so that he can satiate his seamy and salacious avarice."

Achilles's eyes glowed with their inner fire. She felt the embers scorching. He cried out in rage. "I despise bowing to a lesser man, a false and hollow leader, but loyalty compels me."

He knelt in front of her, burying his head in her lap, his arms wrapping around her. She held him and stroked his back, feeling his heat dissipate. She knew how it felt to show respect you did not feel for a selfish, foolish king. She had thought only her weakness as a woman and her forced obligations as wife had sprung the trap. Achilles suffered a humiliation similar to her own, for all his strength as a fighter and power as a king. She had to think about that.

"My husband ruled as Agamemnon does," she said, trying to find the words that would show she understood, without offending him. "You are held by loyalty—not unlike my obligations as a wife. I understand the mortification you feel." He raised his head. "Mine was a more intimate humiliation, but I know what you feel." She remembered Maira's comment that it's hard to be strong and yet powerless to take action.

She pulled Achilles against her and he lifted her out of the chair in an embrace of despair. Her body understood how to sooth his grief as he had soothed hers. They escaped into a frenzy of pleasure and kept the dark at bay.

THROUGHOUT THE AUTUMN and into the winter months, when disease as well as wounds needed her cures, Briseis's reputation as a healer spread. The men brought the injured to her, appreciating her salves and skill at cleaning out wounds, and especially her swift needlework with bandaging. She noticed the men preferred the reassurance of a woman when they came down with the usual illnesses that the cold and dark months brought with them.

When the fighting turned against the Greeks—and those times came and went with no pattern she could understand, unless, as Achilles had said, it was the gods' interference—then she and Achilles worked side by side in a crush of desperation. His skill in taking away the pain of a wound still confounded her. He taught her many of Chiron's techniques, those a mortal hand could perform. He adopted her style of stitching bandages, although it had been difficult for him to master and he was nowhere near as swift with his stitches as she was. She kept to herself her glee over her prowess in this area.

Some days the fighting halted. Sometimes the winter weather made even desperate battles impossible to fight and the two sides could not muster on the plain before Troy. Then everyone huddled inside shelter, and Briseis and Achilles sought their own ways to keep warm through the damp.

At other times the war was interrupted for the grim task of gathering the dead for proper burial or for fruitless negotiations between Greeks and Trojans. These days provided time for Briseis and Achilles to escape in some measure from the war. Healers stayed away from burials unless those near to them had died, and no one would send Achilles on a diplomatic mission—that was Odysseus's job. Like Briseis, Achilles spoke what came to his mind and could not hold his feelings in check. She and Achilles took advantage of these days to wander the countryside renewing their stock of medicinal plants and minerals. His invincibility allowed them to go where they liked.

Along the shore, there was no mistaking his inborn understanding of the sea's plants and creatures. She was in her element when they went into Mount Ida's foothills. Between Troy and Lyrnessos lay a mountain range with Ida's central peak rising above many lesser peaks, sprawling foothills and valleys. She was far from her home, but the woods and springs on this side of the mountains supported the same living things. They quickly added to their stores all the plants and roots that could be gathered in the winter months.

Sometimes, when the fighting went on without a break for too long, she and Achilles slipped out of the Greek camp at night in order to taste the freedom of the mountain. They would choose a clear night when the winter storms had abated. Achilles could walk through the woods by moonlight as easily as midday. He had found a secret route on the ridge above the palisade and gates so they could avoid the guards who would report their actions to Agamemnon, an unwelcome intrusion on their privacy.

She had not wandered so far and freely since before her marriage. She had never done so with a partner as in tune with the forest. Her mother and Maion had taught her the plants they viewed as useful, but Achilles's senses reached into all the life of the forest. He could hear a fawn's breath as it hid in the underbrush and peek at the delicate creature without startling it. By some ethereal hint in the air, he could track a plant by scent. She hadn't thought anyone aside from herself could be so captivated by simple offerings to the senses. To find this mutual celebration gave her peace, and her spirit, broken loose from palace and camp, felt joy without shying away from the wounds and grief that also resided there. In the hidden places of the woods, their heightened sensibilities intensified their lovemaking.

Contentment and purpose filled her days, although war and fate both loomed over her if she did not keep them away by an act of will. She preferred to live as Patroklos had advised, without trying to know what the future held, as though she were not in love with a man who, though more than mortal, was subject to a mortal's fate.

At moments she recognized something else bothering her, some sensibility, like a dream she couldn't remember on waking, that lingered just beyond her understanding, a visceral obligation she had abandoned but could no longer identify. She didn't pursue this uncomfortable inner voice, but even so she sensed some other purpose was trying to find its way to her if she chose to listen. Life with Achilles gave her pleasure enough to shut out anything else.

BRISEIS WANTED to visit Maira more frequently, but the growing tension between Achilles and Agamemnon kept her away. She feared her presence might spark something worse now that she was so closely associated with Achilles, but when she received a message from Maira that Chryseis needed her help, she chose to risk it.

Briseis slogged along the sodden paths, choosing her route carefully since it had rained overnight and some of the paths became muddy rivers. As soon as Briseis arrived at Agamemnon's camp, she saw why she had been called to help the unfortunate victim of Agamemnon's lust.

Slumped and shivering by a cook fire set up inside one of the lean-to kitchens, Chryseis, willowy before, had grown gaunt; her eyes deadened to a haunted emptiness. She appeared even more childlike in her suffering, but still beautiful. Her blond hair cascaded about her face and shoulders in a luxuriance at odds with the thin face, but the sharp definition of cheekbones was still lovely.

Maira whispered, "You see how she is. We can't rescue her from Agamemnon's bed, but is there anything else you can do to help her? What she needs is a resilient spirit, but . . . Perhaps I called you here for nothing."

"I'm glad you did, although I'm not sure what I can do."

Briseis sat down by Chryseis and rubbed her shoulders and arms to warm the girl, but Chryseis didn't look up at her. She wanted to understand this girl with the curious childhood: fostered in a royal household, almost parentless, pampered and privileged, and yet not completely belonging. The intimate wounds Chryseis endured from

Agamemnon could rip out a person's roots. Briseis knew that from experience.

Chryseis responded to her greeting with an unintelligible murmur.

"Maira mentioned you grew up in King Eetion's palace. Tell me about your life. Remembering the people and places we knew before this war can comfort us."

Chryseis looked at her, puzzled. "Why should I tell you anything?" Chryseis's sullen expression made her look even younger, more a spoiled child than an injured woman.

Briseis took a deep breath and held back what she might have said. "Because it might cheer you to talk about happier times. We probably share experiences in common as noble women."

"Not like these serving women." Chryseis tossed her chin disparagingly in the direction of Maira and the other captives. Briseis wanted to shake the girl. How did Maira have such patience, first with Hatepa and now with this girl?

"What did you enjoy?"

Chryseis sagged and her head fell forward like a rag doll's. "I miss my father," she sobbed. "He brought me presents." She raised her head. "Once he gave me braiding from Crete for a new skirt. He paid an exorbitant price—two gold cups. It was even prettier than the trimming on Lady Andromache's wedding dress."

The momentary vitality vanished from Chryseis' expression. "It's all burned up. Maybe my father could buy me more. He's the priest on the island of Chryse, so he wasn't in Thebes when the Greeks killed everyone. But I won't see him again."

"Perhaps you will someday," said Briseis, although that seemed unlikely.

"I was betrothed," Chryseis blurted out. "King Eetion held a feast to seal the agreement between my father and Lord Armati. I watched him from among the women. So tall and slim, very handsome. I couldn't hear what the men laughed about, but he sounded happy, and I know he would have loved me."

So the Greeks had destroyed Chryseis's world when she was on the verge of having what she most wanted, a handsome, carefree husband to love her. She'd been forced into servitude instead. Whatever her marriage might truly have brought, Chryseis would always believe in its perfection, Briseis guessed.

This conversation would not bring Chryseis strength—quite the reverse.

Healing prayers had comforted many of the captives. Chryseis's father was a priest; his daughter might cherish the gods. Perhaps Kamrusepa would bring strength to this child.

Briseis took a piece of kindling from a pile by the fire and lit the tip.

"Chryseis, in Lyrnessos, I was Kamrusepa's priestess. I will pray to her for your good health. She has great power."

Chryseis nodded solemnly and concentrated on her. As Briseis recited the prayer, she moved the burning twig slowly around the girl's head.

"Mother Kamrusepa looked down from the heavens.

'Where is my Chryseis? Why do I hear her call?'

Kamrusepa says: 'Take the fire and touch her with it.

Let her illness ascend to Heaven.

Look! My child Chryseis shines with good health.'"

Briseis buried the burning stick in the dust. To her relief, the prayer soothed Chryseis. *Please, Kamrusepa,* she prayed silently, *care for this girl.* Looking at the translucent, pale skin drawn over the thin bones that defined Chryseis's face, Briseis felt a new foreboding, although she did not see how this girl could be the source of her misgiving.

29

PLAGUE

Alull in the fighting came as the Greeks focused on guarding and unloading cargo from ships that arrived in the small harbor by the fort, now that the worst of the winter storms were over. Agamemnon engaged in a lively trade of wine and foodstuffs with Lemnos and other allies. He exchanged the wealth brought in through Achilles's raids for supplies—which he sold back to the army.

Gossip about one of the Greek ships drew Briseis's interest. A priest had brought gifts in order to ransom his daughter from Agamemnon—this must be Chryseis's father. It had taken time for her father to gather the ransom because his patron, King Eetion, had been killed and the kingdom looted.

That evening Briseis asked Achilles whether Chryseis's father had been successful in his appeal to Agamemnon.

"When the priest appeared before the assembled kings, we thought Agamemnon would take the ransom," said Achilles. "The gods must be honored, and greed has always won out with Agamemnon. To our shock, he told the priest he wouldn't hand over the girl."

"Oh! That's terrible."

Achilles nodded sympathetically. "He insulted him, saying things no father should have to hear—how much he liked her in his bed, even better than his wife. If Agamemnon's wife Clytemnestra hears that, he may regret keeping the girl."

Achilles looked at her with a puzzled expression. "I never paid attention to Chryseis. Is there something extraordinary about her? We told Agamemnon to respect the priest and return his daughter. Her father spoke politely—he asked the gods to give us success in plundering Troy. He offered a huge ransom. Even Odysseus did his best with his crafty words to change Agamemnon's mind and bring him to a wiser choice, but Agamemnon screeched that he'd kill the man if he ever came seeking his daughter again. Shameful to treat a white-haired man that way. The old man seemed like a dried leaf being crushed to nothing, yet I fear his power as a priest. The gods often take offense at the mistreatment of their priests."

"Poor girl. I don't know why Agamemnon wants her so much. She's pretty, but so are most of his captives—and he has so many. She seems to be dying a little more every day. Agamemnon's a pig." Her sense of foreboding returned, stronger than before.

SOON AFTER THE priest's departure, the illness broke out. It made little sense to Briseis. The days were beginning to warm and camp life grew less miserable. With spring on the horizon, disease should have retreated, not taken over the camp. Nonetheless, men lay dying all over the Greek camp, their necks and groins swollen with blackened sores, their strength drained by bloody coughs. Day after day, Briseis, Achilles and the other healers tried in vain to staunch the scourge that ravaged the camp.

BRISEIS SAT BACK on her heels and searched for a pitcher of water among the scattered pots at the soldier's hearth. The sick man groaned as Achilles worked a poultice into his swollen armpit. The smell of rotted meat rose from their patient. Briseis stepped outside to ask a soldier huddled nearby to bring water. "Is he better?" the soldier asked. She shook her head. These men, undaunted in battle, paled before this monstrous disease.

She knelt beside Achilles. They needed water to wash the man's blackened fingers and toes. She removed the linen bandage as gently as she could from his foot. His toes came away with the fabric. Achilles exclaimed in horror. She gagged, turning away to collect herself.

A soldier appeared in the doorway, pitcher in his hand. "What's wrong?"

Achilles stood quickly and took the water before the man could see. Briseis rose and pressed close to Achilles until the soldier turned and left.

They crouched down again by the sick man. The man coughed and choked on his blood. They lifted his chest to help him breathe, but what little life he had, left him.

Briseis wound his body in a blanket, stitching it closed to spare the men this sight as they carried him to one of the many pyres that burned without stop all over the camp. Achilles lifted the bundle, stumbling as he did so. *Achilles, my love, you can run all day without tiring, but now you stumble.*

When they had laid the dead man next to the others waiting to be burned, Achilles turned to her.

"The sun is setting. Has it set two times since we rested? I can't remember."

She nodded. When a soldier approached to bring them to another stricken man, Achilles shook his head.

"Find Machaon or Podaleirios."

Sleep came as soon as they lay down, wrapped around each other. When Briseis awoke, she knew a whole night had passed. No one had called for them. Perhaps death had claimed everyone and that explained the quiet.

Her head rested against Achilles's chest. His breathing told her he still slept. When she moved so that she could look into his face, she saw tears slipping from under his closed lids. She touched his pillow—it was soaked with his weeping. She pulled him tightly against her body, willing him comfort. She too began to weep. Into her mind came an image: the last many days reflected on the surface of a dark pool, the sores and pus, the dead piling up on all sides. She looked into Achilles's despair.

He had failed his men. He was a warrior and a healer. By both he had held off death from them—until now.

Gradually his tears ceased and his face softened. She felt life coursing through her body, holding at bay the darkness they had battled for days. Achilles moved in his sleep, settling against her body. She drew her fingers from the contour of cheekbone and shoulder to the smoothest skin in the hollow where his leg joined his hip, and down the muscle banding from there along his thigh. The wonder of his beauty took her breath away.

When he opened his eyes, she read the despair in them, but she did not let the darkness reclaim him. She wrapped her legs around his hips and asserted the strength of her love with her whole body, sparking his passion to affirm life for this short time.

DAY WAS BREAKING when Briseis and Achilles rose from their bed. They dressed and went outside to find something to eat before returning to the dying.

Eurome was already awake, and over a pot of warm water, a bleary-eyed Patroklos scrubbed his face, chest, and arms.

"Have you been caring for the sick all night?" asked Achilles.

Patroklos nodded.

"Eat a meal with us," said Achilles, "and then go sleep. We have rested and can manage."

"So many are sick—"

Achilles's face clouded over. "Do we save any of the sick? You must sleep. We do little but sit by while the men die—are we healers anymore? Others can keep the dying company since we do nothing more useful than that."

Eurome brought them bowls of stew. She gave Briseis a reassuring hug. "The other women and I prepared a fresh supply of bandages. I'll bring you the basket of them and your satchel."

Briseis thanked her and answered the unasked question. "I'm holding up. A long sleep helped."

"You both looked barely alive when you came back. I kept away the messengers. No point making the healers sick with exhaustion." That explained the peace, thought Briseis.

Patroklos, Achilles and she ate without speaking. An eerie silence from the Greek ships weighed down the morning.

Patroklos scraped up the last of his stew with a piece of bread. He described the unrelenting course of the plague during the night. "We must end this or it will be the ruin of the army."

"Devastation like this comes from the gods," said Achilles. "We must ask for divine guidance about how to make amends."

Briseis felt suddenly cold. She put her bowl aside. She had made similar appeals to the gods for her mother and for Lyrnessos.

"Briseis," Achilles said, "your mother taught you divination, and Kamrusepa is a healing goddess. She will tell you what we must do."

She shook her head. "You are goddess-born and can speak to the gods yourself."

"You misunderstand because my mother and I talk together, but I have no skill at divination. It must be you."

"Don't ask me to perform this divination for you." Already she saw messengers approaching—more sick to attend to.

"You heard Patroklos. We must find an answer. Haven't you seen enough suffering?" Patroklos moved over to stand behind Achilles, his hands resting on his friend's shoulders.

Anger flared in Briseis. "I want this plague to end as much as you do, but you don't understand what you're asking of me. I will no longer make any divinations. I performed many on behalf of Lyrnessos, and it lies in ruins. You talk of my mother teaching me divination, but after I sought guidance through a snake divination, she died of a disease the goddess had given me no help in understanding. The answer to this plague doesn't lie in immortal knowledge. What good has divination ever done you, of all people? Your mother has foretold your death, and yet, much as she yearns to change this fate, she can do nothing. Immortal knowledge does not bring well-being. When you tell me to read the will of the gods, I feel the cold hand of fate."

"I didn't know this about your mother's death, Briseis, and I'm sorry. Still, we must stop this plague, and the only way is through the gods."

She looked at Achilles. "You stay at Troy where you know you will die. Even when the gods give you the clearest warning they could—leave now or be killed—you do not heed it. Why would any divination I perform be different? What good can come from it? Even if the gods shared some truth with us, we would be stopped from changing what is fated. Isn't that what you've learned? Knowledge from the gods brings me grief."

"I must stay at Troy to protect my men—my brothers. This divination would be different. We will find how to cleanse this illness from the men. That is why, despite the grief divination has caused you, you must—"

"No! The Greeks have seers. Let the leaders of this army consult them, if you insist on divination. When the gods confound your wits through the answer you receive, at least I will not have been the prophetess of your undoing."

He looked at her in sorrow. "If I do not ask the gods, the men will die. Would you have me do nothing?"

"What we do as healers is not nothing. Let us use our skills—" She pointed to the bandages and satchel that Eurome had placed next to her. "We'll bring what we are able to these men. We cannot see the end of this, but it will come."

Achilles shook his head. "It isn't enough. I cannot accept the death of so many. If you cannot perform the divination for me, I will seek out one of the Greek seers." He rose and strode out along the main path through the camp.

Briseis went to the messengers who waited impatiently for the healers' help.

SHE WORKED all morning and into the afternoon, going from one dying man to another. A few times she thought she might bring someone through, but each time the angry circles of red bulged forth, their hideous centers turning from white to rotted black. Then the blood ran from the body's orifices and from the putrid sores.

In the middle of the day, she heard the heralds calling the kings to council, but neither she nor the ordinary soldiers who assisted her asked what the Greek leaders discussed. Thus she was unaware that this assembly determined her fate.

By late afternoon, hungry and tired, she returned to Achilles's camp. To her surprise no one stopped her to attend to the sick. Her body dragged. She had not seen Achilles all day and wondered whether he had received the gods' answer from the Greek seer. He would have come to tell her of any good news, surely. She shrugged to herself—no more than she expected. They'd have to fight on as best they could.

Too tired even to greet Eurome, she slipped into Achilles's shelter. She pulled off her cloak and turned into the quiet room.

Achilles lay in Patroklos's arms. She recognized the force of entwined limbs, the use of body to calm the inner tempest. She too had held him like this. The sight stung her. She knew Patroklos had learned this skill long before she had, but she thought he had given way to her. Achilles had told her she brought him a blessed stillness. She had told herself it was a gift that was hers alone to give. Now, seeing them together, she realized the love of Patroklos was equal to her own. Anger burned in her. Patroklos had returned to a place she had thought was hers.

Patroklos saw her. He untangled his legs from Achilles's, and as he rose, Achilles turned, and her eyes met his—they blazed with rage. She backed out of the room, confused and frightened by the force of Achilles's anger. What had happened?

On the porch, she turned when she heard footsteps behind her. It was Patroklos, his eyes flashing in anger that almost matched Achilles's. He stumbled. When she reached out to catch him, she grabbed flesh so hot she feared he must have been overcome with the plague.

"That half-witted winesack. Who does he *always* take from?" Patroklos swung out as though to hit someone. Briseis tried to get him to sit down, but he lurched away and turned to confront her. His voice sounded like Achilles's. "For months that sniveling rabbit's heart has said, 'Achilles, raid this town, raid that town'—never mind that those towns never did anything against Achilles. Did it matter that the Trojans never insulted Achilles, never stole his wife? 'Do all the fighting, Achilles. Bring all their wealth to me, and I will give you some little thing in return—some small insignificant thing. And then I'll take it away. Your honor be damned. That's what our fine king said today. You weren't there when I finally dragged Achilles away from that assembly. Did you have too many dying to attend to? That's the king's fault too, though now there's only a small comfort in knowing."

"What are you saying, Patroklos? Are you talking about Agamemnon?"

Patroklos shoved his face into hers. She stepped back in fear. "He's taking you—you! What a fool he is. He has no idea the harm he's done. At least you won't be here to see—" He tossed his head toward the open doorway. "—what's left when the fire gets through burning." Patroklos held his head in his hands and writhed back and forth.

"Tell me what has happened. What do you mean 'taking me'?" She pulled him down to sit on the porch floor. He slumped against her as though some seizure had finished with him.

"Are you sick? Why is Achilles angry?" As she asked, she understood what had struck Patroklos. Achilles's anger filled him—a fire far too fierce for him to quiet no matter what he took into himself. No waters on earth could quench it. Divinity scorches mere mortals who interfere. She had seen it in her vision, calmed immortal rage as Kamrusepa's little bee. 'I burn up your anger, I sweeten your heart.' She needed to know why Achilles raged.

Gently she raised Patroklos's head and tried to get him to look at her. Beads of sweat ran down his face. "What has Agamemnon done?"

Patroklos's eyes rolled back and his head wobbled on his neck as if its weight were far too much for Patroklos to sustain. Briseis pressed her hand on his brow; he felt cooler now. The fit passed. She glanced through the open door, but she could not see Achilles.

Patroklos sighed and understanding returned to his eyes.

"What has happened, Patroklos? Please, tell me. What has angered Achilles?"

"You didn't hear?" She shook her head. "Achilles and the other kings consulted Calchas, the seer who can read the gods' will from the flight of birds." She could barely hear Patroklos's words. "It was that girl Chryseis. Her father is a priest of Apollo, the archer god, the one whose arrows rain down sickness upon those who anger him. When Agamemnon refused to release Chryseis, her father prayed for our destruction, and Apollo answered his plea. To propitiate the god, Agamemnon has been forced to give Chryseis back. She's gone. The plague will end. Agamemnon has ordered the soldiers to purify the camp now that the source of the plague is gone."

"Why is Achilles angry? This is good news."

Patroklos shook his head. "You were right. Divinations do not bring well-being. The plague may be over, but worse will come. Do you think Agamemnon gave up his prize so easily?" His voice had a bitter edge she had heard only from Achilles when he spoke about the king.

"Agamemnon said he would take a prize from one of the other kings. As soon as he made that threat, he revealed the war for what it truly is—his own selfish stockpiling of wealth. At that point Achilles threatened to stop fighting, to go back to Phthia. He had come to Troy out of camaraderie, not self-aggrandizement. Agamemnon, the half-witted heart of a doe, egged him on and said he didn't need Achilles." For a moment Briseis's heart leapt. They would go to Phthia, deny fate, and live a quiet life of peace. Then she remembered—he would never leave the men, not even for a happy life with her. Either he defended the men or his life lost its meaning. She could not ask that of him.

Patroklos echoed her thought. "Achilles will never leave Troy, abandon his men—he only said that in anger. But Agamemnon doesn't understand that, so when Achilles threatened to leave, Agamemnon had to prove his power over him."

Briseis suddenly knew what Patroklos had meant, 'he's taking you.' Her chest seized. She could not draw in breath.

Patroklos held her hand limply, still drained. "I'm sorry. Nothing could be worse. Agamemnon couldn't resist the perfect insult—to take from Achilles the most famous captive in camp. To him you are only a prize. He does not realize what your loss means to Achilles and therefore to the whole army. Achilles's rage has already grown beyond control. Fire burns indiscriminately—destroying the precious as well as the chaff."

30

HOLDING ONTO FIRE

Briseis needed to speak to Achilles. She would not become Agamemnon's captive. Achilles had to stop Agamemnon before this quarrel went any further. She couldn't understand why Achilles hadn't already put an end to it. She left Patroklos and went inside.

Achilles sat in his chair by the hearth. He stared unseeing, his white knuckles and taut muscles revealing the battle within. She went toward him, expecting him to respond to her presence, but she hardly recognized the being who sat like burning stone. His skin had lost all color, tension had hardened flesh to marble, and yet, even without touching him, she could feel the heat. His rage consumed him, leaving no room for the man she loved, only the god.

She knelt beside him and laid her hands over his. He spoke.

"When he said he would take you, I wanted to kill Agamemnon." Anger contorted his voice. "You as his prize! I drew my sword to run him through. I charged toward his gluttonous belly. Then, suddenly I was caught by the hair, ripped backwards as though I were a child. No man can restrain me like that. I looked in shock and saw the goddess Athena. She, who usually delights in war, stayed my hand and denied me the satisfaction of killing him. I was forced to obey."

An agonized moan wrenched through him. "I cannot turn my hand against my own men—even Agamemnon. He will take you— there is no way for me to stop him."

"What are you saying?" Briseis stood and backed away from him. "You will abandon me?" Her voice rose. "You will let Agamemnon drag me into his bed? That is what you want?" She was screaming— she shouldn't feed his anger, but she couldn't stop.

"No!" Achilles shouted. He leapt from his chair and lunged at her. "No!"

She stood unflinching, and he turned aside, grabbing his chair and hurling it across the room, sending splinters in all directions.

He grabbed her by the shoulders. "I have no choice. I cannot kill that winesack—although I want nothing more. Even if I could forget myself as I did in the assembly, the gods forbid it. Would you have me take up my sword against Athena? I can't stop him from taking you." He pressed her against his chest with crushing force and buried his face in her hair.

His breath scorched her scalp as he spoke. "Since he must take you, all I can promise you is that I will stay away from the fighting and force him to return you to me. He will long for me in the fighting and that longing, if the gods will it, will bring him to his senses. In his great need he will return you."

She pulled from his embrace. Like birds caught in a snare, she saw the trap that closed around them. Only if Achilles stayed out of the fight could he force Agamemnon to release her from the hated king's clutches. And yet, fighting beside his brothers on the battlefield was the one thing that gave Achilles's life meaning. The rage this trap had created would destroy everything. Her body shook so hard she couldn't stand. She sank to the ground.

Achilles began to move around the room and she lifted her head to watch him. He paced liked a lion when hunters have cornered him, ready for the kill. "I will fight again when the swine restores my honor." She saw the man disappear further as he faced his hatred of Agamemnon. Inner fire flashed in his eyes. "The day will come when he is forced to call on me. Then he will restore my honor."

Briseis leapt up. "*Your* honor! What about my honor? My body?" She grabbed his shoulders. Her anger would break the stone that trapped him. It didn't matter to her what fury she unleashed. If he destroyed the entire camp in his rage, she would at least be free of Agamemnon.

"Don't speak to me of your honor. What do you think Agamemnon will be doing to me while you sit by your ships? Picture that disgusting beast forcing himself on me—think what that means to me."

Achilles yanked away from her grip. A searing scream exploded from him. The room shook, the air vibrated. She felt as if a lightning bolt had pierced her center, but she also felt a flash of hope.

She turned to him. He could not bear her abduction and somehow he would spring this trap. Her hope faded. She saw marble fate held him trapped. She would pay the price.

A gentle hand fell on her back and she turned in surprise. She had not been aware of Patroklos's entry.

"Didn't he ever warn you," Patroklos asked her softly, "about his nature?"

Achilles's words spoken on the ridge over a moonlit sea came back to her: "Not all of my nature is easy to hold onto." She had agreed to hold onto fire.

She nodded. Patroklos said, "When a man tells you who he is, believe him."

Patroklos hurried after Achilles, who had gone outside. Briseis stood in the doorway. In the courtyard, Achilles approached two men she recognized as Agamemnon's heralds. The speed of their arrival took her by surprise. She had thought she had time.

Instead she watched Achilles greet the two heralds in stiff courtesy, reassuring them that his anger was at their king, not them. She realized if the selfish beast had come for her himself, Achilles would not have found this control. Agamemnon had disarmed him in this cowardly way, using, once again, Achilles's loyalty to the men's well-being.

She heard Achilles ask Patroklos to bring her outside to the

heralds. How could he do this? He wouldn't even take this last opportunity for a private good-bye? How could he send Patroklos to retrieve
her like some prize to be handed over—that's what she was to
Agamemnon, but not to Achilles.

She turned back inside, fighting the tears. Hurriedly she threw
her small possessions in a sack, tucking Iatros's healing satchel
inside, and then she drew hers over her shoulder. She glanced at her
tapestry, knowing it was safer to leave it in Achilles's camp. Patroklos
waited in the doorway. Eurome appeared behind him and pushed
past.

"You know?" Briseis asked.

Her old nurse nodded, weeping. "All the camp did but you—you
were with the sick. My precious girl, I'll come see you." She shook her
head. "Don't worry, this madness will end, I'm sure." Briseis clung to
Eurome for a moment and then raised her head and followed
Patroklos into the courtyard.

Achilles did not acknowledge her presence. She started to reach
for him and then realized from the hardness of his face that he had
no choice. If he saw her with his heart, nothing would contain his
rage. Kamrusepa had given her the gift to contain the sacred fury, but
she must be able to wrap her arms around the god and cover him
with sweet nectar to do it. To his grief, Agamemnon had interrupted
the rite. The fields and rivers would burn, the bodies would lie in
unbearable piles. She shuddered.

She stood beside Patroklos while Achilles called on the two
heralds as his witnesses and declared, "If ever the Greeks need me to
beat back destruction, they will not find me on the battlefield. I will
be by my ships, and it will be on Agamemnon's head that his men
perish without me." The trap tightened until none could breathe.

DAZED, Briseis followed the heralds. The sun hung low on the horizon. The final line of the Myrmidon ships lay ahead—the end of
Achilles's camp. She saw grim-faced soldiers dragging buckets of

seawater from the shore and scrubbing everything in their camp—purification now that the plague's source had been undone, but at what cost to her? When they reached the last of the Myrmidon ships, she stopped and refused to move. She would not leave Achilles's camp.

Agamemnon's chief herald took her arm, but she turned on him, possessed by rage. "Think what you are doing! You are bringing your own destruction. Do you think Lord Achilles will fight in Agamemnon's war after that wretched king has taken me and stripped Achilles of his honor? What will happen when the best warrior does not fight for you? Think, before you drag me like a sheep to the slaughter."

The two heralds drew away from her in alarm. She knew the tales about her made the men fear her. Perhaps she could terrify them enough to let her go. They certainly had reason to fear what lay ahead if they did not.

"Mark my words. *You* are the sheep sacrificed on fate's altar. You will die if I am dragged to Agamemnon."

She ran toward Achilles's shelter.

The heralds froze. Then she heard the pounding of their footsteps as they chased her down. Her arm jerked back as one of them caught it. She rolled to the ground and they hauled her to her feet, forcing her along between the two of them. The guards at the stockade gates of Agamemnon's camp drew back from them as they came through, and the heralds threw her into one of the women's huts, tossing her to onto the floor as they might a rotted carcass. She heard them clamp a bar across the door.

The last daylight came dimly through the smoke hole. She called softly for help to Agamemnon's women. As the heralds dragged her in, she'd had no chance to see anyone, but Maira must be there. No one came. They'd put her in the hut furthest from the kitchen area. It had only a few pallets laid out in it. She called more loudly, but gave it up when no one answered. None of the huts were very far from Agamemnon's shelter. He always held his possessions close. How could she expect captives to risk his anger?

She lay down on a pallet and eventually slept. The old night-mares returned: burning streets, strangled babies, mangled bodies, and her brothers lying in pools of blood; then, as she watched them die, they changed into one form, Achilles, white, drained of life, unreachable. She awoke damp with sweat from her frantic dreams. Someone dragged at the door's bar. It opened slowly.

She sat up. Against the backdrop of a cook fire's light, she saw Maira.

Maira knelt by her. "I would have come sooner, but Agamemnon's heralds kept watch. How are you? I'm so sorry."

Briseis clutched Maira to her. She sobbed in relief at hearing the gentleness of her friend's voice.

"What am I going to do?" Briseis buried her face in Maira's shoulder and wept. Finally, she pulled away and sat up. Maira poured her a cup of cool water from a pitcher she'd brought in.

"What did you say to the heralds?" Maira asked. "I heard them warning the others to stay away from the seer prophesying evil. Are they fearful of some divination you've made?"

Briseis shook her head. "I made no divination. Achilles believes the only way to force Agamemnon to give me back is to withdraw from the fight. It doesn't take a seer to understand what will happen to them without Achilles fighting. I tried to frighten them into letting me return to Achilles, but here I am. You won't get in trouble for coming to see me, will you?"

Maira shrugged. "Agamemnon called the heralds into his shelter." Through the open door, she indicated the grand wooden structure Agamemnon had ordered built for himself. "I don't think Agamemnon means to keep you locked up, anyway. The heralds just panicked. I'm sure you can come out and sit with us now. You must be hungry. Those foolish heralds can't expect you to starve."

Over food, Maira and the other women reported what gossip they had gathered about the assembly—not much more than she already knew. One of the women, in horrified tones, described Achilles advancing on Agamemnon with his sword drawn, clearly about to kill the king. That part was satisfying—Agamemnon cowering as

Achilles fought to keep her. Then, said the woman, no one knew what had happened—a mist, a cry of rage from Achilles, and then he sheathed his sword. The woman described how Agamemnon claimed a victory and reminded the assembly that he, the most powerful of the Greek kings, would take Achilles's prize. Briseis could see Agamemnon's swagger. No wonder the assembly had filled Achilles with uncontrollable anger.

The others nodded when the woman said it was shameful for Achilles to attack the great king Agamemnon. They mourned their lost families, but if forced to choose sides among the hated Greeks, they already felt an allegiance to the lord who held them captive. The women understood they'd be loaded on ships by their captors whether the Greeks sailed away in victory or in retreat, so they were gradually accommodating the sorrow in their hearts to accept their new master. Briseis didn't blame them, although she could not imagine feeling anything but hatred toward the greedy fool of a king.

Agamemnon's chief herald appeared outside the king's shelter. He looked over at Briseis and hesitated. She sat up taller when he walked toward her. Despite his obvious fear, he told her to follow him. Maira laid her hand briefly on Briseis's arm in support. Briseis's knees buckled as she stood, but she locked them underneath her, unwilling to show her fear before this rat of Agamemnon's.

The massive pine timbers that formed the entryway of Agamemnon's shelter glowered down at her as she followed the herald onto the porch. When she stepped inside, she was taken aback by the tapestries hanging on every wall, the elaborately carved chairs and tables, the conspicuous piles of gold and silver cups, pitchers and platters on shelves.

Agamemnon sat alone. She was shoved forward until she stood directly in front of Agamemnon's chair; then the herald slid outside. She heard the door shut. Agamemnon took a long drink of wine from a gold cup. His eyes moved over her body. He was slavering about his mouth and his hand rubbed slowly at the bulge in his lap. His eyes, when she held his gaze, revealed drunkenness and fear. He reminded her of Mynes.

He leaned forward abruptly and grabbed for her arm. She stepped out of his reach. He lunged at her, grasping her in an iron grip.

"You're mine now." He yanked her closer. She could smell his breath. "Do you hear that, Achilles?" he bawled. "I'm plowing your woman. How do you like that?" She saw his terror.

He feared Achilles. Loathing seared her belly. He would fear her too.

She could not stab him. He wasn't that drunk, and his men would kill her if she did. She saw a vision of a priestess with arms uplifted, calling down a curse from the heavens, and she freed her arm from his grasp. He was a hollow king and she did not need to kill him, only terrify him. Straightening to her tallest, she lifted both arms to the sky and pulled down power as if grabbing hold of lightning. Her eyes blazed as she called down the curse of the wolf.

"I am a sacred keeper of the divine power of the wolves. You have contemplated my violation and have called down upon yourself the ripping jaws and piercing teeth of the wolves' unstoppable violence. Hunters in the pack, they will track you down no matter where you hide. Shiver with terror. The wolves have caught your scent. They speed to your doom."

Agamemnon shuddered and recoiled in his chair. "No!" he cried out. "They killed that priestess! Not you—"

Howling as a wolf celebrating the kill, she loomed over him, drawing her outstretched arms powerfully in and out, their shadows entangling him in winding darkness.

Her words darkened into a menacing growl. "You have offended Kamrusepa, the goddess of the mountain, by contemplating violence against her priestess. Fool, to think you can touch the goddess's chosen one and live! The curse of her ravening wolves will consume you. Their claws will gouge your eyes. Their savage teeth will chew your throat, tear off your ears. In their hunger they will rip out your manhood by the roots and devour it."

He cowered, pulling his purple cloak over his face. The bulge

under his tunic had disappeared. She hoped fear kept him a shriv-
eled worm forever. *Boast about that, great king.*

Briseis turned and left the shelter, not looking behind her. She
began to shake. A figure came toward her in the darkness. Instinctively, she fled from it.

31

HOWLING IN THE DARK

Maira caught Briseis around the shoulders. In the same women's hut as before, Maira wrapped her in a blanket, rubbing her arms and back to sooth the shaking. Then Agamemnon's voice rang out, bellowing for his herald. Briseis felt the bands tighten around her head. Lights flashed and collided in her sight, blinding her.

A moment later the herald's shadow darkened the doorway. "Keep her locked in there. She tried to curse Lord Agamemnon. She goes nowhere. Make the other women move out of that hut so she's always alone. Never near the king at any time. She's a menace. We should have left her cursing Achilles."

"Send her back," Maira said. "I will take her—you needn't fear that you will have to come near her."

"No. It's past that. Lord Agamemnon's honor is at stake. Keep her out of sight in this hut or one of the men will kill her." His voice dropped low. "Then Achilles will never be persuaded to defend us. First Chryseis brings the plague, now this woman threatens us with wolves. At least you can kill a wolf with a sword."

"Not these wolves. I know," said Maira. "I have watched them attack. No man can see them but the one they devour, and that one screams and writhes in agony."

The herald made a guttural sound of horror.

She pulled the door shut, closing him out.

Maira added wood to the fire. She lit an oil lamp and sat next to Briseis. "You don't need to fear Agamemnon," Maira said. "Whatever he did to you tonight, he will not repeat. Calm yourself and remember who you are."

Gradually the warmth stilled her body's shaking. The lights no longer swam before her eyes, but her head throbbed. She wanted to say that Agamemnon hadn't harmed her in the way Maira imagined. But she couldn't speak; her throat and chest ached. She drifted into sleep.

FIFTEEN DAYS PASSED in dreary sameness locked inside the hut, broken only by Maira's brief visits to bring her food. Briseis told Maira what occurred inside Agamemnon's shelter. At first she tried to persuade Maira that she had used the wolf curse only as a trick, but Maira silenced her. Maira had seen the real effects of Hatepa's fears, and in the same way, she told Briseis, the curse had overpowered Agamemnon. When Briseis had needed it, the power came to her from the gods. Perhaps Maira was right.

The rest of Agamemnon's women kept clear of her. The few women who had been living in that particular hut dragged out their pallets, grumbling about having to crowd in with the others. Before this fatal quarrel between Agamemnon and Achilles, Briseis had won goodwill among these women with her healing, but they forgot those feelings toward her now. They believed in the fear they saw in the men and did not trust her. Even without the story of the curse, the antagonism between Agamemnon and Achilles had seeped into these captives. They identified with Lord Agamemnon and saw her as hostile to them.

Briseis had long hours to think.

The wolf curse had spared her being violated by Agamemnon,

but she worried that she had also cursed herself. Agamemnon's terror cut her off from any contact with him, and so she had no way to persuade him to release her. She could have appealed to his greed by reminding him that the only way to gain Troy's riches was to have Achilles fight for them. And the only way he would fight was if she were returned. Trapped in the hut, she could do nothing. If her solitude offered safety from Agamemnon, that safety seemed bound to doom both her and Achilles—as well as the Greek army.

Sometimes in her despair, the recent horrors of the plague filled her mind with bleeding sores, blackened, rotting flesh. She wondered why the Trojans had not overtaken the Greeks while they were weakened with the plague. Had the plague struck the Trojans also? That made no sense. Apollo's anger had been directed at Agamemnon's offense. Perhaps the Trojans had welcomed a respite from the fighting, not realizing the source of their reprieve or the opportunity it presented.

If the Trojans had not taken advantage of the plague's damage to the Greek army, they clearly benefited from Achilles's withdrawal from the battle. During their brief conversations, Maira reported the daily retreat of the Greek army and the massive losses despite occasional temporary successes by individual Greek kings. Such wearing defeat of the Greeks could not go on indefinitely.

She hated her dark prison, but she worried even more for Achilles. The loss of his comrades' lives, when he faced his responsibility for it, would destroy him, molten stone though he had become. He had never been willing to abandon them—not for the promise of a happy life in Phthia with her, not for anything. At some point the weight of his friends' deaths would drive him back to the battle, no matter how much he longed for her return, for his honor. She accepted that—almost hoped for a speedy return to the fighting so that some part of Achilles the man could be left whole, even though that would leave her forever Agamemnon's slave.

Greatest of warriors, Achilles could not use his strength to free himself or her. Greatest of healers, he could not cure their pain. She hated Agamemnon for knowing too well how to trap Achilles and for being too stupid to see his trap harmed himself as much as Achilles. At times she even hated Achilles for allowing himself to be trapped.

She also longed for him. Longed to hold him and drive back the black despair. Enclose him and feel alive again. Waves of desire flooded her and she ached with separation, but he didn't even visit her dreams as he once had. That felt like a betrayal.

She needed to escape this dark tomb, to be out doing things, busy with people, even if she could not be with Achilles. Instead, she stayed trapped in the dim light that came through the smoke hole without even stitchery to pass the time. Thank the gods the days had lengthened so that at least she had a long stretch of light. Sometimes she sat and stared up at that circle of sunshine. More often she paced back and forth in the tiny space over and over, keeping herself from screaming only by throwing herself on her pallet and pounding her fists until her arms ached.

Eurome had kept her promise to come see her, but Agamemnon's men refused to let her speak to Briseis. Maira relayed Eurome's report. Achilles had spent hours weeping at the edge of the sea. The women guessed his mother must have come to him. When he returned to his shelter, he sat alone, grimly determined each day, not fighting. Patroklos could approach him, but no one else dared. Sometimes he played the lyre and sang tales so haunted that Eurome had to block her ears or spend the day weeping.

ON THE SIXTEENTH day of her captivity, the fighting grew so close that Briseis heard it clearly through the walls of the hut. Had the Trojans driven the Greeks to the camp? Such a total defeat of the Greeks would mean slaughter within the camp. With dread she realized neither she nor the other women would be safe in such chaos and confusion of loyalties. It wouldn't be enough that amidst the incoming Trojans might be warriors from their own towns—more likely the Greeks would kill the women to prevent them from helping the Trojan troops. The captive women wouldn't count for much when weighed against the Greek warriors' own lives.

Briseis could no longer hear the sound of women's chores under the battle clamor. She pulled her tunic away from her clammy skin and rubbed her sweaty palms on her skirt. Were the Trojans already in their camp? She pounded on the door, begging to be let out, but no one answered.

The screaming of the wounded and the cries of triumph rose to a crescendo. Then with painful slowness the battle noise receded. Had the Greeks managed to push them back?

Suddenly a thunderbolt cracked and even the air in her hut smelled burnt. What was happening now? Achilles had told her the gods intervened in the battle. Was Zeus, the Thunderer, portending disaster for the Greeks? In answer, the air and earth shattered with three more cracks accompanied by lightning so bright and close it lit the hut through the smoke hole.

Sulfur and ash, despair and death: she knew the king of the gods had declared doom for the Greeks. A moment later the divine thunder echoed in the rumble of hoof and boot as once more the Trojans pushed forward their attack. Horses, mortally struck, screamed. Men bellowed their death throes. The battle crashed against the ramparts that defended the Greek encampment.

She sat alone amidst the terror, her head buried in her arms, through the long afternoon until even the dim light from the smoke hole vanished. With the dying light, the battle screams ceased and quiet fell around her like dew. Whatever cataclysmic forces had been at work, they had stopped when the sun dipped below the horizon.

Into the welcome silence, women's voices, roughly commanded by men, came to her. She stayed silent, unwilling to face those men if someone should respond to her knocking. A woman wailed in grief. Others joined the ululation. A gruff command silenced them. Familiar cooking sounds followed. The smell of roasting meat reminded her that she had not eaten since morning.

The bar scraped across and the door opened. Maira beckoned. She whispered that the Greeks were so defeated and hard-pressed, they wouldn't, she was willing to guess, concern themselves with Briseis and her wolf curse. No guard had been set that day on her hut, in any case. The women were short-handed with all the tasks and wouldn't speak up if she made herself useful. Briseis didn't care what happened as long as she could escape the hut.

She crept forward behind Maira, unsure what she would find. The camp remained whole, but rows of bodies revealed the day's losses. Women washed the dead, wrapping them in their shrouds. Briseis understood the sounds of grief she'd heard—as she herself had, the captive women mourned their own lost families while outwardly giving the Greek soldiers their due. Ordinarily the comrades of the fallen encouraged this honor for the dead. Why silence the women tonight?

The fighting had never come up against the camp before, but now she heard the noise of the Trojan army camped on the other side of the bulwark that ran across the front of the camp between the shore and the ridge. Perhaps by Achilles's ships, further down the shore toward the Hellespont, the sound was not so ominous, but here in the center of the camp, she could distinguish the sounds of victorious soldiers preparing dinner and hundreds of cook fires crackling and sparking, their light glowing up from the plain. No wonder the soldiers had silenced the women. The Trojans would hear the wailing and be glad. Better to withhold honor from the dead than strengthen the enemy.

As Maira had said, the women were stretched thin trying to prepare the meal and attend to the dead. Briseis knelt by the cook fire and mixed bread dough. The women glanced at her; a silence fell over their conversation, but Maira nodded encouragement, so she stayed.

Gradually the others started talking quietly again and accepted her presence. When the Trojan onslaught had come close, they had been taken away from the fighting. The Greeks naturally feared their captive women might view the enemy with sympathy, and they had also been afraid of losing them if the Trojans set fire to the ships and shelters. Briseis shuddered when she realized they'd left her locked in a wooden hut. Why hadn't Achilles come to free her from such a horrific death? Then she realized, Achilles couldn't know she was locked in a hut. There was certainly no communication between Achilles's camp and Agamemnon's.

Briseis heard the women say Agamemnon had called the Greek leaders to his shelter to eat and decide how to save themselves.

She whispered to Maira. "Is there a safe way for you to listen to their plans? Surely they must realize they have to win back Achilles. I want to know how they intend to do that."

Maira nodded. "They'll be arriving soon. I had the same thought. When they left you behind today—to face the flames if they had come—I knew we had to do something. I tried to come back and release you, but they're afraid of the women and kept watch on us, though they don't seem to care about you anymore. I guess the soldiers have met with something more frightening than a wolf. I'm not letting them lock you up again."

The leaders arrived. They would eat before they talked. Henchmen carried spitted meat to the fire inside Agamemnon's shelter. The men had fought all day without eating. No matter how dire their situation, food and drink came first.

Briseis kept out of sight whenever the men came near the cooking area. Sullen, downcast, dreading the morning, they would forget about her if she made it easy.

Women took baskets of bread, trays of food and pitchers of wine to Agamemnon's shelter.

Maira took a wine pitcher and went inside. When most of the women came out with the empty trays, Maira was not with them. If the Trojans' glowing fires on the plain boded the future, the Greek kings would be desperate to persuade Achilles to set aside his anger. They could only succeed if they returned her to Achilles.

Briseis could not hold still. She washed trays and pitched the scrapings where the dogs and birds would eat them, but her eyes stayed on the door, waiting for Maira. It opened.

Odysseus, Phoenix, and Aias came out and left. With Phoenix and Aias in the group, she guessed they were going to speak to Achilles. Odysseus was honored as the best negotiator, a logical choice, except she knew Achilles felt an innate distrust of this man who would say anything to win the day. On the other hand, no men besides Patroklos were as dear to Achilles as Phoenix and Aias. If this was, as she assumed, a delegation to persuade Achilles to set aside his anger, these men might win Achilles's heart.

Maira slipped out of the doorway and blended into the darkness away from the cook fires. Briseis went to her. "What did they say?"

"The kings persuaded Agamemnon to make recompense for the insult he made to Achilles's honor. Odysseus, Phoenix, and Aias have gone to describe the gifts Agamemnon offers and persuade Achilles to return to the fighting. Along with the rest, Agamemnon promises to return you. You should be freed by morning." Maira turned and went toward the other women. Briseis followed, caught up in hope. Maira had been abrupt in reporting this good news and she wanted more.

Her heart beat furiously in her chest. Trying to catch up to Maira, she felt short of breath. She would be free and back in Achilles's arms. If he were still transformed by anger, she would find the man she loved inside and calm the storm so that he could reclaim his mortal self. She longed for the joy of being together again for whatever time they had left. She couldn't help what would come after—she couldn't stop fate.

She called to Maira. She wanted to hear how much Agamemnon was forced to pay out of his greedy store of wealth. She needed him to pay dearly. "What gifts did Agamemnon offer?"

"Seven tripods, ten talents' weight of gold, twenty cauldrons, twelve horses, seven captives, and he promised if they sack Troy, that Achilles may take as much gold and bronze as he pleases to fill his ship and twenty Trojan women besides." Maira turned back toward the women immediately. She didn't hold Briseis's gaze, didn't revel in this good news. Something was wrong. Maira had learned the skill of hiding her feelings from those she served, but Briseis was her friend.

"You've left something out, Maira. Tell me."

Maira shook her head. "You don't want to know."

"Please tell me."

Maira looked at her in concern. "Agamemnon offered in marriage any one of his three remaining daughters along with a huge kingdom, and to be treated equally with Agamemnon's own son."

Briseis burst out laughing. Maira's look of concern deepened.

Briseis put her arm around Maira's shoulder. "Don't look so worried. I haven't gone mad."

"Why are you laughing at the news of Achilles's marriage to one of Agamemnon's daughters?"

"Because it shows how little Agamemnon understands Achilles. For one thing Achilles will never consent to be Agamemnon's son-in-law, not after all that has passed between them—even if he didn't love me enough to say no, which he does."

"He hates the king so much he'd turn down a powerful bond like this?"

"Achilles was born with all the power he will ever want within himself. That's why Agamemnon hates him. Achilles will never trust an offer like this. It sounds like Agamemnon is trying to absorb him into his influence—limit his innate power."

"What do you think will happen?"

Briseis scowled. "Now that I think about it, I'm afraid Achilles will mistrust the whole offer and I'll be stuck here. He never sees the need to negotiate—pull the good from the bad in an offer. It isn't in his nature. His strength keeps him from seeing the virtue in subtlety."

"Unfortunately, he needs you to advise him," said Maira.

Briseis nodded. "And I'm not there."

32

WRATHFUL FIRE

The impenetrable blackness of the sky above and the ominous glow of Trojan watch fires on the horizon pressed in on Briseis as she and Maira sat, waiting for the men to return with Achilles's answer. A rushing sound filled her head, like the cascade of the waterfall in the ravine near Lyrnessos.

Agamemnon's men and captives had eaten their dinners and finished the night's chores. The rest of the women had gone into their huts. Soldiers, somber and exhausted, curled up in their cloaks and slept, leaving it to their leaders to find a way to avoid death. The cold night wind carried with it the only noises: the calling of owls and wolves on the hunt, the settling of the triumphant Trojans.

Finally, Briseis saw Odysseus and Aias approach. Maira stood and slipped inside Agamemnon's shelter, where the Greek kings waited. Briseis's heart sank when Maira returned almost immediately. In this crisis, the leaders wanted no one overhearing their counsels. The two women sat silently, watching for clues.

Then a short, round figure disengaged itself from the shadows around the stockade gate and Briseis heard a familiar voice speak to the guards by the gate. Briseis rose to meet her visitor.

"How did you make your way through the dark camp?" She

hugged her dear nurse. "The men are on edge tonight—you shouldn't have taken such a risk coming here, but I'm so glad to see you." Eurome coughed and Briseis looked at her sharply. "Are you sick?"

Eurome waved away her concern. "It's nothing for you to worry about, just the cool air tickling my throat, that's all. With my token from Lord Achilles, I'm safe around the camp." She held up the leather patch she wore around her neck. "Almost as important as a herald, I am." She chuckled. "I've brung news. Stop fussing about me. D'you hear that Agamemnon sent men to beg Achilles to save 'em?" Briseis nodded. "I hid on the porch outside the door, so I heard what they said."

"Tell me." Briseis's heart thumped hard in her chest.

Eurome patted her hand and let Briseis lead her toward a seat on a rough log bench by the dying cook fire. "First Lord Odysseus told him what a hard place they was worked into and how much they need him—Achilles could ha' seen that for hisself, if you asked me. It don't seem like Lord Achilles trusts Lord Odysseus. When Odysseus got through, Achilles went on about men who say one thing but hide another in their heart."

Eurome settled down by the fire, reaching her hands out to warm them. "I'm jumping ahead of myself. Where was I?" Briseis resigned herself to a long-winded telling. "Oh, yes, then Lord Odysseus told him all the gifts Agamemnon offered—quite a long list that, but Achilles didn't like what he said somehow, as I says before."

Eurome coughed again and gave Briseis's hand a squeeze to reassure her it was nothing. "To speak true, I didn't like the sound of it when, for one of them gifts, Agamemnon offered his daughter for a wedding and all kinds of lands and such with her, when I knowed you two love each other well enough." Briseis gave her a quick smile.

"Come to think of it, maybe that were what got Achilles feeling so contrary, Agamemnon wanting him to be his son-in-law and all. No family love between those two. I can't really say, but whatever it were, Lord Achilles said no to everything."

Briseis sighed and shook her head. It was what she'd feared.

Eurome pulled Briseis close against her. "He were still angry at

Agamemnon and he would no way fight for him. Said he'd fought so many battles and raids—taking care of the men like a mother bird takes care of her fledglings, that's how Lord Achilles put it—and that ungrateful king never gave him anything much in return and now he'd insulted him over much."

Eurome coughed harder.

Briseis leaned closer and listened to the old woman's chest. "I don't like the sound of that, Eurome. You should stay here where I can take care of you."

Briseis saw Maira shaking her head. "Agamemnon's men will herd us up onto the ridge tomorrow as they did today. If Eurome stays with you, she'll be worse off tomorrow, unable to rest in bed. Agamemnon's camp is too close to the front of the battle now. She'll be safer in Achilles's camp."

"Give me one of them healing teas of yours and I'll be fine. Patroklos and Lord Achilles are healers too, you'll remember. I'm no way going to be herded like some old nanny goat by those louts of Agamemnon's."

"I suppose so," said Briseis. "I'll give you some licorice tea to take with you."

"I'll be glad to have it." Eurome gave Briseis a hug.

"If you have your breath, can you tell me what happened after Achilles refused the gifts? Odysseus and Aias couldn't have taken no without trying something more."

"Oh, my little Poppy." Eurome shook her head and her hands fluttered up and down in distress. "Then Lord Achilles said the most confusing, mixed-up things. One breath ugly as could be, the next lovely."

"What do you mean? What did Achilles say?"

"First he called you the "bride of my heart" and how Agamemnon had no right to keep you. That's a pretty thing to say." Eurome brushed back a strand of Briseis's hair, and Briseis smiled. "What he said in the next breath he didn't mean—it were just his anger at that pig talking, I'm sure of it."

"Just tell me what he said."

"After he said Agamemnon keeps his bride, he growled out, 'Let him lie beside her and be happy.'" Bile rose in Briseis's throat. "Don't you go thinking he meant it—more like let him die and be eaten by the dogs, if you listened to the way he said it. Then he pointed out that they'd come to Troy to fetch back Helen, and was Menelaos the only one who loved his wife? He loves you just the same as a queen like Helen, from his heart, as his wife, even though he won you with his spear—those were his words. You ignore anything you hear otherwise."

Yes, but Menelaos had brought an army to get Helen. Achilles seemed willing to leave her with Agamemnon. "What is he going to do?"

"He went back and forth like a teething baby that don't know what it wants. First he were going to sail back to his papa in Phthia." Eurome's coughing interrupted. "Then after Phoenix went on for a long time telling old stories that made no sense I could get hold of, Aias reminded Achilles he couldn't desert the men—you know Lord Achilles is always looking out for his men, or he were until this madness come—so then Achilles says he wouldn't sail but stay by his ship until Hector got to burning the ships. Don't seem quite what Aias were wanting, but he isn't leaving, anyway."

"So I'm left here, and he's going to sit out of the fighting, desert the men, until it's too late—and then he'll fight?"

Eurome shrugged. "That seems about the way of it. He don't show much sense sometimes."

"None at all." Briseis didn't know whether she wanted to weep or scream. She remained Agamemnon's slave. Perhaps worse, Achilles would destroy himself with guilt if he left the men to die. How had Eurome said he'd described himself—a mother bird with her fledglings? Such an odd phrase, but it suited despite the incongruity. And it spoke of the sorrow he would feel when he came back to himself and realized what he had done to the men.

Eurome tried to hold back another coughing fit, but it racked her. Briseis put her hand to Eurome's forehead and cheeks—her skin felt clammy.

"You're having chills, aren't you?"

"It's nothing, Poppy. I'm a little tired out. The night feels cool now that the fire has died down—that's all. Give me some of your licorice tea. It'll mend me up in no time."

Eurome rose slowly. "I better go. I don't want to cause no trouble for you here with Agamemnon. We all know how bad that can be. I'll be in good hands in Achilles's camp."

"I'll give you some willow bark also. Have the women boil both for your tea. You need to rest in bed. Let the other women do your chores." She studied her old nurse in concern.

"I will, little Poppy. Don't you worry about me."

Maira brought her satchel, and Briseis gave Eurome a generous portion of teas. She embraced the old woman.

"Sick as you are, you shouldn't have come to me, but thank you for bringing me news of Achilles's decision. I love you. Go carefully back through the camp. Do you want a torch to light your way?"

"No, the moon has risen—that's light enough, and I can go about unnoticed more easily. I just show my token if anyone growls at me. No one wants trouble with Achilles."

Briseis hugged her again and Maira wished her well. The old woman slipped away.

"Come stay with me tonight," said Maira. "I won't allow you to be locked up again and you saw the way the women reacted. They are cautious about you, but they remember the healing you've done among them."

Before Briseis could answer, the door of Agamemnon's shelter opened, and the Greek leaders emerged. Their silence expressed the gravity of their situation. Maira pulled Briseis into her hut and closed the door.

A small fire burned low in the hearth. By its light, Briseis saw some of the women lift their heads from their pillows, look at her and then lie back down. Maira made Briseis a place to sleep beside her pallet.

THE NEXT MORNING after a hurried meal, one of Agamemnon's henchmen herded Briseis and the rest of Agamemnon's captives onto the ridge above the ships. To her relief the surly man didn't pay any attention to her. He had more dangerous things to worry about than a captive woman, whatever curses he thought she could command.

She and Maira sat with the other women high on the slope from which they could look out at the Greek ships and defensive wall, with the Trojan army positioned terrifyingly close. The Greek army poured out from the camps scattered among the ships. A formidable force gathered to face the Trojans. Briseis peered down to the end of the camp closest to the Hellespont and furthest from the Trojan threat. While all the rest of the camp bustled with soldiers arming and forming into ranks, she saw no movement among the Myrmidons, Achilles's men. She couldn't believe Achilles had come to this.

The two armies clashed on the plain in front of the Greek defensive wall. The captives leaned forward, watching the battle below with an intensity born of their conflicted feelings. Briseis understood what these drawn faces around her meant—the same confusion pulled tight every one of Briseis's muscles. If the Trojans overran the Greek camp, the captives would likely be killed. Yet they couldn't wish for a Greek victory over their own people, either.

The two armies held each other at a stalemate for much of the morning; then, inexorably, the Trojans pushed against the Greek palisade. At midday, Hector, Troy's greatest hero, lifted a massive stone and, with one preternatural blow, brought down the gate guarding the Greek camp. For a confused moment Briseis thought she must be witnessing the fall of her own city again under Achilles's onslaught. She saw Lyrnessos's Great Gate in a pile of rubble and a triumphant warrior raising his golden shield. She shook her head to clear away this vision.

The Greeks responded to the flood of Trojan warriors bursting through the downed gate by climbing high on the ships nearest the wall. From that height the Greeks jammed huge pikes into upturned Trojan faces and searched out the tender spot where neck and shoulder join. Trojans fell in piles below the ships' hulls.

Then, Briseis saw bright torches, carried forward from the back of the Trojan army, heading toward the Greek ships. With a triumphant roar, Hector's men placed a brand in their leader's hand, and Briseis saw the first ship catch fire.

The flames consumed the ship, dry and brittle from being beached so long. How could the Greeks stop the whole fleet from becoming a bonfire? The clouds of smoke and towering flames clogged her breath with remembered ash.

Then, even as the first ships burned, a cheer went up from the Greek side. The captives on the hill looked back and forth in confusion.

"Look, Briseis," Maira cried. "It's Achilles!"

Achilles's glistening chariot, his immortal horses, the familiar armor and shield charged toward the battlefield. Behind him thundered the Myrmidon warriors in such tight formation that their shields and helmets seemed to meld into one creature bent on fighting. Held back against their will for so long, they leaned toward the battle with one mind and purpose. No wonder his exhausted comrades had cheered. The greatest of the Achaians had rejoined the fight.

Briseis studied the heft of shoulder, the legs braced wide as the chariot barreled through the camp, the tilt of helmeted head. Something was wrong—it was not Achilles inside that protective bronze. Patroklos had taken Achilles's place. No one else had realized it, but she understood what had happened.

Patroklos and Achilles had bound themselves so closely together that Patroklos could become Achilles. She had seen him do so when Achilles's anger at Agamemnon had filled him. Now he would fight with Achilles's extraordinary strength. Mistaken for his friend, he would drive back the Trojans. Yet just as Achilles lost all control in the midst of battle except when Patroklos's presence guided him to restraint, so now Patroklos would become ungovernable—and there would be no friend to bring him back.

Briseis turned to Maira. "That's Patroklos, not Achilles." Her heart felt cold as fate took Achilles and her in its inextricable grip. Sorrow and loss whirled toward them, a destructive maelstrom she feared neither of them would be able to survive.

She had reason to fear. Backed by the fresh Myrmidon warriors, Patroklos slaughtered Trojans across the battlefield. Immersed in Achilles as she had also been, she could feel with him the reveling in his borrowed, limitless strength. It was a complete rout. Trojan bodies lay scattered across the plain like autumn leaves in the wind. No one could stop Patroklos. No one Briseis could see. But some other force was at work.

Patroklos made three sallies, cutting down nine men each time, impossible deeds. As he swept in for a fourth time, he stopped as if he had collided with an unseen foe. Achilles's helmet flew off his head and fell into the dust. He whirled in search of his enemy. No one stood near him—not even his own men. His sallies had taken him forward of his fellow Myrmidons.

His spear shattered into splinters in his hand. He looked about dumbfounded. Some hidden force buffeted him back and forth with blows. The mighty shield dropped to the ground, its shoulder strap snapped in two. The front and back pieces of his corselet fell away until he stood naked. Naked, defenseless, alone.

Briseis watched in horror. Some god of Troy had stripped Patroklos. Patroklos searched again for his assailant, but none was visible. Not until a slender Trojan boy broke from the Trojan line, slipped up behind Patroklos and jabbed him in the back with his javelin. A shudder ran through everyone on the plain, Trojan and Greek alike. Then, as though terrified at the sight of the naked and unarmed Patroklos, the boy ran.

She watched as Patroklos, stumbling in pain and confusion, tried to shrink back into the protection of his companions as the Trojans closed in on him. The Myrmidons surged forward, but Hector had seen him. Hector, stalking like a lion toward a herd of sheep, came close and rammed his spear deep into Patroklos's belly. Patroklos fell as Hector vaunted over him. Patroklos lay gored and slaughtered. Even so, he turned his head up and stared into Hector's face before he died. He appeared to speak. Briseis hoped he called Hector a coward for killing an unarmed, wounded man—even one who had left the Trojan dead strewn across the plain.

Briseis wept. The waves of sorrow rose up, choking her in agony. She felt his death to her core. Patroklos had been kind to her, one of the gentlest people she had ever known. With far greater grief, though, she wept for Achilles. He had lost his dearest friend, more than a friend—half of himself. She feared Achilles would rage into battle to get revenge, pursue Hector at any cost. His fury at Agamemnon would be a dim flicker to what would now come. His death must surely follow. Grief-driven, he would be careless of everything, all restraint gone, so that fate would easily destroy what no one could before: a man, more god than man, possessing beauty, grace and fatal anger.

During the long afternoon, through eyes made blurry with tears, Briseis watched the battle over Patroklos's body. First Hector's men held off the Myrmidons while Hector put on Achilles's immortal armor, glorying in his spoils. Then the Myrmidon's first shock wore off and they gathered their strength to prevent Hector from seizing Patroklos's body. Like a ritual dance in honor of some jealous god, the fight over which side would carry the body off the field reenacted the bloody ebb and flow of the war. One moment Hector stood triumphant over Patroklos's stripped body; the next the Greeks shielded the corpse and tried to carry it to their side.

Then, when all seemed lost, and the Trojans had hold of Patroklos's body and would at any moment carry it back to their city to be a source of revenge for their dead, food for dogs and vultures, Achilles appeared on a mound at the edge of the battlefield. Hector had taken his armor. He could not fight. As he stood there, he gave off a golden light, fearful and sacred. His hair became flames climbing high into the sky. The battlefield fell silent. Into that awe, he shouted three times, wordless cries of agonized rage.

With each cry, Trojans fell dead until the body of Patroklos was left undefended. At last the Greeks were able to carry the body of their fallen comrade away from the Trojan battle line. They lifted it gently onto a litter, placing the arms across the bloodied torso. There was nothing to cover the torn flesh, only their tears falling from grim faces consecrated the body. Four heart-heavy warriors lifted the litter and walked to the mound where Achilles stood, his body bent and weighted by grief. The sun, as though reluctant to witness such sorrow, fell below the horizon, one last golden glow shimmering for a moment on the rippling waves of the sea before darkness descended.

33

IMPLACABLE

During the night, the Greek army filled the air with the sounds of lamentation for Patroklos. Forced to stay in Agamemnon's camp, Briseis grieved alone. She pictured Patroklos caring for the injured. His kind and generous spirit had touched everyone—the cries rising up on all sides proved that. She remembered their momentous conversation on the shore. Patroklos had thought that she could quiet Achilles's turmoil. How had he put it—fire calmed by fire? Sometimes. But her fire had also fed his fire. When Achilles needed her most, she had failed him. Patroklos intervened and lost his life.

Even in the midst of Achilles's battle lust, Patroklos had been able to forestall Achilles's fated death. Now death would stalk Achilles with the sure step of a hunting dog on the scent of its prey—the death his goddess mother had dreaded from the moment of his birth. She saw how intimately linked the two men were, how essential to each other. Together they were indestructible, but fate had found this way to separate them.

Caught in a trance of desolation through the night, she gradually became aware of familiar sounds as the camp awoke around her. She found it difficult to grasp that it had been only yesterday that she had seen Patroklos struck down. How could the sun have brought a new morning to the Trojan plain with the weight of such a death fresh upon its soil?

What would this day hold? She pushed herself up from the ground, her limbs stiff and awkward. The women worked around the kitchen lean-to in their usual morning routines, but Agamemnon's courtyard was strangely empty of soldiers. No guards stood by the open gates. Even with all the Greek losses, someone should be left on guard duty. Something had drawn them away.

Briseis slipped through the gate and no one yelled at her. She continued down toward the shore where she saw soldiers muttering in worried clusters. A strange wind trilled around her, otherworldly and terrifying. This sound had pulled the men here. She avoided Agamemnon's men and went further down the shore toward Achilles's camp. The sun rose over the water, making it glow. White caps leapt across the bay's usually tranquil surface. Waves rose up from the blue-green depths and bowed in translucent, shimmering splendor as though paying homage to their god.

The strange wind became in her ears a chant of grief rising from the sea, an echo of her sorrow. It seemed to rise simultaneously from inside of her, and its strangeness did not disquiet her. Female voices lapped against her heart in wordless threnody. From Achilles's descriptions and the consonance with her own sorrow, she recognized the voices; this was the lament of his mother Thetis and her immortal attendants, daughters of Nereus, ancient ruler of the sea.

An immortal mother had begun her eternal mourning. *How strange, it used to anger me that I could not hear a goddess's voice, and now, sharing a goddess's grief, I hear her so clearly it breaks my heart and I wish I didn't.*

On the shore in front of the Myrmidon ships, the waves curled back, forming a dry path that stretched from the depths of the sea to the land. The melancholy voices grew louder. Briseis shielded her eyes as a golden brilliance rose from the sea: radiant, as if held aloft by invisible hands, a glowing armor appeared before them. The one thing Achilles would have asked from his mother—the only thing that prevented him from returning to battle—now glistened before them. And such armor! Only the blacksmith of the gods, Hephaistos, could have fashioned it—and in a single night. She heard a cheer from the soldiers on the shore. Now Achilles could fight for them again. That was all they saw or cared about. What anguish it must have cost Thetis to bring her son new armor, knowing she brought him closer to the death she had foretold. The bitter whip of fate must have scarred her every step.

Achilles walked down that divinely swept path and returned with the armor clutched against his chest. Briseis shivered as the sea closed over the path. The sound of the Nereid lament echoed around her even after the bay had returned to calm. Perhaps Achilles would receive solace from their mourning for his friend—and for him—but their chant had only deepened her own human grief. They expressed all that had been lost, all that soon would die.

Briseis leaned against a ship's hull, exhausted by her grief and sleepless night. She heard a herald calling the men to the assembly. Soldiers moved past her, heading toward the field where the army gathered. Their faces showed relief now that Achilles had returned to them. They had grieved during the night for Patroklos, but their sadness had passed. Everyone had loved Patroklos, but they loved their own lives more. They did not understand how brief a span of life Achilles clung to.

She was startled to hear Achilles's voice, bellowing for the men to come to the assembly. She ran toward the sound. There he was, ranging back and forth, driving the men in front of him toward the assembly. His armor awaited. His impatience was palpable. His fierce glare, the chiseled stone of his muscles, the radiance of enflamed rage all told her his mortal self was submerged deep inside—if indeed it had survived the furnace of his grievous anger. The beautiful shell contained only a god of war and vengeance who would slake his thirst on the blood of Hector and his Trojans.

She was close enough to call out to Achilles, but she did not. She wanted to feel his love for her now, but that wasn't possible. It was true that if he returned to the fight as he clearly meant to do, she would be given back to him. They could be together again. But Patroklos's death had ignited a greater fury. This godlike creature would not return her love. Looking at him, she was reminded of the metals in Milos's workshop. They had two states: hard and immovable, or molten and dangerous.

She followed him to the assembly field where he climbed onto the speaker's mound. Was he driving so hard toward his death that this glimpse was all she would have as farewell? She came closer to get a better look, hiding behind the curve of a ship's hull so that the Greek leaders did not see her.

Achilles addressed the assembly. "I have called you here, my brothers in arms, to act as witness as I revoke my oath to withdraw from the fighting. Agamemnon and I will declare our reconciliation. Agamemnon, was it good for either of us to engage in this heart-gnawing quarrel over a woman? I wish that Artemis, the goddess whose deadly arrows strike down mortal women, had killed her on that day I destroyed Lyrnessos. That way my comrades would not have been laid in the dust while I stayed apart in my wrath. The only ones who gained were the Trojans. Though it is difficult for me, I am putting aside my anger at your insult. It's time to fight. Let's order the men into battle."

Briseis fell back against the ship's hull. He preferred her dead? Would he wipe her from his life like words written in error upon a damp clay tablet, to be scraped away, obliterated forever?

She stumbled back to the women's huts, instinctively heading for Maira.

"What's happened?" Maira asked when she saw Briseis's tears.

"He said he wished I had been killed instead of taken captive."

"Who said that? Agamemnon?" Then Maira's face lit with understanding. "No! He can't mean that." She hugged Briseis tightly.

Not long afterwards, Odysseus came with a group of young men to gather Agamemnon's gifts and bring them to Achilles: tripods and cauldrons, the talents of gold, the horses, the seven women, and Briseis. Maira slipped into her hut. She returned quickly, carrying Briseis's possessions.

The sack of possessions looked oddly depleted. Then Briseis realized why. Maira had pulled Iatros's satchel out of the sack, and she
held it along with Briseis's own healing satchel. Maira lifted the
straps of each of the satchels over Briseis's head so that both rested
across Briseis's chest.

"Remember who you are," Maira said.

This betrayal by Achilles froze Briseis's heart—she knew Eurome
would excuse it, say it came from his grief for Patroklos, his guilt over
so many dead comrades. *He chose to stay out of the fighting,* she countered in her mind, as if her nurse were actually talking with her. And
he'd let Patroklos go in his place. The force of what that must mean to
Achilles hit her. He would never forgive himself. All that anger
turned against himself.

She didn't notice anything outside her as they walked, and so she
was unprepared when they arrived at the wide, sandy area along the
shore by Achilles's camp. There she saw Patroklos's bier, his corpse
lying underneath a white shroud. Achilles stood nearby with his
hands on his divine armor, and she started toward him, but then
stopped. His eyes were locked on the armor—that was his only
beloved now, his means toward vengeance against Hector.

Instead she walked up to Patroklos and gently pulled back the
linen cover to see him. So many gashes rent his flesh. Had every
Trojan stabbed him? Even though his body had been washed, his
wounds filled with unguents, she felt the horror of so many spear
thrusts as if she too had been struck. She slipped her arm under his
shoulders and pulled his body close, rocking him as if he were a
child. Tears flooded down her cheeks, and she shook with grief.

She looked again toward Achilles, longing to have her sorrow
comforted by the person who would understand it best. His gaze lay
now on his dead friend, but he showed no sign he even recognized
her. Briseis wanted to be held in the shelter of his arms, but he
stood like a statue, neither wanting nor giving human solace.
Around him the other kings and his henchmen tried to draw him
up to his shelter to take nourishment before the battle, but he
refused to do anything but arm. He had vowed not to eat until he

had killed Hector. Odysseus signaled the kings and they left Achilles to his fast.

Achilles's face was hard set and even his hands, those deft and gentle hands, formed unyielding fists. She could not imagine them embracing anything. She thought his eyes, fiery abysses, could kill if he looked too long upon her, as his shout had struck down men the day before. His henchmen drew back a cautious distance, waiting for his orders.

Beside him she saw the extraordinary armor his mother had brought. It gleamed so brilliantly that it was painful to look at. The figures depicted on the shield moved as though alive. The circling designs upon the shield contained the whole world. Hephaistos knew the choice Achilles would make when he put on this armor: to give up life. She wondered if Thetis had asked him to depict life in such fullness that it would be impossible for Achilles to put on this armor and fight, knowing that he would die as a result. Whether at Thetis's request or his own vision, Hephaistos had portrayed every aspect of life, not simply the buildings and places of human habitation, but the natural universe also, and the rites of passage in mankind's years, the give and take, the making and the destruction that fills the world.

Hephaistos had depicted the troubles and the joys in life, wars as well as weddings. She'd heard Hephaistos was a lame god, thrown from the heavens by his own mother. That must be why he understood mortals so well. He himself had suffered. Briseis thought it might be the perfect shield—any opponent would run from the sight of it because he would understand in a flash what the cost of fighting truly was.

No one would choose death with that shield in front of them; no one but Achilles. He glanced at it and strapped one greave on his calf, then another. He girded the corselet about his chest and slung the sword over his shoulder. With no hesitation, he lifted the great shield. When he had placed the helmet on his head, she watched him try the armor to see how it fit and moved. It became like skin to him, and he seemed to lift off the ground in it as if he had put on wings and not heavy bronze.

He took up his spear. It had not been lost because no one else could lift it, not even Patroklos while filled with Achilles's fury. He vaulted into his chariot and called out to his horses.

"Xanthos and Balios, bring your charioteer back safely from the fighting this time. Don't leave him dead on the field as you left Patroklos."

Xanthos bowed his head low, sweeping his golden mane upon the ground. Briseis thought this was his acknowledgement of Achilles's words, but then to her shock, the immortal horse spoke in a deep, resonating voice.

"We will keep you safe, grave Achilles, for now, but your day of destruction is near. We are not to blame, but a great god and over-powering fate. For not by our slowness or sloth did the Trojans take the armor from Patroklos's shoulders, but that preeminent god, Apollo. He killed him and gave the glory to Hector. For we two run as fast as the west wind, which they say is the swiftest of all. You also are doomed to be overcome by a god and a man."

"I know too well how soon I will die. I am destined to be killed far from the land of my father, but, nonetheless, I will fight. I was not there to defend my companion when he needed me. Now there is nothing for me in life but to kill Hector and lay his dead body before Patroklos." *Nothing at all?* wondered Briseis. Had he lost every sense of her? Had his self-loathing stripped him of all else?

Impatiently he signaled his horses and they leapt forward.

Briseis took a deep breath. While Achilles had been near, the air felt charged with lightning, too combustible to take in. Now, in contrast, it seemed cool and refreshing. She covered Patroklos with the white mantle again. How soon would she look upon Achilles's torn body?

She turned to join the women at Achilles's cook fires. With alarm she wondered why Eurome hadn't come to the shore to greet her.

34

BURDEN OF GRIEF

Briseis raced into the courtyard and looked at the women working by the cook fire but didn't see her nurse. She rushed to their hut and pushed open the door.

Eurome lay on her pallet. Briseis knelt by her. The old woman's eyes opened slowly, and the wrinkled lines of her face softened.

"How are you, dear Eurome? Did your cough grow worse?" She put her hand on Eurome's forehead. It burned. "I should have been here to take care of you. You are hot with a fever. Didn't anyone make you willow bark tea? I entrusted your care to Patroklos and Achilles. Clearly they did nothing for you."

"Now that—" A cough interrupted Eurome's words. She caught her breath slowly. "Now that my Poppy is here, I'm happy," she said, and panted with the effort. Briseis placed her ear on Eurome's chest, listening. The wet rattle worried her.

Eurome's condition had grown alarmingly worse in the day and night since her nurse had come to her in Agamemnon's camp.

She squeezed Eurome's hand. "I'll ask the women to bring me a kettle of water to boil, and then I'll be right back."

She went out to the other captives. "How long has Eurome been sick? Did any of you make her some of the willow bark and licorice tea I gave to her?"

The women looked puzzled. They didn't know about any tea, and Eurome hadn't complained of feeling sick. They'd noticed she had not gotten up yesterday, but they knew she'd gone across the camp in the middle of the night, so they thought she was just tired. Who had noticed anything today except Lord Achilles's grief? They were eager to help Briseis now that they knew Eurome needed them.

When Briseis returned to Eurome, the old woman was shaking with chills. Briseis wrapped some blankets and fleeces around her and stirred up the coals in the hearth, feeding kindling into the fire until it could sustain the logs she added. One of the women placed a tripod kettle over the coals, and Briseis brewed a tea of willow bark, mullein, and licorice mixed with honey.

She propped Eurome up and gave her sips. Gradually Eurome coughed less often.

"I missed you, Poppy," said Eurome, her voice a raspy whisper. "Almost as much as Lord Achilles missed you." Briseis looked sharply at Eurome.

"I don't think Achilles missed me at all, Eurome. He did nothing to get me back, and he hasn't spoken a word to me since I returned." She ground mustard seed and dried mint leaves to make a plaster for Eurome's chest, smacking the pestle harder than necessary in the mortar.

"He were so sad without you. His songs. If you heard 'em you'd weep."

"Eurome, I was locked in a dark hut. I did weep every day, and Achilles could have settled his quarrel with Agamemnon and gotten me out. Why are you telling me how sad he was? There's enough misery right now."

"'Cause I know he hurt you. You turn stubborn when you're sore. You'll be sure he's in the wrong because your heart's aching." Eurome had to stop to catch her breath. Briseis gave her another sip of tea. "He loves you, and you was happier with him than I ever saw you.

Forgive him. He's so lost he doesn't know what he's doing—" Eurome coughed and the wet rattling made Briseis shudder.

"Eurome, stop talking. It's making you worse."

"I need to speak my mind. He's lost Patroklos; you're all he has. You need him. Revenge on Hector's all he's thinking now. That's a man's way. Wait a bit. He'll remember you. His love. You think sweet about him, I'll be quiet." Eurome looked at her. Briseis nodded and kissed Eurome's cheek, although she wasn't persuaded. She had more important things to worry about with Eurome's illness. Briseis opened Eurome's tunic and spread the plaster across her chest.

One of the women brought in a tray of food. "I thought you might be hungry," she said. Briseis thanked her and laid the tray next to Eurome's pallet.

The old woman shook her head at the cheese and bread. "You eat, Poppy. I'm too tired."

Briseis looked at the food. She hadn't felt like eating in days. "I never feel hungry for breakfast anymore, but you should eat to build up your strength. You always say, food is the best thing for getting better. It's always been good advice."

Eurome opened her eyes and studied Briseis. "How long you been sick over breakfast?" she asked.

Briseis shrugged. "What difference does it make?"

"You're the midwife—"

Briseis took a sudden intake of breath. She put her hand on her stomach. That couldn't be it. It was the darkness, the misery. Then she remembered that she'd felt sick in the mornings even before Agamemnon took her. She'd been in the middle of fighting the plague. She'd seen so much to make a person nauseous. Had it started before then? She tried to remember, but that seemed a life-time ago. When had her last cycle of bleeding come? Why hadn't she noticed its absence?

Eurome was smiling and watching her. "My Poppy having a baby. Now you two will love." She sighed contentedly.

Briseis closed her eyes and put both hands on her belly. A child growing inside her? Achilles had marched out to kill Hector and soon he would lie dead like Patroklos. Her eyes filled with tears and she laid her head next to Eurome, felt the old hand smooth her hair, prayed not to be alone in the world with a child—a child likely to be extraordinary—extraordinarily difficult, she thought with a softness in her heart for Achilles that she had not felt in a long time.

The rasping and gurgling in Eurome's chest was worsening. She sat up. "I must find a way to heal you."

Eurome patted her hand. "You pray to Kamrusepa—outside where you'll feel her."

Briseis hesitated. "I don't want to leave you."

"Go on. Give your old nurse a kiss and then outside. Speak to your goddess. She'll help you."

Briseis gave the wrinkled cheek a kiss. "I love you, Eurome."

She walked toward the shore, and the breeze off the blue water refreshed her. She watched the rhythmic movements of the waves. Then she raised her hands. "Kamrusepa, bring your healing strength to Eurome. Clear her breathing and take away her cough. Restore her good health."

She added another prayer, this time to Thetis. "No one understands the pain of loss more deeply than you. For the sake of my love for your son, heal Eurome."

Her attention returned to the world around her. Across the bay the battle raged. Trojans ran across the plain toward the city walls. Many in their flight had reached the banks of the Scamander River and were trying to make their way across its deep whirling waters. She looked for Achilles but couldn't find him in the battle. Had he already killed Hector and been struck down?

His brilliant armor and size should have made him easy to see. She hunted and peered, straining her eyes. Nearby stood the ships, propped upright on the beach with wooden beams. Using one of the beams as a ladder, she climbed to the stern and looked out from its height. Piles of dead warriors lined the banks of the river and clogged its waters, their bodies forming a horrific dam, holding back the strong current in a roiling, turbid nightmare. The water darkened with blood.

There—she saw a golden flash. Achilles stood in the river surrounded by the dead bodies of his victims. The water crested above him like a lion pouncing on its prey. Boulders and bodies, carried by the water's force, knocked his feet from under him. Troy's immortal river itself engaged him in battle. Achilles reached for a branch of an overhanging elm, but the whole tree wrenched from the riverbank, its dense roots dragging the river bluff with them into the water, nearly burying Achilles.

Surely this was not his fate, to lie folded under mud and stones in the hostile waters of Scamander, but how could even he escape such raw power?

To reach for Troy he had fought against the city's gods for so long; she could not tolerate this river god rising against him also and drowning his beauty in its murk, no matter how many dead he had thrown into Scamander's waters. She strained forward, willing him to escape the river's hold. A wind rose up, hot and blasting. It caught her hair and pulled it toward the river. When she tried to gather her hair in her hand, it scorched her fingers and escaped her hold.

The banks of the river burst into flames. The dead burned in a sudden pyre. The water boiled. The fish leapt upon the scorched banks in a vain attempt to flee the flames that had replaced their watery homes. The tamarisks and elms along the river's edge became monstrous torches.

In the midst of this inferno, she saw Achilles lift his massive shield and spear in victory. Her heart surged. Not even the divine river could stop him. She heard his shout of joy as he raced across the plain, blasting Trojans like a bolt of lightning. Invincible warrior god, unstoppable fire. He lived, but she no longer knew him. The wonder and terror of him stunned her: his flesh with hers. His child growing inside her. She turned away with a sob, stumbling blindly back to Eurome. Achilles was lost to her now.

EUROME WAS DEAD. Briseis knew the moment she saw her still frame, the peace on her face. She had lost everyone she loved. How many was she destined to consign to the flames? Her mother, her brother, and now her dear nurse. If Achilles was not already dead, he soon would be. She was alone now.

Eurome had known. Her wise old nurse had made her goodbye. She had died happy in the knowledge of what she'd discovered—her Poppy happily joined with Achilles by the bond of a child. It had released her. *Eurome, I need you.*

Briseis wept by Eurome's side, unable to move until the rumble of chariots alerted her to the warriors' return from battle. She stumbled down to the shore to see if Achilles had returned alive.

Achilles stood in his chariot near Patroklos's bier, his warriors gathered around him. "Let us honor Patroklos by driving our chariots, stained with enemy blood, around his body three times as a proper offering to the dead."

They took off at once, swooping in tight formation on the wide beach around Patroklos's bier, their horses' long manes flowing back, the bronze armor flashing, the deep-voiced lament of men overlaying the warlike thunder of hooves and wheels. Majestic and fitting for a fallen hero. Then she saw that Achilles dragged something behind his chariot—a corpse. She felt sick.

The third circle completed, Achilles reined in his horses close to the bier. He stepped from his chariot and laid his hands on his friend's chest. "Farewell, Patroklos. I salute you even in the land of the dead. Everything that I promised to do in your honor, I have done. I bring you Hector's body, which I have dragged through the dust to be food for the ravening dogs. I have brought twelve Trojan youths, whom I captured on the battlefield, to sacrifice and burn on your pyre." Achilles untied the torn and mangled body and flung it face down in the dirt. Briseis crouched down and threw up. This murderous warrior was the father of her child.

Briseis left the shore. Near Eurome's hut, one of the women asked about Eurome. Briseis could barely answer her. She went inside and curled up on the floor.

Two women entered the hut. She saw them through half-shut eyes. They murmured some comforting words to her, but she didn't move. They heated water and brought out linen to wash and prepare Eurome's body. As she watched the women work, she wondered where Eurome was, why she was not helping them. Eurome always took charge at times like this. She began to shake.

Loneliness and cold filled her. As the women cleansed Eurome's body, they keened in mourning. She howled with them until she had wailed herself into numbness and the women had laid Eurome's body on a litter.

Having seen to the dead, the women gently brought Briseis outside to the cook fire and pressed her to eat. She sat in a blur.

It had grown dark. The women had gone to bed, leaving her to her grief. She walked around the camp in the gray light of the stars and moon. She saw no one else. The men had fought a long day and must be sleeping. She wished she had thought to send Maira word of Eurome's death. Perhaps Maira would have found some way to come to her in the current disorder of the whole Greek camp. She doubted Agamemnon's men wanted to cause trouble with anyone associated with Achilles.

She walked toward the shore to better hear the soothing sound of the waves. Patroklos's white shroud hung over his bier and gave off an ethereal gleam in the moonlight. On the ground next to it, lay Hector's body. It too radiated light and what she saw chilled her. His skin, which had been torn beyond recognition when Achilles had thrown him down beside Patroklos's bier, was now whole, his face at peace, his wounds gone. Surely this was the work of the gods. She stepped back in fear, but she was glad the gods had given Hector this respect. Grief had driven Achilles mad. Gentle Patroklos would not wish to be honored in this horrific way.

Closer to the water's edge there was something else on the sand— shapes that after a moment resolved themselves into the forms of men. One man, larger than the others, lay in their midst, twisted in a tortured sleep. Achilles slept here, unable to leave Patroklos, and his loyal companions stayed near him. She picked her way to him. His men had washed the gore of battle off their own bodies, but Achilles was still covered in it.

As she stood beside him, he called out Patroklos's name and his arms reached out. Despite the cruel thing he had said and the violent form of his grief, she longed to hold him, to bear his burden of grief and feel him shoulder hers, but his men were close, and she could not bring herself to touch his body with the blood of Trojans on it. She felt a sob rising up and left the beach. If any of his men keeping watch over their lord had awakened and noticed her, she did not want to speak to them.

She returned to her hut and curled up near the litter on which the women had laid Eurome. Her exhausted body pursued a restless sleep through which dreams fluttered: her nurse floated in front of her, smiling but silent. Eurome looked behind, and from the darkness Patroklos emerged.

Though his body bore the gruesome marks of his death, his voice was gentle as he knelt beside her. "I have asked Achilles to attend to my pyre quickly, no longer to put off my burial so that I can pass through the gates of the Underworld and mingle with the souls of the dead. His ashes will soon lie with mine. Remember this and forgive what his torment drives him to do. He must honor me as his spirit requires. His grief burns hotter than any funeral pyre, and it must be given room to rage.

"You have your own sorrow. Tomorrow bid the men who bring wood for my pyre to set some aside, away from the shore where Achilles will burn my body along with many animals and captives that he will sacrifice. Eurome requires no sacrifice but your tears. Tell the men to construct a small pyre. Turn away from my funeral. Leave Achilles to his immortal sorrow for now. Later when you have attended to Eurome's burial, seek him out as a balm for both your spirits."

Patroklos's image dispersed like fog thinning until she could see him no longer. She awoke and remembered her dream, comforted by his guidance.

As the dawn turned into day, she sat in the doorway of the hut, keeping vigil for Eurome and waiting for the wagons loaded with wood cut from Mount Ida's forests. She had heard the men leave early in the morning to cut down trees for Patroklos's pyre. She had taken out her tapestry and laid it over her lap, a meadow of flowers that gave her solace and courage.

She would ask one of Achilles's men to take word of Eurome's death to Maira after they had finished the pyre. Such messages had been Eurome's job—now there was no simple way to get word to her friend while her duty to Eurome's burial held her here. Somehow Maira would find a way to mourn with her.

When one of the overloaded wagons drew near, she called out to the drivers and asked for their help with the pyre. The two men hesitated.

"This timber is for Lord Patroklos," one said. His tone was apologetic.

"I know," she answered. "That is why I ask you. Lord Patroklos himself appeared in my dream last night and told me to use a portion of his pyre wood for another, much smaller pyre up there by the spring." She pointed. The man swallowed and his eyes scanned around her as if Patroklos might still be present.

"I have heard you are a seer. We can spare a small amount if you believe that is Lord Patroklos's wish."

They carried a pile up the slope to a flat area by the spring and laid it out as she requested. She had chosen the spot with care—the best place to overhear gossip since so many women gathered there. When the wood had been laid, Briseis returned to the hut in which they had laid out Eurome. She took a small linen sack from her healing satchel and started up the hill in front of the other women of Achilles's camp who carried Eurome's litter for her.

She climbed up on the pile of wood and kissed Eurome's wrinkled cheek. Then she opened the linen sack and sprinkled dried lavender over her body. "May Antiope's favorite scent sweeten your funeral pyre so that the spirits of my mother and brothers will draw near and guide you into the land of the dead in their dear company. Since I have lost you, the best wish I can have for you is that you may always be with those who loved you."

When she had climbed down, one of the women handed her a

brand and she walked around the pyre lighting it in several places. A light breeze off the sea lifted the flames. She sat next to the spring and wept throughout the day as the fire did its necessary work. She wanted to be anywhere where the smell of a pyre would never reach her again.

Occasionally she looked out at the building of Patroklos's pyre, gigantic to consume so many dead. When the men laid Patroklos at the center of it and she knew they would soon begin the sacrifices— animal and human—she did not look again. Patroklos had given her good advice. She would not witness the violence of Achilles's grief.

When the smoke and heat from the flames made her thirsty, she knelt by the spring and drank deeply of the clean water. A sweet memory came to her of drawing water from the spring in the orchard on her father's estate. How she longed for that life again, part of a loving family there on the slopes of Mount Ida. She wept for Eurome, so central to that family and the one who had been at her side through every struggle in life.

Now she needed to eat. She could imagine Eurome's voice, "Keep up your strength, my Poppy. Eating's important for growing a baby. You know that better'n me. Feed that little one." She yearned for Eurome's chatter.

PATROKLOS'S PYRE burned most of the night, its light flickering against the dark sky. She shuddered at the thought of the sacrifices that had been laid upon that pyre. She hadn't watched, but her mind conjured up more than she wanted. Surely Patroklos would not want twelve youths killed upon his pyre, and yet, on that last day he had killed far more than twelve Trojans as he drove them back to the city walls. He had said to let Achilles grieve as he must. He had also said to seek him out, but Achilles and his men stayed on the shore. Achilles could not yet leave his friend's side.

35

LIFE OR DEATH

The next day Maira slipped into Achilles's camp. Briseis and she embraced. She had left Agamemnon's camp as soon as she could—when she'd said where she was going, the guards were fearful of angering Achilles by preventing her, so she'd had no trouble. They shared a meal in honor of Eurome and talked about the dear old woman together.

Maira described how quickly Eurome had brought order among the servants who worked in the women's quarters of the palace.

"She'd share some bit of gossip with a serving woman," said Maira, "and slip in that she needed the servant to do this or that. Everyone liked her too much to refuse. Was she like that as a nurse when you were a child?"

Briseis shook her head with a smile. "No. She was quite happy to boss me around. I was always trying to outsmart her, but I adored her."

Briseis told some stories about Eurome and the household of her childhood.

"I wonder if I will ever again live in a place that feels as much a part of me as my father's estate and the woods of Mount Ida. It is as if I were born from them as much as from my mother."

Briseis looked at her friend. "Maira, where did you grow up? I don't know anything about your life before the palace."

"I came from the island of Cyprus, far down the coast from here, but I was taken captive when young, and I remember only a little of what it was like there. Pirates made a surprise attack on our town during the night. My father tried to organize the defense of his citadel, but the pirates killed my parents. After that, wherever my sister was, felt like home to me."

"Your sister? I didn't know you had a sister."

"We served together on the estate of the lord who bought us from the pirates until Lord Mynes attended a feast there and forced my sale to the palace."

"Do you know where your sister is now?"

"I hope safe on the estate. I never saw her after Mynes bought me, but sometimes word would come from her through the palace shepherds. I have asked for her throughout the Greek camp. She isn't here. So either the Greeks did not find the estate she worked on or—" Briseis understood.

"Your father's citadel? You were a princess?"

Maira nodded but pointed out that she hardly remembered her life as a princess. She had only the briefest memories of either her father or her mother. It was her sister that she loved and wondered about.

"I should return to Agamemnon's camp now," Maira said. They stood and embraced. "Keep the happy memories of Eurome foremost in your mind."

ACHILLES and his men built a massive barrow to honor Patroklos and contain his ashes. Achilles remained beside it day and night. When Achilles's friends encouraged him to return to his shelter, he turned away, and to the horror of all he continued to drag Hector's body around Patroklos's barrow. Some god kept the body whole, but Achilles's rage still burned too strongly for him to contain it without this revenge.

Briseis rejoined the women in Achilles's camp, but each day felt like a wrenching of her heart in Eurome's absence. Both Eurome and Patroklos had told her to seek out Achilles, but she did not know how, nor did she want to. A maddened god, he did not look or sound like the man she loved. She slept in the bed in Achilles's shelter—if she returned to her old place in the women's hut, it would be an open rejection of Achilles's love, something difficult to undo when they were already so disconnected. So she slept alone in his shelter each night, but she ate with the women outside by the kitchen fire, and she tended to the tasks she had before Agamemnon had taken her away.

Briseis kept her own watch when she could of Achilles's vigil at Patroklos's barrow. At least the spring weather held mild and fair. The elements offered Achilles that kindness in his grief. She waited for a sign that he reached for her. After all the hurt, she needed him to show he loved her. His men seemed to understand her distance and left her alone. She listened as Achilles's men urged him to eat or partake of other normal activities of life. They waited cautiously for moments when Achilles's inner rage damped down temporarily. At those times he acted distant but not rude. Most of the time it seemed as if he did not remember what these human needs were or why his men cared about them. He looked puzzled by their kindness. Briseis saw that his immortal grief did not leave room for these weaknesses.

When she realized that he was incapable of seeking her, she ignored her pain and approached him as he paced along the beach. Achilles was even less able to hold still than he had been in the past. His henchmen feared him these days, so she came near slowly, watching for his mood. He did not slow his frantic walking, but she braced herself and fell in step beside him.

When she spoke his name, he looked at her with an anguished expression. She placed her hand on his arm and told him how deeply she grieved for Patroklos's loss, but he shook his head and answered with a strange question.

"Why do we warriors think that we must seek the battlefield—do we die any less finally because we have overcome great foes while we fought all day long, splattered in blood and weary at heart?"

She knew this war made him sick at heart, and the drive for glory on the battlefield had never made sense to her; but how strange this question sounded from him—the greatest of the warriors, who had plunged back into the battle to avenge his friend, whose honor had seemed more important to him than his love for her.

Before she could think of any reply to his odd question, he went on. "In the span of generations, each man lives only a short time, whether he reaches old age or not. What does life mean if we do not stand by those near to our hearts? Who are we if we leave our companions to be slaughtered, undefended?"

She had hoped for comfort, an understanding between them after so many hurts, but instead he spoke in spasms. Now these two questions that had bothered him before were inextricably weighted with the guilt of Patroklos's death. Had he not refused to fight for Agamemnon, he would have been at Patroklos's side at the critical moment. His words sounded like prophecies, she thought—cryptic and profound and illusive. Like oracles, what he said at one moment contradicted what he said next.

"Welcome death. It is the only escape from agony," he cried as his gaze swept across the white-capped sea.

She wanted to scream *No!* at him, to tell him there would be a child, another reason to live, among so many others, but she could not speak with him of something as tender as a baby while he continued to drag Hector's corpse, while his grief trapped him in such madness that he would not eat, could not even hold a conversation. It might have been possible to speak of it if he would look at her—see her and know her as he once had. But he didn't. Perhaps it was kinder not to hinder his headlong rush toward death—the fate the gods had pronounced for him would drive him along whether he wanted to go or not. She told him how much she missed his company and asked if he would join her at his shelter. He looked puzzled and said nothing. She left him still pacing on the beach.

She tried again another day. This time Achilles seemed no less disoriented except that he greeted her by name and he seemed to want her company. She walked beside him, saying little, letting time and nearness do what they could.

He still spoke of his fate, how near death was—a state he welcomed now that he had failed Patroklos. He granted no room for her in this, no handhold to draw him back to life. She understood that even the news of a child would not be enough to bring him back unless the rage of his grief-driven fire lessened—and his daily desecrations of Hector proved it had not.

He often brought up another subject—her going to Phthia and how old Phoenix would take her there when finally Troy had fallen and the Myrmidons returned in their ships over the sea. He assumed this was her dearest wish because it was his. She knew he intended this plan as a way to care for her when he had died. It was the one way in which he now showed concern for her, and she valued it as such—and besides, she saw no other place she could go besides this strange, far away place that found no answering call in her heart. Yet the more he spoke of Phthia, the colder and more desperate she felt. Once he had seen things through her eyes—he would have recognized her doubts—but now he did not see her in any meaningful way.

Achilles assumed everyone would comply with his wishes once he had died, but she feared everything would change without his powerful presence. He had always treated her as if she were not a captive, but the other Greeks did not hold her in high esteem. She did not believe she would be Peleus's daughter as Achilles thought, but rather a foreign captive in an unfamiliar land.

He described his father's palace and the beauty of the horse fields around it. He told her she would be a comfort to his father. It was hard then not to tell him about the baby, a grandchild for Peleus, but she kept silent. He had hurt her almost beyond repair. Watching him blazing on the battlefield in pursuit of Hector, she had felt he was already lost to her. Perhaps if he turned toward their love when she told him about the baby, she would believe he loved her again, but if even that did not bring back the man she loved, it would be the last blow. Like a tree the woodsmen bring down with one final stroke, her love would suffer that deadly crash. She had to wait until his madness had passed, if death gave him that much time.

ON THE TWELFTH day after Achilles had killed Hector, Briseis rose from her solitary bed in Achilles's shelter. He remained by Patroklos's barrow. As soon as she stepped out of the hut, she felt drawn to the shore and that puzzled her. She stayed away from the beach in the early morning because, after each tormented night, Achilles raged against Hector's corpse, but this morning the sound of the sea called to her and she obeyed.

Where the waves ordinarily rolled upon the beach, the sea had drawn back to form a dry path. Briseis felt a wash of coldness go through her. Achilles stood enveloped in a golden glow. She could faintly see a slender woman in shining garments wiping away his tears with her hand. Thetis had returned. Briseis wondered why she could see the goddess this time and what purpose had brought her here. She glanced around. Few people had awakened this early, and they showed no signs of noticing this divine visitation.

After a moment Thetis spoke.

"My son, I have come from Zeus to tell you he and the other gods are angry that you have not allowed Hector's body to be redeemed. Apollo has kept all harm and decay from the corpse, but this desecration must stop. If you were any other goddess's child, the gods would have stolen Hector's body away, so great is their outrage, but they fear my wrath if they dishonor you. Accept Priam's ransom for his son's body."

Achilles inclined his head. "If it is Zeus's command, I cannot refuse. Let Priam come with ransom, and I will relinquish Hector's body."

"In this you act wisely." Thetis cupped his cheek softly. "But it is not good to go on sorrowing as you are, my son, refusing food and rest. Your life will be short—I do not want to think of it—even in your grief you should savor what pleasures you can in the brief span allotted to you. Why not lie with a woman in love?" Briseis felt Thetis's eyes on her. The coldness inside spread.

The goddess's form began to fade from her sight and she no longer heard her voice, although the strange glow and the parted waters remained for some time. Gradually the sea returned to its accustomed place. Achilles remained in the water, allowing it to rise to his waist before he dove and swam out to the middle of the bay. Perhaps he sought his mother, or more likely, having agreed to give back Hector's corpse, he needed to cool his fury. Finally, he turned and swam back to shore. He pulled off his soaked tunic and stretched out on the beach. The sun glistened on his wet skin.

She felt dizzy looking at his naked beauty. She approached, sat beside him and gently caressed his chest. He turned in surprise. He held her hand and, bringing it to his lips, kissed it. Then he put it in her lap. She read the sadness in his eyes. This hint of connection wasn't enough. She pulled her knees up and wrapped her arms tightly around them.

THAT EVENING, mindful that the goddess had brought her to the sea to overhear, Briseis went to Achilles's shelter at dinnertime to see if she could encourage him to eat. At least he sat in a chair by his hearth instead of raging on the shore. Two of his henchmen roasted meat on spits. Briseis laid out a basket of bread and poured wine into Achilles's cup—the one upon which an image of Thetis rose from the sea. Achilles had suggested in jest that his mother kept her eye on him from that cup. If so, she would be disappointed at how little her son ate. He politely took the food from his men, but almost none of it passed his lips.

Briseis wondered how the ransom would be arranged. Even if Achilles initiated it, who would dare to come into the Greek camp and face him?

36

A FATHER'S KISS

B riseis left Achilles's hut and went outside, tired of watching him refuse to eat. The air was oddly still, and she climbed up onto one of the ships near the shore to catch the breeze. Looking across the Trojan plain as dusk fell, she saw a wagon and chariot approaching Scamander's ford, each holding only one man, although the wagon brimmed with goods. The men who climbed down from the vehicles moved with the care and slowness of the elderly as they let the mules and horses drink from the stream.

From the shadows of the trees along the riverbank, a lanky young man approached them. Briseis observed him intently. Despite the growing darkness, the air around him seemed light, and when he grasped the hand of the old man who had stepped from the chariot, the light stretched out to include the whole group. The god disguised as a young man—for surely, thought Briseis, he must be a god— sprang into the chariot and helped the old man in beside him. The other took his place driving the wagon, and they came toward the Greek camp.

She saw no movement by the ramparts—the guards did not seem to be on duty. She climbed down from the ship and waited in the shadow of Achilles's shelter. An unnatural silence had fallen on the camp. None of the usual noises of men and horses filtered to her. Zeus had sent some kindly god to bring King Priam, Hector's father, safely to Achilles's door. How else could two old men come through the enemy camp?

They arrived in Achilles's courtyard. The aged servant stayed with the chariot horses and wagon, which was piled high with treasure for the ransom. Priam walked heavily toward Achilles's shelter. When she glanced back at the wagon, the young man had disappeared.

She had never seen a man more weighed down with grief than Priam, a heavy load different from Achilles's fiery sorrow. Every line of his aged face, every movement spoke of a shattered heart. He paused in the doorway as if to collect himself and regain some measure of the regal and commanding presence he was known for. When he had stepped through the door, she slipped into the room unnoticed.

Priam knelt before Achilles and took his hand—the one which had killed so many of his sons, and Hector, his most beloved son, protector of Troy. He raised it to his lips and kissed it. Achilles leaned toward him and touched his gray head. The symmetry of their grief was so painful that she had to look away.

Priam spoke. "Remember your father, who is old and defenseless like me. Even now he must be surrounded by troubles since you are not by him to keep them off. And yet, when he hears that you still live, his heart lights with joy. Such happiness will never fill my heart again. I had fifty sons, the noblest in Troy; most are dead, struck down in the violence of war. One remained who guarded the city and her people, the dearest and best of them all, Hector. You killed him while he fought in defense of his country. I have come with gifts beyond number. Honor the gods and remember your father, taking pity on me, who am even more pitiful than he is, for I have kissed the hand that killed my children. Return Hector's body to me."

Achilles bent down to Priam. "As you knelt here, you looked like my father. Perhaps you seem so alike because the grief you feel now is the same that Peleus will feel when I am gone. I have imagined that same expression on his face over and over, and it has torn at my heart." Tears stained both Achilles's and Priam's faces.

Achilles reached out and raised Priam from the floor. "How could you dare to come alone to my shelter when I have killed so many of your brave sons? Your courage and your grief surpass any that the human heart has known, and yet you endure. Seeing your suffering as if it were my own father's pain, I understand that the pain I feel at having lost my dearest companion, Patroklos, is not unique to me, but the agony that we all feel when someone who is a part of our selves—our children, our closest loves—is taken from us. No matter how we long for them, nothing that we do can bring them back. In some way, I thought if I could make Hector suffer enough, Patroklos would conquer death. Sit here upon a chair. Let us put aside our lamentation. Do we gain anything by grieving? The gods spin lives full of unhappiness for us, unfortunate mortals."

Priam shook his gray head. "Do not make me sit in a chair while Hector lies on the ground. Take the ransom and give him back to me so that I may look at him."

The old anger flashed in Achilles's eyes and Briseis drew back in concern for Priam.

"Do not speak of this again," said Achilles. "I have already pledged to return him. Zeus commands it, and I know you did not come without a god to guide you. Some immortal brought you past the guards and all the dangers of the Greek camp."

Achilles turned away, and she saw him will himself back to courtesy. He called to his men to bring wine to Priam while he waited and to prepare a meal as the rules of hospitality required.

She stepped forward, wondering if he had noticed her waiting in the shadows. He nodded as if to affirm he welcomed her presence and said softly, "We must prepare Hector's body." She went outside with him and asked some of the women to help her.

While Achilles's grooms helped the old servant who had driven the wagon stake Priam's mules and chariot horses and give them fodder, Achilles and his men unloaded the wagon.

Briseis and two other women went down to the shore where

Achilles had left the body. As they knelt with basins of scented water and linen cloths, the women murmured at the purity of the corpse. There was little to do, but they washed him. As they finished, Achilles came with a finely woven tunic and a great robe that he had chosen from the treasures to serve as a shroud for Hector.

Achilles himself lifted the body to carry it to the wagon. Briseis saw him shudder as he straightened up with the body in his arms. His eyes burned with that terrifying fire. Then, as if the dire necessity of anger had loosened its grip, he seemed to breathe more freely. When he laid the body in the wagon, he called out Patroklos's name.

"Do not be angry that I gave back Hector to his beloved father." Patroklos would be pleased at this compassion, not angered, thought Briseis.

They returned to the shelter. "I have released Hector's body," Achilles said. "When the dawn comes, you may take him back to Troy. Now we must remember to eat."

Achilles himself brought Priam a plate of roasted lamb, rich with cumin and garlic. He raised his two-handled cup and Priam lifted a fine silver bowl to his lips, and they drank deeply. As Achilles tore off a piece of bread and scooped up the juicy lamb, a look of surprise crossed his face. It was, thought Briseis, as though he had rediscovered some long lost pleasure. The hard edges of his face softened. She had not been able to reach Achilles. The words of his own goddess mother had made no difference. The grief of a father, this old man who wept and kissed his hand, had restored Achilles's humanity.

Later, when they had filled themselves with food and drink, Priam asked Achilles to make beds for his servant and him so that he could sleep before he returned to Troy.

"I will make you beds in my anteroom. If some messenger from Agamemnon comes, he will not see you there and bring word of your presence to the king. Lord Agamemnon would require three times this ransom to release you back to your family, and I cannot permit such an insult. You were forced to perform this duty because I forgot

myself for a time. It is enough that you had the courage to face me."
Achilles gave the orders to make up the beds.

"Before you take your rest, tell me how many days you will need
for Hector's funeral rites. I will hold off the Greek attack for as long as
you require to conduct them as is proper for the son of the king."

Priam asked for eleven days. Briseis wondered at Achilles's ability
to promise a truce for the whole army, but then she realized no Greek
king would ever argue with Achilles again. His word could stand for
all of them.

After Achilles had shown Priam and his servant to their beds, he
came back into the room, and he and Briseis stood in the flickering
firelight together. The others had left them alone. Achilles looked at
her and she knew that he truly saw her for the first time since
Agamemnon took her away.

"So much has come between us," he said. She nodded. "I am not
the same person whom you loved. My wrath claimed too high a price
from everyone. Too many lives gone—was our love also destroyed
while I stubbornly stayed in my rage? Then in my grief I lost all other
feeling. You have borne these weeks alone. I used to understand your
feelings as if they were mine, but now I hardly know my own. I feel
like a visitor in a strange land."

He reached for her and they embraced. A balm for their spirits.
He knew what she had endured—that was enough. So much had
come between them, and yet in his arms she was willing to let those
hurts recede. Loving kindness toward each other made more sense in
the face of all they had suffered. They were both different people
now. They could not return, but they could love in this new territory.

Her face rested against his chest. She slid her hand across the
muscles of his back and down into the hollow at his hip. Her breath
caught with desire. Some things remained the same. She turned her
face up and tasted his kisses.

He drew her toward their bed. She pulled his tunic over his head,
standing on tiptoe to reach high enough, and then she kissed the
powerful shoulder and along the bone until she ran her tongue
within the hollow of his throat and down the modeled perfection of

his chest. He groaned and fumbled with her skirt and tunic, letting her clothes fall to the floor.

He knelt before her, running his hands and kisses slowly up her legs until the intensity of her sensations made her legs buckle underneath her. They gave themselves to the embrace of pure sensation.

When at last they lay content to hold each other in stillness, Briseis felt melancholy return to both of them. Their lovemaking had only temporarily pushed aside the distance between her and Achilles. Sorrow rose in her for her life before captivity. Their love could offer a soothing balm, but not a cure.

He looked apologetically at her. She kissed away a tear that started to run down his cheek. At least, she thought, he was able once again to sense what she felt; he wanted happiness with her, even if it was only possible for brief moments. Perhaps the time had come to tell him she was pregnant. They could share this joy for the time allowed.

But he spoke first. "I may feel the fullness of life at this moment, but I am no longer truly part of it. My fate has been too firmly fixed, too clearly marked in the minds of men and gods for me to do more than taste a meal I will never finish. But you—you are fully alive. Your losses do not diminish what each day offers you. You must find a fresh wellspring for yourself. I cannot help you."

She did not say anything. From time to time since the death of Patroklos, his words had sounded like prophecies, but dire ones, that gave her no guidance out of the darkness. Suddenly he had given voice to the inarticulate longing of her heart. She knew in that moment where her wellspring lay, where it had always been. Lyrnessos. Her city. Mount Ida's forests. She had shrunk from his beloved Phthia. She did not feel like she was meant to sail across the sea to his father's home. Reluctantly, she kept silent. She knew his joy at the thought of a child would be too much for her; she would never be able to refuse to go to Phthia. She felt the presence of another measure of distance between them.

WHEN THEY AWOKE JUST before dawn, Priam and his servant were gone. Briseis saw Achilles's relief that he did not have to face the heartbroken father and the responsibility of getting him safely out of the camp when others might be awake. She did not wonder how the old men had escaped. She remembered the young man whose divine light had brought them to Achilles's door.

She and Achilles shared an early breakfast outside by the kitchen fire that they themselves had stirred back to life. The day promised to be warm and sunny. Achilles was restless.

"I was thinking we could go walking on Mount Ida, but we can't. I agreed to an eleven-day truce. Having given my word, I can't risk a confrontation by wandering through the countryside while the Trojans believe they have no reason to fear the presence of any Greeks."

Instead they walked to the shore. When they stood before Patroklos's barrow, he looked around, unused to having no means to take out his bitterness now that Hector's body had been redeemed. She laid a hand on his arm and he covered hers with his own for a moment, but then he pulled away and knelt by the raised earth, laying his forehead against the dirt. He could not let anyone help him with this pain.

She walked to the water's edge, slipping off her sandals and lifting her skirt so that the cool water could wash over her feet. She smelled the salty tang of the sea air, felt the back and forth tug of the waves as they surrounded her feet and then flowed back into the main body of water.

She considered what might happen if she returned to the ashes of Lyrnessos. Had enough people survived on the surrounding estates that life went on, if in meager form? Maira had spoken hopefully of her sister's survival. Certainly no one had sent the hill estates word to come into the city—Mynes's precipitous launch into battle had assured that, at least. Getting there in safety, especially for a pregnant woman, posed many risks. She might arrive and find the survivors had abandoned the ruins.

She picked up two stones and tossed one across the water. It skipped twice and then plunged below. That plunge to the bottom of the sea felt like her fate if she went to Phthia. She knew too much of palace life. As a captive—once Achilles died she would be no one's wife in Phthia—she could not hold off threats to her child. Many would wish to seize the old king's throne as soon as death claimed him, if not before. Let the threat of Achilles's return vanish and the vultures would descend. What chance did her child have to grow up in safety within those intrigues?

If anyone remained in Lyrnessos, they would welcome her. She held an assured position as ruler and healing priestess. She could give that status to her child. If any of her people had started to rebuild, she had a duty to them. She flung the second stone far out, letting it arc through the air. Better to be queen of the ashes than slave in a foreign court.

37

WELLSPRING OF LIFE

Briseis heard Achilles's footsteps on the beach behind her. Would he realize what she had been contemplating? His words the night before had seemed to give her a kind of blessing, but she didn't want him to know her thoughts. She smiled as he approached.

He took her hand. "We can't go for a long walk about the country-side, but we can climb onto the ridge. From there I can look across the sea and imagine that I can see Phthia. From here, hateful Troy always fills my sight."

She nodded and leaned down to put her sandals on. They walked toward the lower slope. She wasn't sure whether he knew that she had buried Eurome there or not. His grief had been so all-consuming, she didn't think he had attended to her actions, but he stopped by the small mound she had made for Eurome's ashes. His respectful posture eased some of her pain left from that lonely burial.

"It is a custom among my people," he said, "to offer a lock of hair to honor our dead heroes. Patroklos took one of mine with him to the Underworld."

He took his knife from his belt and cut a lock of his hair. He looked at her with a question and when she nodded, he clipped one of her curls. He handed her the intertwined locks. She tugged off the wool thread she had used to tie back her hair and wrapped it around the top portion so that the two locks stayed together. Then she placed them on Eurome's burial where they fluttered in the breeze like a small flame.

They continued climbing to the top of the ridge. She remembered their lovemaking in the grassy nest. They looked at each other with understanding but without speaking of it. The somberness of greeting their dead still held them when they reached the place and sat on Achilles's outspread cloak.

"It would be easier," Achilles said, "if we knew that when we died, we would be rejoined with those who died before us. Some say we wander mindless through the dark, nothing more than gibbering shadows, others imply that we hold some remembrance of our former selves and can recognize our fellow dead. What does your goddess teach?"

Briseis looked at him in surprise. "I never considered it that way —but among my people we provide a pleasant place for the spirits of our dead to return to so that they will linger among the living and give us protection, so it must be that they remember who they were when they lived. I haven't ever considered what death would truly be like. Strange, I suppose, since death has been everywhere around me and we have faced your over-looming fate together."

"You shouldn't think about dying. You will live for a long time and grow into a gentle old age—that has to be true."

She smiled at him. "I hope so. I wish you would grow old beside me. Why does your fate have to hold you here in its grip? So far your fate is only a prediction that has not yet happened. Can't we escape this war together and live?"

He shrugged. "I cannot leave Troy now that I have caused Patroklos's death. I can no longer choose life away from this war—if I ever could have. My fate is the way it must be. The gods—my own mother —have announced it clearly. If I tried to fight it, fate would catch me even more cruelly. You have heard the songs the bards sing about men who try to outrun their fate when they do not like what the oracles tell them. Better to face my death with honor and win immortal remembrance and glory as recompense." He smiled at her. "Perhaps death is like sleep and I will be able to dream about you— then I will choose to dream about the night we spent here and last night."

She had never confessed her vivid dreams of lovemaking to him. When she should have told him, she could not bring herself to mention so intimate and private a subject from her previous life.

Now she told him about the dreams and vision he had appeared in during her girlhood and marriage—her Telipinu, whom she only later realized was him. This revelation first startled and then delighted him. Her descriptions of the dreams broke their solemn mood and inspired new lovemaking, this time slow and tender as they both felt the presence of a new, shared history and dimension in their love. They had, Briseis thought sadly, little future together, so they added more past.

BRISEIS'S CONVERSATION on the ridge with Achilles about the near- ness and unavoidability of his death helped her decide to talk to Maira about returning to Lyrnessos.

For now, she and Achilles had regained some portion of their love, but that would be taken away soon, and then she would be alone. Even now, she sensed Achilles had passed some boundary between mortals and gods and no longer balanced his human and divine sides in equilibrium. Even in their most intimate moments, he lived as a god.

Nonetheless, their old love filled her with gratitude. Without Achilles's healing, she would not have recovered from Lyrnessos's destruction, the loss of her family, the humiliation of Mynes's violence. She would not have become a warrior. He had been the best of healers. Her delight and joy in all that life had to offer had been restored because she understood it was an essential part of her, a strength to listen to.

Now she must live on her own. She had to turn away from his death before it consumed her. Lyrnessos called to her, but was it a foolish madness that she must forget? She needed to try the idea out with someone she trusted. Her sister was Maira's reason to return, and Maira had both good sense and courage. Briseis brought it up when she was able to slip into Agamemnon's camp and visit her friend.

Maira brightened at the idea. "I want to find my sister, but I don't see how we can do this. You're worried about getting safely over the mountain range, but before that how can we escape the Greek camp?"

Briseis told her about the route up on the ridge that Achilles had shown her on their secret night walks. At night she and Maira could escape without anyone noticing.

"If you can escape this camp, why not go to Troy where your father may still be alive?"

"Because Troy will fall and I do not wish to participate in its death. Could you bear to live through another city's sacking? How long would we be free if we went there? My father is honor bound to stay and fight until Troy is no more. If he survives, where else would he go but back to the lands he holds in Lyrnessos? If fate means for us to meet again, this is the surest way to accomplish that in safety."

"How long is such a journey by foot? Half a cycle of the moon?" Briseis nodded. "Do you think we can carry enough food? Life as a Greek lord's captive is not what I would choose, but starving in the forest or being attacked by wild beasts is far worse."

"It is early spring. The woods offer food for those who know what to look for—and I do. There is a great store of weapons that Achilles has stripped from those he vanquished in battle. I will look for two daggers and two light javelins that would suit us."

"You've already proved your power with a sword. We two are not so helpless in the face of danger, are we?"

Briseis smiled at her friend. "No, we are strong. We'll be safe enough from animals. I've wandered through Mount Ida's woods many times without being attacked. I feel Kamrusepa bids me to go home. That sense may be my own wishes persuading me, but I do not fear the dangers of the mountains. I am more concerned that we may find no one when we reach Lyrnessos. What if the survivors were few and they abandoned the area?"

Maira shook her head. "People are living there. I know it. No one told the estates and farms to come into the city. The Greeks will have scoured the area for food, but they cannot have found all the farms hidden away in the side valleys and slopes. The estate where I worked with my sister is far from the city and high on the mountain."

Briseis thought of her father's estate, so close to the main road and in the midst of the richest farm land near Lyrnessos. She had to persuade herself it lay in ruins. She couldn't create a false hope. But talking with Maira had not made her head ache nor did the usual bands of tension tug at her temples.

"Maira, there is one more thing I need to tell you before we decide. I know you will not tell anyone. I'm pregnant."

Maira gasped. She squeezed Briseis's hand. "I'm glad for you, even in these circumstances. Does Achilles know?"

"I haven't told Achilles and I'm not going to. It's a mark of how wedded he is to his impending death that he has not intuited something so important to both of us. He wants me to go to Phthia, but if I do I will always be a slave."

Briseis pressed Maira's hands in both of hers. "I'm not far along and even the sickness I felt in the morning is gone now. But it's another reason to think carefully. We have ten more days during which the Greeks will honor the truce and stay inside the camp. If we go, we should be well away before it's over. I do not think Achilles will come after me—especially during the truce. Agamemnon may want you back enough to send men after us, but he will fear to break the truce Achilles made and wake his anger once more. He's learned that's not worth a slave girl. We have some time, but not much."

"It's frightening to think of such a journey," said Maira.

Briseis nodded. "I know. Can you meet me tomorrow morning at the spring?"

Maira nodded. "I can offer to bring the morning's water."

"Why don't we both think about it overnight? If it doesn't seem foolish by tomorrow when we see each other at the spring, we will have the day to gather what we need before nightfall."

By the time the sun rose again, they had both found their resolve. One glance at each other as they filled their pitchers told them they had come to the same conclusion. They stood apart from the other women and quickly settled on what each would bring. The weapons, a small cooking pot and means to make a fire, two skin bags for water, their cloaks and other clothes, some food and Briseis's satchels. She considered leaving behind Iatros's to save the weight, but she couldn't, and two well-stocked medicine bags would be an asset to her when she returned to Lyrnessos.

After Briseis finished bringing the water for the last time, it took her only a short while to gather everything she needed. She stowed her bundle and the javelins outside the courtyard behind a pile of firewood, covering it with some logs. The gate to the courtyard would be open for her—Maira would send a message at dusk that one of the women was near to delivery and Briseis might be called out during the night. With the truce's quiet and safety, the guards would eagerly agree to leave the gates open so as not to be awakened for such things. It would also explain her departure if Achilles awoke.

The remainder of the day weighed heavily on her. She sought out Achilles's company, but she felt guilty and miserable. How could she abandon him? She reminded herself that he had already abandoned her—first to Agamemnon and soon to widowhood with none of the protections of being his wife, however much he called her that. He would mourn for her loss, but not, she hoped, as much as he still mourned for Patroklos. He had told her to find her wellspring. She prayed he would understand.

Each familiar action, every routine reminded her that this was the last time she would do each of these things. She sat in her chair next to Achilles by the hearth. They ate a good meal together: a stew of mussels that one of the men, freed from fighting, had gathered from the rocks along the shore, roasted meats well spiced the way Achilles liked them and fresh bread just lifted from the hot stones in the cook fire. She could not imagine when she might eat as generous a meal again. She thought of the growing baby in her womb and prayed she had not made a tragic choice.

The message came from Maira about the anticipated delivery. She went out to discuss the opening of the gate with the guards. Maira had stayed sure enough to go ahead with their plan. She would hold fast also. When it grew dark, she would set out.

Achilles's caresses were the hardest part. How could they be the last? She pushed aside her worries and gave herself to their love-making with wild abandon. If it was to be their last, it would have to sustain them both. She wanted him to know she loved him; that her leaving did not diminish how she felt. She wished to make the blow of her departure as gentle as possible. He must know that she was going toward life. She smiled when it came to her how to say all that to him. She knew just what to leave behind.

In the meantime, she thirsted for this last drink of his body. She kissed his lips softly and then more deeply. She wrapped her legs around his hips and held him tightly on top of her.

"I do not ever want to let go," she murmured in his ear. He laughed and smoothly turned them so that she lay on top of him.

"Choose another hold you know so well," he whispered, "and I will be at your mercy." She gave him his wish, guiding their movements with her hips until they lost time and place in pure sensation.

Afterwards, she lay in his arms and he did not fall asleep immediately. She was grateful for this delay and the short reprieve it gave her in this last embrace. Later he slept soundly, and she slipped out of bed to dress. Before she left, she kissed him softly on the cheek and placed her tapestry next to him, unrolled a little so that a meadow of flowers would be the first thing he looked at when he awoke instead of the empty place where she had been. She hoped he understood what it said. *I chose life.*

MAIRA WAS WAITING where they had agreed. They went out of the camp along the ridge Achilles had shown her. He had taught her how to escape—it couldn't have been an accident that he had shown her this route. She and Maira saw the guards below by the main gates, but they slipped away unnoticed.

They met no one as they crossed the plain in the dark and began to climb the foothills of Mount Ida side by side. When the first rays of light began to make the going easier, they reached a meadow hidden away on the slope. At one edge of it, a small spring gurgled up. Watercress and mint grew around its edge. They knelt to drink. Briseis looked up at the high peaks ahead, and as she cupped her hands and lifted the spring's offering to her lips, she felt Mount Ida's blessing.

To receive a **free short story** set in my Bronze Age fantasy world and a **free cookbook** of foods imagined in my novels using ancient Mediterranean ingredients, sign up to my newsletter on Judith's website www.JudithStarkston.com. My newsletter goes out occasionally with updates about new releases, special offers and useful information about recommended books and the background of my Bronze Age world.

And *so* important:

If you enjoyed *Hand of Fire*, the kindest favor a reader can do for an author is to leave a review on Amazon. A quick sentence or two is all that's needed.

Aegean Sea

Hellespont

Places in Hand
of Fire

Troy

Mount Ida range

Lyrnessos

Lesbos

Thebes

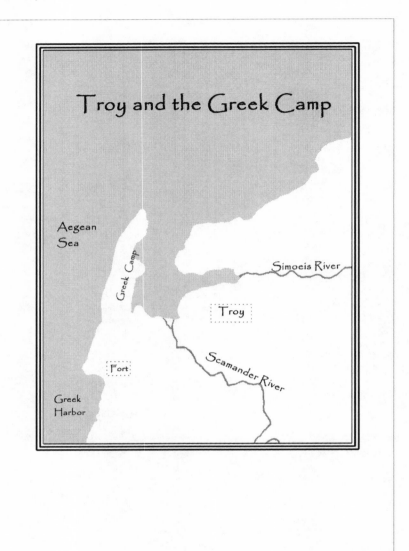

PEOPLE, GODS AND PLACES

Briseis's Family
Briseis: daughter of Antiope and Glaukos, healing priestess of Kamrusepa, betrothed to Prince Mynes

Antiope: wife of Glaukos and mother of Briseis, healing priestess of Kamrusepa

Glaukos: husband of Antiope, father of Briseis, Chief Counselor of King Euenos of Lyrnessos

Bienor: oldest brother of Briseis

Adamas: middle brother of Briseis

Iatros: youngest brother of Briseis, 16 yrs old, one year older than Briseis

Eurome: Nursemaid of Briseis

Milos: Glaukos's metalsmith

Maion: Glaukos's oldest servant, retired overseer of the estate, knows plant lore

Royal Family of Lyrnessos and Temple Staff
Euenos: King of Lyrnessos, ally of Troy

Hatepa: Queen of Lyrnessos

Mynes: Son of Euenos and Hatepa, betrothed to Briseis

Maira: Hatepa's maid servant

Zitha: Resident priestess/servant of Kamrusepa

The Greeks

Achilles: greatest Greek warrior, leader of the Myrmidons; half-immortal son of Thetis, goddess of the sea, and Peleus, King of Phthia

Patroklos: warrior, best friend of Achilles

Agamemnon: warrior, king of the Mycenaeans, most powerful of the Greek kings

Menelaos: warrior, younger brother of Agamemnon, king of Sparta, husband of Helen

Odysseus: warrior, king of Ithaca, best negotiator among the Greek leaders

Phoenix: aged warrior, father figure to Achilles since infancy

Machaon: Greek healer, son of the Greek healing god Asclepios

Podaleirios: Greek healer, son of the Greek healing god Asclepios

Aias: strongest of the Greek warriors after Achilles, cousin to Achilles

Helen: queen of Sparta and wife of Menelaos, taken by Paris to Troy

Iphis: Patroklos's captive woman

Chryseis: Agamemnon's captive woman, daughter of a priest of Apollo

The Trojans

Priam: elderly king of Troy

Hector: oldest son of Priam, greatest Trojan warrior

King Eetion: ally of Troy, king of Thebes (a town near Lyrnessos not to be confused with the more famous Thebes in Greece), father of Andromache; killed by Achilles on a raid of Thebes along with his seven sons

Andromache: wife of Hector, daughter of King Eetion

Paris: youngest son of Priam, who has brought Helen of Sparta to Troy

Gods and Goddesses

Kamrusepa: Lyrnessan goddess of healing, childbirth, fertility of herds and fields

Telipinu: Lyrnessan warrior god, son of the Stormgod; his return from anger is reenacted each year, bringing fertility to the herds and fields

Zeus: Greek king of the gods

Thetis: sea goddess, mother of Achilles, daughter of Nereus the ancient sea god

Apollo: Greek archer god who sends illness with his arrows, intervenes on Troy's behalf in the war

Hephaistos: Greek blacksmith god

Chiron: Greek immortal centaur (half man, half horse), who instructed Achilles in healing skills

Places

Lyrnessos: city on the far side of Mount Ida from Troy, allied to Troy, Briseis's home

Mount Ida: a tall central peak around which spreads a wide mountain range along the southern side of the plain of Troy

Troy: most powerful city on the western coast of Anatolia during the Late Bronze Age; controls the passage of ships and trade through the narrow water course called the Hellespont, which separates the Aegean from the Black Sea region; controls an area called the Troad, a group of nearby towns, cities and islands

Phthia: kingdom in Greece ruled by Achilles's father, Peleus

AUTHOR NOTES

A reader of historical fiction has the right to expect accurate history and to be informed of any divergences from the known record that an author has taken. The case is somewhat complicated for this book because I have delved into both history and into the mythological tradition, primarily as presented in the *Iliad* of Homer. The two are not mutually exclusive by any means—Homer is full of history—but the poem also presents a lot that we would call myth or legend. Including these aspects puts this novel into the genre of fantasy. I have tried in every way possible to present an accurate picture of life in the Late Bronze Age in the area surrounding Troy in what is now Turkey, and to remain true to the Homeric tradition.

First a note about names in my novel. One known mythological "fact" I changed from the Homeric tradition: In the *Iliad* Briseis's father's name is Briseus. I have named him Glaukos purely for reasons of clarity. The names are already complicated enough in this book without two characters with almost the same name. My goal throughout has been to keep the names as simple as possible, although it may not feel that way to you, the reader. Whenever I named a purely fictional character, I picked the shortest names from the handy online list "Repertoire Onomastique," compiled from the extant cuneiform tablets of the Hittites/Luwians, which gave me names that are accurate to the peoples living in this place and time. Occasionally I borrowed names from minor heroes in Homer or I used Greek words, which is reasonable given all the trade between these peoples. For example, Briseis's youngest brother's name, Iatros, means doctor in Greek. He was one of my first characters, and that seemed right for him. Other names, such as Briseis, Mynes, Euenos and Patroklos, are set by the tradition and I kept them, with the exception of changing Briseus to Glaukos. There are many variant spellings of Greek into English. The spellings I chose may differ from the ones you are most accustomed to but are all accepted translit- erations.

While my goal has been to stay true to the Homeric tradition, including how the tradition presents these heroes and captives, the major proviso is that everyone has his or her own interpretation of the *Iliad,* and I have stayed true to mine. I, for example, see Achilles as an existential hero who questions the warrior code and, despite the destruction he causes, is a good man at heart, just incredibly conflicted and confused. Many people see him as a vicious, selfish killer with few redeeming qualities. I cannot see him that way and don't in this book. So you may find yourself disagreeing with my presentation, but that is the joy of this fluid and grand Homeric tradi- tion. We can all make it our own.

I will summarize the relevant "facts" that we do know from Homer and myth and how have I dealt with those. We learn very little about Briseis. She has a handful of lines in this patriarchal poem. In my interpretation of Homer, it seems clear that Achilles loves and respects her, and she returns these feelings. Over many years of teaching, this struck me as odd. Suggestions of some ancient version of Stockholm syndrome simply don't work for the Achilles I know from Homer, so I went exploring to see who Briseis might be to explain her love for the man who destroyed her family and city. I ended up pulling largely from the archaeology of this time rather than from Homer because so little is mentioned about her in the epic.

From Homer and a few other references in later ancient sources, we know Briseis is married to the prince of Lyrnessos and thus presumably can become Lyrnessos's queen. Her husband is called Mynes and he is referred to as the king of Lyrnessos at times. We know Briseis's father survived the attack on Lyrnessos, but her three brothers, all born of the same mother, did not. One other mythological "fact" that I changed is that Briseis's husband Mynes is said in a post-Homeric author to have a brother. In my book he doesn't. To be honest, I totally forgot that this mythic brother is ever mentioned and by the time I realized my mistake, Mynes was so clearly an only child in my tale that I just left it. We know from Homer that Briseis mourned Patroklos's death and that Patroklos told her early in her captivity that Achilles would marry her as his "legal" wife and take her back to Phthia with him. We know she particularly mourns her brothers. In various parts of the novel here and there, I include events from the *Iliad* as Homer gives them to us, but I have told them from Briseis's point of view, so they often feel quite different from the *Iliad*. That's pretty much everything we know about Briseis from Homer and myth, if such a person ever really lived and isn't the product of a creative bard in the oral tradition of the ancient epics. The rest was up to me.

Even if no such person named Briseis ever truly walked the earth —and I like to believe she did—I have constructed a young woman who could have lived as I have described in this time and place. I created her carefully from the most current historical and archaeological understanding of the peoples living near the city of Troy during the Late Bronze Age. At no time did I consciously have Briseis do anything that a woman of that time and place and her social status wouldn't have done. I've had this book read by excellent historians who are far more knowledgeable than I am and they concur. But, given the fragmentary record of this time and place, I have also had to imagine much of what is on the page. My mind is a modern one, so I'm sure that I have inadvertently included some inaccuracies and unlikely behavior for people of this place and time. I guide my imagination as tightly as I can by my research, but it's still my imaginings. For example, in the first chapter, Briseis performs a rite to save her mother's life. There are hundreds of such rites recorded on cuneiform tablets. This rite is not taken word for word from any of those. I know of no "Breath of Life" incantation. However, this rite that I "made up" is very similar in language, idea and intention to the many that do exist. I must admit that in "real" Hittite/Luwian life, most of the rites go on for a very long time. I have shortened them for the sake of good storytelling. The Spring Festival, for example, is modeled on many such that we have in the record, but the historical ones went on for days and often moved from place to place, etc. Taken directly from the tablets, they are incredibly repetitive. After the fiftieth identical sacrifice you would have thrown the book at the wall.

Briseis is bi-lingual in Greek and her native tongue. The best current scholarship believes that she would have spoken Luwian, but we may never know for certain. Like Greek, Luwian is an Indo-European language, a sister language to Hittite. Hittite is the language of the dominant empire to the east of Troy, an empire to which Troy was allied or subject in greater or lesser degrees over time. From Luwian's structures etc, we can tell it is pretty closely related to Greek. Its written form, cuneiform, is borrowed from the Near Eastern world and applied to this language, so it looks utterly different from the Greek letters most people are familiar with, but that is merely the form used to represent the language in writing. The Greek alphabet is a much later invention than this time period. To the extent that the Mycenaean Greeks of the period portrayed in this book wrote anything down, they used a system called linear B. Linear B was a sort of accountants' system used for keeping track of the royal wealth. It was not used for recording religious rites and sacred tales, or anything "literary," such as we have in cuneiform both in Hittite and Luwian.

I have also drawn from the myths of the Hittites in creating Briseis's tale. I believe the myth of Telipinu, a young warrior god who is famous for his sacred and cosmically disastrous fury over his insulted honor, probably served as a source or influence as the legends about Achilles formed up during the centuries of oral composition of the *Iliad* tradition. I used this connection to draw Briseis and Achilles together.

If you are wondering whether there ever was a Trojan War, or how the Hittites and the Trojans are related or how a woman would be literate and powerful in the ancient world, the best place to go is my website, www.judithstarkston.com, where you will find a wealth of information and an informal bibliography of books about Troy and the Hittites. Turkey has an extraordinary number of active archaeological digs with unimaginable treasures being found each season. So, if this intrigues you, subscribe to my website and I'll do my best to keep you informed of breaking news in a down-to-earth way, along with writing fantasy re-imaginings of these exotic lost worlds. Subscribe to my newsletter and receive a free short story and a cookbook of ancient Mediterranean foods mentioned in my fiction.

ACKNOWLEDGMENTS

This book has had a long evolution and there are many people to thank. From early on, I banded together with two remarkable women, Diane Benitez and Carolyn Allport. We met over Diane's kitchen table every other week for years, critiquing and learning to write from each other.

Without these two friends, there would be no book. I can't express my gratitude properly for their friendship and guidance. Diane and I continue to read each other's every word and give the quick cheer or redirect as needed. I'd be lost without her constant willingness to spend time with my tortured prose. Recently I have also been working with a larger critique group under the leadership of MaryLee MacDonald; the group's comments on several chapters were tremendously insightful and gave a polish towards the end that I couldn't have achieved on my own.

Thanks to Amy Dominy for giving me a much-needed lesson on how to write dialogue and an orientation into the world of writers. My physician, Robert Bloomberg, read an early draft and clarified many of the medical issues. The information about Bronze Age medicine is scant, and his essential expertise about wounds, injuries and disease combined with that meager scholarship to steer me on a sound path. When I traveled to Turkey to research this book, Sevil Çonka, able archaeologist and art historian, skillfully led my family and me around the key sites, including a delightful trip to the area where Lyrnessos is traditionally thought to be—nothing like being asked to take your tour to a mythological city. Several friends read my manuscript and encouraged me on the long and often disheartening path to publication: Rachel Diamant, Dora Diamant, Sue Ochs, Janine Skinner and Patty Carlin. So many writer friends in the historical fiction world gave me advice, space on their blogs, recommended me and cheered me on. I can't list you all, but you are essential, from all around the world. To my own local writer friends in the Arizona chapter of the Historical Novel Society and in the Desert Sleuths chapter of Sisters in Crime, thanks for your friendship. No writer can write without community.

A number of scholars gave me votes of confidence about my research conclusions or answered key questions: Susanne Ebbinghaus of Harvard University, Harry Hoffner, Jr. of the Oriental Institute of the University of Chicago, Billie Jean Collins of Emory University, and Eric Cline of George Washington University. I had a series of editors on this project and they dedicated countless hours and creative energy to refining my book. I am so appreciative of their generosity: Jennifer Sawyer Fisher, MaryLee MacDonald, Tinney Sue Heath, Bonnie Pike and Nancy Bilyeau. Thanks go to Susan Spann for donating her expertise in finalizing my contract with my publisher. And then there's the man who has given me support of all sorts, my dear husband, Bob. Thank you, most of all.

ABOUT THE AUTHOR

Judith Starkston

Judith Starkston has spent too much time reading about and exploring the remains of the ancient worlds of the Greeks and Hittites. Early on she went so far as to get two degrees in Classics from the University of California, Santa Cruz and Cornell. She loves myths and telling stories. This has gradually gotten more and more out of hand. Her solution: to write wild stories, magical and fantastical, set in the exotic worlds of the past. Fantasy and Magic in a Bronze Age World. *Hand of Fire* was a semi-finalist for the M.M. Bennett's Award for Historical Fiction. Her upcoming *Priestess of Ishana* won the San Diego State University Conference Choice Award.

Judith has two grown children and lives in Arizona with her husband. Because writing is best done with community, Judith belongs to her local Desert Sleuths chapter of Sisters in Crime, the Society of Southwestern Authors and the Arizona chapter of the Historical Novel Society. Judith is represented by Richard Curtis.

For a **free short story** set in her Bronze Age fantasy world and a **free cookbook** of recipes inspired by the ancient Mediterranean foods in her novels, subscribe to Judith's newsletter on her website www.JudithStarkston.com. The newsletter goes out occasionally with updates about new releases, special offers and useful information about recommended books and the background of my Bronze Age world.

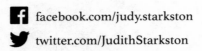
facebook.com/judy.starkston

twitter.com/JudithStarkston

Made in the USA
San Bernardino, CA
16 October 2018